Searching For Emiliano

Ryanna Hammond

SEARCHING FOR EMILIANO

RYANNA HAMMOND

"The details in Hammond's debut novel, of an authentic and raw young love, are carefully written...and through Hammond's Spanish narration, I have been given a new perspective of Mexican American culture."

– J. A. Bishop, author of Her Colored Scars

This novel has a soundtrack.

When you reach a song while reading, scan this QR code
to go to the novel's playlist. Listen to that scene's
respective song to feel more immersed in the narrative.

SEARCHING FOR EMILIANO

RYANNA HAMMOND

To the man whose presence in my life changed me in more ways than I could imagine

If light is love, then fear is its shadow.

-    L. J. Vanier

PROLOGUE

It's curious how people can live in the same town nearly their entire lives and yet their paths will never cross. As one exits the parking lot, the other has just parked. As one orders an ice cream cone, the other walks out of the shop looking down at their phone. As one goes from aisle five to aisle six examining their grocery list, the other brushes past them into aisle five.

And this truth is no different for the residents of Old Oak, California; what with its nearly 40,000 residents any two people could be under each other's noses quite often and one or both of them may never know it.

One person who never notices such things is Rachel Williams. She tends to be aloof, a bit in the clouds. Not in the way of an idiot, but in the way of an overthinker. Everywhere she goes, her body is in reality, but her mind is somewhere else. And that's why she never notices people.

As it turns out though, people notice her. They have an affinity for her upbeat spirit and intellect. She's got the kind of personality that Curiosity wants to taste, that Misery wants to tarnish, that Pain wants to kill. On top of her character, she's got an athletic physique that turns heads and a natural beauty that shines with or without makeup.

One such person who has *always* been drawn to Rachel is Javier Aguilar. He grew up just four blocks away from her, and prior to her moving away for college, he would see her all the time. They went to the same elementary school, and that's where he first saw her. She was in third grade, he in sixth. And, unfortunately for him, their age gap meant they would never be in middle school together. By the time he was off to high school, the boundaries within the city limits that designated which school one would attend changed. Rich neighborhoods were popping up just over the hill, so the cutoff line became the main road between his house and Rachel's.

She went to Old Oak High School and he went to Ten Pines High School, the next town over.

Now, he is twenty-six and she twenty-three, and he is still trying to meet her. However, outside of the elementary school setting, their near run-ins were never by accident. Javier *wanted* to run into Rachel, and often sought her out. In middle school, he would walk by her house every morning on the way hoping to meet her. In high school, he would try to hang around the same crowd as her or go to her soccer matches, hoping to enter her circle. Some might think that to be embarrassing or ridiculous, others may believe it to be charming. He stopped trying when she moved away to college over half a decade ago and set his sights elsewhere. He has no idea that she has been back for a year.

Another such man who has had near run-ins with Rachel is Emiliano Morales. However, unlike Javier, his near run-ins with her were never planned; rather, they were coincidence, random, accidental. He went to middle school and high school with Rachel and would often pass by her in the hallways, see her playing in her high school soccer games, or spot her occasionally at a party.

In the grand scheme of school life however, it wasn't truly that often. They were from completely different crowds, cultures, and lifestyles. Unlike Rachel or Javier who belong to the dominant American culture and live in middle class neighborhoods, Emiliano is heavily immersed in his Mexican heritage and is first generation in the United States.

Growing up, his family often relocated from one rented room to another, until he turned fifteen and a half and was able to get a job. By that point, with his sister being seventeen, they both worked. And—finally—he, his mother, and his sister, were able to afford their own condo with the help of an undocumented immigrant and her son who paid rent to them under the table for one bedroom. From the time he was sixteen to now, age twenty-two, his immediate family has lived in that same condo, in one of Old Oak's few *barrios*, which is nestled between the 101 freeway and the town's only true *Mexicano* shops.

His life has been filled with hustle, grind, and labor for as long as he can remember to help his family survive. So, no, he hasn't thought about Rachel since high school, and truly he rarely thought about her then. He had no breaths or seconds to waste thinking about the beautiful Rachel Williams from an entirely different world who didn't even know he existed. She was merely a pretty White girl with privileges he could only dream of. It wouldn't matter to him whether or not she is back home from college or that she even left for college in the first place.

However, on this oddly serendipitous October morning, Rachel Williams, Javier Aguilar, and Emiliano Morales have all planned to attend the same pickup soccer game at a park in Old Oak. In just two hours' time, all three of their paths will cross—the match that, when lit, will spark inevitable change in each of their lives forever.

1 sss

For the third time this weekend, Emiliano finds himself being reminded by his mother, Adriana, about their lunch plans in Los Angeles with his *tías*, *tíos*, and *primos*. The first time was in passing on the staircase, the second when she was leaving the house hastily to run errands, and now—in a more thorough manner—as he munches on Fruit Loops at the dining table.

He wouldn't say this is unusual of his mother, to remind him of an upcoming event like a notification popping up on a cellphone. In fact, she works for an event planning company. And outside of work she can be found creating and organizing plans for their family. If there is one thing Adriana has grasped tightly to in her forty-two years on Earth, it's that family is everything. Through thick and thin. And family must stick together. It's something she naturally instilled in Emiliano—not by way of words, but through action and devotion. Thus, to him, family banning together is simply a way of life, *the* way of life.

After lots of nods in response to her questions, he confirms that he will be home by 11:00 a.m. His time stamp of course only sparks more questions from Adriana: what are you even doing up so early on a day off from work? Where are you going? She was not surprised to hear that he is going to shoot hoops with Pablo, but she does make a questioning look when he says he is going to play soccer afterward—Emiliano hasn't kicked a ball in a few years.

"All right. Well, don't forget you gotta be ready by noon, mijo."

"I won't, Ma. Don't worry," he says, getting up from the table.

"Good. You better not!" She chuckles. "And you better not leave that bowl right there either!"

"No, Mamá. Imma clean it right now before I head out." Emiliano looks at his mother bashfully as she takes a bite of a *concha* that's dusted with pink powder.

She is a true *Mexicana*: round chestnut eyes, long dark brown hair, and a bronze honey complexion. Aside from a few facial features and their matching hair color, the two don't look much alike. Emiliano has jade green eyes and a fairer complexion, a light-skin or *güero* or *miklo* as many *mexicanos* would say.

Emiliano takes the bowl to the sink as his mother turns on the local Spanish news. He half-listens to the weather update and a report on a fiery car collision. By the time the newscaster begins explaining a fraught civil case, he has finished cleaning his cereal bowl, along with other dishes.

As he puts the last item in the cupboard, he looks over at his mother—who is intently watching the news—and notices her royal blue top. "That much pride, huh?" he says teasingly, gesturing to the Dodgers shirt. As she looks down to see what she is wearing, he reminds her that their family's favorite baseball team didn't make the playoffs.

"All right, Mr. Lakers…Well you better watch yourself, otherwise you're not coming with me to a game this year, huh?" Adriana says with attitude, her forehead wrinkling. They both laugh; that's just the way their playful, banter-filled relationship goes. "Oh, mijo, before I forget…you riding with us or taking your own car to lunch?"

"I think with you guys. I don't wanna take my car far. I got a small leak last night on the boulevard with my homies."

"Aye…a leak how?" Adriana's eyebrows raise. "Doing something you shouldn't be doing, trying to impress girls?"

Emiliano chuckles. "You know I don't even try with girls, Ma. We was just cruisin', then got some tacos from the food truck."

And he's telling the truth. He *never* goes out of his way to try with girls. In fact, he never makes it past the most basic talking stage with any of them, even when the females pine over his plump lips, thick hair, and captivating personality. The young man is like a cross between '50s-lover-boy, '80s-too-cool-for-school, and '90s-Los-Angeles-*Chicano*. What young woman wouldn't be intrigued by him?

Emiliano slings his athletic bag over his shoulder, then gives his mother a kiss on the cheek before reiterating that he'll be home *and ready* by noon. As he opens the front door, a waft of cigarette smoke passes him. He looks up and waves to his neighbor who's taking a long drag on the porch of the condo above his. One day Emiliano won't live in a condo or have neighbors above him. Well, that's the plan anyway.

He looks across the back alleyway scanning his neighborhood. Large peppertrees. Tall, freshly trimmed palm trees. Lots of trucks. Familiar brown faces. People walking their dogs. Lots of cars. Music, laughter, and other lively buzzing. Everything is as it should be. He props up the garage door and eyes his most prized possession: a black 1976 Pontiac Firebird. "Still got lots of work to do, but you lookin' real firme," he says, patting the roof before getting behind the wheel.

As he backs out, a group of children run behind his car. "¡Oigan, Niños! Get outta the street!" a neighbor yells. Emiliano abruptly hits the brake pedal. The slew of children run onto the grass and continue playing. He cautiously looks around for other youngsters while making his way out of the neighborhood, wind dancing through his wavy dark hair.

For a few moments, he fusses with the stereo knobs, even though he knows they won't work. The stereo has been broken for months. A small grumble of annoyance escapes him. At the stoplight he pulls out his phone, puts on "Major Tom" by Peter Schilling, and bobs his head to the beat. Gazing out the window, a few things catch his attention: the brightness of the sun, a mint green house on the corner of the street, and—

And that's when he sees her for the first time in five years—diagonally to the left of the intersection in a modern white Acura is Rachel Williams. A memory of her suddenly flashes in his mind from years before: she was running down the athletic field to shag a ball during a high school soccer game, her long ponytail swinging back and forth. She was absolutely gorgeous. She still is. Almost as if on cue, the light turns green. Without another thought of Rachel—who he deems is out of his league—he looks back toward the road and follows behind a trail of cars.

As Emiliano's old black car goes through the intersection, it draws Rachel's attention. She doesn't catch a glimpse of the driver—another near miss between them—but her eyes are drawn to his car until an incessant, monotonous ringtone sounds through her stereo. She does a double take of the vintage car before answering the call from her mother, Shannon.

"Hun, where'd you go?" Shannon asks. "I just got home from running errands and your car's not here."

"I'm getting breakfast, then heading to the park to play soccer, Mom."

The light finally turns green and Rachel heads through the intersection as her mother tells her to stay safe and have fun. Both women exchange goodbyes with a fast stream of bye-bye-bye-bye-bye before ending the call; it's a tradition in their family to say bye not once, but five to seven times. Like NSYNC's "Bye Bye Bye" but on steroids.

Rachel blasts one of her favorite Hall & Oates '80s songs as she gazes out the window. It's only a few days into October and, for some reason, early birds are putting Halloween decorations on their porches and front lawns: carved pumpkins, fake spider webs, and various other things like tombstones and witch cauldrons. Some people get *so* into the holiday season. Rachel is no Scrooge, but she also isn't super festive. The holiday season just seems drab to her. It's the same old thing year after year.

A few minutes later, she pulls into the café, eager for her solo breakfast date. She takes her food to an empty barstool table outside. Around her are tables full of couples, friend groups, and families; it's a typical Saturday. Rachel's Saturdays never look like this. She is the type of person who does things *alone*, and finds immense joy in diving into her many solo hobbies.

She pulls a self-help book out of her bag, one about living an honest and meaningful life. A young surfer-looking guy with bleach blonde hair walks over, looking her up and down. She clears her throat loudly so that he *knows* that she *knows* he's there. To his dismay, his effort did not elicit the response he was looking for—and, to her dismay, neither did hers.

After an awkward interaction, standoffish Rachel resumes eating and starts reading, though she can't focus on the book. What is it with guys? She would never entertain someone who can't stay interested in meaningful topics for more than five seconds. If he wanted to know her, wouldn't he ask about her interests, like the book she is reading, instead of immediately using a basic pickup line about her looks?

You're so hot I get a tan just looking at you. She adds it to the list in her mind of ones she's heard recently. *It must have hurt when you fell from heaven. You must be a ticket, got "fine" written all over you. If I could rearrange the alphabet I'd put U and I together.* She's heard them all. And they all suck.

With a glance at her book, she notices the next section is about an important life lesson: while we cannot control the events around us, we have full control over our reactions and responses. Ah, interesting, Rachel thinks. If only she knew how to put that into practice. She doesn't lift her head again until she realizes there's nothing left in her breakfast bowl. And she has just enough time to make it to the park for soccer.

When she reaches the community recreation center, she passes by a row of large oak trees, then parks between two huge dirty suburbans loaded with softball gear. She eyes a group in the distance and assumes they are softball fans watching from the outfield. However, as she gets closer, she realizes they are all wearing cleats. There's at least twenty players, all of whom seem to be around her age in their early- to mid-twenties.

The only person Rachel tries to find is her best friend, Hannah Evans, and it doesn't take long; it's hard to miss Hannah's long bleach blonde hair and tan skin. With a smile emerging, Rachel beelines toward Hannah, when suddenly— due to her typical fixated vision—she collides with another body, with Javier Aguilar's body. What she doesn't know is that he saw her coming and purposely got in the line of fire. After so many years, this young woman was going to meet him, dammit. And now they've officially made contact.

"Oh my gosh, I'm so sorry. I didn't see you there," Rachel says, a worried expression on her face. She takes one glance into his eyes thinking that he and his mocha-toned skin look familiar, though she is sure she's never seen him before.

"No, it was my fault." His eyes seem to fill with a spark of gratitude, as if this is all he's ever wanted. "I'm Javier," he says, reaching out his hand.

"Rachel," she replies with a small smile before scurrying off to Hannah.

After a quick hug and greeting, Hannah remarks that the crowd is larger than she expected. Rachel nods in agreement, then shares that when Fabian—their friend from high school who organized the event—reached out to her, she was under the assumption it would just be a soccer get-together with five or six people.

Fabian Romero played on the Old Oak's team in high school and graduated the same year as Rachel and Hannah. He then went on to become a fitness instructor and a soccer trainer. A few weeks earlier, he had gotten the idea to reconnect with old classmates and teammates, and that's how they all ended up at this field today.

"Honestly this will probably be more fun than I expected," Hannah says.

"Yeah, I'm really excited to play again. It's been a while since I touched a ball," Rachel replies. "Also, how's everything been going with Brax?"

Brax Kingston is Hannah's boyfriend—a tall, beautifully dark-skinned man of Caribbean descent. The two had met at USC in undergrad almost two years ago and they've been together ever since.

"Oh, you know. Same old. Up and down like always. I've just been enjoying lots of wine…*lots* of wine," Hannah emphasizes with wide eyes. Her perfect, thick brown eyebrows raise. They share a giggle, put on their cleats, and head to the field to warm up.

Right then, Emiliano and his best friend Pablo Rivera walk over from the outdoor basketball court and sit down. Another near miss between Emiliano's and Rachel's paths.

"You had the dopest shot today, esé," Pablo says.

"Sheesh. Yeah, that was smooth…but I still lost to you anyway," Emiliano says, his lips smacking, making a clicking sound.

While leisurely putting their cleats on, Emiliano scopes out the faces around him. At the table full of guys, a few are his friends, some he played with in high school, and others he doesn't know at all. Then he notices Javier under the tree and they briefly make eye contact. He doesn't look too familiar, though maybe their club teams once played one another. Emiliano's eyes then drift to the people warming up on the field. Some guys are passing a ball around and two young women are doing dynamic stretches and—holy shit, he thinks. It's her, again. It's Rachel from high school. And her best friend, Hannah. He takes an extra moment to admire Rachel's ponytail, her long straight hair swaying from side to side, just like the first time he saw her.

"You coming bro?" Pablo hollers.

"Yeah, let's hit it." Emiliano quickly ties his cleats, then catches up to Pablo, ready for their warm-up lap around the field.

Just as they begin to cross Rachel's vision—though upside down from her vantage—she comes out of the downward dog stretch. Yet another near miss of some sort of interaction between Emiliano and Rachel.

"Then he told me I couldn't talk to my friend at work anymore because my friend is a guy," Hannah says. "And I thought that was just ridiculous. First of all, we are coworkers and I'm not attracted to him! But secondly, Brax has loads of friends who are girls, so that just doesn't seem fair to me."

Rachel shakes her head, disapproving of Brax's double standards. She begins to do arm circles and her attention drifts away from Hannah's story. She hears a crow squawking and searches for it. Though, her eyes don't find a black bird. They land on none other than Emiliano Morales as he rounds the corner of the soccer field.

She catches a full glimpse of Emiliano for the first time, noticing his luscious hair, then his facial features: his high cheekbones, his symmetrical nose with its perfect bridge. How does a nose like that even exist? Then she examines his clothes. How could someone look so attractive in athletic attire? Eventually her eyes make their way to his bare skin—his muscular arms and his defined calves. Surely, she is transforming into the heart-eyes emoji in front of everyone on the grass.

"Have you gone deaf?" Hannah asks.

Rachel mutters a half-fake laugh still staring into the distance. After a moment, she looks over at Hannah. "Sorry, wait what? What'd you say?"

"Eh, doesn't matter. Rachel, you never find guys attractive! Do you think he's cute?"

"Oh no, of course not." Rachel awkwardly laughs. "I was just staring into space."

"Space?" Hannah muses, nodding.

"Yes…There was a bird…um…a crow…and—" Rachel smiles.

"Yeah fucking right!" Hannah laughs, playfully pushing Rachel. "I'm your best friend! Come on, you gotta know you can talk to me about these things."

"OK, fine," Rachel whispers, implying if this information were leaked it would probably be more life-threatening than top secret government data.

"Hey, guys! I have some important news!" Hannah yells obnoxiously to the whole field. Some people look over and Rachel's eyes widen, conveying a plea for Hannah to *please* be an adult about this.

Hannah smiles as she hollers, "It's almost nine. We should seriously start because I have a lot of shit to do today!"

Rachel squints at her best friend. "Nice one."

"Oh, did you think I was going to spill your big secret?" Hannah says sarcastically. "Rachel, of course I'm not gonna tell a soul."

Rachel shyly smiles.

Everyone around them begins placing the balls behind the end lines or next to the goals. The pair of best friends exchange one more glance, then head to their positions. Rachel looks across the field to admire Emiliano again. And, over the next two sweaty hours, she steals glances of him again, and again, and again.

When they're finished playing, Fabian Romero gathers everyone into a huddle. He believes their session was so fun and worthwhile that he makes a texting group chat on the spot titled "SSS" for Soccer Saturday Sessions. Then he adds each of the players to it. Now, Javier Aguilar's, Emiliano Morales's, and Rachel Williams's phone numbers are all together virtually.

As Fabian concludes his powwow, Javier can't help but have his eyes on Rachel; Rachel can't help but glance over at Emiliano; and Emiliano takes a peek in Rachel's direction exactly one time.

The next two months unfold in this same way: each Saturday morning, Javier eyes Rachel, Rachel eyes Emiliano, and Emiliano isn't trying to focus on anyone, yet can't help himself from glancing at Rachel.

2 A Breath of Fresh Air

Of all Emiliano's jobs, his favorite has been working at the auto shop; though, truly, he's been able to find joy and gratitude in each of them. Movie theatre cashier. Restaurant busboy. Utility worker. Any job—for Emiliano—could be described in three simple words: getting. it. done. He's treated each position the same: respect the work, respect the boss, get in the zone, work hard, then go home.

He likes his current job as an auto mechanic the most because of the perks. For one, Pablo's father, Miguel, owns it and Pablo works there. Who wouldn't want to work with their best friend? Mr. Rivera hired his son and Emiliano the day they graduated high school, and they've been working for him ever since. And that's another great thing about the job: comfortability. Both he and Pablo have been there so long that they know what to expect and how to do pretty much anything on a car. Mainly though, he likes this job because it has the best salary; he can help his mom with rent, groceries, and anything else their family may need. It was a big task to become the man of the house at such a young age, but he accepted the position gracefully and with so much pride.

Most weeks, Emiliano works six days, and sometimes he works upwards of ten hours a day. Today has been fairly busy—along with oil changes and conducting routine maintenance, he replaced a starter, and is working on a second one. However, most shifts he probably couldn't even recall all that he does; he tends to get so in the zone at work, efficiently moving from one task to the next, that time simply slips away.

"Hermano, can you pass me the wrench?" Emiliano calls out.

His coworker Santos thumbs through a rusty red toolbox. "Which one?"

"Uh—fourteen millimeters." Emiliano scoots out from under a car and wipes sweat off his forehead with a nearby towel. His blue coveralls are stained from head to toe in oil, dirt, and grime.

"Aquí, hombre," Santos says, holding out the wrench.

"Gracias." Emiliano stalls an extra second before going back under the car. "It's damn hot today." He removes some wiring, then twists the wrench to get the retaining bolt.

"Yo, homie. Aren't you done for the day?" Santos asks. "It's 4:06."

Pulling out from under the car, Emiliano glances at the clock on the far wall. "Damn. 4:06? Forreal?" He stands, wiping his gloves against his coveralls. "You think you could finish up this starter?"

"Sí. We'll figure it out. See you tomorrow."

Emiliano heads into the locker room that smells like grease, sweat, and labor. There are four lockers marked with names written on manilla tape: Emiliano, Santos, Jimmy, and Pablo. Jimmy is around the same age as Emiliano and Pablo, and is the only non-Mexican worker at the auto shop. Emiliano doesn't see him often since their shifts aren't usually at the same time these days.

Emiliano changes out of his dirty work clothes, then heads into the restroom since he won't be able to shower until later tonight. All he sees when he looks in the mirror is fatigue. He splashes water on his face, then reaches into his backpack for deodorant and lathers his underarms while humming "Everything She Wants" by Wham!. Mid-hum he lets out a yawn. No surprise. He has been awake since 5:00 a.m. (Not to mention, he has the earliest work shift out of his whole household.)

As he exits the restroom, he abruptly stops humming as he runs into Pablo. "Mi hermano! What's good?"

"Trabajo, esé," Pablo says, exchanging a handshake and fist bump with Emiliano.

"Didn't know you was workin' today?" Emiliano says.

"Ah, my dad just called me, asked me to come in for a little. I was jus' around the corner anyway. So, I guess some cabrone couldn't finish a starter or somethin'." Pablo playfully punches Emiliano's arm and they laugh. "I'm just messin', I know you been here all day. You wanna shoot hoops tonight?"

"I don't think I got time." Emiliano shrugs. "Maybe tomorrow?"

"Mañana," Pablo confirms. "Later, bro."

On his way out of the auto garage, Emiliano looks at the clock again. Half-past four, already? He picks up his pace. At least the commute is convenient; he lives just a few miles from the auto shop.

After getting in his Firebird, he puts on "Everything She Wants," since it won't seem to leave his mind, then waves to his coworkers before heading down the steep parking lot. Once on the main road, he sings the lyrics that take him back to an eerie time in his life. He would listen to this song angrily a few years back while working on cars, thinking about his ex-girlfriend from high school. They dated for a couple years. She cheated on him and broke his heart. Though the worst part was that she got pregnant with the other man's child.

So deep in the memory, Emiliano doesn't realize he's home, in his crowded and lively neighborhood. He waves to an elderly next-door neighbor watering plants, then hurries into his house, pulling up his jeans that are a size too big.

"Mila," he whispers to his pit bull, who's asleep on the couch. "Let's go outside, girl."

The dog follows him until they make it to the nearest patch of grass. She sniffs until she finds the best smelly spot to mark her territory. And, as soon as she finishes, he quickly ushers her back inside. "I'm sorry, girl. I gotta run errands. We'll go for a walk tonight." He rubs her whiskers with his knuckles before heading back to his car.

Surprisingly, no neighbors are mowing, smoking, barbecuing, or watering plants, which is good because if anyone he knew were around, he would feel compelled to stop and talk, even though he's in a rush. The first thing on his agenda is the florist, well *florista*, which thankfully is just around the block.

The side of town where he lives is home to all the things that remind him of his Mexican heritage—the street carts, the meat market, and the local *panadería*. Also in the area are all the United States necessities—the auto shop, the town's grocery store, and the overpriced name brand shops, like Nike and Vans, that Emiliano loves.

Pulling into the nearly empty lot, he parks in front of Flores de Felicia, which is between the Mexican *panadería* and the American grocery store. Truly, he has always considered the florist shop to be a breath of fresh air—and it's not because of the flowers and plants. It's that there is no place he feels more like himself than right here, on this sidewalk, teetering between his two vastly different cultures.

"Hola, Felicia," he says, stepping into the shop.

"Emiliano, ¿cómo estás?"

"Bien, ¿y tu?"

"Bien, pero ocupada." Felicia shakes her head as the phone starts ringing from the back room. She holds a finger up to Emiliano and says, "Lo siento, uno momento." Her landline has been ringing so much it could pass as the store's background music—from the world's worst radio station. A few minutes later, Felicia hurries back into the room. "The ringing has been driving me loca!" she says, muddling through the orders, looking for Emiliano's.

"Been real busy, Felicia?"

"Sí, a funeral is coming up. A young woman was found in the mountains. Between the girl's family and friends, and the typical weekly orders, I been absolutely swamped!"

Emiliano's brows knit together. "Aw, no. That's terrible."

"Sí." A wary look crosses Felicia's face as she walks over with a bouquet of white roses. "Para tu novia?" she asks, handing Emiliano the flowers.

"No." Emiliano chuckles. "Para mi madre." He hands her some cash. "Gracias, Felicia."

As he walks outside, his phone rings.

"Hola, Mamá," he says.

"How was work, papicito?"

"Good, Ma. You on your way home?" He hopes not because he wants to surprise her with the flowers, all prepped and perfect, inside his mom's vase on their kitchen table.

"Not yet, I got caught up at work. Can you go to the store for me, por favor?"

"Yes, Mamá." The familiar response slides off his tongue without hesitation. "¿Qué necesitamos?"

"Paper towels, paper plates, toilet paper." Adriana pauses. She can't think of anything else to add. "Sí, todas las cosas de papel," she says with a laugh.

"¿Todas las cosas de papel?" Emiliano repeats, chuckling. "OK, Mamá. I'll see you tonight." He goes to hang up the phone then brings it back to his ear. "Get home safe." That's a sentence he always makes sure to add when talking to his family and friends. After all he has seen and been exposed to thus far in his short life, it's no secret to him that life is fragile.

When Emiliano lays the flowers on the passenger seat of his car, an irresistible aroma suddenly finds his nose. He instinctively leans into it until he's directly facing the window of the *panadería*. The richness of *pan dulce* wafts through the air as someone exits the bakery. He glances inside to the customer at the counter, then to the bag of edible gold in his hands. The customer's smiling from cheek to cheek—a smile so wide one knows it has everything to do with the fact that he's about to indulge in delicious sweet bread. Emiliano has been smiling all day, but his smile's not as wide as the one initiated by the comfort a bakery brings to one's taste buds and *panza*. He feels at his back pocket and pulls out six wadded up dollar bills and some change.

Maria Nuñez, the woman working, waves to Emiliano through the window. The bakery was opened by her father in the '80s and has been on the corner of the shopping center ever since. The Nuñez family lives in Emiliano's neighborhood and they have known him since he was in diapers.

"Hola, Maria," Emiliano says as he enters the store.

"You were standing out there so long, I knew you'd come inside amigo," she says with a smile. "What would you like today?"

Emiliano scans the array of options with intensity. They have everything from savory *bolillo* bread to sweet *tres leches*. And he loves all of it. "Un niño envuelto, una galleta de choco chip, y tres polvorones por favor."

Maria tosses the desserts in a large brown bag. "Bueno. Son cinco dólares y cincuenta centavos."

Emiliano hands her the money, telling her to keep the change. As he heads for the door, Maria advises that he not eat it all in one sitting or he'll get a stomach ache. With a thoughtful smile, he looks back at her, then continues out of the store.

Handfuls of people are filtering in and out of Flores de Felicia. Emiliano furrows his brows, wondering whether or not he has missed a vital holiday—Christmas is still a few weeks away.

"Shit. There's no way that's all for that funeral," he mumbles under his breath.

Abruptly, his body shudders, partly in thinking about a young woman's funeral, partly because of the breeze that has grown crisper since the daylight began fading. The surrounding world has slowly dwindled into dusk. The hairs on his arms begin to raise and immediately that's enough cold weather for the next century. He *hates* feeling cold and grabs a hoodie from his car before taking a single step toward the grocery store. His mother's list loops through his mind until he is just outside the automatic doors that seamlessly glide open.

After quickly gathering the paper items, he walks under the dull fluorescent lighting to self-checkout, tuning out the awful elevator music. A few people are in front of him in line, giving his mind time to wander.

There is still so much to do before he can get to sleep tonight. Dinner. Laundry. Dry cleaners. Walk the dog. Probably more. It seems there's always so little time, and the unfinished tasks from one day roll right into the next. Maybe he'll get an hour to himself tonight, just before sleep, to listen to music and relax.

When it's finally his turn, he quickly scans the items and slides his debit card into the machine. He glances out one of the large tinted windows while waiting for the store to take hard earned money out of his bank account. A white Acura pulls into the parking lot. An image of Rachel smiling flashes in his mind. Could that be her? Could he randomly run into her outside of soccer? It's already random that he sees her on a weekly basis after not seeing her for years. The self-checkout machine incessantly beeps. Emiliano pulls his card out, unsure how long it had been doing so. He quickly grabs his bags, heads outside, and—go figure. It *is* Rachel. And she is heading his way. Maybe she won't say anything. Surely she doesn't even know him, wouldn't recognize him.

When he looks up, they make eye contact.

"Emiliano from soccer, right?" Rachel asks. "What's up!?"

"Oh—hey, Rachel." He shoots her a smile. "Nothing much. Nice sweat pants," he says, staring at the Lakers emblem. "You watch the Lakeshow?"

"Is that something on Netflix?"

"No." He chuckles. "The Lakeshow! Lakers games? You never heard that before?"

"Nope." She laughs. "Uh, yeah my friend actually gave me these. Sometimes I wear them with a Clippers hoodie. I also don't watch the Clippers, but apparently it's a no-no in L.A. to rep both teams, especially at the same time."

"Aw man." Emiliano shakes his head. "Nah, Lakers all the way!"

"Big fan?"

"Huge!" Emiliano looks down at his phone, realizing it's later than he thought. "I better get going. I'll see you on Saturday, yeah?"

"Yeah, I'll be there!" She waves goodbye before walking past him. Her cheeks flush at the simple fact that he knows her name, knows who she is. After crushing on Emiliano every Saturday, they finally had their first conversation. Before entering the grocery store, she looks back at him as he gets in his car.

After buckling, Emiliano glances toward the grocery store, catching a final glimpse of Rachel. That is one beautiful woman. One beautiful, out-of-his-league woman. His stomach lets out a growl. He pulls the chocolate chip cookie out of the bag of *pan dulce* and takes a bite when he reaches the stoplight, chewing slowly to savor its goodness.

He pairs the sweetness of the second bite with thoughts of Rachel. Her long cinnamon brown hair. He takes another bite. Her athletic physique. He takes another bite. Her laugh and smile. He takes another bite, this time reflecting over the thought that the smile she elicits in him is better than the one induced by baked goods. He finishes the cookie as he pulls in his driveway, though the idea of Rachel still lingers in his brain.

And so begins the symbiotic attraction between Emiliano Morales and Rachel Williams. Her eyes are on him and his eyes are on her.

3 The Heart Will Do What It Wants

While the young men make their way to the field, Hannah and Rachel sit at the table for "Hannah Storytime," one of their common best friend hobbies. Hannah rubs at her eyes, yawning. She's never been much of a morning person, plus she was partying late at a friend's house. She shares her and Brax's night in detail: hot tub, alcohol, card games.

"And he was fine until he got wasted, then he ignored me all night. I could have sworn he was flirting with this girl too. He was laughing a whole lot, more than he does with me, and was like playfully pushing her in the pool." She demonstrates Brax's behavior, pushing on Rachel's shoulder. Before Rachel can get a word in, Hannah continues, "At the end of the night I confronted him about it. Then he started yelling and told me I'm crazy and way too obsessive. He said this is why we have so many problems between us."

"Aw, Hannah. It's not your fault. A relationship takes two people! If I were you I would have asked him the same thing." Rachel shrugs, wondering how she can help Hannah, knowing the heart will do what it wants.

"No, it was my fault. I mean, I shouldn't be so obsessive. He's right. I need to trust him. I actually apologized when we got in the car. He was reluctant at first, but then he accepted my apology."

"He plays a role too. Don't forget that!" Rachel adds.

"I think I just overreacted, honestly." Hannah's gaze drifts to the sidewalk, noticing a familiar figure heading her way. "Babe!" she calls out.

Brax walks over with a pair of Hannah's cleats, a half-crooked smile emerging on his face. Rachel glares at him; she isn't a fan of Brax at all, and only acts civil toward him because she doesn't want to jeopardize her relationship with Hannah. Both she and Hannah are sensitive girls and they know that about each other—that's why they support each other's decisions, even if they think the other's decisions are terrible.

"Sup, Rachel," Brax says.

Rachel nods, her way of saying "sup" to him.

"The black cleats in the trunk were the ones you needed, right?" Brax asks Hannah as he sits down next to her. "I couldn't remember which pair you said. Look at me though, getting you your cleats," he says with a laugh while running a hand along his short curls.

Rachel rolls her eyes. She hates watching Brax act like he is boyfriend of the year for something so trivial.

"Yeah, these are the right ones. Thanks for going back to my car to grab them, babe." Hannah looks at him longingly, then leans in for a kiss.

On the far side of the field, Fabian mentions that the game will pick up speed once Rachel and Hannah join in. As he is about to call them over, Javier tells him that he can do it. Yes, this makes him look like a helpful guy, but truly he has another motive. This would be a great opportunity to start his first conversation with Rachel in a nice, subtle way.

"Hey, are you two coming?" Javier calls out. "We already warmed up and started playing, Ms. Chatterboxes!" He was going to just ask the question, but then thought maybe it wouldn't be so memorable, and that's why he added the slightly flirty and bubbly comment that maybe Rachel would appreciate.

He'll never know that Rachel wouldn't notice or care about such attention or fine detail, well not from him anyway. She doesn't find Javier attractive, so in no way is he on her radar. Cupping her hand at her mouth, Rachel shouts "I'm coming!" having no clue just how much that response means to Javier and how much it boosts his confidence.

"That's what she said," Brax jokes.

"Is it?" Rachel snaps. She wants to say something sassy to him like *is that what the girl said in the pool last night*, but holds her tongue knowing that it would only cause issues.

Javier feels like he is on a roll, so he continues. "We've got 3 on 3, so you each put on a different colored pinny!"

Rachel gives him a thumbs-up, then grabs the blue and white mesh scrimmage vests. "You'll be out in a second?" she asks as she lays the white one on Hannah's bag.

"Thanks! And yeah, be out in a bit." Hannah stays behind to talk to Brax about why he drove to the field separately. Their apartment in L.A. is over thirty minutes away and it just didn't make sense to drive two cars. A bad feeling rots in her stomach as he insists that he has work in a town near Old Oak and will be busy all day.

Rachel jogs out to the field, scanning the players to see who else is wearing blue—Pablo, Emiliano, and Fabian. After crushing on Emiliano every Saturday, they are finally on the same team. An internal scream of excitement wells through her body.

For a few minutes, she jogs around lightly to warm up before joining in. When Pablo passes her the ball, she assesses the field, then gives Fabian a through ball. He takes a touch past the final defender and has a wide-open shot on the small goal. (Since there's only eight players, they aren't playing with goalies today.) Fabian scores and the blue team cheers.

"Nice goal!" Emiliano yells.

"Let's go blue, keep it up!" Rachel claps. "What's the score?"

"Four to three," Pablo says quickly, keeping his eyes on the game. "We're up. And we're taking a water break when someone gets to five."

Hannah comes jogging over in the white pinny and joins the game without warming up. Cold-legged, she shanks her first pass to Pablo on the other team. He launches it to Rachel on the other side of the field. After dribbling down the line, Rachel cuts in front of Javier, then looks up for a pass. Emiliano is wide open; he'd been running alongside her the whole time, but she hadn't seen him.

"One-two, one-two," Emiliano shouts as he points to where he wants the ball. Without hesitation, she passes it, then quickly runs around a defender. Javier pushes up against Rachel shoulder to shoulder as Emiliano one-touches it back to her. She takes a shot and scores.

"Ayyy!" Emiliano yells excitedly running up to her. "Nice work!"

He jumps in the air for a chest bump. Instinctively, she follows along. As their bodies touch, a lightning bolt of energy shocks through her entire body. Then his entire body. They land and awkwardly laugh.

"Yeah, nice play!" Rachel says, tightening her ponytail. She walks off the field feeling like one million butterflies just exploded in her stomach. After crushing on Emiliano every Saturday, they finally touched for the first time.

As the group sits down at the table, they pull out their water bottles and Gatorades. Pablo gives everyone on his team a fist bump for winning. All the boys start talking about the NFL because playoffs will be starting within the next month.

Rachel and Hannah look at each other knowing they each don't know a thing about football.

"Where did Brax go?" Rachel silently mouths to Hannah.

"Oh, I thought he was going to stay but I think something important came up, so he had to leave." Hannah scratches the back of her neck while looking down at the ground.

Rachel can tell Hannah is hiding something but doesn't want to pressure her for more information. They veer their attention to the men's conversation. They've switched from NFL to cars. Another lost topic.

"Yeah, I've been a mechanic for around five years now. You can bring it in the shop, and I can take a look for you," Emiliano says to one of the guys.

"You work with cars?" Rachel asks, her eyes lighting up.

"Yeah…what's that excited look for?"

"Well, I need to install new windshield wipers. Mine leave gunk all over the glass and I can barely see when I drive. I was going to attempt to put new ones on but didn't want to break something." Rachel looks at him nervously. "This might be a silly question, um, do you know how to install windshield wipers?"

Emiliano laughs. "Yeah. I've installed many before."

"Would I be able to bring my car to your shop and pay you for it?"

"You don't need to go to a shop for that." Emiliano chuckles. "It's real quick and easy."

"Ohhh," Rachel says, feeling embarrassed at her lack of car knowledge.

"I can, um, definitely switch them out for you though. Swing by your house sometime. Just let me know when you're free! You can get my number from the soccer group chat." He smiles softly as he looks up at her.

"OK. Thanks," Rachel says, grinning. "Does anyone know what time it is?"

Unfortunately, most of the young men are distracted. Javier started making bets about who will win the next game after the water break. One of Javier's prominent qualities is banter, especially in a group setting. He knows how to be the center of attention and connect with others through poking and prodding.

"$10 on blue," one guy yells. "$10 on white," another person shouts.

"Nah, let's do $20!" Javier exclaims, a deep laugh erupting from his belly.

"It's almost eleven," Pablo calls out to Rachel as he looks at his watch.

"Damn." Rachel reluctantly stands. "Have fun, guys. I have to head out."

Hannah gives her a hug before heading out to the field. A handful of others, including Emiliano and Javier, say goodbye as well.

"Don't forget, we won't play next week, Rachel. Most people will be out of town for Christmas!" Fabian says.

Rachel throws a thumbs-up as she leaves with her bag slung over her shoulder. The group and all the rambunctious energy on the field become inaudible as she makes her way into the busy parking lot thinking about the goal she made with Emiliano's help.

4 Not One For Instant Gratification

Rachel tosses her bag in the trunk, slips into fuzzy gray slippers, and gets in the car. As she backs out of the recreation lot, she glances over at the pile of textbooks, study material, and electronic devices on the passenger seat. They truly are like passengers. Like the best friend you take everywhere, or maybe the friend who never wants to leave you alone. Her mind is always on the Graduate Record Examination (GRE), the placement exam for graduate school, which is less than two months away. That's why she left soccer early today, to study for a few hours at The Coffee Bar.

If studying were considered a full-time job, Rachel is sure she would be filthy rich. It seems like all she does is study; and on the odd occasions where she *does* grant herself free time, it's never for long and most likely educational—reading, watching documentaries, or listening to true crime podcasts. Though, she doesn't mind her lifestyle. She is not one for instant gratification. It's always been an easy trade-off to bypass the partying, the staying out late, the group hangouts—all the typical things people do in their twenties.

Rachel turns on the radio and puts on one of L.A.'s oldies stations. The song that's on is "Let Your Love Flow" by The Bellamy Brothers. She opens her sunroof, lowers the windows, and dangles a hand outside to feel the breeze. Her hair knots up, flying everywhere. She feels free and alive, and wishes the lyrics could blast through the town.

The song reminds her of the purest type of love that generates from the center of one's being for all creatures and Mother Earth. She feels that if everyone were to live their lives from that place—where they are a wellspring of love, always flowing, making connections with everything they touch and everything that touches them—the world would be a better place. If only she knew how to live that way all the time. So often she is caught up with overthinking things that she can't control—like Hannah's romance life or whether or not everything will work out with school and her future occupation.

She turns into a parking lot and admires the beautiful shopping center. It's her favorite one in town, new and fairly small with just four businesses. There's a Chinese restaurant; a massage spa; a modern ice cream shop with KETO, gluten-free, and vegan flavors; and The Coffee Bar, a hipster hangout spot. Rachel studies here a few times a month, whenever she wants to dive deep in the study zone. She prefers this coffee shop because they have freshly made in-house syrups, delicious avocado toast, all the dairy-free milk one can imagine, and the ambiance is perfect for studying.

With her backpack and pile of study materials, she walks inside and sets her stuff down on an open seat at the chic wooden bar. The barista greets her from behind the register. "Back again? You've been in here a lot recently."

"Grad school studying." Rachel looks to the heavens as if pleading to the Gods for help.

While Rachel scans the drink options, the barista tells her about a new matcha drink that's not on the menu yet, handing over a card with health information about the beverage. Rachel smiles as she takes the infographic and reads about the many benefits of matcha.

"I'll have to try this sometime! I think today I'll just get a hot decaf latte made with oat milk. And can I get a pump of the organic vanilla syrup, please?"

"Perfect. And what size?" The Barista enters the information into the cash register.

"Um...medium should be good," Rachel says, nodding.

After paying nearly $7.00 for the beverage, Rachel sits down and glances at the funky abstract art on the walls. This place really is something special, she thinks. Often, when she's here, the coffee shop is playing lo-fi beats, which she deems to be the perfect study music: light and subtle, accompanied by the occasional coffee house chatter or a utensil clanking from behind the coffee bar.

She opens her textbook to chapter eight: Society and Culture. Just as she begins reading, one of the baristas walks over with her latte. She admires the forest-colored mug and the foam artwork delicately displayed on the top layer. Cupping her hands around it, she instantly feels the warmth.

Slowly, the people, the music, the smells all fade as she focuses on the text. She recalls a lot of the mentioned terms from classes she took during her undergraduate degree: cultural appropriation, assimilation, ethnocentrism. Rachel can't help but think this textbook would be beneficial for everyone in the United States to read, as the country has such a unique society—a beautiful blending where many subcultures coexist.

For over an hour she doesn't lift her eyes from the pages, occasionally reaching one hand out for her drink. Only when she finishes reading the concluding summary and making flashcards for the chapter's vocabulary does she finally lift her tired eyes.

With a hardworking yawn, she collects her things and heads to the car. Unwilling to put the radio on as a temporary distraction, she lets all her thoughts of the day's events surface, to process during her time behind the wheel. What was Hannah hiding at the table? And where did Brax go? What could have been more important than supporting his girlfriend for once? Just as the curious questions stop, new thoughts arrive. This time about Emiliano. She is eager to see him again. What was that feeling that came over her when they touched? It was something she had never felt before. Did he feel it too? And as quickly as those thoughts come, they leave without lingering.

Her study session makes its way to the forefront of her mind. More specifically, what the textbook said about cultures and subcultures. Rachel wonders if there will be a day when cultures can accept and celebrate one another as opposed to repel and look down on one another. Though, she thinks, perhaps that's an easier statement to say for someone who has the same skin color as those who massacred the entire planet.

The familiar scenery of her street snaps her out of auto-pilot driving. She passes Prius after Prius and parks on the sidewalk in front of her house.

"Hi, honey!" Shannon yells from the front lawn as she bends over to water a group of plants. "I just went grocery shopping if you're hungry."

This statement is pretty indicative of Rachel's upbringing and the kind of parents she has. She's lived in this same house since she was three months old. She's always had the security of shelter, food, and water. She's always had two loving parents—who minimally fought—and were committed to doing the best they could.

"OK, thanks Mom." The coffee curbed Rachel's appetite, so she just smiles as she watches her mother. The petite woman in her early fifties with platinum blonde hair fusses with the knob of the hose until it goes from stream to trickle to nothing.

The two chitchat about dinner plans as they head inside the house. Ultimately, they settle on the idea of split pea soup. Since there is still a few hours until supper, Shannon decides to relax in the living room. She turns on the TV and a corny Hallmark Christmas movie blares on the screen. Rachel glances at it before going upstairs to her room. She doesn't watch a lot of TV. And, if she were to, it definitely wouldn't be a corny Hallmark holiday film.

Rachel lies down on her bed and—like clockwork— her dog comes running in, wagging her tail. "Hi, Moo!" Rachel says.

Her dog's name is Cece, but Rachel nicknamed her Moo because of her white coat with brown spots. (And the extra chub from all the treats Rachel feeds her.)

Cece jumps on the bed and licks Rachel's nose, cheeks, and forehead. "Thank you, Moo Moo!" Rachel laughs, moving her face away from the licking. The dog quickly rolls over into a *please give me a belly rub right now* position and Rachel complies. She rubs Cece's tummy, then asks her if she wants to go for a walk.

Cece tilts her head at the infamous four-letter w-word, then proceeds to spin in circles. She practically races Rachel down the stairs toward the harness and leash that hang by the front door.

"Please be careful!" Shannon cries as Rachel and Cece enter the foyer.

"I will, Mom. I always am."

"I'm serious. When you go out after dark, don't be out too late. Be mindful of who you're with. Be careful where you go."

"OK…" Rachel says, confused by the seemingly random statement. She cranes her neck to see what her mom is watching. Not the whimsical holiday story, but the local news. A search team and helicopter somewhere in the outskirts of Los Angeles. The red headline at the bottom of the screen reads "Unsolved: Young Woman Found in the Mountains."

Her mother isn't typically a paranoid person, but things like this worry her. Especially since L.A. is so close to home. Then again, L.A. has always been a hot spot for crime and that crime rarely ever makes its way to the suburbs of Old Oak and Ten Pines.

"I'll be safe, Mom. Be back soon!" Rachel opens the door and Cece follows her outside.

Fairly quickly into their walk, Rachel scrolls through the "SSS" group chat to save Emiliano's number. She already knows which one is his since there are texts mentioning early Saturday basketball and Pablo, his favorite sport and his best friend. She wonders if it will be weird to text him. He did tell her to though, after all. For a bit, she contemplates how to start the conversation, then sends a short, simple message.

Hey, is this Emiliano?

A few minutes later, at the corner of a main road, her phone buzzes.

Yes! Is this Rachel?

The bright phone screen is like a spotlight illuminating her giddy smile. Immediately, she types a response with an eager yes and a blushing emoji.

With such focused attention on her phone and Emiliano, she doesn't notice that someone is walking on the other side of the main road. And that "someone" happens to be Javier Aguilar. He planned on waving to her, but upon noticing how absorbed she was into her phone he continued on his way.

As Cece stops to mark territory on a bush, Rachel's phone buzzes again. Another quick response from Emiliano, this one with a grinning emoji. After a few more back-and-forth surface-level texts, the two start talking about soccer, then they make plans for after Christmas, for him to help change her windshield wipers.

5 Hundreds of Stars Twinkling

With two cups of hot cocoa in hand, Rachel walks to the curb, dressed in a chic navy blue sweatsuit. Emiliano pulls up to her house in his mother's car, a newer gray Hyundai Sonata. As he steps out, she studies his outfit under the dimly lit street. He is decked out in pure comfort: a black Lakers sweatshirt, gray Nike sweats, and colorful Nike high-tops.

"This is for you," Rachel says, gesturing a cup toward him.

"What's this?" Emiliano asks.

Rachel goes on a rant, a bit nerdy and cute, about the vegan hot cocoa that she made from scratch. What she doesn't tell him is that she had purchased all the ingredients earlier that day from Whole Foods and spent over $50.00 on the highest grade hot cocoa ingredients just for him. (Since he came to help with her car, she figured the least she could do was make him hot cocoa on a cold night.)

"Thank you! I don't know if I've ever had vegan hot cocoa before." His nose scrunches. "Actually, I don't even think I know what vegan hot cocoa is."

Rachel explains that vegan simply means there are no animal products. He takes a sip, and she watches nervously.

"Wow, this is reeeeal rich and smooth," he says. And, while the cocoa is tasty, the excitement in his voice mainly comes from the fact that he is stunned she made it *just* for him. "So where are these new windshield wipers?"

Rachel's eyes widen. For a moment she forgot that's why he came over. She grabs the package from the back of her trunk.

"You think you can hold this for me while I work?" he asks, gesturing to his cellphone as he turns on its flashlight.

Rachel takes it. "Just let me know where you need me to point it."

"I guess we'll start with the directions?" Emiliano takes his time reading about how to install the windshield wipers, even though he already knows how. Throughout his life, he's done this too many times to count. He wants to stall as long as he can to spend more time with Rachel; he's so curious about the woman from another world.

After removing the old windshield wipers, he fiddles around with the new ones and all their plastic attachments. "I think this part clips into this one," he says, even though he knows the two parts connect. "So, uh, what do you do for work?"

"I'm actually between jobs right now. Looking to go to grad school, so I've been studying a lot." Rachel isn't quite sure why she said "between jobs" because truly she's never been "between jobs." It's just…she doesn't want Emiliano to see her as some spoiled girl. She had part-time gigs in college, but school has always been her main focus and her parents were willing to continue paying her way until she was finished with school.

"Nice. School for what?" he asks.

"Cognitive-behavioral therapy."

"Why therapy?"

"To help people with their mental struggles." Has Rachel finally met a man who shows interest in *real* topics? She doesn't say anything else because watching Emiliano's hands is distracting. He keeps messing around with the windshield parts. She wishes she was the plastic in his hands—being touched and fondled by him.

"For some reason, I keep confusing these parts. They aren't fitting into each other," he tells her. Truly, it's just another way to stall time. He might not be alone with this girl ever again.

Rachel wonders why he is confused, recalling that, at soccer, he mentioned he'd installed many before. "It's OK, take all the time you need."

Seeing that as an invitation, Emiliano puts the windshield wiper down, then sips the hot cocoa and licks his lips. He bets Rachel is probably as warm and tasty as the beverage. Before his mind can take that thought deeper, a brown suburban turns onto the street and parks across from Rachel's house, stealing their attention. They watch the silhouette of the driver as he jumps out with a large paper bag, making a food delivery to her neighbor's house.

Emiliano squints. "I think that's my homeboy!?"

Rachel stares, trying to get a better look at the short delivery man.

"Pablo?" Emiliano calls out.

Pablo looks across the street, then continues walking to the car, thinking he wouldn't know anyone in this neighborhood.

"Pablo?" Emiliano repeats.

"Emiliano?" Pablo says, in a tone that suggests he's just as confused as Emiliano. "Rachel?" Pablo adds. "Whatcha guys up to?" He looks at the two of them, trying to figure out why they are together.

"I'm just installing her windshield wipers," Emiliano says. "You was delivering food or something?"

"Yeah, that order was from Acai Cruisers. I started doin' Uber Eats to make some extra money."

Rachel's eyes light up. She loves Acai Cruisers and promptly begins raving about it.

"Yeah that place smacks," Pablo says. "I better get goin'. I got another delivery."

After exchanging goodbyes, Rachel and Emiliano head back to her car while Pablo's suburban rumbles up the street.

"What a crazy coincidence!" Rachel says.

"Right? For a second I was wonderin' if my eyes were workin' properly." Emiliano takes a sip of cocoa, then picks up a windshield wiper. "So you like Acai Cruisers?"

"One of my favorite places," Rachel says.

"Me too!" Emiliano replies. "So, um, this should clip in right here." He leans over the hood and snaps in the first windshield wiper, then walks to the other side of the car. Rachel follows behind with his illuminated phone flashlight. Seamlessly, he snaps in the second one.

"Well, that should do it," he says. "You might want to make sure they swipe properly."

Rachel gets in her car while Emiliano stays in front of the hood. She stares at him for a few moments, then leans out the window. "You wanna come in?" she offers. "We might need two sets of eyes on this thing."

Without answering, he gets in, gliding his hands across the slick black leather seats, studying her car. He wonders why she invited him in, why she invited him *here*. It just doesn't make any sense to him.

Rachel looks over at Emiliano, lifting her hand to her mouth like a microphone. "Testing, testing in 3, 2, 1." He smiles at her goofing around. She flicks a lever and her windshield wipers go back and forth perfectly. "It's nice to finally see clearly," she says. "I appreciate you helping. Are you sure you don't want me to pay you?"

"Of course not, the cocoa was more than enough." Emiliano wishes he could see her for longer, but wouldn't even know how to approach the subject. "It's been great to see you tonight." He opens the door, initiating a goodbye.

"Wait! Emiliano…don't you think we need to take this car for a test drive to make sure the windshield wipers work?" she says jokingly.

Emiliano's cheeks flush. Is she into him? There is no way. She couldn't be. A smile spreads across his face as he stares at the stunning woman in front of him. "As someone who works on cars, my expert opinion is yes." Each word comes out slowly, lingering in the air. "Replacing the windshield wipers definitely means it's time to test drive the car?"

They shyly laugh. Windshield wipers and test driving? Both he and Rachel are not making any sense. And both of them know it.

"Perfect, you drive!" Rachel says.

After the two trade places, Emiliano asks, "Where to, Rachel?"

"Hmm, since it's dark we can park at the trailhead," she suggests.

Nerves well inside him as they leave the curb. He tries to hide his unease. Rachel doesn't even notice, basking in his masculinity, believing he presents himself so confidently. They make their way toward the mountains on a lightly trafficked back road that eventually turns into a dirt parking lot. Usually, the area is packed at night for stargazing, but tonight the lot is oddly empty. He parks at an angle where they can stare into the light of the full moon.

"What kind of music are you into?" Rachel asks eagerly. "Ooh actually, let me guess!" She looks Emiliano up and down, slightly squinting as if to read it out of his body. "I'm sensing an oldies vibe. Like '70s and '80s music."

"What makes you think that?" Emiliano says with a smirk.

"It's just your aura and your style that gives me that impression."

"That's wild. I love oldies music. '70s and '80s. I also love the '50s and '60s too. I used to be obsessed with Elvis, even styled my hair like him all the time." His eyes light with passion. He's not used to talking about himself. It's not often people ask him questions about who he is and what he enjoys, and Rachel surprised him.

"You're gonna hate this, Emiliano, but…I don't know much about Elvis. I've probably only ever heard one song."

"No way! What? He's a legend! Which song do you know?"

"Uh…the one about dogs. Who let the dogs out?" Rachel murmurs unconfidently.

Emiliano tries to keep a straight face. "That is *not* by Elvis." He howls with laughter, leaning closer to her, his head briefly resting on her shoulder. "How old even are you if you don't know Elvis? You must have just had your fifth birthday," he jokes.

"Fifth?" Rachel giggles. "For your information, I am an entire woman, twenty-three years old." Suddenly the song title clicks in her mind. "Hound Dog," she says with conviction. "I swear I meant Hound Dog." Rachel joins in his laughter.

"Wow, you're older than me? I'm still twenty-two for a while." Emiliano scrolls through the music on his phone. "You know, I think I just gotta show you my favorite Elvis song."

He puts on "Such a Night" and starts dancing to the rhythm in his seat. As Elvis's voice comes in, he unashamedly belts the lyrics with his crackly, off-pitched voice. His gaze drifts to Rachel's brown eyes, then to her long, perfectly straight hair. She is one of the most beautiful girls he has ever seen. Lyrics about the moon fill the night air. He rolls down the window, throws out an arm, pointing and pleading as if the moon is his lover and he's performing a solo to her.

Rachel sits still as a stone wall, intently staring, having never met someone so authentic who easily and gracefully embodies themself. She realizes that the handsome man in front of her is an enigma. A puzzle—not with a hundred pieces, but with thousands. A down-to-earth human with quite the persona to offer the world. She takes a mental note that she has found a piece to his puzzle. A piece somewhere in the middle, close to his heart. A piece named Elvis.

Matching the famous singer's pitch, Emiliano remains lost in the song, almost as if he has forgotten that he is in the presence of another human. A poetic line about kissing comes next. Rachel fixates on his lips. All she can think about is kissing his lips. His plump, juicy, perfectly pink-toned lips.

The seat warmers and heat from the vents start to make Rachel sweat, though those aren't the only things making her hot. She rolls down the window and leans into the cold. It's a beautiful night. The breeze is light, yet crisp at the same time. There are hundreds of stars twinkling down on them. A reminder to her that they aren't alone in the dirt lot. There's an entire universe watching them. She wonders what the stars think. Are they smiling down? Are they feeling warm inside? She peers at the full moon. It's one of those nights where it appears cartoon-like, closer and bigger than it normally looks. Knowing this is a memory she will cherish forever, she takes a mental photograph of Emiliano singing out to the moon.

As the song concludes, Emiliano's vibrant grin withers into a slight smile. He remembers how he used to sing it to his ex-girlfriend. Someone who he thought was the love of his life. Someone who he thought he was going to marry. Someone who turned out to be nothing like who she said she was. He hasn't loved since and definitely won't let Rachel see his emotions, nor share the memories that are coming back.

Instead, he gives her his cellphone. "Show me whachu got, Rachel."

Their hands slightly touch as she grabs the phone, causing the infamous butterflies to flutter in both of their stomachs. He patiently waits while she scrolls and scrolls through the tunes. After a bit of contemplation, a hint of musical instruments enters the atmosphere. Rachel sets the phone down on the center console, repositions herself, and looks over at Emiliano as "When Doves Cry" by Prince heads into the first verse.

Rachel harmonizes with the high-pitched singer to the best of her ability. She swivels her torso, letting herself get lost in the music. Her hands glide up and down her stomach and the outside of her breasts as she sensually dances and moves her hips, mirroring the energy of the lyrics.

"Oh, OK!" Emiliano shouts, hyping her up. He can't help but stare at her. She's sexy. She's athletic. She's smart. She's, well, everything.

Rachel points to Emiliano, then motions him toward her. Simply and utterly soaking in the joy of the song, she remains lost for another verse the same way he had been. Then, not wanting to get too carried away, she halts her dance moves and shyly laughs.

Emiliano pauses the music. "I gotta show you some real cool bands sometime…like Chicano Batman, El Chicano, Malo. I wonder what you'd think of 'em."

"Who are they?" she asks.

"They are the sound of California Chicanos and Mexicanos."

Rachel couldn't be more enthralled by his statement. She finds learning about other cultures to be such a wholesome and inspiring experience. "So, are you fully bilingual?"

Emiliano nods.

"Do you think you'd be able to help me with a few translations?"

"Yeah, of course! What are you translating?"

"I've been reading this book..." Rachel pauses, reaching into her back seat. There's a stack of books and each one has a bookmark. After lifting the top two, she grabs the third, then swiftly flips through it until she finds an excerpt with some Spanish. "Aha! Right here...Florecita."

"Little flower," Emiliano says.

"Cuentos."

"Stories."

"Si Dios quiere."

"God willing."

"El Cucuy and La Llorona." Rachel terribly mispronounces both words.

"The book talks about El Cucuy and La Llorona!?" Emiliano questions.

"El Cucuy and La Llorona?" Rachel repeats, following Emiliano's pronunciation.

He nods. "So you never heard of either of those?"

"No, I haven't."

"El Cucuy is a Mexican urban legend. Terrifying. A boogeyman who makes children disappear. Growing up our parents would say things like 'You better be sleeping otherwise El Cucuy will come get ya!' or 'Don't be naughty you know El Cucuy will come around here looking for you.'" He says the words in a parental tone, briefly reliving moments of his childhood.

"Did you ever see El Cucuy?" Rachel asks.

"Nah, El Cucuy ain't real. But you know who *is* real? La Llorona. No doubt in my mind!"

"So...who is La Llorona?"

"La Llorona is a woman, a ghost roaming earth. She's always crying. Weeping. Mourning the loss of her children. Forever searching for them. There's been sightings of La Llorona all over Mexico. In some places, late at night, you can hear her cries and screams in the distance. The history of La Llorona...I'm pretty sure...goes hundreds of years back."

Rachel lingers on every word he shares. "I can't believe I've never heard of this before."

"Are there any legends or folklore stories that were passed down to you?"

"No. Nothing of the sort." Her face drops into an empty look.

Emiliano glances at the clock. "We should go. I gotta be up in six hours for work."

They pull out of the lot slowly. The street is foggy, making it hard for Emiliano to see past the first twenty or so feet out the windshield. Neither of them says a word as they soak in their night spent together—the laughs, the conversations, the surprisingly smooth way they just clicked.

After parking along the curb by her house, they exit the car and walk toward one another. Each of them wonders what their goodbye is about to look like, unsure what to expect as everything about the night thus far has been, well, *unexpected*.

"Thank you again so much for helping me with the windshield wipers," Rachel says. "Oh, and for the Spanish lesson!"

"It's no problem at all. I had lots of fun tonight." He walks toward her, his arms open.

Leaning in, they hug, her nose nestling into his shoulder. The cologne on his shirt smells incredible, like deep smoky wood and fresh air.

"Goodnight," she says before heading up the driveway.

"Goodnight," he replies. After unlocking his car door, he looks back at her. "Hey! Make sure to close your closet and check under your bed. Gotta be safe out here. You don't want El Cucuy to come get you!"

Rachel laughs at his clever joke. "Get home safe." She waves from the porch, still relishing the incredible night with Emiliano Morales.

6 The Lucky Man

Taking a large knife out of the butcher block, Emiliano's *abuela*, Martina, steadies her hand as she makes the first cut into the colorfully adorned *Rosca de Reyes*. In Spanish, she hollers to her family to join her in the kitchen. Martina doesn't know much English. She was born and raised in Mexico City. It wasn't until her mid-twenties that she, along with her husband and four children, made the long journey to the States.

Conversations die down. People finish the last few bites of the holiday feast and head into the kitchen. Emiliano's family is quite large, so they spill out into the hallway and living room of Martina's small, cozy house. Martina places slices of the *pan* on paper plates and hands them out. "¿Quién necesita un plato? Vengan aquí niños flacos." She waves, motioning everyone to come get a slice of bread.

Emiliano and his older sister, Samanta, are the last to grab theirs. With their plates in hand, they sit on each side of their mother on the couch. Samanta looks strikingly similar to Adriana: same smile, same facial bone structure, same thick dark hair.

While everyone takes their first bites of the bread, Emiliano's *tío*, Antonio, stands with his glass of agave tequila. Antonio is a hefty man in his early forties. The most noticeable things about him are his cowboy hat and thick dark brown mustache. "A mi familia," he says, raising his glass. Everyone old and young smiles, extending their cups of *champurrado* in the air. "Familia!" they holler in unison. Uproars of laughter sing through the kitchen, hallway, and living room.

Emiliano takes a few more bites and suddenly crunches down on something hard. He takes the bread out of his mouth and picks a small figurine out of it. "¡Me salío el niño Jesús!" He holds the plastic baby in the air. Gasps of excitement fill the room. One of his little cousins points up to the baby Jesus, mouth open wide.

Adriana rubs the back of Emiliano's shoulders. "¡Eres un hombre afortunado!"

Antonio glances their way. "¿Jefe?" He motions for Emiliano.

With his empty plate in one hand and the last bite of sweet bread in the other, Emiliano walks over to his *tío*.

"You are the man of your house. And now you are a lucky man too. Do you know what that means?" Antonio looks deeply into Emiliano's eyes, proud of the young man he sees before him. Emiliano looks back with reverence, unsure what his *tío* is talking about. A smile ever so slowly spreads across Antonio's face. "¡Tequila, el jefe!"

Emiliano chuckles. It seems hard liquor is his *tío's* answer to everything. Sad? Drink. Happy? Drink! Lucky? Definitely drink. Truth be told, Emiliano's never been much of a drinker; it never looked appealing to him.

Antonio pours two shots from the bottle of Corralejo Resposado. One for Emiliano. One for himself. He pats his nephew's shoulder as he slides one across the table. They lift the shot glasses evenly in the air. "Para el hombre!" Antonio shouts, professing his approbation of Emiliano. After clinking their glasses, they cock their heads back and take the shots, celebrating their manhood. It goes down like water for Antonio, while Emiliano shudders.

"Gracias, Tío." Emiliano coughs into his elbow.

"Don't worry, niño. When you get old like me, it'll go down easy!" Antonio winks.

Emiliano's head shakes back and forth, his body still processing the tequila.

"Emiliano, Emiliano!" a young voice calls from the kitchen. Emiliano looks in the direction of the voice, then back to his *tio*. Antonio sends him off with a head nod.

In the kitchen, Emiliano is greeted by his little cousins. Two of them run past the refrigerator laughing and chasing each other. He dodges their path, then walks over to Alicia who's sitting at the kitchen table. She is sporting her skateboarding helmet, her long black hair tied back in a ponytail.

"Can we pleeeeasseee go skateboarding? I reeeealllyyyy want to show you my new tricks!" Alicia imparts with eagerness, clasping her helmet buckle together.

"It's getting reeallllyyyy dark out, Alicia. I do want to see them though. You want to show me the next time I see you…when it's daytime?" He shoots her a smile as he holds his hand out for a high five. Alicia's cheeks get rosy pink. She nods, fast and methodical like a bobblehead, then slaps her hand to his, sealing the deal.

"So, word on the street is you're about to be ten," Emiliano says, his eyebrows raising.

"Sí." Alicia shyly smiles, then takes off her helmet and joins the other kids.

Emiliano watches the youngsters as they laugh and run in circles. They are another reason why he's not much of a drinker. He wants to be present with them, and a good influence.

As he walks back through their play zone into the hallway, his mom is walking through with a stack of used paper plates.

"You ready, papi?" she asks.

"Si, Mamá."

"Perfecto. Let me just grab my purse."

Adriana walks past her son and the darting children to throw the trash away. Emiliano continues into the living room and spots his mother's purse on the couch. He walks over and casually slips it over his arm.

Tía Camila watches him, her head tilting, her short brown hair dipping past her shoulder. "You know you looked just like your papá right then."

Emiliano looks up and realizes she's addressing him. "Oh, really?"

Camila doesn't add anything else to the statement but continues reminiscing with the same look of nostalgia. A flashback from high school twenty-some years ago comes to mind—her gorgeous older sister, Adriana, a junior, was dating a handsome senior, Emiliano's father. They would all walk home together every day. He would grab Adriana's backpack for her and sling it over his shoulder, the same way Emiliano just had. Camila was just a freshman then, watching, and hoping that one day she would have a boyfriend like her big sister. It was shortly after that when she found out she was going to be a *tía*. During Adriana's senior year, she gave birth to Emiliano's sister, Samanta. Then Emiliano came eighteen months later.

"Here's your purse," Emiliano says to his mother as she rounds the corner.

Adriana looks at her son with admiration and thanks him. They wave goodbye to everyone in the room, including

Samanta and her heavier-set *Chicano* boyfriend, Marcos, who drove over separately. A symphony of goodbyes resound from the sea of waving hands. "Can't wait for el Día de la Candelaria, Emiliano!" one of his family members yells as they exit the house.

Shoot, Emiliano thinks. He almost forgot about that tradition. The meal. The task for the finder of the plastic Baby Jesus. As he and his mother walk down the driveway, they stare at the concrete, exchanging no words.

After a few beats, Adriana says, "The lucky man," breaking the silence.

He smirks, placing his hands in his jacket pockets. Truly, the second they had shut the door was the second his mind left the Epiphany celebration, was the second his mind turned its attention to Rachel Williams.

7 Falling Fast and Falling Hard

As soon as Emiliano and Adriana get in the car, Emiliano pulls out his phone and calls Rachel to invite her to Acai Cruisers. When she answers the phone, he greets her eagerly. A beat later though, he fears how that eagerness may come across to Rachel, so he clears his throat, lowers his voice, and proceeds in a cool and calm demeanor. He's young and inexperienced so acting like he doesn't care—when he truly does—is just his M.O. After ending the call, he nonchalantly slides the phone into his pocket, as if nothing out of the ordinary just happened.

Adriana glances over, noticing a twinkle in his eye. "Who's that?"

"Oh, just my friend from soccer."

"Mmm," Adriana mumbles, nodding.

A few minutes later, they pull in the driveway, blocking Emiliano's car in the garage. Instead of going through the hassle of pulling her car out, propping up the garage door, pulling his car out, lowering the garage door, then putting her car back in the driveway—a process that takes about fifteen minutes—he asks his mother if he can borrow her car.

"Uh…sure, mijo. Be careful. Be home by midnight. I have work very early tomorrow. Gotta be up even before you!" Her eyebrows raise as she hands him the keys.

Emiliano gets behind the wheel and taps his pockets, double-checking that he has everything—keys, phone, wallet. Once his mom gets inside safely, he leaves the neighborhood, multitasking while he drives. He smiles at the rearview mirror, making sure there isn't anything in his teeth, then lightly combs through his hair. He wants to look good for Rachel, however he will not admit that to himself.

When he reaches Rachel's dimly lit street, he parks underneath a lamppost across from her house. A nervous sigh escapes him. He can't help but wonder what Rachel sees in him or why she said yes to seeing him again.

Thrilled for their date, Rachel quickly gets off the porch swing. She is wearing ripped baggy jeans and a dark green sherpa jacket, and hopes that Emiliano will like her cute and casual outfit. She feels pretty, and is excited to see him again after they hit it off the night he changed her windshield wipers.

Once inside the car, Rachel scans him from bottom to top: leather Converse, dark blue Levi jeans, Lakers windbreaker, backward Lakers hat. There's something about his style that she just adores, and she isn't quite sure what it is. "I like your outfit," she says with a shy smile.

"Thanks! I was at a family thing."

"What was your family doing?"

"Well today's a holiday." Seeing no cars coming their way, he pulls onto the street and heads for the main road. "Día de Los Tres Reyes. It's also called Epiphany." He explains the tradition in detail, telling her how it's based on the three wise men visiting baby Jesus. His family eats a special Mexican bread that has a plastic baby inside, which is meant to represent Jesus at the manger. Whoever gets the slice with the baby has good luck for the rest of the year. "And this year I got the baby Jesus!"

"Woahhh! So how do they bake a plastic baby inside?"

"You know, I always ask myself that same question. I'm like, 'How come it doesn't melt while it's baking?!'" His nose scrunches, and they both laugh at the thought. "Along with my luck, I also get to bake a meal for my family's next holiday celebration."

"Oooh…I know a great Italian dish you could bake!" Rachel finds a photograph on her phone of the delectable cuisine from the last time she baked it. At the stoplight, he looks over at the huge pasta shells dripping in red sauce, various cheeses, and green onions.

"That looks good! I have to make tamales though…for Día de la Candelaria."

"Why tamales?"

"I don't really know why. It's just the way it is…same with a lot of things."

They pull into the parking lot and drive down a stretch of parking spaces. Emiliano spots his friend Ricardo's truck and sees two silhouettes inside. Presumably, it's Ricardo and his girlfriend Sofía. They always eat at the pizza shop next to Acai Cruisers. Instead of parking, Emiliano turns down another row of spots. He doesn't want to run into Ricardo and Sofía while he is with Rachel. For one, they are just hanging out and barely know each other so why would he want to introduce her to his friends? Secondly, it would make him feel uncomfortable and awkward and he wouldn't know how to act.

"My friend Ricardo was back there with his girl, Sofía," Emiliano says after parking.

"How funny running into one of your friends again. You want to say hi?"

"Nah. They busy, we busy. It's all good, I see Ricardo all the time…Maybe we should call in our order that way we can wait in the car while it's being made?"

Rachel shrugs, feeling it's neither here nor there. They decide what they each want and Emiliano makes the call. Rachel listens in, surprised and slightly grossed out by his smoothie order—he requests a smoothie with an orange juice base and asks for extra oats. As soon as he gets off the phone, she pokes fun at his terrible taste buds.

"You know what? Now you don't get any!" he says.

They laugh and their eyes meet. Rachel quickly looks away. She knows that if he looks into her eyes, he will see the truth: she likes him and is already falling for him. She's notorious for falling fast and falling hard. Reclining her seat, she gazes into the boring gray car ceiling, as if it were the night sky on a clear night with thousands of stars to be explored. "So, tell me more about Epiphany."

Following her lead, he reclines his seat and gazes at the main road through the windshield. "Well in some Chicano communities here, and for my cousins in Mexico, Epiphany is like how Christmas is in the United States. The three kings, instead of Santa, come in the middle of the night with treasures and goodies and treats and stuff."

Rachel soaks in his words for a few moments. "That's neat. The whole thing. The family gathering, the bread, the plastic baby, the goodies." She smiles, imagining the richness of his culture. "It makes me wish I was…part of something…or…had family traditions."

"You don't have anything like that?"

Of course, she does. She is third generation in the United States and deeply engulfed in the middle-class American values—self-discipline, thriftiness, ambition, Christian household, family-oriented—and the country's traditions: Halloween, Thanksgiving, Christmas, Easter. Since Rachel has only been in and experienced her own culture she doesn't see her culture as a culture. Meeting

Emiliano and learning about his Mexican American way of life, on the other hand, feels like true culture. And, it's different than reading about cultures in her psychology textbook. It's real. Intriguing. Special. Sacred.

"Well, I haven't heard much where my ancestors came from," she says. "I mean…my White ancestors? What were most of them focused on anyway? Colonialism? Classism? How to turn the Earth and its People into monetary gain? I don't think my ancestors were anything but trouble to our own culture and others."

"I mean…I can't disagree," Emiliano says sheepishly. "You know, I had no idea there was a White person like you out there."

"What do you mean?" Her gaze shifts from the car ceiling to Emiliano.

"I just didn't know there were White people who thought like that."

"Oh." Rachel pauses. "Well, um…" She trails off and stillness sweeps through the car.

For a beat an awkwardness infiltrates the air. And, as if it were some sort of pest, Emiliano shoos it away by changing the subject. "So how long you been playin' soccer, Rachel?"

Almost immediately, the intense mood—still tickling through the air—lightens.

"Since I was seven. I asked my parents if they could sign me up because I wanted to run and I wanted to win." She smirks. "How about you?"

"Shoot, I been messin' around with a ball since I could walk. Soccer's just part of my culture, somethin' I was born knowin'."

And with that, they head inside the nearly empty Brazillian shop decorated in purple and green décor. Emiliano pays before Rachel has a chance to offer, then holds the door open for her as they leave.

She really likes this; she really likes *him*. His kindness is beyond anything imaginable. Paying for her food? Holding the door open? Men from her past never treated her with such respect. With a sweet smile, she whispers thank you to her cute date, hoping that he *is* her date.

Once back in the car, she scoops a hefty spoonful of fruit into her mouth while he takes a large sip of his smoothie. Then, hoping to elicit some flirting, Rachel makes a joke about his gross smoothie flavor. Of course, he flirts back. He knows what she is doing and he likes it. Rachel is hot, cool, fun, out of his league, and she is initiating flirting with him.

"You talkin' so much crap 'bout my smoothie. C'mon jus' try it."

Rachel stares at the purplish-brown drink with chunks of oats, contemplating whether she should. It truly does look and sound disgusting to her. She hesitates before reluctantly reaching for it and taking a nervous sip. Her eyes grow wider the longer her mouth is on the straw. After she swallows, she goes in for more.

"Hey, gordita! Don't drink it all!" he says jokingly. "It's so good, right?"

"Did you just call me little fatty?" She laughs. "Honestly, it's better than I expected."

"Keep hangin' with me and I'll be puttin' you on all the things," Emiliano retorts.

"Oh reeeeally? What kind of things?"

"You name it. Drinks, food, restaurants, hangout spots, movies."

"You're going to think this is preposterous, but I don't watch movies. I'm always studying." She sighs, feeling slightly embarrassed. "Basically, I can almost guarantee that if you name a specific movie, my answer will be 'No, Emiliano, I haven't seen it!'" She speaks the words theatrically as if she is rehearsing an all too familiar line from a movie.

"You got a pen and paper?" He starts looking around the car.

Rachel reaches into her purse nestled between her feet and digs around until she finds a pen and a mini paper bag. She holds up the potential makeshift "paper," then places it on the center console and steadies the pen before looking up at Emiliano.

"Um…*Blood In, Blood Out*. We have to watch that one! And *Freedom Writers*…Hmm…What else? *Boyz n The Hood*…" He looks up in deep thought as he sips his smoothie, speculating other movies they could add to the list. Rachel writes each one as he says it, as if she is listening to a professor, taking notes in a lecture hall. Emiliano looks over to her list and sees *Boys in the Hood*. "No, no. It's *Boyz n the Hood*," he says, emphasizing the parts she misspelled.

Rachel scribbles through her words disconcertedly, as if she just found out she got an answer wrong on an exam. After rewriting the title—the correct way—she looks up, unsure if he has more suggestions.

"*American Me, American Graffiti*…and *Colors*, that's a great one! And…*Mi Vida Loca*. Have you heard of any of these?"

She adds the latter half of titles to the cumulative list, then puts her pen down and takes a bite of her acai bowl. Scanning the titles, she racks her brain for memories of any of them. "No, Emiliano, I haven't heard of a single one," she says, not so theatrically.

"Good. We'll watch one soon." He smiles, his insides warming as if he's been touched by fresh morning sunshine. He loves that Rachel is interested in learning from him and learning about his culture.

"So why these specific movies?" she asks.

"Well some of 'em are just good, classics. Others will give you a glimpse into the Mexican American culture, also classics." Noticing the time, he puts his seatbelt on. "I gotta get home and get you home. It's late."

After a quick defrosting of the windshield, Emiliano pulls onto the main road. Rachel tucks the paper bag into her purse. How cool to have a list of movies, she thinks. *Their* list of movies. He turns the radio on and the chorus of "Head

Over Heels" by Tears for Fears hums through the stereo. Rachel can't help but feel like she is falling head over heels for Emiliano. He is everything and more; she already knows and feels it.

And, she feels it even more when they pull up to her house because Emiliano randomly suggests that they create a special handshake *just for them*—for when they see each other, for greetings and goodbyes.

"Like a secret handshake?" She chuckles, sticking out her left hand.

"Woah!" He puts his hands up by his chest, then points at hers. "Not with the left hand. Left is disrespect…And the handshake is because we in Cali."

This time, she offers her right hand. He slides his palm across her palm and instructs her to curl her fingers. Their right hands conjoin into an interlocked fist. Then, he twists out of the fist and makes an L shape with his thumb and pointer finger. Slowly, she creates an L with hers. Their fingers slide into one another until the bridges of their Ls meet. Rachel is pleased that she successfully grasped all four steps: slide, interlock fist, twist, interlock L. Their Ls stay touching for a moment before Emiliano pulls out.

"And then we snap," he instructs, breaking the gorgeous, serendipitous silence as he clicks his fingers together.

"OK. Let's try it faster, from the beginning," she says, eager to perfect the handshake.

They repeat the steps again, snapping at the same time during the finale. Then, they smirk, pleased with their smooth delivery.

"All right. Have a good night, Emiliano."

He leans across the console for a hug, squeezing her extra tight in his arms. His body warms from the inside, starting with his heart. "Goodnight, Rachel," he says coyly, with longing in his voice. A type of longing that suggests he doesn't even know what it is he longs for.

8 Left Alone to His Business

Javier wouldn't say that he loves his job. He also wouldn't say that he hates his job. Working as a data entry technician in a laboratory has its perks and its downfalls. Perks: sit most of the day at a computer, have little to no interactions with other humans, and occasionally work from home. Also, he has been at the same company since he graduated college so he makes a decent $26.00 hourly wage. Downfalls: the work is tedious, monotonous, and boring. He basically spends eight hours per day, five days per week, turning paper data into computer files or typing customer information into spreadsheets.

Truth be told, when he got a bachelor's degree in communications, he never thought he would end up doing data entry work. Pretty much he does the opposite of "communication" on a daily basis. Like most people who don't know what they like to do, he ended up here for the salary and then just stayed. He got caught in the trap of middle class America: working a 9–5, doing something he doesn't like, hating Mondays, getting excited for Fridays, and repeating the cycle every week for years upon years.

Today, Javier had to come into the lab because the company had a meeting about a new software system they would be using. This didn't make him happy because he is unfamiliar with the system and will have to spend ample time studying all its intricacies. Around 4:58 p.m., he finishes double checking his final spreadsheet for the day. His brain feels warn out and sucked dry from so much monotony. He grabs his bag and jacket, pushes in his chair, and heads for his car.

The only thing that makes today better is that it's Thursday, which is better known as Friday Jr. That means it is almost time to play soccer and party. He spends each of his weekends in pretty much the same way: playing soccer at some local gathering and hanging out with friends at bars and breweries with alcohol. He has a lot of acquaintance-type friends, and is always making people laugh or making them feel special.

This weekend will be slightly different than the average weekend though because he and his parents are attending a *quinceañera* for a second cousin on his mother's side. Javier has only ever been to a few *quinceañeras* and feels out of place at each one. He is unfamiliar with the traditions. And, to make matters worse, he conjugates Spanish sentences incorrectly, which often results in people poking fun at him. He is darker and more Mexican-looking than most, so when they speak to him in Spanish and he cannot understand what they are saying, he feels like they give him a disapproving look, as if he has betrayed them. English has always been his primary language; he is third generation to the U.S. on his father's side of the family and second generation on his mother's side, therefore while his skin and facial structure scream Mexico, his mind and spirit scream assimilated to the United States.

He has attended many U.S. sweet sixteens, but truly those aren't any better. Every so often, some White father would think Javier was getting at his daughter and seemed to outright disapprove of him because of his skin tone. Or, there would be the drunk asshole White teenage boys who would tell him to go back to where he came from. Truly, he feels nobody ever accepted him. Not Mexico, not Mexican Americans, not the United States. That's in part what led to him becoming so outgoing and bubbly, because underneath he doesn't really allow people in. He's disconnected from his emotions and seems numb to feeling. This history of rejection has led to him only feeling good when he's the center of attention, flirting, or drinking alcohol.

On the way home from work he stops at Kohl's to get a new tie for the dreaded *quinceañera*. When he pulls into his driveway just before 6:00 p.m., one of his roommates is getting into their car. As always, the two exchange half-smiles and waves. He's lived with the same two guys—the street over from his parent's home, his childhood home—for the last four years and the most they've ever interacted is greetings and waves in passing. Javier likes to be in his room with his door locked, left alone to his business. He heads into his house and up the stairs to his room that echoes plain-Jane: medium blue walls with nothing on them, a bed with a white comforter, a closet with mirrored doors, and a nightstand with a lamp and alarm clock.

He spends his evening the way he spends most week night evenings: eat dinner while watching TV, take a shower, watch more TV, and end with a long walk in the dark night. His nighttime route is never the same; he usually just goes wherever his feet take him. Though, often, he does end up walking through a park, passing by Rachel's house, and strolling by his elementary school.

Tonight, he walks a new route by a small shopping center. He heads into 7-Eleven and purchases a hotdog, which he eats on the swingset at the park. After throwing away the wrapper, he walks through the streets of his neighborhood and strolls by Rachel's house. Through the curtains of her upstairs bedroom, he sees her bare back as she is changing into a sweatshirt. He would hate to look like some sort of creep, so he continues walking down the street after glancing at her for just a measly few seconds.

As he heads home, he can't help but think about how ravishing Rachel is. He could do, and would do, so many things to her body—of course, in time—if only he were to get to know Rachel, if she were to let him get to know her. Unfortunately, he has been trying, or wanting to try, for years and hasn't been able to get anywhere other than stranger. He decides it's time to move on and set his sights elsewhere.

9 Giddy Like a Virgin

As Rachel rolls over, pulling a thick, fluffy blanket off her body, the sun creeps through the bedroom window and warms her skin, bringing her into a state of consciousness where she is no longer asleep but isn't quite yet awake. A nostalgic scent spreads through the vents in the house. She slowly opens her eyes, knowing her mother must have made her favorite breakfast—a meal Shannon's been making since before Rachel could even talk. She ties her hair in a messy low bun and inhales the aromatic tease of what she is about to eat.

After putting on slippers, she saunters down the stairs. In the kitchen, she is welcomed by her mother in an apron, mid-pulling the glass platter of heaven out of the oven. "Good morning! Were you up late?" Shannon asks, noticing Rachel's tired demeanor.

"Good morning, Mom. Yeah, just studying."

Shannon nods, carrying the warm pie-shaped glass to the table. "Charles, breakfast is ready," she calls to her husband in the living room. There is no reply but a chair rustles, the TV is silenced, and footsteps proceed down the hall.

Rachel sits down at the head of the table and rubs her eyes. She stares at the heat dancing out of the top of the meal. Her stomach growls, begging for a taste. A beat later, Charles, a tall, muscular man in his mid-fifties, walks in. He gives Shannon a peck on the lips, then sits down and announces it's time to pray. As with any ritual, they know the steps and follow his lead: link their hands together, bow their heads, and close their eyes.

"Heavenly Father, thank you for this meal we are about to receive. Thank you for my wife, my daughter, our beautiful family who are with us in spirit. May you help us to walk in your light every day and be humbled by your presence. Amen."

After a brief pause, Rachel and Shannon acknowledge the prayer with a nod and a smile. "Amen," they say together.

Rachel stares at the layers of salty, savory yumminess—the thick deep-dish style croissant crust, a layer of organic eggs mixed with tomato, bell pepper, garlic, onion, and various spices, and a final tier of bacon crumble: half real pig, half plant-based. The clinking of forks, knives, and glassware resound like an offbeat symphony as they all dive in.

Rachel glances at her father's gelled brown hair speckled with hints of gray. "Do you work today, Dad?"

"Yeah, not until the afternoon. We've got a big rig we're setting up for a sitcom tonight. I should be home around midnight." He sighs deeply. "What are you doing today?" he asks Shannon.

"Work, gardening, cooking, cleaning, arts and crafts…the usual."

"This is delicious, Mom. Thank you for breakfast!"

"Of course," Shannon says. "How has studying been going, Rachel? Do you know what schools you're going to apply for?"

"I haven't decided on schools yet. Studying has been good. I've been looking into the foundations of clinical psych and various aspects of social psych. Like recently I've been reviewing social influence. How conformity and groupthink can shape our decisions."

"Groupthink?" Charles questions.

Rachel's eyes shut as she tries hard to recall how the book described it. "When people are encouraged to shy away from their thoughts and are persuaded to follow along with the group."

"Well, I can tell you've definitely been studying!" Shannon says enthusiastically.

"You're going to build yourself a great career." Charles nods firmly, then takes a large bite. "And then you can move out of my house!"

Rachel fake laughs, wondering if he really wants her out of the house, living on her own, fully supporting herself.

Shannon's eyes shift between Charles and Rachel. She doesn't like the subtle tension that pervaded the atmosphere after her husband's statement. "Do you guys want to go for a hike sometime this weekend? We'll just make sure to stay away from Bluffs Peak, Rachel."

Both women look at each other and explode into laughter, thinking about the last neighborhood annual hike up Bluffs Peak. Charles is unaware of what they are referring to, as he wasn't able to attend. This is typical of their home life. For nearly thirty years Charles has worked as a grip in Hollywood and Los Angeles. Setting up lighting for TV shows and movies sets typically meant early mornings, late nights, long hours, and sometimes weekend shifts, sacrificing his time and body to help the family stay afloat.

"What happened?" he asks, grimacing. Halfway curious, halfway nervous.

Rachel lifts her sleeve and points to a scar on the underside of her elbow. "I tripped over a rock, sprawled down the trail, then came up with blood on my knees, stomach, and arm."

"Ow! That doesn't sound funny?" Charles says.

"Well, that's not the funny part," Shannon interjects.

Rachel continues, explaining that she had to use the restroom shortly after the fall, and Shannon was the lookout. She stands and begins acting out the scene. "I pulled down my pants, spread my legs out to pop a squat. Then, suddenly, this old man, about seventy-years-old, comes around the corner and sees everything, and I mean *everything*!" She exhales. "And then he walks past us and—like a sports announcer—says, 'God, that's gotta be the best thing I've seen in years!'"

"Oh wow. That's hilarious!" Charles lets out an elated sigh.

After one more good laugh, Rachel puts her plate in the sink, then heads upstairs to get ready for the busy day. First on the agenda: a trip to Los Angeles to help Hannah set up her new TV. Then: an early dinner with Emiliano that's already making her nervous. She wants to look nice, but not too nice because her parents or Hannah might ask questions. Tight jeans and a colorful blouse it is. Straight hair, combed, nothing out of the ordinary.

She hurries downstairs, mentioning she's heading to Hannah's apartment. Before she reaches the door, Shannon peeps her head out of the kitchen, noticing her daughter's outfit. "Why are you dressed so nice?!"

"Oh…I didn't think it was that nice? I guess just in case Hannah and I decide to do something…like…go to dinner!" Rachel shuts the front door and hurries into her car hoping her mother didn't think her answer seemed fishy.

When she gets on the freeway, the beautiful suburb that she calls home slowly disappears in the rearview mirror. The drive is typically anywhere from thirty minutes to one hour from her house to Hannah's apartment in the hub of Los Angeles, all depending on the 101 and the 405 freeways, which typically turn into stop-and-go city traffic.

Her car comes to a halt next to an offramp where she can see the nearby street—part of Skid Row—one of the largest populations of people experiencing homelessness in the United States. Tent after tent after tent is lined along the bridge. Occasionally, there is a gap in the tent housing where there's someone just lying on a dirty blanket. A man walks out of a tattered blue makeshift shelter holding a glass bottle wrapped in a brown bag.

Rachel immediately recalls something she read in her textbook: roughly 60 percent of people experiencing homelessness in Southern California don't have access to medical or mental health care. When the cars move, Rachel's eyes move too. Away from the poverty, away from the despair, away from the sadness.

She merges onto the 10, drives a few more miles, then exits into a picturesque neighborhood bustling with palm trees and hipster people in designer clothes like Gucci, Louis Vuitton, and other brands Rachel can't recall. What a stark difference from here to the homeless sector. How interesting that just a few miles can change so much about the lifestyle and scenery. Aha! Gentrification, Rachel thinks.

Hannah lives near USC's Health and Science Campus, next to some of the coolest restaurants, historical museums, and eccentric bookstores. Neither Skid Row nor Hannah's neighborhood resemble Old Oak or Ten Pines, the nature-filled suburbs full of hiking trails. She examines the concrete jungle metropolis until inside the parking structure at Hannah's complex.

"Rachel! Perfect timing!" a familiar voice calls out.

Rachel spots Hannah by the elevator, holding an overly full black garbage bag.

"I'm just taking the trash out, then we can go inside!" Hannah walks down a staircase to the apartment's trash bins while Rachel gathers her things and waits by the elevator. A few moments later, Hannah comes back up the staircase.

"Sorry you missed Brax, he just left for a business trip. He'll be out of town until Friday."

"Oh, that's all right, I mainly want to spend time with you, anyway!" Rachel says, relieved to hear that she won't have to see him. They lean in for a hug, then enter the elevator. Hannah pushes the button for the third floor and steps back against the railing. Rachel stares at the concrete slats, admiring the contrast between the large buildings and vibrant palm trees until the elevator doors close. "I love your apartment. It's so beautiful here!"

"It is!" Hannah says. "I wish you could live here with us."

Rachel smiles. A few months prior, Hannah had invited her to move into their two-bedroom apartment, but she politely declined because she didn't want to live with Brax. Since they still haven't found a renter for the empty second bedroom, they are essentially paying for unused space. Although, neither one of them pays rent. Both Hannah's and Brax's parents have high-paying corporate jobs and co-pay the apartment.

"Yeah, how is the roommate search going, Hannah? Have you guys found anyone yet?"

The elevator dings and the door opens. Hannah walks out, looking over at Rachel with a somewhat concerned look on her face. "No, we don't have one yet…I think we have a potential prospect though."

"Oh, that's awesome! Who?" Rachel asks.

"Uh…actually it's one of Brax's friends. Some girl. Some friend. Good friend, apparently. He met her at USC." Hannah hides her trepidation and tries to think positively. "It might be fun to live with a girl, we can go shopping together!"

Hannah unlocks her apartment and Rachel follows her into the spacious living room. A large flat-screen TV sits in a box next to its stand. While Hannah pulls out the instructions, Rachel studies the mount and all its intricacies. Then, they sit down in the mess of it all and start working.

"So, what have you been up to, Rachel? I haven't seen you in…what…two weeks? Way too long!"

"Studying," they say at the same time. Hannah nods, aware of Rachel's rigorous routine.

"How'd you know?" Rachel laughs.

"But seriously…your cheeks are glowing. What have you been doing other than studying?"

"It must be…my mom's breakfast pizza."

"Breakfast pizza? You're telling me you look giddy like a virgin who's about to get laid for the first time over breakfast pizza?" Hannah's eyebrows raise.

"The plant-based bacon crumbles will do that to you," Rachel says, unwilling to disclose that she has been spending time with Emiliano. She wants to see if their friendship progresses into something more, or to find out if he's even interested in her in that way.

Hannah drops the subject as they successfully screw the TV into the mount and plug it in. "Now for the Wi-Fi set-up," she says, hoping the network won't cause too much trouble.

Rachel sits down on the couch and examines the overwhelming panel of buttons on the remote. "What have you and Brax been doing lately?"

"Oh my gosh…Rachel…He did the sweetest thing for me the other day." Hannah leans in as if she's about to divulge a secret. "My company was catering a wedding from 7:00 a.m. to 9:00 p.m. and by the time I got home, I could barely stand because my feet were so sore. I walked into our bedroom and he had drawn me a warm bath, put a bath bomb in it, laid out my favorite book, and lit so many candles."

"That's sweet of him," Rachel says, making the kind of face someone would when seeing an adorable puppy.

"Right? We have our ups and downs but when he does things like that I can't help but fall in love with him over and over again." Hannah looks off longingly, only snapping back to reality once the remote is handed to her. She pulls out a paper with her Wi-Fi password and slowly enters the long list of letters and numbers on the screen. The loading circle spins and spins.

They sink deeper into the couch and start talking about soccer. Hannah insists that she and Rachel be on the same team the next time they play. "It's fun since we've played together forever, but mainly I love to watch boys squirm when they get absolutely wrecked by girls. It crushes their egos…and totally inflates mine!" Hannah smirks.

"Sometimes their uber-masculine egos are too fragile though," Rachel says. "Last weekend, I dribbled around that guy Javier and he seemed to be upset about it. He pushed into my shoulder hard, and I think it was on purpose! I held my ground though, and that was around the time when me and that other guy, Emiliano, made that play together." She hopes the way she brought up Emiliano's name was subtle.

"Ew." Hannah makes a disgusted face. "Honestly that's so annoying. Don't guys realize they have more muscle mass and are genuinely bigger than us? That's so rude. Now I don't like that guy Javier at all and I never will."

"OMG. Hannah." Rachel starts laughing. Truly though, she loves Hannah's protection and constant support. They both snicker, then look at the TV. The loading circle is still on the screen, spinning around and around. Then, finally, a white screen pops up, informing that the connection was successful.

In honor of setting up the TV and the Wi-Fi with no major issues or hiccups, the young women sink into the couch with fluffy pillows, fuzzy blankets, a single glass of red wine each, and a bag of movie theatre butter popcorn. They watch the tail end of a Nicholas Sparks movie, and both cry even though they missed most of the plot. Then they watch two episodes of Family Feud and pose that if they were to go on the show with three other people, they would win the big bucks.

"Well, I wish I could watch TV with you all night Hannah but I better get going," Rachel says. "I should—"

"Study?" Hannah cuts in.

"Yes, exactly."

After saying goodbye and getting in the elevator, Rachel's stomach growls. The popcorn wasn't enough of a lunch. She's been hungry for a little while but of course has been awaiting her nighttime plan: Emiliano, early dinner, sunset. The mere thought of it really does make her giddy like a virgin. How is Hannah always on the nose with these things?

10 The Moment She Knew

As Rachel heads toward Old Oak, she lowers the windows and opens the sunroof to feel the Southern California sunshine. The stopped traffic during rush hour would typically stress her out, but she doesn't mind knowing it might help Emiliano; if she ends up arriving a little late to his house, he'll at least have more time to relax after work.

With eyes fixed on the road and mind fixated on Emiliano, she is oblivious to the group of young men rolling by in the lane next to her. The passenger waves persistently out the window, trying to get her attention. After his fourth attempt, Rachel finally looks over.

"What you doin' tonight, Mami? We got a party going on here in the Valley, you should come through." The group of White boys all smirk. One in the backseat playfully hits the guy in the passenger seat.

"I don't live around here." Nonplussed, Rachel switches lanes, hearing a faint *C'mon, baby!* as she rolls up the window.

To further drown out any outside chatter, she puts music on. Specifically, a '60s song that Emiliano recommended to her recently over text. It doesn't take long for her to appreciate the lyrics and rhythm of "Put Your Head On My Shoulder" by Paul Anka. Almost instantly, she starts daydreaming about Emiliano. An image flashes in her mind of him resting his head against her shoulder when they were in a laughing fit the first time they hung out. It only lasted for a brief moment though because then he eagerly began singing Elvis lyrics to the moon. And now that image plasters itself in her brain. That was the moment she knew she would fall for him. The moment she *did* fall for him. The memory of the night is still crystal clear: his cheery smile, his hand gestures to the moon, his contagious upbeat energy, and best of all his crackling singing voice.

Rachel exits at the freeway offramp that leads to both her house and Emiliano's. To get to her house: turn left and drive for a few miles. To get to his house: turn right and it's basically right there. She makes the turn and her heart begins beating faster than the speed of her car. She has never felt so excited about seeing someone before. The feeling is foreign, and also a bit scary.

As she turns into his neighborhood, she notices lots of children playing and running around. Along the curbs there are no parking spaces. Everything is completely packed bumper to bumper. She follows her GPS down a cul-de-sac, eyeing both sides of the road to figure out which condo is Emiliano's.

Inside his home, Emiliano says goodbye to Samanta. She asks where he is going, but he doesn't tell her. After he shuts the door, she lifts the curtain that hangs over the window on their front door and watches her younger brother. A curious look crosses her face; he is walking to an unfamiliar white Acura with an unfamiliar White woman inside it.

Emiliano gets in Rachel's car wearing both an undeniably huge smile and a plush Spiderman blanket—one typically marketed to young boys. Before he says anything he reaches his right hand across the console for their special handshake.

After their snaps, Rachel examines Emiliano's unique choice for an overcoat. "Nice blanket." She nods approvingly.

"You know I'm warm-blooded, but I always come prepared. I just hate being cold, Rach. Can I call you Rach? I been meaning to come up with a nickname for you."

"Yeah, Rach is fine," she says, giggling. "Is there a party in your neighborhood? There are so many cars here!"

"Hmm…Maybe? There's always a lot of cars here. Lots of people live here. And there's never any parking!"

"Oh…" Rachel pulls to the end of the street and looks both ways for oncoming cars.

"So…welcome to the hood!" he says proudly, lifting his arms.

"The hood?" Rachel questions curiously, having only ever heard that term used in a negative connotation.

"Yeah. The hood! This is my hood, my neighborhood. And these are my people!"

Rachel never knew *hood* was short for *neighborhood*. She nods and gives him a sweet smile, unsure of the proper way to respond. "So where do you want to eat, Emiliano? How about something vegan?"

"Vegan food? I don't trust fake meat!" He was thinking more along the lines of burgers, tacos, burritos, or pizza. He loves his meats and cheeses.

"There's a lot more than fake meat…like beans and rice are vegan. Vegan just means no animals were harmed."

"Uh…I don't think I can do vegan food." He has already stepped out of his comfort zone enough. Not only has he been hanging out with a female, which is surprising, but a female from outside of his neighborhood and even his culture. Trendy food and trendy diets are not going to be on his menu. But then he looks at her and can't help himself. "All right, all right. Fine, Rach. I'll try it…just for you," he says with a dismissive face.

They pass by the shopping center that has the grocery store, Flores de Felicia, and the *panadería*. Emiliano glances out the window, noticing the *panadería* looks like a ghost town. There are no customers inside. And there are no cars outside—except for two run-down ones that have been sitting there for a few weeks. He stares as the shopping center fades in the distance, hoping the Nuñez family had a lot of business today. He would hate to waste his money elsewhere— especially on something vegan—if his neighborhood shop needed his support.

"How was work today?" Rachel asks.

"Sweaty and busy. Couple oil changes, brake repairs, worked on an engine." Emiliano pauses and smiles. "Just livin' the dream, honestly! I love it. I love working hard to live here in the most beautiful area of the country. Feel so lucky to call this place home."

Rachel admires his gratitude. He follows up with a few questions about her day and she briefly mentions the breakfast pizza and the trip to Los Angeles to visit Hannah. What she doesn't tell him is that he's been on her mind *all day*. Though, truly that's an inaccurate statement, because he's actually been on her mind *for months*, ever since the first moment she laid eyes on him.

When they pull into the food court parking lot, they pass by a megachurch. A protruding half circle on the front reads Elation's Outreach in large block letters. "Have you heard of this church before, Rach?" Emiliano points at the massive building.

"No, I don't think so."

"They've done a lot locally for my Chicano community. They help people get off drugs and alcohol and help during the holiday season."

"Do you know any of the people they've helped?" she asks as she pulls into a parking spot.

"Nah, but my family friend knows somebody who knows somebody. This guy was an alcoholic, I guess. Got baptized in the ocean. Said the church saved his life. So I got alotta respect for Elation's Outreach."

As they get out of the car, they gaze at the sky. It's full of fluffy clouds and has hues ranging from purple to pink to orange. The almost blinding sun is slowly heading over the mountain peaks. Emiliano opens the door of the food hall for Rachel and they turn to continue gaping at the mesmerizing sky as they walk inside.

When they finally turn around, they don't realize that they have stepped into a rock planter in the center of the walkway. At the same time, they both trip, instinctively grabbing onto each other, somehow managing to save one another from smashing into the ground. After looking around at the elevated gravel, they both make funny faces and laugh.

"How did we end up in here?" Rachel asks.

"I don't know?" Emiliano says. He spins around, scanning the scenery. "Rach, how did we not see *that!*" He points to a big yellow cone in front of the rock planter. Not only is the bright cone itself a warning sign, but there are exclamation points all over it and an image of a person tripping. Rachel scoffs teasingly. Clearly, they were both so lost in the beauty of lilac and cotton candy hues marrying tangerine colors of the sun that they didn't see what was right in front of them.

"I'm glad neither of us fell," Emiliano says, now shaking his head. Though, he is quickly realizing there is nobody he would rather fall with, or fall *for*, than this girl who somehow entered his life out of seemingly nowhere. However, allowing himself to fall is an entirely different feat.

Walking into a spacious room they are greeted by smells from all sorts of cuisine. There are four restaurants, all from different ethnic backgrounds: Thai, American, Mexican, and Korean. "I've had food from all four, but this is the one I was talking about." Rachel points to the American vegan joint. They scan the menu and Rachel finds six or seven meals that sound intriguing while Emiliano has a hard time finding interest in a single item.

"I'm going to run to the restroom before we order," Rachel says.

Emiliano nods, then watches her backside sway from left to right as she scurries down the hallway. Once she is out of view, he glances back at the menu, then politely hands it to the cashier and walks over to the Mexican spot.

"Hola," Emiliano says, scanning the menu plastered in large font on the wall. "Me puedes dar los nachos de pollo con arroz, frijoles, jalapeños, y salsa verde?"

"Sí." The cashier faces the kitchen. "An order of chicken nachos with rice-beans-jalapeños-and-green-salsa," he hollers hastily, the toppings morphing together, sounding like one ingredient.

"Y una horchata, por favor." Emiliano tries with Spanish again, wondering why the cashier translated the order to English. Who would be cooking his Mexican food? Someone who doesn't even speak Spanish?

"Vegana o no?" The cashier points at two separate pitchers.

Great. The place is definitely more American than it is Mexican if there are vegan options. "No, regular." Emiliano pays for his food, then sits down at a nearby table after receiving his horchata.

A few minutes later, Rachel walks back in the food hall and asks Emiliano if he's ready to order. Sipping his cinnamon rice drink, he gestures to the Mexican place (though loosely Mexican in his eyes), letting her know that he already did. Part of him feels bad that he didn't attempt vegan food, but honestly it was just too much and he probably wouldn't like it.

He stands to pay for her meal, but she insists that he doesn't, especially since vegan food can be pricey. She orders a vegan rainbow roll, feeling bummed that he won't be trying it. She wanted to expose him to something new, the way he's been sharing aspects of his culture with her. Nonetheless, she is happy he found something he'll enjoy.

As she joins him at the table, he mentions they could eat in the car to watch the sunset. Perfect. Just what she was hoping for—something romantic. After a few minutes of silent glances, quirky smiles, and unintentional (yet enjoyed) footsy under the table, their food orders are called.

On the walk to the car, meals in hand, Rachel notices *Metallica* written across the center of Emiliano's black tattered shirt. "You like heavy metal?" she asks, gesturing to it.

"Yeah!" Emiliano looks down, admiring his tee. "Do you?"

"No, I don't think so...I haven't heard much of it honestly."

Emiliano isn't surprised by her answer. It didn't take long for him to gather that she is isolated from many things—like him—but in a different way. And, if anything, that drew him closer to her because he enjoys introducing her to new things. Though, on the flip side, he doesn't much care to be introduced to new things.

They get in the car and Rachel unwraps her food while Emiliano pulls out his phone and messes around with the Bluetooth. As she puts a piece of sushi in her mouth, tasting a mesh of delicate vegetable flavors, a deep thumping sounds through the car's bass. She looks over at the center console, where he set down his phone, and reads "The Four Horsemen" by Metallica across the screen. He bangs his head like a rockstar to the beat.

"On Guitar Hero, I mastered this song," he brags, rapidly playing a nonexistent guitar in his hands.

"You're such a goober!" Rachel laughs, watching his gorgeous hair flip every which way.

Emiliano bites his bottom lip and continues playing the air, his head bobbing up and down. He wonders if her statement was a compliment; upon seeing her mesmerized eyes, he is sure it was. He lowers the volume, wooshes his thick hair back gracefully, then opens his food tray to find a deliciously sloppy mess of nachos. He searches for the largest chip full of the most ingredients. "So, now do you like heavy metal, Rach?"

"It's interesting…but I don't think I'd listen to it in my free time, no." She chuckles. "I like your wide array of music though. It's like every time I see you, you're showcasing new bits of your personality." She smiles as she pops another piece of sushi into her mouth. It's been cool getting to know someone vastly different from her. It's been unexpected. It's been like a real life classroom without desks and tests and papers. It's been *real.*

Emiliano looks over at Rachel's side profile, studying her nose and the natural pout of her pink lips. She's so different. And intriguing. She truly accepts him the way many people never have. He feels like part of him is just inches away from holding her. But another part of him is miles and miles away—his life was going so well without romance in it. And romance has always only ever messed things up.

Rather than sharing their thoughts and epiphanies, the two just smile at one another before shifting their gazes to the sun, now sinking below the mountain. On the other side of the road, two Mexican American children ride by on colorful bicycles. Emiliano takes a bite of his nachos while observing them. They enter a parking lot to meet with other youth who all have the same styled bikes, each in different colors. The large group of friends exchanges various handshakes.

"Look!" Emiliano points. "You see those bikes?"

Rachel nods, leaning forward to get a better view.

"My cousins and I used to ride those same bikes, Fixie Bikes, around my neighborhood and the town…just like them! Getting into typical crazy kid stuff." He pauses, still staring, inhaling a breath of nostalgia and memory. "A new generation of young kids like that? Not all-consumed by technology? I can't even believe it," he says. "Dude, it's the coolest thing! You can customize any part of the bike you want…handlebars, pedals, and wheel rims."

"What color Fixie did you have?"

"I think black and blue," he says, his nose scrunching.

"¡Negro y azul!" Rachel shouts.

"Hey! How'd you know that?" The statement makes him grin.

"Well, I took three years of Spanish in high school, then one in college. I remember some words, not as much as I would like though…I'd love to be bilingual some day!" Rachel looks over at Emiliano, then down at his food tray. For the last few minutes, he's been poking around the center with his finger, picking up chips then putting them down. She glances at her almost empty tray in comparison. "Do you like your food, Emiliano?"

He shakes his head. "This isn't authentic Mexican. Look at this shredded chicken." He holds a piece up, far away from him, as if he is holding a dead rat. "It shouldn't be like that. And they got the spices all wrong." He tosses it back into the nachos.

Rachel extends her sushi across the console, offering him a piece of her food. He hesitantly takes a piece, thanking her. As he chews, sporting a multitude of facial expressions, Rachel watches attentively. "Wow, Rach! That's vegan? It's good…better than I expected."

She eagerly tells him that he can have more, but he declines and reaches back into his messy meal. He piles a chip with jalapeño, chicken, rice, and beans, then chomps on the familiar flavors. Observing his sizeable bite, Rachel wonders why he would immerse himself back into something he doesn't like when there is something he truly relishes right in front of him.

11 A Holy Attraction

The basketball rim vibrates in a low hum as the ball ricochets off the hoop and bounces into the grass. Pablo jogs over to get it, bummed over his missed shot, while Emiliano stands at the top of the key anticipating with his hands in front of his chest. They are talking about work, and can't believe they've been at Pablo's dad's shop for almost five years.

When Emiliano gets the ball, he springs up for a shot, curling his wrist as he releases. "Nothin' but net!" he hollers. It sinks effortlessly. And so have his last twelve shots today. He's more than heating up, and feels like the best street baller in Southern California.

"And did you see that fool who came in the other day?" Pablo asks.

"What foo?"

"The White fool who came in with his new beamer. Acting all *I'm better than you* type shit." Pablo scoffs, then mimics the customer's mannerisms. First, he walks like a red carpet is beneath him. Then, he pretends to pull down sunglasses and toss car keys toward Emiliano. Worst of all: he taps a finger at Emiliano with an attitude, a snobbish look, and an aura that screams *you are a peasant.*

"Man, I hate foos like that," Emiliano retorts. "Musta been after I left or somethin'."

"Speakin' of you leavin' and disappearin' and shit, where you been lately?"

"Just out here," Emiliano says.

Pablo nods, used to his best friend's vague responses. "You was with that soccer chick, Rachel, when I was delivering food. Y'all um…you know?" He waves a finger in the air, questioning the new relationship.

"Nah, esé, we just friends. She ain't into me like that."

Pablo nods again, though he doesn't quite buy what Emiliano is dishing out. He dribbles to the three point line and takes a shot, hoping to turn his shooting luck around. He just barely misses again. The ball hits the rim at an awkward angle and shoots off into the grass. "Man today is not my day," he grumbles as he walks over to it.

Off in the distance, the group is gathering at the table and a few lingering players are walking over from the parking lot.

"Yo, Emiliano," Pablo hollers, nodding toward the soccer field. "Everyone's gettin' ready to play."

Emiliano glances over, almost immediately spotting Rachel in the crowd. It looks like she and Hannah are about to warm up. He can't help but feel eager to see her, to be closer to her. They grab their athletic bags from the wet bench, still misty from the morning dew, then walk through the long stretch of grass that separates the two sports areas.

"How am I already tired? I feel like I been hit by a truck," Pablo says, rubbing at his neck and trap muscles.

"I feel you, hermano. It's gotta be from work. My back's all fucked up." Emiliano reaches his free hand over the base of his spine, rubbing the tender areas in circular motions.

Feeling sore and drained is not uncommon for either of them. Working in the auto shop has always meant lifting heavy objects, squeezing into small spaces, or twisting one's arm or body in weird ways. They've gone home with kinked necks, strained backs, chemical burns, irritated eyes, and more. That's just the life of a blue-collar worker.

When they reach the table, Pablo greets some of the guys while Emiliano fixes his attention on Rachel warming up. The whole of his being—mind, body, eyes—are drawn to her without hesitation. It's like some magnet or external force is doing the thinking for him, like he is a puppet, and the puppeteer is love. He doesn't want to admit it to himself, and he definitely won't admit it to her—the feelings are too scary. And it's not like he and Rachel can be together realistically; they are too different and from two different worlds.

"Hey, um, wrong sport!" Rachel calls out teasingly, pointing to Emiliano's basketball.

He chuckles as he pulls his mud-stained cleats out of his bag. "Rach, I'm sure I could take you at both sports."

"Your confidence is laudable, but…I'm clearly more athletic," Rachel retorts, keeping her eyes focused on the passing drill with Hannah.

"Laudable?" he questions.

Hannah passes the ball to Rachel, then looks at Emiliano. "Laudable is like…commendable or praiseworthy," she offers.

"Praiseworthy? Nah. I'm just telling the truth. I know I'd win, Rach!" Emiliano says.

Rachel playfully rolls her eyes, kicking the ball back to Hannah.

"My money is on her," Hannah says. She traps the ball at her feet, then starts jogging off the field. "I'm gonna grab some water. I'll be right back, Rach!" she hollers, naturally adopting Emiliano's nickname for her best friend.

In all the years Hannah's known Rachel, Rachel never liked or accepted nicknames. She is the kind of girl who likes her life orderly, rigid, and predictable. She has only ever been Rachel or "11" on the field since that has always been her number. Something must definitely be going on between Rachel and Emiliano, Hannah thinks, because "Rach" is now something she responds to, something he made happen.

"Rach, we gotta hoop sometime forreal," Emiliano says.

"Honestly, you'd laugh at my basketball skills, or lack thereof. A five-year-old would be better at dribbling than me." Rachel takes a seat across from him at the table.

After their handshake and synchronized snaps, Emiliano begins to study Rachel's appearance. Infatuated by her long French braids, he traces them with his eyes. He starts above her forehead, traveling around her high cheekbones, down the sides of her neck, then shoulders, atop her breasts, until he reaches her ribcage, where his eyes stop—because the table is so rudely in the way—but his mind doesn't. His mind hasn't stopped since it started. And it started the night he changed her windshield wipers when he realized he'd finally met a girl who matched his level of authenticity.

"I'll teach you how to shoot a basketball," he finally says, offering her a grin; the kind that goes from cheek to cheek where teeth become objects of study.

Rachel stares at his perfectly shaped white teeth, wondering what makes teeth beautiful, as she's never considered someone's calcium-filled enamel to be attractive. Studying his face, like she has multiple times before, she realizes there is not one single feature that is even remotely unattractive. All of him is wholly attractive—maybe this is a holy attraction. Something of worship. His forehead? Attractive. The slight pink pigmentation of an acne scar on his cheek? Attractive. The almost unnoticeable stubble underneath his lower lip that she would never find attractive on anyone else? Attractive. His thick long eyelashes? Attractive. His striking green eyes that make her feel like she's lost in the Emerald City, where she never wants to find her way home? Attractive. She stops herself, knowing there would be no end to the list. Her thoughts of his magnetism are as bountiful as there are blades of grass on the field where their feet are planted.

"We should get going before the clouds part and the heat becomes unbearable," one of the guys says, abruptly interrupting both Rachel's and Emiliano's daydreams. Pablo, Javier, and a few others at the table start heading to the field.

"Is she playing with us?" Emiliano asks Rachel in a low voice, tilting his head toward a girl who's leaning against a nearby tree.

Rachel shakes her head. "She came here with Javier. I think just to watch?"

"Yeah, Jemma's with me," Javier says, walking over from the pinny bag. He leans in and lowers his voice, "I met her at a quinceañera. I'm hoping we'll be more than friends soon." With a wink he puts on a blue pinny, then hands them each one: Rachel white, Emiliano blue. Before heading out to the field, he waves to Jemma—the youthful, beautiful, and petite *Chicana*.

The only player who has yet to put on a pinny is Hannah, per usual. Up on the hill, Brax is explaining to her that he has to leave for about thirty minutes while she is playing, but that he will be back to watch the end, and then they can go home to get ready for the party they will be attending. A sad expression washes over her face. She wonders why he always has to leave during her game. Then, she remembers that she bought a new dress for the party and eagerly shows him a picture of it, mentioning she likes the way it makes her body look.

"Come on, stop being so conceited." Brax scoffs.

Hannah apologizes, shrugging off everything from him not staying to him not celebrating how she looks in her new outfit. The only part she holds onto is him calling her conceited—she feels conflicted and would hate to fracture their love by being too vain. Before she stands, Brax pulls passionately on her arm, drawing her in for an ardent kiss. A warm smile radiates from her as Brax inhales her love. She blows him a final kiss as she walks over to Rachel and Emiliano, who are still conversing at the table.

"So, you ready to lose, Emiliano?" Hannah teases as she picks up a white pinny.

"Yeah…I think we got this one!" Rachel exclaims.

Emiliano rolls his eyes playfully as they head to the field.

Rachel scans the white pinnies, then the blue, sizing up both teams before heading to her position, playing forward. The white team starts the kickoff: Hannah passes the ball to Rachel, who one touches it behind her to Pablo.

The next time Rachel gets the ball, she dribbles down the line and takes on Emiliano. Confidence, adrenaline, and flirtation arise in her body. She never would have correlated coquetry with soccer before; it has always been strictly business. Yet, here she is, changing definitions and thinking in new ways because of this intriguing man.

Emiliano crouches down steadily, making sure not to dive in too quickly. She attempts to fake him out, but he keeps up with her moves. Until suddenly, he leans a bit too far to one side. Rachel cuts the ball past him and sprints down the line until she gets to the corner where she crosses the ball toward the goal.

Hannah, who always finds her way into the right spots, jumps between two defenders for the header, and scores. The best friends run to each other, ecstatic over their incredible play. They simply go together undeniably like two peas in a pod, peanut butter and jelly, cookies and milk.

"Nice play dude!" Pablo exclaims, jogging over and giving Rachel a fist bump. "And nice goal!" he adds, pointing to Hannah.

"Let's keep it up, white!" Rachel hollers.

Javier starts the kickoff for the blue team. Eventually the ball makes its way to Emiliano. It feels natural and comfortable at his feet. He jukes Pablo with a fake pass and Rachel runs up to defend. He tries pushing the ball past her, but she blocks it, sending the ball flying off the field.

Fabian meanders over to get it, hoping to give everyone a few seconds to catch their breath—typical mindset of a group leader. He throws the ball to Javier, who quickly notices Rachel out of position and launches a through ball to Emiliano.

Realizing her mistake, Rachel runs twice as hard trying to catch Emiliano. Her mind stating self-insults and *shit shit shit* on replay. She reaches him at the corner but takes too big of a stride. He nutmegs her, then sends the ball in front of the goal. Fabian laces it into the back of the net, and the blue team whoops and hollers.

"Damn. Sorry guys, that's my bad," Rachel says, shaking her head.

"That's **OK** guys, we'll get it back!" Hannah shouts, heading over to start the kickoff.

Both teams get zoned in, extra focused and competitive, since the game is tied one to one. As they continue playing, the sun breaks free from the clouds. The temperature gets increasingly hotter and almost everyone's shirts become soaked. Foreheads cry tears of sweat. The blue team steals the lead for a while, then the white team does.

Eventually, the game is tied four to four. The intensity rises, as both teams are eager for the win. Javier accidentally passes to someone on the white team. Without thought or intention, the player toe-pokes the ball, sending it back to the blue team on the other side of the field.

"God, a toe-poker," Rachel mumbles under her breath. She would never do such a thing, and she expects better from anyone on the field. In all aspects of her life she has high standards and that is no different for soccer. "Guys, we gotta look up before we pass!" she calls out passionately as she sprints back to cover the open space in the midfield.

Javier traps the ball, then attempts to pass a through ball to Emiliano, copying what he did earlier in the game. Rachel reads the play and blocks the passageway. Collecting it at her feet, she finds Hannah in the middle. When the ball ends up at Pablo's feet, Rachel cuts toward the goal and he chips the ball nicely in front of her.

Emiliano runs up to defend Rachel, a look of confidence radiating from his eyes. She does two scissors over the ball, then pushes it past him, takes a shot, and scores.

"Fuck yeah, Rach!" Hannah yells.

Some people eagerly hurry off the field to get water. Others lower their heads and amble, upset over losing.

"Can't believe you megged me," Rachel says to Emiliano, her cheeks flush.

"Can't believe you dribbled around me twice!" Emiliano replies.

Rachel smiles, proud of her slick moves and winning goal. She grabs her water bottle and lies down in the grass, spreading her arms and legs, as if to make Southern California snow angels in the January heat.

Javier walks over to Jemma, who's still sitting against the tree. He chugs an entire water bottle, then throws it in his bag. "We should call it a day. Nobody wants to do a second round, right? It's way too hot," he calls out.

"Are you OK?" Jemma asks.

"I just get heated when I play, that's all," he says, a bit of attitude in his voice.

Silence ensues and nobody answers Javier's question. Finally, Emiliano suggests that it might be nice to end early. Though, he has an ulterior motive: see if Rachel Williams is free to hang out. A few more players agree and start collecting their things. Pablo gives Emiliano a fist bump before leaving.

Rachel slowly unties her cleats, sporting a look of disappointment. Soccer is practically the only thing she wants to do on a day off from studying. As she gathers her things, she notices Emiliano walking toward her. Well, maybe it isn't the *only* thing she would want to do.

"You got any plans today, Rach?"

"Just dinner later with my mom."

"So…you're free right now?" he asks.

"Yeah, I'm free right now." She nods as she slips her cleats into her bag.

"Well…do you want to do something?" he asks, unsteadiness in his voice.

"Sure." She smiles, finding his nervousness and multitude of questions to be adorable.

Javier overhears their conversation as he packs his bag. He's glad he set his sights on someone new because Rachel clearly is occupied with Emiliano. He wonders what their chances are of making it as a couple, or if they are even a couple at all. He decides to keep a tab on the Emiliano and Rachel situation, and pursue Jemma in the meantime.

Rachel and Emiliano head up the hill, making a plan to meet at Emiliano's house. They pass by Hannah and Brax who are still sitting in the grass. Rachel waves to them, wondering if they will think anything is going on between her and Emiliano.

As soon as Rachel and Emiliano are out of earshot, Hannah whispers to Brax, "Something's going on there."

"Or maybe they're just friends, Hannah. Guys and girls can be *just* friends." He sighs, hoping Hannah's questioning mind will stop because his best friend Alexis is moving into their apartment soon.

"I guess." Hannah shrugs, keeping her eyes on them as they fade in the distance. Rachel playfully pushes Emiliano's arm. The gesture looks oddly similar to how Brax and that one girl touched each other at the pool party they attended. Maybe she has been overthinking. Maybe Brax's relationships with other girls are harmless. Maybe Rachel and Emiliano aren't flirting. Maybe guys and girls can be just friends—maybe, maybe not.

12 Beaming from the Rendezvous

Rachel trails behind Emiliano past stop signs and through traffic lights until they pull into his neighborhood where the fully packed curbs make it seem like a professional sports game is going on nearby. In the back alleyway, he pulls his car slightly onto the grass and concrete, squeezing closely to his mom's car in the driveway.

Rachel stops in the middle of the road wondering where to park. Since the nearby streets are so packed and there are only driveways in the back alley, Emiliano offers to pick her up at the Nuñez's *panadería*. She doesn't want anything to be a hassle though with more driving, relocating, picking up, and dropping off. Ultimately, they decide on leaving the neighborhood in her car and she can just bring him home later.

Emiliano hurries inside his house to put down his soccer bag. A few minutes later he comes outside with a blue baseball cap and wallet. He combs through his hair then puts the hat on, facing backward, before getting in the car. "You wanna swing by the food cart, Rach? My ma wants me to pick up some esquites for her."

"Yeah! Um…where is that and what is that?"

"It's right around the corner. You've never had esquites?"

"You have a food cart in your neighborhood!? And no, I've never heard of it."

"What! What about chicharrones?"

"I've heard of that one. But I've never tried either of them."

"Wow…" Emiliano says. "Well, you're going to make a left here, then another left, then it's about fifty feet up."

Rachel follows his directions, driving slowly to scan for parking. As they make the second turn, coming up to the Mexican street vendor, they still haven't found any open spots.

"Oh, right there!" Emiliano points to an open space on the corner where two streets meet.

"Are you sure I can park there?"

Emiliano nods confidently.

Rachel attempts to parallel park three times before finally squeezing her car into the space, with the front wheel slightly up onto the slanted curb.

"Esquites is a common Mexican snack," Emiliano says. "Grilled corn topped with mayonnaise, cotija cheese, a slice of lime, and tajin powder." He adds up the ingredients on his fingers.

"Sounds delicious!"

"Do you want some?" he asks.

"I'm lactose intolerant, Emiliano. I can't have dairy."

"Ah, I'm sure I'm lactose intolerant too, but that ain't stoppin' me!"

Emiliano gets out of the car and waits in line behind two *Mexicanas* and one of their daughters. The women order a bag of *chicharrones*. When the young girl stands on her tiptoes to tell the street vendor her order, Emiliano looks over at Rachel and waves, gesturing for her to join him.

Excited at the invitation, Rachel gets out of her car. The women and the child stare at her while they wait for their food. Rachel awkwardly addresses all three of them with a shy smile.

"¿Quién es ella?" The street vendor asks Emiliano.

"Es mi amiga del fútbol."

"Ah." The street vendor nods while swirling hot sauce into the bag of *chicharrones*. "Ella es buena?"

"Sí, sí, mucho mejor que yo. Ella tiene pies tramposos. Ella va de izquierda a derecha, izquierda a derecha rápidamente y luego dispara la pelota con mucha fuerza!" Emiliano says passionately, shaking his head.

The street vendor and the two women laugh. Rachel stands silently with a soft smile on her face, wondering what they are talking about.

"He asked me who you were and I told him you were my friend from soccer. Then he asked if you were any good and I told them about your tricky feet, and how you scored that goal today," Emiliano whispers to Rachel, who immediately blushes.

The women and child receive their snacks. After taking a bite of the spicy fruit, the child reaches up for her mother's hand. They walk down the street and the young girl turns around twice to look at Rachel and Emiliano.

"¿Qué se te ofrece, Emiliano?" The street vendor asks, wiping his hands clean on a towel.

While Emiliano orders a bag of *chicharrones* and two *esquites*, Rachel scans the neighborhood, admiring the vibrant, close-knit community—the smiles and warmth, the language she can't understand, the lifestyle that is absolutely foreign to her—just three miles from her home, yet seems worlds away.

The street vendor hands Emiliano a bowl of *esquites*, then flips up the plastic lids. He starts whipping up the second bowl, corn bits flying on the cart and the nearby ground. Emiliano scoops a huge spoonful into his mouth, making sure to grab a little of every ingredient. He focuses all his attention on the array of creams and spices invading his taste buds. After savoring the richness, he extends the spoon to Rachel.

"You wanna try a bite?" he asks.

She smiles, then grabs the spoon as she looks into the mixture of goodies. One bite won't hurt, she thinks.

"Make sure you reaalllyy dig in there, get all the ingredients!" Emiliano says, pretending to scoop a huge spoonful in the air.

Rachel digs in deeply. The spoon comes up with a mound of every color it can muster—yellow and cream topped with *verde, blanco, y rojo*. Emiliano intently watches as she chews for a minute, her head dancing back and forth.

"You like it?" he asks.

"So good! And not what I was expecting it to taste like…"

"Hell yeah! We gotta getchu eatin' all the Mexicano food." Emiliano nods proudly.

Rachel nods in return. She likes Emiliano so much that she is willing to watch anything, learn anything, or try any food, even if her lactose intolerant body shouldn't have it.

The street vendor places the second bowl of *esquites* on top of the cart, then shuts all the plastic lids. He unhooks a bag of *chicharrones* from the side of the cart and opens it. Swirls of hot sauce marinate the orange pinwheels. After shaking the bag, the street vendor swirls one more round of hot sauce before swiftly tying the bag in one seamless movement.

"Aquí tienes, vato," the street vendor says, placing the *chicharrones* on top of the cart.

Emiliano thanks him and puts a few dollars in the tip jar. He knows the vendor well; he comes into the neighborhood to sell every day for five or six hours straight. Most of the money he makes gets sent to his wife and three children in Mexico. He's been trying to work to move them to the States, so of course it was a must for Emiliano to give him a good tip before heading back to Rachel's car.

After barely squeezing out of the tight spot, they head for Emiliano's. He pulls out a pinwheel full of hot sauce and offers her the piece of puffed wheat.

"It might be spicy!" he says quickly, as she raises the pinwheel to her mouth.

Rachel chews for a moment then sticks out her tongue, breathing heavily. "Holy cow! That's hot!" She barely manages to utter the words. Emiliano snickers as he places a pinwheel in his mouth, then a second and third, casually chewing as if they are regular tortilla chips.

"You don't think they're spicy, Emiliano?"

"No, not to me." He lets out a chuckle as they pull up to the front of his house, where Adriana is waiting outside.

After a quick introduction, Rachel and Adriana exchange a handshake, both smiling. It's immediately apparent to Rachel where Emiliano got his good looks from. Adriana's thick dark brown hair is the same rich chocolatey color as his. Also, she has beautiful large brown eyes and soft youthful skin. Rachel hopes she'll look half as good when she is a mom.

"So is this the badass girl? The one who's super good at soccer?" Adriana says with a smirk.

"Yep. That's the one, Ma." Emiliano sheepishly smiles, a pink hue rushing to his cheeks. Hoping to put an end to the conversation, and his embarrassment, he hands the *esquites* and *chicharrones* to his mother.

"Thank you, son." Adriana looks down at the food. "I'll have to run this off later at the gym. All right, you kids have a great time, and nice to meet you, Rachel!"

As they head back to the car, Rachel adores everything about Emiliano from the way he is dressed to his bubbly personality to the sheer confidence in his step. And, she can't help but feel enthused; he actually talked about her to his mother?

"Rach, we should go to The Peak of the Earth."

She looks at him puzzled. "Is that the overlook everyone talks about on top of a mountain?"

"Yeah! You never been, Rach?"

"As if this answer will come as a surprise…no."

"My goodness, chica. We gotta getchu out more! Head to the main road and I'll tell ya how to get there."

As they drive down the street, Emiliano notices one of his neighbors—who's also in his early twenties—standing outside. He rolls down the window and yells "Sup, vato!" as he sticks his head out. The boy waves back as they turn out of the neighborhood.

"Turn right here," Emiliano tells Rachel. He pulls out his phone, scrolls through his music, then fusses with the stereo and Bluetooth. "This is Chicano Batman, one of the bands I told you about."

"A Hundred Dead and Loving Souls" serenades the atmosphere. For a few verses, they remain silent, listening to the soft and soulful tune. At the next stoplight, he mentions the overlook is at the top of the windy road. The long instrumental in the middle of the song fits impeccably with the peaceful drive up the mountain.

She parks at the top and they look out of the windshield, scanning the expanse of their beautiful California suburb. The cars look like mini toys zooming down the freeway. Emiliano pauses the music, then points to his neighborhood in the distance. Rachel leans closer to see where he is pointing, then searches for her own neighborhood, quickly realizing the mountain blocks it.

"Isn't it so beautiful?" Emiliano says.

"I'm mesmerized!" Rachel continues staring out into the layers of trees, houses, mountains, and roads. The afternoon's sinking sun is like a spotlight shining on everything.

Two crows fly overhead and land on a tree branch fairly close to the car. Rachel smiles; she can't help but feel like the birds are a symbol representing her and Emiliano.

After watching the birds cock their heads while staring at one another, Rachel looks over at Emiliano; he's still admiring the view. She gazes longingly at his lips that look like fluffy pillows she could rest her lips on before falling asleep forever.

"I've been thinking about your lips for a minute." The words slip out of her mouth, as she is unable to contain her desire any longer.

"What?" He looks at her like he is starstruck.

"I just…I…really want to kiss you, Emiliano."

"Well, this is, um…news to me." He smiles softly.

"News? You didn't read the paper?" Her lips curl inward.

He lets out a sharp breath. "That just…don't make any sense to me."

They sit wordlessly for a few seconds.

"I'll meet you halfway," he says, in a low voice that isn't quite a whisper, with desire overflowing in his eyes.

They lean in slowly, looking at one another's lips until they get within an inch. Then, their eyes shut and they pull toward each other, *each* the lure to the *other*. His lips caress around her bottom lip, while hers cradle his top lip. She passionately touches his cheek, sending shivers through his body. Their tongues meet for the first time, swirling around each other, getting acquainted in a dance.

Emiliano pulls back his tongue, then rolls it across the inside of her mouth, like he's walking down the hallway of a new home for the first time. When he finishes, he sucks on her top lip while reaching over and gripping the skin on the outside of her hip. His entire body leans over the console, over her, as if to say he cannot get enough of her love.

They kiss again, this time her lips hugging his bottom, his lips hugging her top. Holding the kiss for a few seconds, they breathe in their shared passion. She sets both her hands gently against his cheeks, now fully locked into him.

"You are so beautiful," he whispers, his eyes studying her face. Leaning in toward her puckered-up lips, he wraps the top one between his, sucking intensely for a few seconds, before slowly letting go.

She opens her eyes and, for the first time, gulps an overwhelming feeling of fear. She fears her feelings for him—so intense, so like a forest fire. She fears the future. They were having fun, just hanging out, and it was all light-hearted. Now suddenly there is more weight, more pressure, and no way of knowing what is to come. Most of all she fears her attachment to him. The minute his lips touched hers, her heart was officially placed in his hands, and what if he breaks it?

Emiliano looks into her eyes and she lowers her gaze to his lips. Then, she lathers his cheek in the love of twenty kisses—some slow, others fast, a few where you can't tell when one ends and the next begins.

"Cheek kisses make me feel warm," he whispers. "They make me feel loved."

She repeats her kisses on his other cheek, hoping he'll feel as warm as a freshly baked cookie.

Overcome by the waves of kisses that overflow from her ocean of love, he leans back, a mystified and sorrowful expression on his face. "Baby, what do you want to do with me?" he asks.

"What do you mean?"

He sighs. "You're way out of my league. You know that."

"No I'm not." Rachel pulls back, perplexed he would even say such a thing. "Don't think like that. If I'm out of your league, then you're out of my league, just the same."

Emiliano practically chokes on his pride, wondering why an intelligent, athletic, goofy woman would want anything to do with him. "You know, I thought the girls I dated were pretty, but you…" he pauses, "Rach, you are something different, something special, and you're like a twelve outta ten." He tucks her hair behind her ear, then places a hand gently on the outside of her cheek and pulls her in for a soft, delicate peck. Neither one of them can tell if they are holding the kiss for a few seconds or an eternity. Perhaps the kiss belongs to both sides of the time paradigm.

When he opens his eyes, he pulls away, spotting someone lingering near the driver's side of the car. A middle-aged White man is oddly close to the side mirror, half-heartedly picking up an empty bag of chips in a bush.

"Why is he so close to us?" Rachel asks.

"I don't know." Emiliano's uneasy look is evidence that he is not approving of the man's invasion of privacy. He takes his hat off, combs his hair back with his fingers, and steps out of the car. "Can I help you, sir?" Emiliano says politely, holding his hat against his chest.

"I'm just picking up the trash, there seems to be a lot of it up here!" The White man's eyebrows raise. "You look familiar," he says in an interrogating tone.

"No, sir. I don't know you," Emiliano says politely.

"Yeah. This is my hill, I live here. I see you and your friends come up here all the time trashing this place! Loud! Through all hours of the night and you never pick up after yourselves!" The White man scoffs, self-assured that he recognizes Emiliano.

"No, sir. I would never do something like that. I love my city. I would never trash it. We just came up here to enjoy the beautiful view," Emiliano says politely.

"Well, I'm just gonna call the cops! You can't be up here!" The White man threatens.

"We aren't doing anything illegal, sir. Maybe you should leave," Emiliano says sternly, looking into the man's eyes—showing him that while he is polite, he will not be challenged.

The White man shakes his head as he carries the empty bag down the hill.

Emiliano waits until the man gets into his car before getting back into Rachel's. He sinks into the cushion, takes a deep breath, and puts his hat back on.

"Thank you." Rachel barely manages to get the words out, in awe of Emiliano's manly behavior. She looks in the rearview mirror; the White man is sitting in his car, still staring at the two of them.

"No problem," Emiliano says, looking over his shoulder.

The White man slowly reverses his car down the hill and disappears in the distance.

"Do you think we should leave, Emiliano?"

"Yeah…we probably should."

The low rumbling of the engine reverberates in the quietness. Rachel and Emiliano glance at each other, beaming from the rendezvous between their lips. She makes a U-turn as Emiliano presses play on the music. The remainder of "A Hundred Dead and Loving Souls" echoes from window to window as they drive down the winding road.

13 Cycle of Fear

A few days after their first kiss, Rachel is lying in bed journaling. She rubs her hand across her bottom lip and smiles; she swears she can still feel a lingering touch of his kiss. Then she remembers the fear she felt just before they went home. Her anxiety settles in—she wants to know where their relationship is going, but feels scared to ask and doesn't know whether it's too early. She and Emiliano have been texting pretty much all day, whenever they have been free. On her next reply, she musters some courage, and writes and rewrites a few times before pressing send.

Hey Emiliano. Can I ask you a question?

A few moments later, her phone buzzes.

Sure. Anything!

His reply makes her feel relieved, and some of the tension in her body releases. Again, she writes and rewrites trying to find the perfect words.

I really like you. Where is our relationship going?

Her message brings up a lot of fear in Emiliano. He has never made it past this stage with a girl since high school. In the last few years, when other girls have gotten to this point, he has run for the hills. He does not want to lose his independence. He does not want someone to rely on him. He does not want to mess up. Also, he thinks Rachel deserves a lot more and is out of his league. He takes a little while to respond, trying to find the right words, the most truthful words.

I'm just still getting to know you. I like getting to know you.

When Rachel reads the text, fear rumbles through her belly and up to her heart. He didn't give her a straight up answer. He didn't say yes that it was going somewhere or no that it wasn't going somewhere, which makes her feel like she is at the other end of a string that he is holding. The anxiety and overthinking habit that takes over her external life—never noticing people around her, sticking to a small inner circle—is the same anxiety and overthinking habit that easily infiltrates her romantic life. She begins thinking about all of her and Emiliano's plans, and believes that she has initiated almost everything in their relationship. The windshield wipers: her idea. The late night drive to the trailhead: her idea. The first kiss: her idea. Asking about where they are headed: her idea. Now, this is turning out to feel embarrassing.

Her anxiety begins to spin into a tornado. She thinks he must not like her, that he is using her, that he must laugh about this with his friends thinking it's hilarious that she is practically all over him. She starts to cry, now completely in fear, and overwhelmed. She neglects to recall nearly half the things they have done were his idea. Getting acai bowls: his idea. Driving to The Peak of the Earth: his idea. One day playing basketball together: his idea. Their sunset and dinner plan: mutual idea. Yet, all of these slip into the cracks.

The next time he texts her, she ignores it for a few hours. There is no way that she is going to be someone's laughing stock!

Emiliano doesn't mind the distance because unlike Rachel, he has a knack for avoidance. When she does finally respond, he tells her that he will not be able to see her over the weekend because he has a lot of work, car stuff, and family stuff. While he does have some plans, this is an over-exaggeration of how busy he will be. He liked when they were just enjoying each other's company, nothing being too heavy. Now, he is feeling claustrophobic in the downstairs living room of his condo, which is full of plenty of air and breathing room.

Her anxiety worsens when she receives his text about being busy. She texts him back and says it's no problem because she also will be *very* busy and has a lot of studying to do. It is true that she will be studying—her exam is just under a week away. However, she is not *that* busy to where she wouldn't be able to see him; she, of course, only said that out of fear.

Her response makes Emiliano feel lighter on his feet, like a two-ton weight is falling off his back.

* * *

Over the next two days, their texting grows sparse. Emiliano does not mind it. Rachel absolutely hates it. The cycle of fear between avoidance and anxiety begins to whir like a washing machine set on heavy.

When Saturday comes around, neither one of them goes to the Soccer Saturday Session. Emiliano goes to lunch with his family at his *abuela's* house and Rachel has a long study session at The Coffee Bar.

When she finishes up and heads for her house, she is full of anxiety. Yes, about the GRE, but mainly about Emiliano, which right now seems more important. She doesn't know how she will be able to focus on the exam if she doesn't gain some semblance of clarity with their relationship. Just before reaching the freeway onramp, a sign on the road catches her eye—a nearby mystic shop is offering palm readings, tarot readings, and more. Rachel is not much of a believer in that kind of stuff, thinking it's all woowoo. Yet, she turns on her blinker and makes her way to the shop.

When she enters, the place is full of curtains, tapestries, and intricate spiritual designs on the walls. A peaceful and subtle guitar instrumental hums through the room. A lavender aroma wafts through the air from an incense holder at the front desk.

An older woman with an olive skin tone comes through one of the curtains and walks over to Rachel. "Hello, my darling. I've been expecting you."

"Really?" Rachel's brows knit together. She is sure that is a line that a mystic woman would say to anyone and everyone who enters their shop.

Truly, though, the woman had received a premonition in her mind's eye that a young woman in a light yellow shirt would be coming into the shop today in need of a tarot reading. And here she is: young, light yellow top. "You are here for the tarot, my girl?"

"Uh, yes. I think so," Rachel says. "I've never had a reading done before."

"No problem," the woman says. "Follow me." She takes Rachel behind one of the tapestries and into a small nook with a wooden desk, two chairs on either side of it. A deck of tarot cards is already on the table. Rachel wonders if the woman truly was expecting her.

They sit down and Rachel watches as the woman closes her eyes and begins to hum. She flips through the cards, feeling each one. Slowly, over the next few minutes, five cards are placed upside down on the table, making a plus symbol. The left card: the past. The middle card: the present. The right card: the future. The upper card: the heavens. The lower card: the underworld of dreams and magic.

"Now, dear, before I start, I must tell you how the tarot works." She explains each card placement to Rachel, then tells her it's not just the card in a specific place that matters, but also how the card is positioned: upright or facing down could signify completely different things. Also, some things are more intuitive while others are more straightforward; she won't know until the cards are flipped over. "Now, let's begin. So long as you are ready, dear?"

Rachel nods, lightly folding her arms.

The woman flips over the card representing the past. "Ah. I see. In the past, you have had some emotional and mood disturbances, such as anxiety. It led you to escapism in many ways, and to pursue romantic relationships with those who couldn't see you, those who had no care for your emotional well-being. This only fed your emotions and anxiety more. You struggled to tell the difference between your intuition and paranoia."

Rachel's eyes grow wide. "Yes...that's true...How can you tell?"

"Well, my dear, if you look, you see this queen is upside down. If there were anything in her cup, it has all been spilled out. Also, do you notice how she is facing out, her back against the card in the present position?"

"Yes."

"This also means, darling, that you need to be aware of your past-self neglecting to see how she is showing up in your present. Are you not following your intuition? Are you choosing paranoia? Are you struggling with emotional disturbances? These are questions to ask yourself." The woman flips over the card in the present position; another woman, a younger looking one, is also upside down. "My dear, you might be connecting your life-force and well-being to another human. This is not safe. See how that cup is still empty?"

Rachel nods. She knows that the reading is referencing Emiliano. That ever since their first kiss, her fear and paranoia have taken over. She knows she needs to put her focus back on herself. Her attraction and love for him should not mean neglecting her emotional well-being and her career. "This is spot on, and bringing a lot of subconscious things to the surface. Thank you," Rachel says.

The woman flips over the card in the future spot and her brows furrow. Needing more clarity, she flips over the cards in the upper and under world. For a few moments she studies the three, meditating on the message coming to her mind. "My dear, this is important. In the future is the three of swords, and I see a love triangle of sorts. A vision came into my mind's eye of a younger man, a bit younger than you, with lighter skin. And an older man with darker skin. One or both of them are Mexican, or have a Mexican lineage."

Rachel's ego gets stuck on this news. A love triangle? Two men? Mexican? The younger one must be Emiliano, though she has no idea who the older one could be. Are two men going to fight over her? She is only half way listening when the woman continues, "In the underworld, in the realms unseen of dreams and of nightmares, I see a storm coming. You will see the dark rain clouds. You must beware to not go into the clouds because lightning will strike."

When Rachel hears the word "lightning," she thinks of the first time she and Emiliano touched. "Are you sure the lightning hasn't already happened?"

"Yes, my child. I'm sure."

Rachel speculates over what the thunder and lightning could be. Will the two men get in a fist fight over her? Will she literally have to choose between them, choose who she wants to be with in her future? She is sure that no matter who it is, or what the circumstances are, if one of the triangle points represents Emiliano she will choose him.

The woman takes a deep breath. "Above you, in the heavens, you have angels helping you, dear. They want you to reach spiritual victory. Take care of your emotional well-being, only then will you know which path to choose when the two men are in front of you."

"OK." Rachel nods, then thanks the woman for the helpful and telling reading, knowing there is no way she would choose another man over Emiliano when or if the time comes. She takes out her wallet and the woman shakes her hand, informing her that the reading is free.

When Rachel gets home, she lies down on her bed and looks through her recent journaling entries. Most of which are about Emiliano. She vows to herself that she will work on her anxiety toward their relationship, as the tarot reader suggested. Her phone buzzes and she glances over, excited to see it's Emiliano. Their scarce texting had given him room to breathe and he felt ready to reach out again.

I have been craving In-N-Out fries, Rach.

She smiles at the message, thinking she must have been anxious over nothing. Without overthinking, she types a response.

Haha. They do have great food!

Less than a minute later, Emiliano texts back.

Do you want to go get some soon? I just gotta figure out which day I'm free.

Rachel tells him that sounds great, including a blushing emoji in the text.

Their conversation picks up from there, out of the darkness, out of the cycle of fear.

14 In the Time Continuum

Emiliano heads down a main road in Old Oak in his old Firebird, glancing in the rearview mirror a few times to make sure he's looking crisp; of course—no matter how many times he looks—his hair is still clean and orderly and his face is still smooth and shaved. When he turns onto Rachel's street, he exhales, nervous to see her.

Like always, Rachel is already waiting outside, anticipating. They haven't seen each other in almost two weeks, which is an awfully long time for people who just shared their first kiss. She's dressed in high-waisted Levi shorts and a white crop top that accentuates her beautiful, athletic figure. He pulls up to the curb and she gets in, elated to enter Emiliano's stylish black car for the first time.

"Your hair looks amazing," he says.

"Thanks." Rachel combs through her wavy locks that just came out of French braids. Immediately, she throws a clothing compliment his way in return, like a boomerang; his tucked in tees are always a sight for sore eyes, at least to her eyes anyway.

Before buckling, she holds out her hand. Without him realizing it, he's following along with their handshake, as if she's one of his guy friends initiating it. When they snap, he looks up with a shocked, yet impressed, expression. "Did you just initiate our handshake?"

"I think I did," Rachel says confidently.

"Bet! That's sick." Emiliano chuckles. "You ready to grub?"

"Ready as I'll ever be," Rachel says.

They head toward In-N-Out, Emiliano feeling glad that Rachel isn't asking about the future, and Rachel feeling glad that her anxiety has subsided about the future. After all, the only place they can ever truly *be* in is the present, and thankfully that's where they are now.

Everything felt better for her once their In-N-Out texting conversation turned into flirting over fast food: first they had made bets about who would win in an eating competition, then they told each other which fast food item they most resembled. Emiliano told Rachel she was like ketchup, good with anything. Rachel told Emiliano he was like soda, sparkly and fizzy.

"I took the GRE and I'm anxiously awaiting the results!" Rachel says, crossing her fingers. "If my test scores are good enough, I'm gonna apply to Brown, UNC-Chapel Hill, and Boston College."

"I'm confused," Emiliano says. "I thought you already went to college."

"Well, yeah. For a bachelor's degree in psych. Now I'm getting a master's degree in counseling."

Emiliano confesses that he doesn't know the difference between the two. Rachel explains that a master's is a higher degree and will lead to a better job. It also could be more narrowed to a specific field—like how her bachelor's was in psych, but her master's could be anything under the umbrella term "psychology."

They pull into the parking lot and get in the drive-thru line that is at least ten cars long. Emiliano puts the car in park while they wait.

"So why do you want to be a therapist? Just cause?"

"No, I struggled with mental health when I was younger, and now that I've—for the most part—made it to the other side, to a happier life, I want to help other people with that too," Rachel says. After a breath, she continues, "So…how have you been lately?"

Emiliano shrugs. "Same old. Workin' a lot and been workin' on my car in my free time."

Glancing around his car, Rachel notices the entire panel is off the passenger door. She touches her fingers across all the metal parts—some big, others small, some so tiny they're tinier than her fingernail. She looks at all the pieces that attach to the lever of the lock. "This is cool. I've never seen what the inside of a car door looks like."

"I have a lot of work to do. That's the next thing on my to-do list."

"Oh…I kinda like the rugged look." Rachel shrugs, then asks what he'll fix next. He tells her about his broken stereo and how he wants to install a new system. Then, he shows her how he currently listens to music. He sets his phone on the dash with its speaker facing against the windshield, which helps to amplify sound.

A few cars pull forward and Emiliano slowly follows. He rolls down the window then leans out trying get a look at the menu. "You getting a shake?" he asks.

"I don't consume dairy," she reminds him. "I think I'm in the mood for Sprite."

"You're gonna get the most boring soda flavor ever?" he teases.

"How do you figure that? What's your favorite soda, Mr. Emiliano?"

"Dr. Pepper."

"Oh…you're one of those guys…" Rachel jokes.

"Well, no, I'm not like your *typical* Dr. Pepper guy." Emiliano awkwardly chuckles.

"Oh…what's the *typical* Dr. Pepper guy?"

"You know…The one you described! Just like your *typical* Dr. Pepper guy." He scoffs, as if to make fun of and separate himself from such a character. "And I'm nothing like him!"

Rachel laughs, finding his ego to be oh so cute and fragile. "I was kidding, Emiliano!"

"No, there actually is a typical Dr. Pepper guy, Rachel!" He laughs coyly, but then notices Rachel smirking. "I'm serious, Rach!"

Space opens and Emiliano pulls up, waiting for the worker's cheery voice to come through the speaker. He orders two hamburgers, a tray of fries, and a Dr. Pepper.

When Rachel leans over—into Emiliano's physical bubble—to order, he is delighted for her to invade his space. He gazes at her mouth while she orders a tray of fries, Sprite, and the veggie—a feeble excuse for a burger as it only contains lettuce, tomato, and grilled onion on a bun. For a moment, Rachel lingers there, close to him. He remains enraptured by her physical closeness and confused by her food choices.

When they get to the pay window, Rachel pulls out her debit card, but Emiliano acts like he doesn't see it and hands money to the cashier. She playfully rolls her eyes, though is pleased with the kind gesture. They park again, for a final time, waiting for one more car to receive their food from the last window.

"Do you think you could outlast me in a staring competition?" Emiliano asks.

"A stare off? I'll probably win."

Emiliano looks into Rachel's eyes, as he has many times before. She has never met him eye to eye and doesn't want to give anything away, believing eyes are the windows to the soul. Their eyes meet, but she is guarded, refusing to let him see anything. Her concentration remains on the surface—admiring how many shades of green are in his speckled eyes. She estimates there are perhaps at least fifty-four. Emiliano tries to read her, tries to see the young woman beyond the color, beyond the light-brown eyes.

They stare for a few moments without blinking. At the same time, their resting mouths turn into smiles. Rachel blinks first.

"I win!" Emiliano exclaims. "I almost blinked because that serious face just doesn't match your sweetness, Rach!"

The car in front of them finally exits and Emiliano pulls forward. Each tray of hot food that the young worker hands over gets exchanged with a thank you.

"We should eat here," Emiliano says. "I'm hungry."

"OK." Rachel shrugs. "Sounds fine to me."

He pulls into a spot in front of the bike shop across from In-N-Out. The sun has set and darkness slowly envelops the world around them, except for the neon blue bike shop sign that illuminates the car. He takes a huge bite of a burger, secret sauce spilling on the sides of his mouth as he chews.

"So," Emiliano says between bites, "when you comin' to a car show with me?"

"Whenever you invite me." She puts a small handful of fries in her mouth.

"Have you ever been to one, Rach?"

"No. I don't even know anything about car shows."

"We definitely gotta go sometime then! They got all the classic cars there, some are revamped real nice. They also got new cars to show off. There's racing…and lots of food!"

Rachel begins unwrapping her veggie, daydreaming about a car show. Something she never thought she would daydream about. "Since they don't have a patty in here they should rename this. Veggie *sandwich* seems more fitting." Rachel stares at the thin stack of veggies lying between two perfectly soft buns.

"Or they could call it a suh-lad," Emiliano jokes.

"Suh-what?"

"A suh-lad! Don't you remember that SpongeBob episode, Rach? When SpongeBob makes a salad."

She shakes her head, disappointed and embarrassed that her answer is always no.

Emiliano takes his fresh-cut, warm, greasy fries out of the bag and places them on his lap. As he goes to drop a handful in his mouth, he accidentally tips the tray over. Fries spill everywhere, landing on the seat, in the crack, and all over the floor.

Rachel covers her mouth, trying to hold in a laugh. He's been craving these fries for a week, and now he won't have any.

His brows furrow as he looks down at the mess all over the driver's side. "Damn. I spilled just like you, Rach."

"What? I didn't spill!"

"Yeah, last time I saw you. Spilling the beans about wanting to kiss me."

"Wow. You know what, Emiliano...the beans were just on the counter. I simply nudged them off!"

"No. The beans were in the cabinet. You took 'em out and flung 'em all over the kitchen!"

They both laugh as Emiliano pulls a fry out of the crack between the driver's seat and the console. Unashamedly, he eats it.

Rachel sets her tray between them to share. They reach in and their fingers graze each other's. Two weeks is too long to go without a physical touch. It feels bubbly like the first sip of a carbonated drink. They nervously pull their hands away, then Emiliano opens the door.

"This 'bout to be a bitch to clean..." he says, trailing off with a sigh.

The fries seem to be playing hide-and-go-seek under the driver's seat, by the brake pedal, sprinkled across the floor. Rachel reaches into a crack to help find them.

"I might need…" Emiliano says, struggling to get the words out, "help on this side." His body is wedged in the car, examining the area underneath his seat.

After finding a few fries, Rachel gets out and walks over to help him. His hips are in the air, greeting her. She enjoys the view, admiring the shape of his butt and how the jeans hug his hips.

Emiliano turns around, catching Rachel checking him out. "Were you just staring at my ass?" he asks, holding a wad of French fries, decorated in fuzz, hair, and the like.

"Maybe I was," Rachel says. "Did you get them all?"

"I think so."

After throwing all the trash away, they get back in the car and, for the first time all evening, neither one of them has anything to say. Though, it doesn't feel awkward. Rather, it feels refreshing, welcoming, safe, and shared. Furthermore, Emiliano's soft smile and curved lips say everything words never could. And, per usual, Rachel admires all things Emiliano.

They gradually drift toward each other, almost as if electromagnetic currents are pulling them together, just as any two forces would be pulled by the law of attraction. When they are an inch apart, they linger intimately close to one another, their eyes still open, staring at each other's lips; once they gently meet, their previously acquainted tongues join the soiree, twirling in circles. Together, they create one beautifully sloppy wet masterpiece.

As they wipe off their mouths, they start laughing.

"You smell like burger, Emiliano."

"You smell like onion, Rachel."

She looks out the window, noticing it's now completely dark outside. The last morsel of light has vanished without the smallest trace. Neither one of them noticed, since they've been so lost in each other—somewhere in the time continuum, where hours feel like seconds and seconds feel like hours.

"You wanna get ice cream or go to the overlook by the freeway, Rach?"

"Hmm. Both sound good. And they're right near each other. Maybe we can just drive that way and decide when we get in the vicinity."

"Vicinity! What the heck is a vicinity?" He chuckles. "You got a big vocabulary. Always sayin' things I don't know." Emiliano pulls out of the parking lot, leaving behind the neon blue sign and the wasted tray of fries.

"Vicinity means like the surrounding area."

"Where you learn all these words?"

"I don't know, Emiliano. I don't notice them! I probably pick them up while reading."

As they get closer, Rachel tells him that she is honestly too full; she has no room for dessert and would rather go to the overlook.

He nods, then turns onto a quiet road with a steady incline. They drive past a few warehouses, a church, and their town's post office. At the top of the road is a cul-de-sac. There's only one other car up there, so they park a few car lengths in front of it.

Emiliano cracks the front windows and turns off the headlights. The wind lightly whisps into the car. They both look out toward the freeway, watching the seemingly endless flow of red and white lights and listening to the distant fast-moving traffic. Past the freeway are lampposts, traffic lights, and porch lights flickering in the ever-present darkness.

"I wish we could be closer." Emiliano fixes his gaze on the center console—the only physical, ridiculous impediment between them.

"You can always come over here," she whispers, gesturing to her seat.

Emiliano contemplates the offer, then agrees to it and gets out of the car and walks over to her side. The seat only fits one and a half bodies though, so they squeeze together, Rachel sitting slightly on top of him.

Instantly they grow quiet, both realizing this is the closest they have ever been. He wraps his arms around her, squeezing her in a warm bear hug, one as tight as he can manage. So tight he even lets out a slight grunt. Rachel gently wraps her arms around his neck and holds onto him firmly. They can feel the sexual tension radiating off their bodies to one another and through the car.

Making a bold move, Rachel repositions herself and straddles her legs on each side of Emiliano. He stares up at her with yearning—for this moment, for her body, for all of her. She twists her hair into a messy bun on top of her head.

He watches silently, completely hypnotized by her as she combs through her short baby hairs. "How is it possible that you look so amazing with every hairstyle?" His words slip out in a whisper as he marvels at her head full of silky brown hair. He places his hand to her chin, then moves in and delicately wraps his lips around hers.

They make love with their lips, feeling no need or desire to physically be naked. She gently presses her body closer to his, sliding a hand down his chest to grab a fistful of his shirt.

"I wanna get to know everything," he whispers.

Their heads tilt, their tongues contort, and their mouths mingle, becoming students of each other. Emiliano keeps his hands on her hips, not once daring to place them anywhere without her approval.

As they continue French kissing, Rachel grips the skin underneath his shirt, as if to say *I'm never letting you go*. With her other hand, she tilts his face. He tries to turn back for more kisses, but she shakes her head slowly. He complies. She gently grazes her puckered mouth across his cheek, then licks his ear and lightly breathes into it before sucking tenderly on his ear lobe. Moving down to his neck, like she's following a trail, she gifts sloppy, wet, passionate kisses—some sweet pecks, others hickey instigators.

"Baby, baby, baby," he mutters the hymn slowly, eyes closed, indulging in her passion.

She meets him back at his lonely lips and they continue the slow dance between their mouths, hands, and bodies. Again they get lost in the time continuum, drifting away somewhere that isn't here, somewhere that isn't quite anywhere. A place neither one of them can name nor wrap their brains around.

Emiliano looks at the clock, seeing that over an hour has passed by without their knowledge. He gulps slightly as he looks at Rachel, realizing he's never felt so drawn to a woman before. To calm his nerves, he pulls out his phone and puts on "Wicked Game" by Chris Isaak. The lyrics speak the words and feelings he could never manage to say aloud. He sets his phone on the dash (its speaker facing the windshield to amplify the volume), then gazes into Rachel's eyes. She stares at his nose and mouth, still unwilling to look at him that intimately.

"Kissing you feels like I'm on a roller coaster," Emiliano says in a low voice, holding her head between both of his hands. "Like I'm lost and spinning with my eyes closed. Like energy is moving all through my body."

"Kissing you feels like I'm lost in the universe—in a place where nothing exists. No time, no space, no colors…nothing," Rachel whispers, leaning in for a hug, for a haven in his arms, knowing the sensations he gives her are extraordinary and slightly terrifying.

He welcomes her in and squeezes tightly, his body language saying *I know you'll never let me go, and I'll never let you go either.*

15 Pause the Movie

Emiliano sprays and wipes the countertops and cabinets in the kitchen, then scans the room for any discrepancies. The house must be tidy and welcoming because Rachel is coming inside for the first time. He throws a few used towels in an empty laundry bin behind the table, then tucks a few papers and bills into a drawer before making his way to the living room. He is almost satisfied with the level of presentability. The pillows on the two adjacent couches get straightened and the plush blankets get folded.

While tidying up Mila's toys and dog supplies, he thinks about Rachel and her soft lips. After their date to the freeway overlook, they've been texting nonstop. He likes sending her good morning and good night texts each day. The past few weeks they haven't been able to keep their hands off one another. They went for an ice cream date and had a heavy make out session. Then they went for a long drive through the mountains to the beach and there was even more making out. One night they intended to do something yet couldn't make it out of the alleyway because they were so enraptured with one another they made out in every seat of Rachel's parked car.

Emiliano touches his lips, which are still tender and sore from all the love and passion they've been puckering onto various locations of her face. With the last item cleaned and put away, he goes to sit, but the doorbell rings. Rachel's striking silhouette is just on the other side of the square glass on the front door. Illuminated by the porch light, she looks like something holy and glowing. She waves as he walks over.

"You got here real fast! You found parking?" he asks.

"A spot had opened up just as I turned onto your street."

They hug, and Rachel notices his dog lying on the floor in the living room.

"This is Mila." He gestures for Rachel to come inside. "She's very timid."

"Hi, Mila!" Rachel reaches out, allowing the dog to sniff her. Mila retreats behind Emiliano. Hoping to not scare the shy creature, Rachel walks slowly toward his pet.

"Well if ya walk too slow, she gonna think you're suspicious." Emiliano walks past them and grabs a bone-shaped biscuit from a jar. "Tell her to sit and give you a handshake," he says, handing Rachel a dog treat.

Mila loosens from her timid stance and gives Rachel her paw.

Emiliano smiles, enjoying the cordial interaction. "Now if you grab that she'll love you forever!" He points at Mila's stuffed animal sloth toy.

Hoping to initiate a deeper bond with Emiliano's furry friend, Rachel immediately picks up the sloth. Mila finishes chewing her biscuit, eyeing the stranger's hands that just stole her toy. Unsure of how to play with the dog, Rachel shakes the toy a few times, then tosses it up in the air. Mila, somewhat amused, runs over and bites it. A smile emerges across Rachel's face. She hopes to make a good first impression—yes, with the family members, but also with the dog too.

"¡Mira!" Emiliano calls from the dining table. "¡Mira!"

Rachel looks over and sees him holding a stack of movies. She wonders if *mira* is a pet name, maybe something like *baby* in Spanish.

As she walks over to Emiliano, he thinks to himself that he's glad she knows what *look* means in Spanish. "Which one do you want to watch, Rach?"

Scanning the movies laid out on the table, Rachel's eyes light up. She quickly realizes they are movies from their list: *American Me, Mi Vida Loca, Blood In Blood Out*, and *Colors*. How romantic that he did this for her, she thinks. She lifts each one, scanning the descriptions on the back covers. After a long silence, she finally says, "*Blood In Blood Out*."

Emiliano grins as he happily takes the movie into the living room. "You can sit anywhere you like."

Instead of sitting, Rachel studies the family pictures on the wall. There are a few circular framed photographs from the same photoshoot above the TV. She looks at the black collared shirt younger Emiliano is wearing and smiles. "How old were you here?"

"I was prolly fifteen…I hate those photos. Don't look at 'em, Rach!"

"Who's that?" She points to a woman with orangish-brown hair and minimal wrinkles.

"That's mi abuela."

"Your grandma? She looks so young! What's her name?"

"Martina."

Rachel walks closer. "And who's that?" She points to a handsome man in a marine outfit.

"That's Juan, my mom's brother."

"And her?"

"My sister, Samanta."

Rachel nods as her eyes shift to Adriana, whom she recognizes. "Your mom is so beautiful." After taking one last look at fifteen-year-old Emiliano, Rachel sits down and watches Mila walk in circles on the other couch. Eventually, the dog lies down after a few good spins.

Emiliano finishes the pre-movie tasks like turning off the lights, grabbing the remote, and getting comfy next to one of the most beautiful girls he's ever seen.

"Where is your family, Emiliano? Sleeping?"

"No. My mother's outta town in Tijuana and my sister basically lives with her boyfriend, Marcos, at his apartment. Only comes here to shower or grab clothes." He pauses, a wary look on his face. "Now listen, I wanna let you know beforehand…this movie is pretty heavy."

"That's what I figured from the description I read on the DVD case."

Since she doesn't seem to have any apprehension, he presses play. The commercials blare for a few minutes—time they use wisely to flirt with their eyes and accidentally brush up against each other in completely non-accidental ways. When the three-hour movie commences, they are immersed into a world of crime, drugs, violence, and prison, based just outside of their suburb in the mecca of California: Los Angeles.

After the three main characters make their initial appearances on screen, Emiliano pauses the movie. "Did you see how his name was Miklo?" he asks. "Miklo is a nickname for a Chicano person who looks white. Growing up people called me Miklo, cause I got light skin."

"Oh…interesting." Rachel wishes she had more to say, but is unsure how to properly respond. She doesn't want to offend him and isn't sure whether the term is considered a good thing or a bad thing, or if it is just a neutral thing.

They resume watching and Rachel tries to keep up with the movie's Spanglish, sensing the scenes by observing body language. When a violent scene with blood, knives, and guns arises, she turns away, unable to watch, burrowing her face into Emiliano's shoulder.

"Can you pause the movie really quick?" she whispers. "I just have a question."

He pauses it, then sits up a bit straighter.

"I've obviously heard about gangs before, but I've never known anything about gangs or seen gangs or seen anything like this. Is this fictionalized? or dramatized? or fabricated? or…is this actually what it's like? Does this go on in LA?"

"Parts of it might be dramatic for the film, but absolutely. This is real life. This goes on everywhere…all the time," Emiliano says.

"I can't even wrap my brain around the depths of it. It's so foreign to me." She sits silently for a moment. "Thank you for pausing."

He presses play once again and the movie settles into calmer scenes with underlying themes of friendship, family, and love. Since Emiliano has seen the movie many times, he stops focusing on the film and instead focuses on Rachel. Attempting to read her facial expressions, he wonders what she thinks of him and his culture. Her unblinking eyes and fixated stare are evidence that she is absolutely engrossed in the film. He is almost in a state of disbelief that she, a White woman, is watching a *Chicano* movie with him. In an instant, he is overcome by Rachel's aura, enraptured by her outer appearance and captivated by her inner beauty and intellect. He pauses the movie yet again.

"Why'd you pause it? Press play!" she says, not taking her eyes off the screen.

He doesn't respond—instead, he just gazes at her, mesmerized and smiling. After a few moments, she looks at him.

"Can I please kiss you?" he whispers.

"Yes," she says softly, her bashful smile glinting.

Emiliano places a hand gently against her cheek as he slowly moves in for a kiss. Their eyes shut and they get lost in each other's lips.

"Baby, I wish I had a place of my own to take you," he says achingly.

"Like an apartment?"

"No, baby, just even a bedroom."

"Don't you have one upstairs?"

"N-no," he says hesitantly.

"Where do you sleep then?" She looks at him, confused.

"Anywhere."

"What do you mean?"

"Anywhere. The couch. The floor. That bed." He points to a twin-size bed underneath the staircase. "Wherever there is room."

"Well, where are all your clothes and shoes and things?"

"Over there." He points to a closet behind them in the kitchen.

Rachel doesn't respond, brows squeezing together. How could such a hardworking man, who busts his ass day in and day out, not have his own bedroom? He deserves to have a space to claim as his own. A place for only him, for his things, his privacy.

"I know this is a long movie. We still got an hour left," Emiliano says, breaking the silence. "Did you want to keep watching or save it for another time?"

"No, I—I want to keep watching!" Rachel lies down with her head resting on Emiliano's lap. Two images won't leave her mind: a bed under the stairs and a closet in the kitchen. He combs a hand gently through her long locks as they settle back into the film.

More turbulent scenes arise and devastating deaths occur. Rachel experiences a range of emotions from fear to sadness to shock, and even tears up a few times. Emiliano watches, holding her and comforting her. The concluding scene holds a theme of forgiveness. When the credits roll, Rachel is not finished, eager to dissect and unpack everything she witnessed. She contemplates in silence while Emiliano turns on the lights.

After seeing her perplexed look, Emiliano asks, "So what'd you think of the movie?"

"Heavy. Heartbreaking. Full of imperative themes," she says succinctly. "I'm confused by this whole concept of gang mentality though. They call themselves family but would kill one of their own under some circumstances? Or the concept *blood in blood out*. They kill someone to get initiated in, and once they're in, the only way out is by getting killed? Almost like a cult?"

He nods. Recognizing Rachel's naivety on the subject, he knows she will only be able to grasp the tip of the iceberg. "I also don't know some of it myself. I never got into that lifestyle."

"Are there gangs here?"

"Yeah. They always recruitin'. A few people in my hood was in the local one. And my sister's boyfriend, Marcos, was in that same gang too. That was before they got together."

"How'd he get out?"

"I'm not sure, Rach. Some gangs got different rules." He pauses for a beat. "When I was twelve or thirteen, me and my homie was getting recruited. We were out walking, on the way to meet up with the gang, and something inside me said, 'Turn around and walk home. Don't do this to your mom.' So that's what I did. I turned around and I've stayed turned around."

Tears fill Rachel's eyes. She doesn't know what to say. Furthermore, she's never seen or heard of gangs in their town. Ever. As she continues to ponder the reality that's stumping her, she lets out yawn.

Emiliano gestures to the small bed under the stairs. "We can, uh, lay down? If you want?"

Rachel nods, rubbing her eyes. "Do you have sweats I could borrow? I'm freezing."

He walks into the kitchen, opens his closet, and grabs a pair of black Nike sweats. "The restroom is the first left upstairs." Emiliano ducks under the staircase and lies down in bed to wait for her. As he closes his eyes, he hears the bathroom door creak to a close, then swing open, then footsteps scuffle down the stairs. She stacks her clothes by the couch before lying with him.

"Rach, remember that tree called El Pino in the movie?" he whispers, eyes still closed.

"El Pino. Yes. That means pine tree, huh?" She scoots closer to him, closing her eyes.

"Yeah. It's the biggest tree in East L.A. Really important to the Chicano culture. It's like the tree of life. I gotta take you there sometime." Emiliano yawns. "You can sleep over tonight, baby."

As he begins drifting off, he moves closer to Rachel and wraps his arms around her. She nestles into him, her leg sprawling across his body. Their lips slowly find each other in the darkness. Together they make a symphony with their mouth, cheek, and forehead kisses, a silent sort of love song composed by the harmony of their intimacy. With their lips pressed together and their bodies entwined, they drift off into a peaceful slumber in the area underneath the stairs, enclosed in their capsule of love.

* * *

Mila barks, hearing footsteps outside. The door jangles and Samanta comes into the house. Immediately she notices not one, but two bodies in the bed underneath the stairs. "Get up! Get out of that bed!"

Rachel abruptly wakes up, startled. Looking over at Emiliano, who's still sound asleep, she lightly shakes his arm.

Samanta clears her throat as she walks into the kitchen, still eyeing them. "Emiliano! Get up right now out of that bed!" She raises her voice a bit higher. "Now, I said!"

"Emiliano, we gotta get up," Rachel whispers into his ear.

He rolls over grunting.

"¡Levántate! ¿Qué estás haciendo?" Samanta hollers sternly at her younger brother. She begins to wash her hands, fixating her eyes on Rachel's folded shorts and shoes next to the couch.

"¡Ay! ¿Qué?" Emiliano hollers, rubbing his eyes.

"Why are you two in that bed? Get up and clean those sheets!" Samanta wipes her hands on a kitchen towel, now scowling at the two of them.

Emiliano gets up and starts taking the pillowcases off the pillows. Rachel looks around confused, an uneasy feeling in her stomach. She moves over to the couch and watches Emiliano frustratedly remove the rest of the things off the bed. When she notices her shorts and shoes piled neatly next to the side table, her eyes shut in frustration. Samanta will not have a good first impression of her; she probably thinks they openly had sex in their living room.

Samanta hasn't moved, still staring. "Like I said the other day…that's fine if she comes here. But stay on the couch. Don't get in that bed."

Emiliano doesn't answer, continuing to throw all the blankets and sheets into a mountain on the floor. Rachel sits silently, waiting for him to say something—anything—to her. As he grabs the last item from the bed, leaving it to a bare mattress, he glances her way. "So when you leavin'?"

"Oh…um…whenever you want me to?" Rachel looks at him, confused.

"You takin' off my sweats?" He looks at her expressionless, mouth straight as a pin.

"Um…yeah." Rachel walks upstairs with her shorts, feeling humiliated.

Samanta stares at Emiliano and doesn't say a word. He takes the pile of bedding to the laundry unit on the backside of the house. When he returns, he waits for Rachel, who drums down the stairs quickly with his neatly folded sweats.

Even after Rachel hands them over, he remains quiet. How does he have *nothing* to say, she wonders. What possibly could have changed from before they fell asleep to now? Is he embarrassed that his sister found them cuddling in bed? Or tired and grumpy that she made him do laundry in the middle of the night? Or is he just plain rude?

Emiliano puts the sweats on the couch, then walks Rachel to her car. Neither of them say a single word. Once behind the wheel, Rachel shuts the door hard. Not quite a slam, but almost. Emiliano knocks on the window, pointing a finger down, asking her to lower it. Irritated, she pushes the window lever.

"I'll see you soon, OK?" Emiliano says. "Have a great night and get home safe, Rach."

"Okaaay?" She refuses to look at him as she starts the car.

He leans in and kisses her cheek. In her hurt state, the peck is unwanted, almost unwelcomed, though delicate and lovely. Before he has a chance to initiate their handshake, she raises the window and hastily backs out of the parking spot. The unfavorable situation leaves their hands cold and untouched. He tucks his hands into his pockets and watches her car exit the neighborhood.

16 La Raza

Marcos gets out of Samanta's running car and hurries across the street into his girlfriend's house. "¡Qué demonios! What's taking so long? And who was that güera?" he says irritably as he opens the front door.

"Lo siento, Marcos. I was getting my jacket, but had to deal with my brother and that girl."

They look at Emiliano, who's crouching underneath the stairs pulling the last corner of the clean sheet over the bed and putting the pillows into new cases.

"She's just my friend," he mumbles.

"Fucking lies! I saw her clothes on the floor!" Samanta yells.

Emiliano throws the last pillow on the bed, then faces his sister, arms folded with a blank face. She rolls her eyes, letting out a scoff. Without saying a word, she walks out of the house, jacket in hand.

Marcos follows behind her, stopping when he gets to the front door. "Don't mess around with a güera, carnal.

You're just a plaything to a güera. She won't never take you seriously." His gaze lowers and he lingers for a second. "And she won't never understand la raza." And with that, he closes the door behind him.

Emiliano sinks into the couch and sits in pure silence—a silence so chilling there is nowhere to hide from the echo of the night's events. Could Rachel ever understand *la raza*? Does she know what it's like to uproot her life to a new country? To speak a language that wasn't meant for her tongue? To make a grueling journey like his *abuela, tías*, and *madre* did, alone, at separate times: long days, even longer nights, walking through hot desert or mud or rivers, praying to *La Virgen*, hoping to make it to their family, hoping to not get caught, hoping to not die? Does Rachel know how that kind of experience lives in an entire family's bones? Their lives are nothing alike, nothing at all. And he can't think about it anymore. He eyes his basketball on the far side of the TV and decides he'll let off steam in the best way he knows how.

"Come on, Mila."

His dog follows him outside. He passes the basketball from hand to hand around his torso. Once in the cul-de-sac, he starts dribbling, getting lost in a beautiful sort of meditation—allowing his brain to rest without impeding thoughts of Rachel, the night, or their cultural differences. He jumps up, curling his wrist—as if about to shoot—but doesn't release the ball. Mila runs over eagerly. He dribbles around, allowing her to be a defender, and attempts to fake her out.

When Emiliano turns around, a young guy is walking toward him. Someone around his age, early twenties. He's wearing baggy shorts that hang below his hips, a white tee, and a blue backward-facing cap. Holding the ball between forearm and hip, Emiliano watches the guy, who's walking with a rhythm and hop in his step. As he passes under a lamppost, Emiliano catches a glimpse of his face and doesn't recognize the guy from his hood. "¿Quién eres?"

"Ay, hombre!" The guy's fingers contort into gang symbols across his chest. "Estas con nosotros?"

"¡Lárgate de aquí!" Emiliano points down the street. "This ain't your hood."

The guy continues strutting toward him.

"I said get the fuck outta here!" Emiliano stomps forward, pumping his chest.

The guy swiftly shuffles, pulling at his pants before bopping around the corner.

"Come on, Mila." Emiliano heads inside his house, not wanting to be in the wrong place at the wrong time. After locking the door, he walks into the kitchen and closes the curtains on the windows. He looks at the clock on the microwave, frustrated to see it's well past 1:00 a.m. on a work night.

He lies down in bed, wishing Rachel were next to him, keenly aware of the extra space where her body lie just a few hours earlier. He stares at the underside of the staircase, unblinking, listening to the not-so-soothing snores from Mila. When he eventually shuts his eyes, he tosses and turns, going in and out of restless sleep. Rachel. Sleepover. Samanta. No sleepover. Güera. Plaything. Basketball. Gang member.

After what seems like only a few minutes, his alarm goes off. He rolls over, feeling confused, disoriented, and absolutely tired, then rubs his eyes and stands, knowing there is no time to complain. He hastily changes in the kitchen, then heads outside, where there is still no sign of the sun. As soon as he props up the garage door, he notices a puddle of liquid. Almost instantly he knows his Firebird is leaking again. Second time in four months. He combs irritably through his hair, then pulls out his phone and dials his sister's number.

Of course she answers. Of course she understands. Of course she will give him a ride. Of course she will be there in five minutes or less. That's the definition of family—no grudge, no questions asked. He puts his phone back in his pocket, then delays for a second before leaving the garage and slumping over on the curb.

A few minutes later, Samanta comes down the street. Their eyes meet briefly before he gets in the car. She studies the dark bags under his eyes. "Did you get any sleep, hermano?"

Emiliano lightly shakes his head, then gazes out the window for nearly the entire ride, until they make it up the steep parking lot entrance and pull in front of the auto shop.

"I'll watch Mila today and take her to the park."

He rubs his eyes. "I appreciate it."

Reluctantly, he gets out and watches his sister's car disappear. With an exaggerated step forward, he heads into work, hands in his pockets.

"Buenos días, Emiliano." Pablo's father looks up from a messy pile of papers at the register.

"Buenos días, Don Miguel."

Pablo's father smiles, then immediately dives back into his paperwork.

Emiliano heads into the locker room, wishing his work shift were already over so he could take a nap.

"Hey, dude!" Jimmy says, combing his hands through his dirty blonde hair. "Haven't seen you in a minute."

"What's good, bro." Emiliano gives his coworker a fist bump. "I know man. I haven't been picking up weekend shifts lately."

"Well, it's good to have you back!" Jimmy says. "Let's hoop on our first break?"

Emiliano nods, then watches Jimmy exit the locker room. Not wanting to linger, he quickly gets ready before heading out into the spacious, yet cluttered, garage in his coveralls.

"Can you start on those, hermano?" Santos points to a dirty red Nissan and a black Toyota in the shop. "Just changing the oil and checking the fluid levels."

"Aight, man." Emiliano walks over to the Nissan, lifts the hood, and immediately starts working on the oil change: open, unplug, drain, replace, fill, check for leaks. After finishing, he inspects and adjusts the coolant levels and brake fluid. Having done this countless times, he goes into autopilot, and refuses to think about Rachel because relationship problems and fixing cars never mix well for him.

He moves efficiently through both cars, then grabs a nearby towel and wipes the sweat off his forehead and the back of his neck. An older white GMC Sierra pulls up, and he instantly recognizes who's inside. Emiliano's friend, Ricardo, and his girlfriend, Sofía, hop out. While Ricardo greets Emiliano, Sofía stands a few feet back chewing on gum.

"I saw y'all at Acai Cruisers a little while back," Emiliano says.

Sofía looks at him, disappointed. "Why didn't you say what's up?"

"I was jus' in a hurry," Emiliano replies. "Anyway, somethin' goin' on with your truck, Ricardo?"

"Yeah, the check engine light came on." Ricardo lifts the hood. "Was tryna figure it out myself but it was takin' too long."

Emiliano double checks the gauges and car battery, then walks over to examine the engine. Sofía steps in front of her boyfriend and looks over Emiliano's shoulder. She crosses her arms, annoyed, and glances back at Ricardo. When they make eye contact, they speak to each other through their eyes. After a few moments, Ricardo shakes his head.

Sofía turns, saying to Emiliano, "Why don't you just check the gas cap?"

Ricardo scoffs. "It's not that, Sof."

Emiliano leans out of the hood. "Well did you check it?"

"Hadn't thought of it, carnal, I—"

Sofía interjects, "I thought of the gas cap over thirty minutes ago and told him it might need to be tightened." She looks at them with pursed lips and a face that screams *attitude*.

"Well, the gas cap keeps the vapor from escaping the tank." Emiliano walks around the car and opens the hatch that covers it and—it *wasn't* tightened properly. "Pendejo…didn't tighten the lid," Emiliano says, smacking his lips.

As Emiliano screws the cap on, Sofía rattles off a rapid-fire of "I told you so" statements to her boyfriend. Instantly, he regrets dismissing her opinion. Now he knows he will never hear the end of this.

"So because I have a pussy, I don't know shit about cars?"

"No, mamacita. I'm sorry. I shoulda listened to you." Ricardo walks closer to Sofía, arms out for a hug. She puts her hand up, telling him to keep his last sentence in mind the next time there is trouble. As she gets in the passenger seat, she thanks Emiliano for the help. Under her breath she mumbles that at least *one* man out there listens to her.

"Imma go make love to this woman," Ricardo whispers to Emiliano. "And hopefully she won't give a damn bout none of this in five minutes."

Emiliano shakes his head, chuckling. While exchanging a handshake, they make plans to hang out soon, then Ricardo hops into his truck and backs out of the parking lot.

Santos walks by, letting Emiliano know he can take his first break. Eager to get outside with Jimmy to let off steam from the drama of the last twenty-four hours, Emiliano hurries to the locker room, taking off his grimy gloves.

* * *

Rachel looks down at her watch, knowing Emiliano still has a few hours left of his Saturday shift. She is kind of bummed that he couldn't come to soccer, but also feels relieved since their interaction the night before left their relationship in an awkward position. She walks across the field, scanning the crowd for Hannah: a handful of sweaty players are sitting at the table, Javier is making Jemma a bracelet of plucked flowers underneath the tree, and Hannah is in her usual spot on the hill, though Brax isn't here. Not in the mood to talk to anyone else, Rachel beelines for Hannah and plops down next to her.

"You weren't playing like your usual self today," Hannah says.

Rachel sighs. "I know. I didn't get any sleep last night."

"How come, Rach?"

"Well…can I talk to you about something?"

"Anything."

"I've been seeing Emiliano for a while."

"I know." Hannah chuckles.

"What? How?"

"Your face was glowing at my apartment, then he was calling you Rach, then you guys left together to the parking lot after the game, so…it doesn't take a rocket scientist."

"Yeah, that's true." Rachel smiles. "Sorry I didn't tell you. I just wanted to see where our relationship was headed first. He is just…such an amazing person. Hardworking. Appreciative. Gentle. Generous. Funny. Respectful toward me and my body. And I love learning about his culture, his family, his history! I—I didn't want to jinx it."

"I totally get it," Hannah says. "So are you guys boyfriend and girlfriend now?"

"Kind of. I mean, not yet. It's going well though. Well, for the most part. Something weird happened last night." Rachel proceeds to tell Hannah about the night in detail. She starts with them falling asleep, and makes sure to include his comment about sleeping over. Then she describes the energy in the air when Samanta walked through the front door while they were in bed. She ends with rolling up the car window, and how she cried the whole way home.

"Have you guys talked since?" Hannah asks.

Rachel shakes her head.

"Well, you guys were sleeping when she impolitely woke you up. He was probably confused and half-asleep, the same way you were. I wouldn't think too much about it!"

"Yeah, you're probably right." Rachel bites the inside of her cheek. "How about you? How are you doing?"

Hannah looks at the clouds, rolling her eyes as she mentions that Brax's friend, Alexis, moved in. They've all been getting along, but she's been having to practice broadening her horizons because Alexis isn't her typical kind of female friend—Alexis is all consumed with fashion, trends, celebrities, reality TV. Hannah's not much into any of those things.

"So how do Brax and Alexis know each other, Hannah? USC is a huge school."

"They had a class together and *apparently* became good friends. Recently he told me that they fucked once…but he said it was a long time ago before I even knew him."

"Wait, what! They fucked?" Rachel's mouth drapes open.

"Hey, anyone in the mood for some nature? A hike?" Jemma calls out.

Hannah and Rachel exchange glances. Both of them typically would say yes, since they love hiking, but they are too tired from playing. "Maybe next time! Thanks for the invite though," Hannah hollers before she and Rachel gather their belongings and walk to the parking lot, continuing to discuss the latest drama of Hannah Storytime.

"They all just played soccer. I'm sure nobody wants to come," Javier says to Jemma. "Plus, I'd prefer it just be the two of us." He picks up his bag and heads for the hill. "C'mon, Jemma."

Jemma doesn't respond but follows behind him, thinking Javier clearly doesn't know how to be *just friends* with her. He's always wanting it to be more than what it is, more than what she wants. As they enter the parking lot, she walks to her car instead of his. "Lo siento, Javier. I forgot my mother needs my help at the restaurant making tamales."

"Come on." Javier walks toward her, nerves welling inside of him. "I've been dying to spend some time alone with you. I really like you!"

"No, I…I can't." She pulls out the key to her early-2000s silver Corolla. Before she can unlock her car, Javier glides a hand against her hip. Enough waiting, he thinks. He leans in to kiss her, hoping it might change her mind about him, about spending the day with him.

"Javier! We're just friends. What are you doing?" she pushes his chest and he backs away, feeling insecure and rejected. A car pulls into the parking space next to them, so Javier retreats to the curb. Jemma quickly gets in her car and pulls out of the parking space. Javier watches until her car disappears out of the parking lot, and Jemma will never contact him again.

17 The Heavenly Oasis

Rachel sits on the front porch swing, mounds of nervousness and anxiety stirring inside her. She taps her foot to the beat of the obnoxious ring-back tone coming through her phone. It's been a week since she's seen Emiliano or heard his voice, though they have texted a bit here and there, the energy off and odd. After what seems like ages, he answers and the ringing ceases.

"You were very rude to me the other day," Rachel says quickly, as if she wouldn't be able to get the words out if she waited any longer.

"Aw, please don't think that meant anything. I was just tired, Rach."

"Tired? You treated me like I was a two-dollar hooker! You didn't say a word to me for ten minutes, then those two questions?" Rachel scoffs. "Come on!"

"I was shocked, OK? Wasn't expectin' for us to be woken up…don't know why my sis was bein' a bitch."

"This isn't about your sister! Do you think I will tolerate that for one second? You will never treat me like that again or you won't be in my life!"

Emiliano sighs. "I—I'm sorry, baby. It won't happen again, I promi—Holy shit!" A loud thud and a screech come through the phone. Rachel looks down at the screen to make sure Emiliano is still on the line. For a few moments he doesn't respond. Light traffic and white noise crackle from his end. After clearing his throat he starts speaking, but trails off, revealing nothing.

"Are you OK?" Rachel asks. "Emiliano?"

Brows furrowed, Emiliano watches a hobbling squirrel that he hit with his mother's car while driving into his neighborhood. One of its back legs is broken. It makes it to the sidewalk feebly, then into the grass safe from traffic.

In dismay, he tells Rachel about the poor squirrel. Silence creeps through both ends of the phone conversation. He feels terrible and can't let go of the image as he gets back in the car.

"Poor little guy," Rachel says before another bout of silence hums through their phones. Suddenly, their small quarrel now seems trivial to them, as life—and near death—bustle around them.

"Well…how you doin', Rach? What you got planned today?"

For a moment she stalls before answering, gazing at swaying leaves and the houses across the street. She still feels sour over what happened at his house. "Well, we had soccer this morning. Missed seeing you there," she says, purposely ignoring his question.

"You know, the main reason I like going is to spend time with you," he replies.

The subtle flirting loosens them up a bit. Rachel giggles; Emiliano laughs. She tells him that she got her GRE results back and other than starting her master's applications she has no plans. Other than cleaning he has no plans either, so he suggests that they both do what they need to do, and then they could go to a record store in L.A. once they're done. "Oh…the only thing is…we gotta take your car, Rach. Mine's not working."

"From hitting the squirrel?"

"Nah, I hit the squirrel in my mom's car…borrowing it for work. Mine broke down last week. I can tell you more about it when I see you."

Eager to see one another, they hurry through their tasks, attempting to make time move faster. Rachel types away on her computer—as if she is trying to break the record for fastest amount of words typed in one minute—and Emiliano scrubs every square inch of the carpets.

After finishing, they both get ready for their date. Rachel looks at her outfit in the mirror in her bedroom. She's wearing a tight white dress, a light green puff jacket, her favorite silver necklace, and suede sandals. Emiliano adjusts his hair in the bathroom mirror as he puts on a navy blue cap that has a red strip across the rim. He's wearing his favorite vintage gray Lakers hoodie, dark blue Levi jeans with his black belt, and black leather high-top Converse. They look at themselves one last time before leaving the mirrors. Grabbing her keys, Rachel walks outside to her car. Picking up his wallet and a spare jacket, Emiliano heads outside to wait for her.

When Rachel pulls onto his street, they find themselves together again, all at once, exchanging glances, sharing smiles.

"Is there any way you would want to drive?" Rachel asks.

Emiliano doesn't answer but gives her a facial expression that says *of course I'll drive*. Once inside, he extends his hand across the console and apologizes for what happened at his house. Rachel half-smiles as her hand meets his—their handshake, a symbol, representing the conclusion of their mishap and the reestablishment of their bond. Emiliano gives Rachel a peck on the lips, then heads out of his neighborhood.

The first thing Emiliano is eager to hear about is her GRE. She shares that she got a score of 710, which is really good for someone at the master's level. She will be able to apply to all three of her top schools, and today she finished the application for Boston College, her top choice.

The first thing Rachel is eager to hear about is his car. Emiliano tells her about the leak, and how that happens often since his car is old. He explains that this fix won't be easy because some of his car parts are stock and some are aftermarket. She, of course, knowing nothing about cars, does not know what the terms mean.

"Stock means the original part from when the car was made. Aftermarket means a new updated version of the part. I gotta replace my stock pump for an aftermarket pump because then the line to my carb can hook up properly."

Rachel lets out a laugh. "I don't know what any of that means."

"Yeah, just car stuff." Emiliano chuckles. "If my car was runnin' this past week, I woulda come by your house to see you."

"Really?" Rachel's cheeks blush as she gazes out the window.

While on the freeway, they converse about all things oldies music. Emiliano shows Rachel '50s and '60s songs she's never heard of, and Rachel shows Emiliano some '80s songs she thinks he'd want to add to his repertoire. As they enter Los Angeles, each of them admires different aspects about the city: Rachel, the skyline; Emiliano, the graffiti art. And both of them adore the strings of palm trees.

"Have you ever heard of the restaurant El Tepeyac?" Rachel asks. "I guess it's a really popular Mexican food spot in East L.A. I've never been but my grandma Tilly and my parents rave about it."

"Nah, I haven't…which is weird cause I know most things around here. I wonder where it is. El tepeyac means hilltop," Emiliano says. "My favorite place is El Huero. I go there with my homies all the time."

When they reach the hip, new age record store, the line to the entrance goes out the front door and around the corner. Rachel squints as she reads a sign on the front of the building that says "Grand Reopening" in bold letters.

"Damn, Rach! Of all the days we choose to go to this record store…"

As they round the corner, their eyes follow the store line. Not only does it continue through the length of the building, but it continues down the street for two blocks. Upwards of 200 people are standing there idly, willing to wait for the reopening. After exchanging glances, they agree that it'd be foolish to wait a few hours just to get in the doors.

As they pull up to the next stoplight Emiliano takes out his cellphone. "Rach, let me know when the light turns green!" He juts out the window, believing the absurd line to be hilarious, and starts recording a video of the sea of people—old and young, dark-skinned and light-skinned, eccentric and conventional.

Rachel nervously stares at the traffic light, scared that they could potentially get in an accident or be pulled over by the police. She nervously checks the side mirror, then quickly focuses back on the light. "Green!" she yells, with a twang in her voice, at the split second she notices the light color change.

Emiliano ends the recording, gets back in the car, and hauls through the intersection. The few-second video, now on a loop, begins to play aloud. Among the wind and outside chatter sounds Rachel's nervous voice, "Green! Green! Green!" The audio echoes through the car.

Embarrassed by the apparent unease in her voice, Rachel's cheeks flush. She stares out the windshield refusing to look at Emiliano. He laughs, then yells, "Green!" She joins in his laughter, admiring how he so easily and gracefully brought her out of her embarrassment.

"Hey, I think I actually know a place we could go," Emiliano says.

He drives by a small record outlet nearby that he's been to a few other times. Thankfully, there are only a few cars in the lot. Rachel muses any record store, even one with few options, would be better than one with a line as long as the Disneyland entrance.

When they walk inside, they immediately head in different directions: Rachel toward the '80s R&B, Emiliano toward late '70s hip-hop. After thumbing through four stacks of records, Rachel pulls out an intriguing one with a vintage-style black and white cover. She reads the front and back of "We Are One" by Pieces of a Dream. The romantic song titles "You Know I Want You" and "When You Are Here With Me" persuade her to buy the record, opposed to any of the other thousands in the store. With the record carefully in hand, she walks over to Emiliano and shows it off.

He glances at the cover. "Awesome! Is that one of your favorite bands or somethin'?"

"No, I've actually never heard of them before." She wraps her arms around the record, pulling it into her chest. "Did you find one yet?"

He continues scanning the '70s hip-hop. "I been lookin' for this specific one…it's a second edition with an all-black cover." Emiliano continues flipping through the box of tattered records. He pulls out "We Rap More Mellow" by The Younger Generation. "I don't think I'll be able to find what I'm looking for. This vinyl looks coo though. It's from 1979, got a hip-hop, funk sorta feel…I think Imma get it."

They head to the cash register and Emiliano (of course) pays, and Rachel (of course) thanks Emiliano as they walk out of the store together. Courtesy on top of courtesy—it seems to be their foundation.

Once back on the busy, noisy road, they head deeper into East Los Angeles, where the lively and thriving *Chicano* culture becomes more and more apparent. As they go through a stoplight, they both gasp and shout, "El Tepeyac!" noticing the restaurant at the intersection.

"And now we know why it's called hilltop. It's on a hilltop!" Rachel says.

For a few more blocks, they drive straight, before pulling into the parking lot of El Super. Rachel looks around the shopping center, then to the one across the street, noticing everything is written in Spanish.

"My family goes there all the time." Emiliano points down the road to a market and deli called Los Cinco Puntos.

"The five...points?" Rachel asks.

"Yeah! Named because of the surrounding streets. See how there are five directions where the roads meet at that corner?" Emiliano points at the intersection. Rachel stares at the market, impressed by the owner's ingenuity, and by Emiliano's knowledge of the area.

"And look over there!" Emiliano points into the sky about a quarter mile away. "After we get some drinks we can drive up there!"

Rachel looks off, spotting a familiar-looking massive tree with long fanned-out branches on the hill. "El Pino!" She smiles, looking at him with admiration. He is so romantic, bringing her here to this place that holds a special spot in his heart.

She follows him into a small market, decorated with colors of the Mexican flag, called La Princesita. They immerse into Emiliano's primary world. He heads to the drink section while Rachel absorbs the foreign scenery—familiar soda bottles with Spanish labels, spicy Mexican candies, and various seasoned meats behind the counter that have a mouthwatering smell.

Emiliano takes a couple sodas to the counter while Rachel continues examining the foods and reading the labels. The dark-skinned female cashier with thick brown hair stares brazenly at her. An older man working at the meat counter also watches her as he dries the kitchen utensils with a towel.

Emiliano resets one of the drinks on the counter. The loud clank compels the woman to divert her attention from Rachel.

"Hola ¿Eso sería todo?" she says, scanning the first drink.

"Sí, señora. Gracias." Emiliano hands her a wad of cash, then picks up the sodas. Rachel is now reading a Spanish nutrition label from one of the bags of chips. She looks up and smiles, then walks over as he holds the door open for her.

"Thank you, Emiliano. And one of these days you need to let me buy something!"

On the way back to the car Emiliano ushers Rachel to a Mexican street stand to check out homemade *aguas frescas*. It would mean the world to him if Rachel could try it. While they scan the pitchers of brightly colored drinks, a teenage girl putting on a new pair of gloves greets them.

"¡Hola!" Emiliano says. "¿Nos puedes dar una agua de piña y pepino?"

"Sí, seria cuatro dolares." The girl pours the drink into a large plastic cup. Three adult women behind the counter look at Rachel, then Emiliano, then the two of them together.

Emiliano notices them staring as he pulls out his wallet. He only has two dollars, so he asks Rachel if she has any cash. She reaches into her purse, stalling for a moment to decipher the Spanish, feeling a little nervous and on the spot. After handing Emiliano two dollars from her wallet, he exchanges the money for the bright green concoction. He takes a sip, then hands the cup to her, informing her it's pineapple cucumber flavored. She tries it, loving the familiar flavors that have been conjured into something foreign and new.

When they get back to the car, Emiliano lets out an embellished sigh as he sinks into the driver's seat. "Did you see everyone staring at us, Rach?"

"Umm…no? I didn't notice anything odd." Rachel takes another sip.

"Well, they were all staring at you…at us."

"I didn't see anything, Emiliano."

"It's because I brought a White girl here."

Rachel looks out the window, wondering why he is accentuating the differences in their skin colors, when mixed couples have been around for generations.

"I mean, maybe they were staring because you're beautiful, I don't know." Emiliano reverses the car and turns out of the parking lot, hoping to leave that conversation and comment near El Super. El Pino gets closer and larger as they drive up the hill. "I'm surprised nobody hangin' around here on a Saturday," Emiliano says as he parks in front of the expansive tree.

Rachel's brows crease together. "The street looks different than it did in the movie."

"That movie was filmed in the '90s, so a lot has changed…even since I been coming here as a kid it's changed." Emiliano points along the pathway where the wood and steel fences used to be in the movie—now it is a paved walkway with steps that lead up to the special tree. Some would say it's become modernized, but truly this is gentrification at work. He points to the end of the street, where a car was parked in one scene in the movie—it is now unreachable by car, as the nearby houses have infiltrated the area with landscaping, walkways, and driveways.

"It's crazy how twenty years can change so much in some ways, and yet change so little in other ways," Rachel says. Like how entire streets and cities can change, but people still can't change their mindsets about each other.

"Like how El Pino always been the same, but the street looks different."

"Yeah…something like that." Rachel slightly smiles.

Drinks in hand, they walk toward El Pino. They crane their necks, their heads nearly at 90-degree angles, to stare at the top of the tree where the leaves fan out like a male peacock's feathers.

"You know, apparently they were gonna take El Pino down back in January, but my Chicano Angelinos signed a petition and saved the tree."

"That's amazing! What does Angelino mean?"

"Someone who lives in Los Angeles, or who was born there."

Rachel soaks in the atmosphere as the sun sets. She stares down the hill into the surrounding boulevards, thinking that Emiliano has a special, tight-knit community. Looking up at El Pino again, she is overcome with joy, appreciating Emiliano for sharing himself, his heart, and his culture with her. A gust of wind blows through the neighborhood, and Rachel shivers, rubbing her arms and legs.

Emiliano grabs his spare jacket from the car and lays it across her lap. "Also, I meant to tell you this earlier, Rach. You look beautiful and I love your outfit."

Rachel leans closer to him until their lips meet. They share a kiss underneath East Los Angeles's tree of life. He wraps his arm around her and for a few minutes they sit peacefully in silence. All the while, he wonders once again what she thinks of him and where he comes from.

"Emiliano…" Rachel says, a bit of nervousness in her voice.

"Yeah?"

"I know we kind of already talked about this once before, but, um…I really like you. I like spending time with you. Where do you see our relationship going?" she asks, her heart now thumping in anticipation for his answer.

"Oh…uh…I really like you too, Rach. I'm still getting to know you. There's a lot to learn." Emiliano gazes over his shoulder, then leans in and whispers, "I want to show you something."

With a smile and curiosity, she stands. His non-answering answer is good enough for now. They walk past El Pino and turn onto the adjacent street, one that Emiliano's walked many times before. He gapes at a seemingly average two-story beige house with a white fence, a look of longing shining through his eyes. "You see that house?" Emiliano halts, chin lifted, vision focused. "Imma live there one day."

"Really?" Rachel says.

"Yeah…it's always been my dream home since I was little. I'll wake up to El Pino every day. I'll be a real Angelino…It's my dream to live with my people in the city." His eyes remain glued, refusing to look anywhere but the beige house.

"I'm sure you can make it happen!" Rachel looks at him, imagining that one day it could be *her* alongside him in his dream.

"Maybe one day." He lowers his gaze, putting his hands in his pockets. "We should get going, I don't think we should be around here when it gets dark."

They walk back toward El Pino, and the only sound is the shuffling of their feet as they stroll across the pavement and gravel. Emiliano ruminates on his dream, wondering if there is a way he could ever see Rachel being in it, if their cultures could ever collide in that sort of way. He wishes they could, but he has no idea how he could make that happen.

"Thank you for letting me borrow this!" Rachel's voice draws him back to the present moment as she hands him his jacket. They take one last look at the voluminous tree before getting in the car, driving past his dream home, and exiting the heavenly oasis. As they turn onto the freeway, Emiliano leaves half his heart in East L.A.

18 The Apex of Love

There is no traffic heading into the suburbs. Across the median, the freeway is packed bumper to bumper for those driving into the big city. Rachel yawns, sitting sleepily in the passenger seat after their long day of adventuring in East L.A. Emiliano reaches across the console and their hands slowly interlock.

"I wish one of us had an apartment," he says. "I wanna lay with you without having to go through what happened at my house."

Rachel nervously bites her bottom lip. "We can go to my house tonight, Emiliano. My parents are out of town visiting family in Oregon."

Emiliano opens his mouth to speak, then pauses for a moment. "OK, baby." He presses the gas pedal a bit harder, hoping to make it home a little earlier. When they reach the exit that leads to both of their houses, he turns left—toward Rachel's. The long windy road slowly builds their anticipation until they are parked in her driveway. He finds his hands are getting clammy and takes a deep breath.

"I'll be right back. I'm going to bring my dog out here to meet you."

He waits patiently at the base of the porch while Rachel goes inside. Barking ensues followed by a high-pitched voice from Rachel. When the door opens, forty-five pound Cece runs out, fully prepared to attack any intruder. She barks incessantly, running down the steps toward Emiliano.

"She's just acting like Miss Aggressive. She won't do anything," Rachel says.

While most people typically cower or flinch at this point in an interaction with Cece, Emiliano gets down and meets her at eye level, unafraid and radiating openness. "Hi, girl. I know this is your house." He extends his arm, letting Cece smell the back of his hand. The dog leans forward, sniffing for the slightest reason to declare him an intruder.

"This is why I was so cautious around your dog, Emiliano. I didn't know if your pup would be anything like mine. They're total opposites."

"Yeah, they are!" Emiliano gets up and walks toward the porch. Cece immediately barks while backing up, guarding Rachel and the house.

"Cece, be nice!" Rachel hollers.

"It's OK, Rach." Emiliano lowers again, this time widening his arms like he's getting searched with a metal detector at the airport. "You can sniff anything you need, girl." Cece circles around his body, sniffing his arms, clothing, hat, and shoes.

Emiliano looks at Rachel during Cece's interrogation. "I want her to know that I respect her..."

Rachel nods, shyly grazing her thumb against her top lip. Once again, she finds herself in awe of Emiliano's character. A type of man she never thought existed, in fact, exists. He is kneeling before her.

Cece runs past Rachel inside the house toward her bin of toys; Emiliano officially got cleared to enter. He wipes off his jeans, then follows Rachel inside. Cece greets Emiliano with her favorite pig toy as he steps into the foyer. He leans down next to the chestnut piano and pulls at Cece's pig. The dog playfully growls, shaking her head back and forth. After a few seconds he releases the toy—letting her win the tug of war—then rubs her snout and whiskers. Rachel watches their friendly interaction, admiring the two beings who have captured her whole heart.

"Oh yeah, you love the whisker rub," he says in a baby voice.

"The whisker rub? That's innovative. I've never heard that before," Rachel says, walking into the living room. She takes a seat on the plump dark brown couch. Emiliano sits on the cushion next to her while Cece jumps onto the reclining chair adjacent to them.

"Wow…" Rachel says. "Cece *never* lets me sit next to boys. She always jumps in between."

"Cece must love her mama!" Emiliano exclaims.

Rachel smiles, looking over at Cece, then over at Emiliano. "She must really trust you…"

For a moment, they sit quietly looking in each other's direction. A TV remote sits on the living room table eager to be touched. Emiliano looks at it, hoping Rachel won't grab it. Rachel looks at it with no intent to reach for it. Silence sweeps through the room, capturing everything except the old red clock that continues its faint ticking. Emiliano's eyes wander from Rachel's beautiful face to her stylish outfit to her stunning figure to her warm ivory skin.

"I wish I could get you the moon!" he says abruptly.

"What?" Rachel chuckles, confused.

"I wish I could get us tickets to New York!"

"New York?" Rachel's chuckles are now accompanied by a cheerful smile.

"I wish I could," Emiliano says in a low voice, looking down at his feet.

"I don't know about the moon, but maybe someday we can go to New York!" she says.

"Rach. I know I only known you for a few months, but...I don't ever wanna lose you."

Rachel softly smiles, wrapping her arms around Emiliano's neck. He leans in and squeezes her tightly. They close their eyes, embracing the fullness of their love. She combs her hands through his hair and slowly moves toward his ear. "Then don't do anything to lose me," she whispers, a passionate ache in her voice.

Emiliano turns toward her, both of their eyes still closed. Their lips navigate toward one another. A first kiss turns into a second, third, eighth, twentieth. She holds the base of his neck, then traces down his chest and abdomen, wrapping the bottom of his sweatshirt in her hand. He grazes a hand gently across her cheek. They linger on another kiss, holding their lips together to remain in love's abyss.

As they open their eyes, Rachel holds out her hand. Emiliano looks down at her palm, then up to her face. He slowly interlocks his hand with hers. She leads him through the living room and the foyer. His eyes are spellbound by all things Rachel. When they reach the staircase, she looks his way for a brief moment, then continues up the steps. He follows closely behind, not letting his hand slip the tiniest bit from her grasp.

At the top of the stairs, Rachel stops in front of the first door. Keeping her eyes low, she leans forward and kisses him. The door to the spare bedroom slowly creeks open as she turns the knob behind her back. Emiliano, now fully enraptured by her, places both of his hands sweetly on her cheeks. He gives her a trail of kisses until they reach the bed, where he bends down and picks her up. Her legs wrap around his waist and their lips remain locked.

After setting her tenderly on the bed, he gives her a mouthful of sloppy wet kisses. Her mouth wraps around his tongue, sucking in to pull him toward her. Then she releases, leaving his lips to ache for more as she leans over to the bedside table and turns on the stereo. "Weak for Your Love" by Thee Sacred Souls serenades the room.

Slowly, he climbs onto the bed and gets on top of her. Her eyes follow his every move. With nothing but passion in his eyes, he plants soft kisses on her lips and cheeks. She takes her jacket off while he continues leaving delicate kisses along her neck and ear. Then he interlocks his hand with hers and pins her arm above their heads. She pulls her dress up a bit, then gives Emiliano a look. One of longing. Of lust. Of love. An invitation to assist.

He leans back and grazes his hands across her thighs as he slowly slips her dress past her waist, stomach, breasts, and head. His eyes linger across her near nakedness. Then, he leans back for a moment and takes off his hoodie. Rachel watches, admiring Emiliano's lean stomach and strong upper body. He moves closer and lays on top of her, his bare stomach now touching hers. Each following kiss precedes the removal of a clothing item until they are both lying in their raw, unaltered nakedness.

Emiliano looks into Rachel's brown eyes. She holds her gaze low, sweeping her thumb across his plump bottom lip.

He lightly places a palm to her cheek. "Baby, you never look me in the eyes," he whispers.

She bites her bottom lip and continues looking down, afraid.

He kisses her affectionately, then lifts her chin. "Baby, look at me," he whispers.

She swallows her nerves. Her eyes gradually make their way past his stomach, his chest, his lips, his nose, until she meets his green eyes for the first time, her love now unmasked, no longer able to hide. Neither one of them moves.

They don't kiss. They don't blink. They just stare—fervently into each other's souls. Their eyes speak a language that words never could.

"You sure, baby?" Emiliano looks for any signs of hesitation from Rachel.

"Yes, I'm sure," she says in a low voice.

They hold their gaze intently as he slowly enters her.

"Is that OK, baby?" he whispers.

She nods as he slowly moves in, consummating the home they have found within one another. He rubs his hands across her neck and down her breasts, slowly rocking his hips back and forth, back and forth, feeling the pulsing welling inside of her. She holds his face, his perfectly chiseled face, in her hands. Their eyes stay locked, refusing to waver for a single moment.

Admiring each other's beauty beyond physicality, their souls continue making art with their bodies: touching, tasting, licking, gripping, feeling, aching, and more aching. A poignant ebb and flow between masculine and feminine energies unfolds. They guide one another to the apex of love, before falling asleep serenely, wrapped in each other's naked arms.

19 Portraits

"Y'all seriously gonna ride that thing?" Emiliano shouts across the back parking lot of the auto shop.

"Hell yeah, bro!" Jimmy hollers. He and Pablo hop into a rickety, abandoned golf cart. In the driver's seat, Pablo muddles through the key ring. The fifth key that he tries fits into the hole. He hits the accelerator, jerking the cart forward. They travel at 14 miles per hour, a low hum reverberating from the motor. Both Pablo and Jimmy whoop and holler excitedly.

Emiliano whips out his phone and starts recording a video of his friends. "Where y'all goin?" He holds his phone out, chuckling as he walks closer.

"We on the way to get some girrrrrls!" Pablo shouts. He looks over his shoulder, keeping his foot on the gas.

"Oh shit!" Jimmy yells.

Pablo swiftly turns around, yanking the wheel, attempting to steer away from the large company trash bin. The front of the golf cart crunches as it smacks the corner of the green metal box. Jimmy hurls forward, the seatbelt tugging against his waist. Pablo, who didn't buckle, falls out. His loosely tied shoe flies off his foot, exposing his faded white cotton sock. Emiliano jogs over to the collision, still recording. He zooms the video in on the car hood, Pablo on the floor, then his lonesome shoe a few feet away. In unison they all burst out laughing.

"Y'all some fuckin fools!" Emiliano hollers as he finishes the video recording.

"Daaaaamn, no girls for me today," Pablo says, wiping gravel off his shoulder and elbow.

"Or any day!" Jimmy jokes.

"Ay, fool!" Pablo hollers.

"Vato, you need new kicks." Emiliano stares at Pablo's worn out black shoe with its tattered laces lying on the asphalt.

"Perfect timing, esé. Imma get those new Kyrie 7s." Pablo smirks as he walks over to pick up his shoe.

"Those aren't new, dude," Jimmy says. "Those were released back in November."

"Nah, bro. A new March drop came out last week." Pablo excitedly palms his fist. "Nike Kyrie 7s. Chinese New Year. They sick, man."

They all walk to the front of the crash. The mystery golf cart that randomly showed up in the back lot this morning is now a wreck with its crunched hood and loose front wheel. They pick up pieces of the plastic hood and headlight from the surrounding area.

"Ay, Pablo. Your dad gonna be mad?" Emiliano asks.

"Nah esé, we ain't on the clock and it ain't like it's his cart or somethin'."

They shoot all the scraps into the bin, curling their wrists the same way they would in basketball. After Emiliano tosses the last piece, they head to the trail of cars parked along the side of the building. Emiliano wishes his car was among them. He and Pablo get in Pablo's suburban and trail behind

Jimmy out of the lot. Emiliano looks out the window as '90s hip-hop blasts through the stereo, hating the now familiar view from a passenger seat. For the last few weeks, other than the few times he has been able to borrow his mother's car, he's had to rely on rides from Samanta and Pablo to and from work. While he feels grateful for their help, he simultaneously feels like a burden.

"Well, see you soon," Emiliano says as they reach his house. "Gracias, hermano." He gets out and watches the suburban exit the neighborhood, checking to see if any cars might be entering. Any *white* cars.

Seeing none, he hurries inside, greeting his dog while he thumbs through his closet, contemplating what to wear. Of course he settles for a typical Emiliano outfit: dark-wash Levi jeans, a Lakers windbreaker, black high-tops, and a backward-facing cap—the blue one with the red strip across the rim.

"You ready for the park?" he asks Mila, grabbing her toys and his basketball. Her ears perk up and she chases behind his heels to the front door and into the back alleyway.

Right on cue, a familiar white Acura pulls into Emiliano's driveway. He looks down at the concrete, feeling emasculated that the woman he's seeing is picking him up too many times in a row. He feels it should be the other way around.

They load everything into her car, including the dogs, then greet one another with a smile and hug. Immediately, the dogs wearily circle around the backseat sniffing each other's behinds, their loose gray and white hairs decorating the black leather seats. Once the dogs finish, they separate: Cece behind Rachel's seat, Mila behind Emiliano's.

Emiliano takes an extra moment to admire Rachel's outfit: light-wash high waisted jeans and a slouchy brown crop top. She is looking good as ever. He reaches across the console for their handshake; they slide, curl, interlock, cross their fingers in an L shape, and snap effortlessly, somehow more in sync than they've ever been before.

"I know it's only been a few days, but I missed you a lot," Emiliano says, looking into Rachel's eyes.

"I missed you too," Rachel replies, with newfound post-sex confidence in her voice.

They lean in and their lips mesh together in the most perfect and cliché way, like two puzzle pieces that obviously fit together. When they pull back, ever so slightly, they sit in silence for a moment, communicating through their eyes without the use of words.

Their relationship has now gone much further than any of Emiliano's in the last few years. Recognizing the depth of their connection and intimacy, nervousness engulfs him. He breaks eye contact and takes off his baseball cap. "Do you see this strip of red?" Emiliano glides his finger along the rim of the cap. "That's the only red you'll ever see on my body. Got no red in my closet."

"Why not?" Rachel asks.

"I just can't wear red. Don't wear red…I wear a lot of blue though."

Rachel doesn't say anything, contemplating what he means.

"It's just not safe to be wearin' certain colors out here in these streets."

A horn honks, abruptly interrupting their delicate conversation. Emiliano spots his mom's car waiting at the base of the driveway. "Damn. We in mi jefita's spot. We gotta back out." Emiliano waves to his mom. "Imma go talk to her real quick, Rach."

Rachel backs out and pulls next to the curb. All the while, Mila whimpers for Emiliano from the backseat, leaning out the window staring at him. When Emiliano gets back into Rachel's car, Adriana pulls into the driveway. Her two-inch black heels step out of the dark gray Hyundai Sonata. She is dressed in gray slacks and a black blouse carrying a stack of work materials. Rachel waves to her, then apologizes for being in her spot.

Adriana shrugs. "It's no problem." The women both ask how each other has been, and each of them says good, just as most people when asked that question. "I told Emiliano you guys should come in and watch *King Kong* with all of us," Adriana says. "But he said, 'Heeeeelllll no!'"

"Oh, really? You said, 'Heeeeelllll no?'" Rachel repeats, looking over at Emiliano, curious about his strong level of rejection to his mom's invitation.

Feeling embarrassed that his mom shared that, his cheeks flush red like a tomato.

"You kids have fun!" Adriana hollers before heading into the house.

Emiliano hurriedly rolls up the window. "Rach, it's the middle of the day! It's a long movie! It's not even a good movie! It's crowded in the house, that's all!" Between each excuse he gets flashbacks of Samanta from the night of their first sleepover. He pauses when he sees Rachel's understanding smile, then continues in a calmer tone, "And when I said no to the movie, my mom said 'Well stop sitting in the driveway with her and go take her to the beach or something!'" He mimics his mother's voice and points his index finger.

"Well, you can take me to the beach some other time," Rachel says.

They look at their dogs in the backseat; both of them are panting, eager, patient, and deserving of some fun. Emiliano rubs his knuckles against their noggins as they finally make their way off his street. A few neighbors stare at them as they drive by.

Once out of the neighborhood, Emiliano fusses with the Bluetooth and puts on "Rockstar Made" by Playboi Carti, eager to showcase another side of his music taste. "Now, listen…I know this is ignorant music, OK?" Emiliano says. "I don't know why I like it, but I jus' do sometimes."

Rachel can't help but laugh at the weird song that is so much different than everything else on Emiliano's music palate. He starts telling her about some major artists in the industry and she gladly listens even though modern rap is not her go-to genre. He even mentions a photography book he's been eager to get called "Portraits" by Gunner Stahl. Many of his favorite rappers are in the book, including Playboi Carti. Rachel recites and repeats the book name and author in her head, thinking it would be a great present to give him some day.

They pull up to the small park's entrance and the dogs whine with excitement, staring at the vast, empty field of grass between the swing set and basketball court. Emiliano opens the rear door and the dogs sprint for the grass. Leashes, toys, and basketball in hand, Rachel and Emiliano head over to a large tree planter, exchanging stories about how they ended up with their dogs. Emiliano got Mila when she was two months old from a breeder. He potty trained her and raised her, and they've been together for almost seven years. Rachel got Cece in college, just after Cece turned two, from some guys who lived in the apartment below her. One day they just offered Cece to her, and now they've been together for three years.

Rachel gives Cece her ball while Emiliano launches Mila's out into the grass. In a deep baby voice, Emiliano tells Mila she's a good girl as she chases after the toy.

"Do you always baby talk to Mila? That's how I talk to Cece!"

"I do sometimes." He chuckles. "Honestly, I mainly try to talk to her like a human though, tryna build up her confidence in the world ever since she was a baby."

"You wanted to help build her confidence? I think you might be the coolest person I've ever met, Emiliano."

"No, I think *you* might be the coolest person I've ever met, Rach."

Cece and Mila bark rambunctiously, their neck hairs rising. Mila protects her rubber ball, thinking Cece is trying to steal it. Rachel and Emiliano watch as the two dogs face off, wearily circling each other a few feet apart. To ease the tension, Rachel launches the tennis ball, and Cece forgets about the standoff, watching it fly through the air. Kicking up blades of grass, Cece sprints through the open field toward the ball with Mila close behind her.

"You should run with Mila. She'll love you forever!" Emiliano exclaims.

"Run where?"

"Just down the field, call her name while you run!"

Rachel takes off running. "Mila, come on! This way, Mila! This way!" Both Mila and Cece chase after Rachel, quickly catching up to her. They run on each side of her until she reaches an oak tree on the other side of the park. Emiliano's heart warms, watching Rachel and Mila together. All three of them sprint back to Emiliano, the sun shining on Rachel's long cinnamon hair. Emiliano cannot take his eyes off her.

"Your turn!" Rachel says with a smile.

"Nah, I can't run in jeans."

"Aw, come on, Emiliano…I did it!"

Emiliano slowly leans forward, as if to question whether or not to commit, until his foot plants into the ground and he takes off. After a few yards, he turns around running backward, shifting his gaze from one dog to the other. "Mila, come on! Let's go, Cece!" He turns back around, both dogs chasing after him as he sprints to the tree.

Rachel doesn't take her eyes off the three of them as they run around the massive oak and come back toward her. She takes a mental photo—Emiliano, with his perfect smile, holding up his jeans, and the two dogs looking up at him with their tongues out—knowing this will be yet another memory she will cherish for the rest of her life.

When they make it to Rachel, the two dogs lie in the grass. Emiliano and Rachel join them, and they all look like a young and happy athletic family. Rachel glances over at Emiliano, feeling sturdy in their love, like nothing could ever come between them. Perhaps everything will be smooth sailing from here on out and there won't be any more odd incidents or exchanges.

The sun begins to set over the mountain and light peeks through the green oak leaves, shining warm, orange sunset hues across the park. Emiliano notices there are no lights or street lamps anywhere around. "I wanna hoop before it gets too dark."

They head down the hill, their dogs trailing close behind. Emiliano dribbles around for a bit, sinks a few baskets, then throws the ball to Rachel. She has no idea what she is doing and looks like she is playing hot potato with the ground as she dribbles. She does *not* like being bad at things and quickly gives the ball back to him.

Emiliano shows her a jump shot and an overhand lay-up, encouraging her to give them a go. After a few tries with each move, she gets the hang of it and scores.

"Ayyy! Nice work, Rach!" Emiliano gives her a fist bump.

"That was all you, coach!"

Emiliano dribbles the ball toward Rachel, acting like she is a defender. He passes it around his waist, dribbles it through and around his legs, then playfully pushes up against her shoulder. With a swivel, he fakes her out before swishing the ball. Cece runs onto the court, barking at Emiliano for pushing up against Rachel. Mila follows behind, running into the center circle.

"It's OK, Cece! Thank you for protecting me." Rachel runs into the grass to lure the dogs back over to the enticing green field. Though, by now, almost all the sunlight has faded. "It's getting hard to see. You think we should get going?"

"OK," Emiliano says with a nod. He carries the ball down to the three-point line to take a few more shots. Three baskets in a row. Then a fourth, and a fifth. While he finishes playing, Rachel collects their things.

"Aight. Let's hit it."

They share a kiss before walking out of the park, their tired four-legged children following behind them to the car. Rachel feels like everything about their park date was serene, easy, and perfect. Their love finally seems serene, easy, and perfect, like if it remains like this, everything will be fine.

As Rachel and Emiliano leave the park, Javier and a young woman arrive on the opposite side with a blanket and picnic basket. For dinner they are having charcuterie and wine. Since things weren't moving along with Jemma, he met some of his soccer friends at a bar over the weekend, and that's where he met this cute girl with platinum blonde hair and a button nose.

They uncork the wine and Javier compliments her outfit. The girl is in a red and white gingham dress; she almost looks like a walking snack, a walking picnic blanket. As they clink their glasses together, she whispers that she has a secret: she's not wearing any underwear. Javier smiles, thinking about how Jemma and this girl are both lovely—light, warm, and beautiful. However, at the top of his list is still Rachel Williams. He has no idea how he could possibly get her attention though, since she is wrapped up in another man's arms.

20 400 Heart-Shaped Pizzas

"Put your left hand on top of your chest and feel the beautiful heart that's beating inside of you." The young yoga instructor pauses, taking a large audible breath. "And place your right hand on top of your belly. Start to feel how your breath moves through you."

The overwhelming silence seems to be a source of beauty for some and an absolute nightmare for others. Rachel, on her forest green mat, intently listens and follows the instructions, a serene expression washing over her face. Unable to focus, Hannah keeps her eyes open and looks around the mirror-filled room, firmly pressing her fingers into her turquoise mat. She looks like she has been watching a gory horror film for the past hour, rather than stretching her body in an afternoon yoga class.

"Everyone may return to a sitting position." The yoga instructor bows her head as she gently clasps her palms together. "Namaste."

The yoga class attendees imitate, bowing their heads and repeating the expression. While everyone rolls up their mats, the yoga instructor—decked out in Lululemon attire—turns the lights on.

"Sorry I was late getting here, Rach," Hannah says.

"It's no problem…Are you doing OK?" Rachel couldn't help but notice her best friend's knotted up hair and lack of personal hygiene throughout the yoga class.

"Uh…kinda." Hannah grimaces as they carry their rolled up mats out of the yoga studio. "I know you have plans with Emiliano soon, but do you have time to walk over to the café next door? I really need to talk to you."

Rachel gives her a silly look, as if to ask if that was a real question.

In the small café, Hannah snatches an open table while Rachel orders two green teas. The man working clanks the register's bulky buttons entering the order and Rachel veers her attention to Hannah: she's resting her elbows on the table and staring deeply into the dark brown wood pattern. What could be going on with her? She's never been this distraught before. The cashier places two white paper cups with biodegradable lids in front of Rachel. She thanks him before walking over to Hannah.

"So…what's up?" Rachel asks.

"Well, you know how Brax's friend Alexis moved in…" Hannah looks Rachel in the eyes, giving her a kind of look that only a best friend would understand. "I was folding laundry and found a red lacy thong that wasn't mine." Hannah sighs. "I folded it and walked it over to her bedroom. Alexis awkwardly laughed and said, 'It must have been left in the dryer from before you put all your clothes in.'"

"Oh no. Do you think they…" Rachel trails off. "It's hard cause that could make logical sense right? If you share laundry machines." Rachel shrugs, sipping her tea.

"Yeah. I can't stop thinking about it. I haven't slept. I don't remember seeing anything in the dryer when I put our clothes in." Hannah pauses briefly, then repeats the phrase, despising the feelings that come with it. "I don't remember seeing anything in the dryer."

"So you think he's cheating on you?"

"I can't imagine that he ever would."

"Then it's probably fine, Hannah! Maybe she was telling the truth?" The same silence from the yoga room seems to have followed them into the café. "I would just follow your intuition." Rachel gives Hannah a gentle hug.

"Yeah…my intuition," Hannah says, with angst in her voice, unsure which voice is her intuition. It's just that Brax used to treat her like she permanently walked on a red carpet. And, occasionally, he still does. Maybe they are just out of the honeymoon phase. Maybe Alexis and Brax are just friends. Maybe she should trust him because what is a relationship without trust?

"I can cancel my plans with Emiliano. He would completely understand."

Hannah shakes her head. "I would never think of such a thing. Just because my relationship is going through shit doesn't mean I should stir up yours. Your advice was just what I needed, Rachel."

After a few more sips of green tea, the young women stand, their chairs screeching across the floor as they push them in. The unpleasant sound mimics Hannah's unsettled nerves. A bell on the front door chimes as they exit the café.

"Thanks for the tea, Rachel. Such a life saver!"

Rachel waves goodbye, then gets in her car hoping her best friend will follow her intuition. Only Hannah would know whether or not she can trust her boyfriend, and Rachel has no way of knowing the truth. The red thong could have been in there because they really *did* cheat. It could have been an accident like Alexis said. Or, who knows, maybe Alexis is a psychopath and purposely placed it there to taunt Hannah.

Rachel glances at the bumper of Hannah's car as it exits the lot, then she heads for Emiliano's house.

When she pulls onto his street, two young *Chicanas* are playing with a large rubber ball on the grass. There are no open parking spaces, so Rachel rounds the cul-de-sac and parks next to the cars that are against the curb, essentially in the middle of the road.

One of the girls passes the ball a little too hard. It flies over the other girl's head and smacks the hood of Rachel's Acura. They let out gasps, covering their mouths. One of them runs into the street to get it. She looks into Rachel's eyes with a look that says *please don't be mad at me*.

Rachel smiles and rolls down the window. "It's OK! I know you didn't mean to!"

The girls smile sheepishly, then, spotting Emiliano, they greet him with high-pitched *hola*s as he walks down the sidewalk. He waves to them before getting in the car.

"I am huuuungry!" he says, settling into the leather seat. Rachel laughs, mentioning how she's been thinking about pizza all day. They do their infamous handshake, then their synchronous snaps ensue—Rachel's cue to drive. She does so cautiously, watching for any children or rubber balls that may jump in front of her car.

"Thank you for picking me up. Hopefully my car will be fixed real soon."

"Of course. How's that going, Emiliano?"

After a brief pause, he explains how he doesn't have the time or the money to get it done. He knows what to do, but he just can't do it. And that's one of the most frustrating places to be—in limbo, unsure where to go, how, and when.

"At least the job itself isn't a mystery," Rachel says, hoping to find a glimmer of positivity in his unfortunate lack-of-time-and-money debacle.

Emiliano nods, staring out the window at the passing oak trees, palm trees, and street signs, until they pull into a modernized plaza containing some of the west coast's most popular chain restaurants: Chipotle, Islands, Starbucks, MOD Pizza, and Jamba Juice.

"Island's fries have *the best* seasoning," Rachel says.

Emiliano shrugs. "I've never been there."

"You've *never* been to Islands?" she asks, pulling into a parking spot.

"Nah, that some White people shit." Emiliano isn't trying to be rude about their cultural and racial differences; it's just that he likes being immersed in his own culture, immersed in places that don't involve White people appropriating, stomping on, or demanding something.

Unsure how to respond, Rachel doesn't say anything and gets out of the car.

Side by side they walk through the dimly lit parking lot. The evening sun has disappeared and everything around them is now full of dark blues, grays, and black shadows. Emiliano hurries a bit ahead of Rachel to open the restaurant door for her, a wide, cheesing grin across his face. She thanks him for his courtesy, her eyes overflowing with reverence.

A young high school aged boy, whose voice hasn't dropped yet, greets them from behind the counter. Fully gloved and hair netted, he flattens a piece of pizza dough, then asks Rachel what she'd like. She begins listing off vegetables. The boy nods, reaching into bin after bin as she recites what seems to be a produce grocery list.

Emiliano makes a disgusted expression with each odd new vegetable topping. "Rach got a suh-lad again!" he jokes.

She shoots him a goofy look across the ordering station, then heads to the cash register while he chooses his pizza toppings. Secretly she pays for his meal too. While the cashier taps a few buttons on the register, Rachel looks longingly at Emiliano. He is conversing with the young high school aged pizza maker about the Lakers. Of course that's what he's doing, she thinks. She can't help but smile at the loyal, local fans.

Behind the counter, Emiliano's pizza is getting heavily decorated: a mountain of sausage, Canadian bacon, and pepperoni built on the foundation of mozzarella cheese.

It looks like it was ordered from an entirely different restaurant.

"Here's your card and receipt, Miss."

Rachel smiles at the worker, then walks to the nearest bench to wait for Emiliano. She looks at the receipt, glad to see both of their pizzas on it, knowing he wouldn't have wanted her to pay. But she felt it was important to treat him, as a way of saying thank you—for him just being him. Emiliano just being Emiliano. Funny, goofy, genuine, sexy, protective, respectful, kind, generous Emiliano. She knows every morsel on the pizza could never symbolize her gratitude for him. It would take at least 400 heart-shaped pizzas, and even then, that could never exemplify what she believes he deserves.

"Thank you, man," Emiliano says to the young worker.

Hearing Emiliano's voice, Rachel snaps out of her thoughts. She looks up just as he reaches into his back pocket for his wallet. "I already got it, Emiliano."

"Aw man! Are you forreal?" Emiliano says, surprised. "Thank you, Rach. I appreciate it." He looks deeply at her— cute nose, a freckle on her cheek, soulful brown eyes. A beam of reverence now radiates from him.

A few minutes later, their piping hot pizzas are ready. While walking to the car, Emiliano stares at Rachel's long luscious hair, thinking about how much he likes her. He feels like maybe he doesn't deserve so much love from her. And he doesn't want to get hurt. Maybe she would leave him anyway, thinking there's some White guy more suitable for her. And, honestly, he still can't see any resolution between their cultural differences.

"Are you OK?" Rachel asks as they get inside her car. "You seem quiet."

"Sometimes I'm quiet and just don't got nothin' to say," he mumbles.

Rachel doesn't add anything to the silence.

"You heard back from those schools, Rach?" he asks, leaving his thoughts behind for now.

She tells him most colleges have long decision making processes, so hopefully she'll hear back sometime in the next few months. A smile softly spreads on her face. She is ecstatic at the mere thought of her future occupation and getting accepted into graduate school.

"You gotta keep me in the loop. Lemme know what happens." Emiliano's eyes slowly make their way from Rachel's face down her yoga crop top, to her exposed belly button. Leaning over the console, he grips the skin on her tummy. "Mmm," he mumbles. "Rach, you are so sexy."

She bashfully smiles, though Emiliano can't see her shyness in the dark. He moves within inches of her face and sticks out his tongue. She follows along. Their tongues circle each other, much like two boxers in a ring at the start of the match before the action has commenced. He makes the first move, putting his hand on the base of her neck and gently pulling her closer to him. Then he kisses her mouth—now a home he is familiar with, the corridors he's walked many times, yet has not grown tired of exploring further. After leaving a few juicy, wet smooches on her lips, he kisses the area of skin where her chin, ear, and neck meet: the Bermuda Triangle of sensual pleasure.

Rachel can't help but get lost in his energy and passion. Her light breaths turn into deep sighs. "Baby," she mutters achingly. A close translation to *Oh my god, I'm so fucking in love with you.*

Emiliano immediately pulls back, assuming her ache was a call to stop. He combs a hand through his hair as he leans back into the seat cushion. "Sorry, I got carried away, Rach."

She opens her eyes, snapping out of her dream. "It's OK." A feeling of relief takes over her body. She is in love with him, and the words almost slipped out. She doesn't want him to know, because she has no idea if he feels the same way.

"That's my bad. I know we're in a public parking lot," he says.

"No, it's fine. I was actually about to take my shirt off," she says, half-jokingly.

"Rachel doing that? No way in hell!"

"Oh. You don't believe me?" Rachel places her hands at the base of her top. Slowly, she lifts, lightly grazing her fingers across her skin, until the underside of her breasts are exposed.

"Rachel!" Emiliano gasps, his eyes widening. "I could never imagine you being so naughty!"

She giggles as she lowers her tight shirt. "Guess you just bring it out of me."

They look at each other briefly, exchanging smiles.

"Aight, let's hurry to my place so we can grub," Emiliano says.

They pull out of the parking lot and roll up to a stoplight. When the light turns green, Emiliano yells "green!" and they share a laugh. Both of them warm at the thought that they have an inside joke from the special L.A. trip. For the entirety of the drive the pizzas on Emiliano's lap taunt them with decadent smells of sauces, spices, and oven-baked goodness.

When they make it to his neighborhood, he tells her to park in his driveway because nobody is home. His mom and sister drove to Tijuana to visit family. He couldn't go because he couldn't miss work. Well, couldn't miss the money that work provides.

"You wanna watch a movie after we eat, Rach?"

"One from our list?" she asks excitedly.

"Of course from our list."

They are greeted by Mila as soon as they enter his house. "Hi girl!" Emiliano says. Rachel bends down to pet her, but the dog shies away, still behaving timidly. Mila follows them to the dining table, at the ready in case they drop anything.

"Rach! I forgot I gotta show you somethin'," Emiliano says after taking a bite of his pizza. He walks around the back of the table to a pile of items. She watches as he moves stuff around and picks up a heavy gray circular item. Her eyes scan across the intricate designs, a mystified look on her face.

"Babe, it's an Aztec calendar! Mi madre got it for me the last time she was in México."

Rachel looks at the odd shaped calendar, stunned. "Do you know how to read it?"

"No." Emiliano chuckles. "I wish." He sets the heavy calendar on the floor, then sits back down. "Wanna hear something crazy? People have stuffed drugs in 'em. They used Mayan calendars, which look similar to the Aztec calendars. A few years ago like twenty pounds of meth was found in Orange County disguised as all sorts of Mexican decor."

"Damn. Was it one drug dealer who had that much stuff?"

"Nah. It was a whole set up. It involved alotta people in the drug ring down there." Emiliano looks over at the calendar. "Sometimes I think, imagine if this one is like that. Full of drugs or somethin'. And one day if I accidently break it, all these crazy drugs will fall out!"

They both laugh, imagining the ridiculous tale.

"Oh my God. I would be so scared. I'd have no idea what to do!" Rachel says.

Their laughing ceases as they bite into their pizza slices. A mouthful of vegetables invade Rachel's mouth as she stares at the glass table in deep thought about Emiliano, his culture, and their differences he tends to point out, or accentuate. "I really had so much fun with you in East Los Angeles," Rachel says, slowly lifting her gaze. "I hope we can go there again sometime."

"EasLos," Emiliano says.

"What?"

"East L.A...It's called EasLos," he says, a particular Spanish curvature on his tongue.

"EastLos." Rachel sets down what's left of her pizza slice as she attempts to speak in an accent that she can't quite grasp.

"EeeeeeceLowce." Emiliano draws out the sounds.

"EastLowce," she says slowly, her pronunciation improving, but still too *American English speaker*.

"Why are you saying it like that? There's no T, Rach."

Rachel mumbles the phrase silently a few times to practice before reciting it to Emiliano. "EeeeeeceLowce," she says with mediocre confidence.

"Nice! Now faster. EasLos," he says, bobbing his head forward.

"EasLos," she finally says.

"Pretty good, Rach." Emiliano smiles, proud of her, then takes a large bite of his pizza. "We should watch *Mi Vida Loca* tonight."

"My crazy life," Rachel says. Slowly but surely, her beginner-Spanish translations are getting better, getting surer of themselves.

They finish eating, then head into the living room, where the movies from their list are piled in a stack, separate from the other movies on the shelf. Rachel sits down while Emiliano thumbs through the DVDs. "I remember watchin' this movie all the time when I was real little, like two, three years old. This was mi mamá's favorita...I think it was real relatable to her." He puts the disc in the DVD player, then hands Rachel the movie case. "Read the back to make sure you wanna watch it."

Rachel scans the case of the 1993 drama based in Echo Park. The description highlights young *Mexicanas* and *Chicanas* who are mostly single in early motherhood, facing romantic turbulence and economic struggles in gang-filled neighborhoods. "It sounds good," Rachel says, looking at the young women on the cover. "So where is your dad, Emiliano?"

"He lives in Texas."

"Do you ever see him?"

"I went out there a few summers when I was growin' up."

Rachel nods, not wanting to pry. Suddenly, the knob on the front door jangles. She instinctively looks at the curtain over the square window, blood pressure rising, scared it could be Samanta. The anticipation ceases when a young boy comes through the door.

"Getting home after dark? Better have been with a chica," Emiliano says teasingly.

The young boy laughs shyly, then greets Emiliano in Spanish before heading upstairs.

"Is he your younger brother?" Rachel whispers.

"No…he's, um, kinda like a cousin. His mom lives here too." Emiliano would never, could never, tell Rachel that people rent a room from his family. He presses play and leans back, relaxing into the couch. Rachel turns her gaze to *Mi Vida Loca* as she lays down with her head resting on his lap.

21 A Sort of Lovers' Meditation

Rachel walks off the field looking down at the yellow grass. Her hand is held high blocking the unforgiving sun from her eyes. Behind her, Hannah and Javier walk almost side-by-side, both of them silent, looking past Rachel at the unoccupied tree and vacant hill where their main tag-a-longs used to be.

"Where is that beautiful girl Jemma?" Rachel asks, turning to face the other two.

"I guess she just didn't see us going anywhere," he says, shrugging.

"Aw. I'm sorry to hear that," Rachel replies. "Yeah, I kinda get what that's like. It sucks when people can be wishy washy about you."

Javier heads toward the tree mulling over Rachel's comment. Was she talking about her past experiences, or is she talking about her present one? Maybe her and Emiliano aren't as solid as he thought. Maybe he will be able to find a way into her sphere. Maybe he should test the waters and see what happens.

Hannah and Rachel sit down at the table where a few players are still packing up. "The game had such a different vibe today," Hannah says. "Main supporters not here, vital players not here, playing in the late afternoon instead of the morning…and this new group of faces?" She tilts toward a few men in their early twenties. "Pretty decent. I hope they play with us more."

"Yeah their style of play was different. It felt really fresh! Hopefully Fabian invites them again." Rachel looks Hannah up and down, trying not to show an overwhelming amount of concern. "Have you been getting more sleep?"

"Sometimes." Hannah looks down at the metal table and starts gnawing at her nails. "It's just Brax and Alexis," she says. "More boring Hannah Storytime."

"Hey, Hannah Storytime is never boring," Rachel retorts. "I could sit at this table all day with you."

The three new players swing their bags over their shoulders, say goodbye to the young women, and head up the hill, speaking in Spanish about the game. Javier quickly grabs his bag and jogs to catch up with them.

"Me gusta tu Barça balón," Javier says.

The group of young men chuckle. One of them replies, "Gracias, pero es balón de Barça no Barça balón."

They weren't intentionally trying to hurt Javier, of course—but the Spanish correction immediately feels like a slash to Javier's heart. Once again he is reminded that he is not Mexican enough. But he also knows he isn't White enough. He's also not Mexican American enough. He's just not enough of anything. Javier's cheeks turn a deep red. He glares at the young men, angry that they laughed about his mix up.

The young men continue to talk in fast, indistinguishable Spanish as they walk into the parking lot. They exchange a laugh about one of them tripping over a patch of grass during the game. Javier can't fully comprehend their conversation.

"What's so fucking funny?" Javier shouts.

"We just laughin' bout the game, man," one of them says over their shoulder.

"Don't bullshit! You're laughing at me!"

The three players exchange confused looks with one another.

"Do you know I can get girls that you guys can't even dream about?" Javier sneers.

"¿Qué chicas? With a face like that?" the boy holding the Barcelona ball hollers back, now laughing at Javier's attempted disrespect.

Javier's face sinks into an empty expression. "You pussies don't even know." He scoffs. "I get any fucking girl that I want."

The men brush him off as they get into a beat-up red Toyota Tacoma. Javier watches the taillights as they back out of the parking space and cruise to a stop sign. Rachel and Hannah stroll in front of the small red truck and wave goodbye to the new, friendly faces. Javier's gaze shifts from the taillights to the women as they walk to their cars in the distance.

Hannah finishes her final vent about Alexis and Brax, hoping to get some magical and solid best friend advice. Rachel again emphasizes the importance of following gut feelings and intuition. Hannah nods, then they hug each other tightly before getting into their cars.

Rachel sinks into her Acura and pulls out her cellphone to call Emiliano. She has no idea why he wasn't at soccer, and she's pretty sure that he wasn't scheduled to work. She wants to make sure he is OK. As she's about to dial, an incoming call comes in from her grandmother, Tilly.

Hard of hearing, her grandma says hello multiple times into the phone.

Rachel chuckles, then raises her voice, "I'm here, grandma. Hi!"

After briefly discussing a recent mass shooting and a family member's promotion, Tilly invites Rachel to come visit her in Arizona where she lives. "I want to hear about your applications, the GRE, and maybe, if we have time, we can visit the Hualapai mountains. What do you think?"

"That sounds great, Grandma. One of these upcoming weekends I will." Rachel clears her throat. She's eager to get off the phone. "I better get going, I have a call to make." Both women say bye-bye-bye-bye-bye at the same time, then Tilly blows kisses into the phone.

The warm smile across Rachel's face quickly fades into a sharp gasp as a figure just outside her car startles her. She places a hand over her chest, feeling an immense pulsing as she hastily rolls down the window. "Javier...I didn't see you there." She lets out a slight laugh. "What's up?"

"Um...hi. Sorry for startling you. Do you want to maybe get some dinner tonight?"

"Sorry, Javier, I can't. Maybe one of these weekends we can all go out to lunch after we play though?"

"OK! Raincheck." Javier taps his hand on the rolled down window. "Bye, Rachel." He walks toward the playground, decoding her response. She mentioned a group activity, which means she is still with Emiliano, unfortunately. However, she didn't say no flat-out. Doesn't that mean that one day—if things don't work out with Emiliano—he might have a chance to hang out with her?

Rachel rolls the window up, watching him for a few moments in the side view mirror. Slowly, her eyes pull away and she picks up her phone. Her eagerness builds with each second, as her phone call to Emiliano has now been derailed twice. As the ringing starts, she bobs her head back and forth, anxiously awaiting to hear her favorite voice.

"Hello?" A sick sounding voice comes through Rachel's phone.

"Emiliano? Are you sick?"

"Yeah." He sniffs. "I'm so stuffed up. How was soccer?"

"It was good! I missed you being there. I hope you've been resting!"

"Yeah," he groans. "Been layin' with Mila all day. My throat hurts real bad."

"Have you had anything hot to help soothe it?"

"No," he mumbles.

"Ah, Emiliano! Let me take you to get some hot cocoa right now."

"Will that help, Rach?"

"Well, it's a hot drink…also, I want to see you."

"No, I don't want to get you sick."

"I won't get sick, Emiliano!"

"Well how do you know that?"

"I don't."

Both ends of the rapid-fire conversation go silent for a moment.

"Aight, fine. But I ain't kissing you, Rach!"

"Fine. I didn't want to kiss you anyway," she says teasingly.

They exchange goodbyes as she exits the recreation center. The final glimpse of the sun's rays vanish behind the mountain.

When she nears the entrance to Emiliano's neighborhood, two White policemen are standing in the middle of the road. Their suburban style cop cars nearly block the neighborhood's entrance. One of the officers, sporting a pair of jet black sunglasses, has his arms folded in an intimidating stance. The other is using a pair of binoculars, fixating on one particular house. Rachel drives past them, brows knitting together, as she slowly navigates down the street. What on earth could they be doing?

The neighborhood is oddly quiet. Only a few people are outside watering their plants or washing their cars. There are no children running on the lawns or in the streets. Cars still line the curbs bumper to bumper. Rachel turns onto Emiliano's street, rounds the cul-de-sac, and pulls up in front of his house.

After a few minutes of waiting, she looks down at her watch, then puts on her hazard lights. A look of concern crosses her face. Emiliano is usually outside and ready, or comes out fairly quickly after her arrival. Is everything OK around here?

Inside the house, Emiliano is still getting ready. After quickly lathering on deodorant, he hustles around the living room looking for his leather Converse. Samanta is sitting on the couch watching *Corázon Salvaje*: a romantic telenovela based in Mexico in the 1990s. Emiliano lifts a few blankets and looks under the couch.

"¿Qué estás buscando?" Samanta asks, looking at her brother crouched by her feet.

"Mis zapatos negros."

To his dismay, the shoes are nowhere in the living room. When he walks over to his closet in the kitchen, Samanta's cellphone starts ringing. He picks it up from the counter by the sink and hands it to her through the kitchen bar. "Es Marcos," Emiliano says.

Samanta answers the phone and starts talking while still watching the telenovela.

Emiliano tries to focus through the commotion, knowing Rachel is probably outside waiting for him. He scans his closet for a second time. Still no luck. Then he spots the leather high tops hiding behind the dining table. His lips smack as he walks over to grab them. "How did I not see 'em?" he mumbles to himself, bringing the shoes to the couch adjacent to Samanta, where Mila is sleeping. He puts the shoes on in silence, listening to his sister's phone conversation.

"Sí…OK…Te amo Marcos. See you soon."

After tying his laces, Emiliano glances at the TV. Two Mexican lovers are passionately kissing. He intently watches the lustful exchange, then waves goodbye.

As he opens the front door, he sees his second favorite car in the world. (His first favorite is his non-running Firebird. The white Acura is his second only because his favorite girl is inside of it.)

Rachel admires Emiliano's outfit as he walks down the sidewalk: a black t-shirt tucked into his dark blue jeans with a black belt hugging at his hips. She stares at his head full of thick brown hair. For once, it isn't covered by a baseball cap.

"Hey Rach!" he says, a mixture of excitement and sickness in his voice. "Sorry for the wait, I couldn't find my kicks." They perform their routine greeting: handshakes, snaps, smiles, and hugs, then he looks into her eyes.

"What's wrong, baby?" His brows furrow.

"Nothing." She shakes her head. "There's just some cops acting weird at the entrance of your neighborhood. I just keep thinking about what they could be doing."

Emiliano's face turns from cheery to fuming in less than a second. He immediately buckles his seatbelt. "Let's go. I wanna see 'em."

Rachel heads down the road, and the cops and their cars slowly come into view. Emiliano grumbles and growls like a lion protecting his territory. He mumbles in Spanish under his breath. Rachel watches, wondering what's going on in his mind.

"The fuck is 12 doing here?" He scowls, staring at the cops. Even as Rachel's car slowly trickles forward through the half-way blocked exit, he twists in the seat to continue his glare. The cops remain motionless, fixed in the same positions they were in when Rachel first entered the neighborhood.

They drive past the Nuñez's *panadería*, Flores de Felicia, and the grocery store. For a few miles a stretch of oak trees and palm trees line the road. Eventually, they turn into a Starbucks drive-thru. There are no cars in line, so they pull around to the ordering station, where they are greeted by a cheerful voice through the speaker. Their order consists of two hot cocoas—one made with oat milk and one made with cow milk.

Emiliano pulls his debit card out of his pocket. Even after Rachel insists on paying multiple times, he stretches his card out to her, equally as insistent that he should pay for their beverages. Reluctantly, she provides his card to the cashier at the window.

After getting handed their hot cocoas, Rachel parks the car in the back of the lot where minimal light from the street lamps can reach them. To set the right atmosphere, she opens the sun roof and he scrolls through his music. Once connected to the Bluetooth, he lowers the volume so the tunes are merely subtle background noise.

As he watches Rachel take a sip of hot cocoa, a spellbound look overcomes him.

She lowers the cup and wipes her top lip. "What are you looking at?" A small smile curves across her face.

"Rach, I just got major déjà vu." Emiliano sniffles as he leans back against the window. "You. The cocoa. That smile. What you said. All of it. Like it's happened before…but it hasn't."

"I love when I get déjà vu! I always feel like it's something from a past life."

The two sit quietly pondering the concept. Rachel holds the warm cup steadily with both hands. She feels like she's known Emiliano for many lifetimes.

He looks at Rachel's ivory skin, then takes a sip of his cocoa. He has a lot of feelings for her, but he feels like he has to face reality. "You know this is a no-no right?" he says abruptly.

Rachel giggles, her eyes moving from his lips to his cup. "What's a no-no? Drinking hot cocoa while being sick?"

"No, *this* is a no-no. Me and you. Us." He gazes out the window, not wanting to look at her. The truth, the fears, the expectations all bubble to the surface, like a sneeze tingling the nose, right on the brink of gushing out of the body.

"What do you mean?" she asks, concerned.

"Just in my culture. I'm supposed to marry a Mexican woman. Have fully Mexican babies. Have Spanish be their primary language. Live in my community. Keep the bloodline pure. Continue my heritage." Images flash in his mind— Samanta speaking *Spanish* with her boyfriend, *Mexican lovers* kissing on the TV, *White cops* lingering in his neighborhood.

Rachel's ears nearly bleed. Slight sighs and scoffs and sharp breaths come out of her as she sets her cocoa into the cupholder. She's unable to form real words or sentences, and looks out the window, arms crossed. An overwhelming sense of fury and despair rush through her mind, heart, and lungs.

Emiliano looks at her out of the corner of his eyes, waiting for her to say something. This isn't a situation he ever imagined he'd be in. She's *white*. He's *brown*. She eats a lot of *vegan food*. He is a *meat eater*. She's *school smart*. He's *street smart*. Could they be any more different? She loves *reading*. He loves *movies*. She knows *English vocabulary words*. He knows *Spanglish*. Yet, despite it all, here he is. And here she is.

"So is that going to stop you?" she says in a sad tone. "From this? From us?"

"No," Emiliano whispers, "it's not."

"Well what did you do about this in the past?"

"This ain't ever happened before. I only ever been with Mexican girls, Rachel."

Hearing the starting instrumental of "Make It With You" by Ralfi Pagan, he raises the stereo volume. Their eyes lock, and they remain locked as time disappears. Pure trust radiates from both of them. Slowly, they move toward each other, but not with their lips. As their foreheads meet, lightly resting against one another, their eyes close in a sort of lovers' meditation. Communication occurs, though their lips never open. He carefully tucks Rachel's hair behind her ear, not wavering from their other worldly prayer.

Neither one of them wonders what is occurring between them, as the fluidity of the sentiment simply *is*. Simply exists. The power of love pulses through the car—their bodies the electrical currents. It's not *his* love. It's not *her* love. It's *their* love. *That* love. An indescribable existence separate from, and yet connected to, both of them. After minutes that feel like seconds, they slowly lift their heads and passionately kiss—lips, tongues, hands, saliva, breath, and all.

"I shouldn't kiss you, I'm sick," Emiliano whispers.

"I don't care," she says.

They continue caressing, marrying into the love that emanates from their souls through the atmosphere, fusing an invisible and unforgettable link between them. Rachel leans out of the intoxicating ecstasy, a small smile on her lips. "I should get you home so you can rest."

The tires begin to roll. Among the music sounds the crackling of gravel, rocks, and twigs below the car. They both sip on their now lukewarm cocoa on the drive back to Emiliano's. When they get close to the entrance there are no cops loitering around. The streets are still unusually empty. They pull into the back alley by his house and a quietness envelops the car.

Emiliano gives Rachel a peck, then they do their handshake.

"Please get home safe, Rach," he says, his palms clasped together in prayer hands. After getting out of the car, he puts his hands in his pockets and heads for his house.

Rachel watches his figure slowly fade in the darkness. Feeling a sudden pang of pain from their cocoa conversation, she lowers the window. "Emiliano!"

He turns around, a questioning look on his face.

"One more kiss?" Rachel asks longingly.

With a smile, he saunters over and sticks his ridiculously mesmerizing face through the window. They share a long, delicate kiss, leaving their lips puckered for an extra moment upon the release. Before exchanging another goodbye, Emiliano whispers that he'll see her on the following Friday. A glaze of love covers her eyes.

He steps back and watches her car roll down the street. When it goes out of view, he looks up at the moon, then some palm trees, then—he does a double take. A neighbor across the street is standing outside at the base of a driveway looking at him. Emiliano waves. The man half-smiles; his arms are crossed. Emiliano can't help but think his neighbor's eyes are all-pervading. Is his look stern and grave? Feeling like he is betraying his culture, Emiliano stares at the ground as he slowly walks up his driveway.

22 Begging for the Antidote

Women and men of all sizes, shapes, and shades of brown sway to the rhythmic beat of the cumbia music. Emiliano and Ricardo lean on Ricardo's truck, scanning the crowd from the parking lot. Sofía is sitting next to Ricardo, dangling her feet out of the truck bed while chomping on a piece of gum. All three bob their heads to the music.

Many people at the crowded outdoor concert are sporting Lakers and Dodgers attire—including Emiliano, with his Lakers hat and hoodie. Ricardo isn't representing any sports team. A plain white tank hugs at his long, skinny torso and tucks into his black jeans. Others are wearing plaid shirts, boots, and sombreros.

Sofía, who's highly fashionable, is in tight black jeans that accentuate her thick thighs. *La jefa* is written in cursive across the front of her light gray shirt. The most notable thing about Sofía though is her sassy mouth that's coated with black lipstick.

"¿Quieres bailar otra vez?" Sofía asks as she jumps off the truck.

Emiliano and Ricardo exchange glances.

She twirls a finger through a lock of her thick brown hair. "No tengo tiempo para esperar." Sofía snaps her gum loudly. "Otros hombres bailan conmigo, Ricardo." She shrugs, then walks away, heading toward the entrance.

Unwilling to witness his girlfriend alone on the dance floor, or accompanied by another man, Ricardo immediately follows behind Sofía, gladly, like a puppy. They both flash their stamped hands to the worker at the entrance by the chain link fence.

As they enter, Ricardo grabs hold of Sofía's hand. They jog lightly toward the crowd, the local band, and the loud speakers. The DJ has switched to playing reggaeton.

Emiliano watches his friends dance, their legs straddled between one another's. The smell of tortas and quesabirria tacos from the food truck waft through his nose. He breathes in the delicious Mexican cuisine, for a moment lingering on the thought of what to do: dance or eat. Reluctantly, he closes the tailgate and heads to the entrance.

"¿Decidiste bailar?" Ricardo calls out.

Emiliano hollers something as the worker checks his stamp, but Ricardo can't hear him over the music. He shuffles through the crowd toward his friends, fully aware that beautiful women grace the dance floor. Naturally, he looks at a few of them, but does not approach a single one. Instead, he dances by himself, next to Ricardo and Sofía, thinking about Rachel—who he ditched this weekend. For him, it was the only logical explanation. Rachel couldn't come with Ricardo, Sofía, and him to an event like this in EasLos. Too many people would stare, and Rachel wouldn't fit in. Emiliano tries to dance away his blues to the upbeat tune blasting in his ears. Three songs come and go, and his thoughts of Rachel never cease. He wishes he could dance with her, that she could be here.

"Estoy cansada," Sofía says loudly into Ricardo's ear.

"¿Listo?" Ricardo asks Emiliano.

Emiliano eagerly nods.

They walk out of the small outdoor concert and head for the truck, Ricardo and Sofía holding hands. Sofía pops her gum out, aiming toward a nearby trashcan. It lands just short of the bin. She briefly glances at it, then looks away as they continue through the parking lot.

Once in Ricardo's truck, Emiliano sinks into the cushion of the backseat. Right as he buckles, his phone starts buzzing. Maneuvering around the seatbelt and through his tight pockets, he inches his way to it. A short, bland text message from Rachel is on the screen. He sighs, then puts his phone back in his pocket. There is no way he's dealing with that right now.

He joins in with Ricardo and Sofía's conversation: they're talking about getting food. They all decide they should swing by El Huero, one of their usual spots, for some late night grub before heading toward Old Oak. The restaurant is really popular. It's open 24/7, and is usually packed on weekend nights.

When they pull into the drive-thru, they're all surprised to see that it isn't super busy. They only have to wait a few minutes before pulling up to the large bright menu. Emiliano is the first to speak up, ordering a *carne asada* burrito. While Ricardo and Sofía still decide on their meals, Emiliano continues scanning the overwhelming list of food options. On the far right is a list of vegetarian and vegan dishes. He reads about the veggie burger and its ingredients, thinking it would be the perfect food option for Rachel if she were here.

The indecisive couple finally settles on sharing a plate of *carne asada* nachos. Emiliano doesn't pay attention to the chit chat going on in the front seat because his mind is still on Rachel. He wonders if she knows what *carne asada* is, or if she has ever had it before—and not the Americanized version, but real Mexican *carne ranchera*. He fantasizes that one day she'll try at least a small bite of his family's specialty flank steak.

When Ricardo gets the food, he hands the containers to Sofía before pulling out of the drive-thru. For nearly a mile they are all teased by the delicious smells on Sofía's lap as she fusses with the radio. Skipping past a few gospel stations—all in the middle of saying things like *hallelujah, Jesus, lord on high*—it lands on a rock station. Sofía does not know the genre well, and some ACDC song (that she would never know) is currently on. She reaches down for the nacho tray as she tunes it again; it lands on the local news. The reporter says another body was found in the mountains. Police don't currently know whether or not the incidents are related.

"What the hell? I'm not listening to any of this shit." Sofía turns the tuning knob again, and it lands on a Spanish station. The tail end of the announcer's statement is about how there will be an hour straight of Selena's top hits. "Finally," she says dramatically.

Sofía hands Emiliano his food as they turn onto the freeway. For a few minutes, the only sounds are Selena, the crackling of chips, and approving *mmm's* about the food. Between each bite, Sofía hums along to the music or loudly belts out Selena lyrics.

"Ever gonna bring a chica with you to one of these dances?" Ricardo asks.

"Yeah, true that. I'm sick of hangin' out with two boys!" Sofía pokes her head behind the passenger seat. "¿Por qué no tienes una novia?"

"I do have a girl!" Emiliano says. "A few weeks ago we was in EasLos at El Pino."

"¿Qué? Why not bring her then?" Ricardo looks over his shoulder then switches lanes to merge onto another freeway. Both he and Sofía reach into the nachos, eager to hear more about Emiliano's mystery woman.

One of Selena's most popular hits, "Amor Prohibido," comes on and Sofía raises the volume.

Emiliano takes a large bite of his burrito, stalling as he comes up with an excuse. "She was busy tonight," he says loudly between chews. Then nods, pleased with his basic answer.

"Darn! Well, at least now I got a girl to shop with!" Sofía says.

"Y'all don't got the same style, Sofía." Emiliano takes another large bite to ease the awkwardness he feels welling inside of him.

"C'mon don't be loco, Emiliano. I'm sure we do."

"I don't think so," Emiliano mumbles.

Sofía sighs. "Well, thank you." She turns back around and gazes out the windshield as she picks up another nacho.

"Thank you?" Ricardo questions, glancing over at his girlfriend.

"Well yeah. I mean if Emiliano sayin' my style is *that* good...that it don't even compare..."

"That's not what I said, Sof." Emiliano chuckles.

"Well, that's what I heard," Sofía says.

"Eres una chica atrevida." Ricardo laughs.

"Y por eso me amas." Sofía leans over and kisses Ricardo's cheek.

As they get close to the suburbs, they coast on the freeway, only hitting a few pockets of light traffic. They all finish their meals and continue listening to Selena's top hits. Emiliano looks out the window and thinks about Rachel and her beautiful white skin. Beautiful white skin—three words he never imagined he'd group together.

A nervous ache arises in him, knowing that with each second they get closer to his house, he is one second closer to facing Rachel's text message. Confrontation was never a pleasant thing for him growing up. Family members and ex-lovers all moved on from issues without solving them, fostering a "get over it" attitude. The dynamic made confrontation hard for him, as the only types he knows about involve break-ups and unfavorable emotions, and sometimes knives or sirens.

They exit the freeway and pull into the neighborhood, each noticing some of the houses are extra lively—lots of lights on, loud music, people funneling in and out of wide open front doors, and a few dogs off leashes. Emiliano unbuckles as Ricardo rounds the cul-de-sac.

"Thanks for driving. I'll hit you up this week, man." Emiliano gives Ricardo a fist bump then exits the car. Sofia waves goodbye, then places a new stick of gum in her mouth. After a few good pops, she sinks deeply into the seat as they drive off.

Emiliano pulls out his phone and rereads Rachel's message—so short and full of contempt. He decides he'll put off the confrontation until tomorrow, then goes inside his house.

After greeting Mila he lies down on the couch and can't help but ruminate over the outdoor concert and Rachel, and what that interaction would have looked like. Rachel just won't leave his mind. Rachel. Rachel. Rachel.

Then, his phone rings. Of course it's her name lighting up the phone screen. His finger lingers over the answer button as he mentally prepares himself. And then, he answers.

"What the hell? You made plans with me then didn't see me?" Rachel slams her front door and walks down the porch steps to go for a walk.

"I—"

Before Emiliano gets a word in, Rachel continues, "Don't make plans if you're going to stand me up. That's rude!"

"Well don't get so attached to me!" Emiliano says rashly.

"What?" Rachel wonders what he means, as they clearly have built a romantic attachment over the last several months. Plus, as a psychology student, she has learned so much about this in school: attachment is simply part of human nature, something our ancestor's needed to survive, something every human needs.

Emiliano doesn't answer. He doesn't know what to say.

"What are you so afraid of?" she says.

Feeling overwhelmed, Emiliano puts up his defenses like he's going to emotional battle, and prepares to keep Rachel at a distance like she is the enemy. It feels like his two worlds—his culture and his love—are crashing. "I bet you just want any guy in your life. You don't even care if it's me!" he hollers.

In shock, she refuses to muster an ounce of energy defending herself, knowing that he too knows the truth. Nothing of their love is fabricated. Not one detail dramatized. Not one element made up. She remains silent and stunned.

"I bet you just want somethin' for fun…not even thinkin' long-term!" he yells. "And you don't really feel for me! You just fantasize about us!"

"You know none of that's true." She scoffs. "So you're just afraid of love, Emiliano?"

"God, you're so annoying!" he yells.

"No. You're so annoying!"

Again, they find themselves enveloped by silence, but this one feels the most sour.

"Hold up for a sec," Emiliano says, attitude in his voice. "I gotta look up why my dawg bein' so anxious."

"What's going on with Mila?" Rachel asks.

"It's like…I'm just tryna *take this girl out for a walk* and she keeps *freakin' out* and gettin' *way too concerned with random things*."

Rachel's brows furrow. Reaching the stoplight, she presses the pedestrian button.

Emiliano continues, "Well, she is an *American* dawg, so that makes sense. Next time Imma just get me a *Mexican* dawg."

Rachel's brows are still squeezed together. Just trying to take her out? Concerned with random things? Is she overanalyzing this or… "You're not talking about Mila are you? You're talking about me?" Rachel's voice lowers, her stomach now churning, feeling like curdled butter.

"You're a fucking fool. Of course I'm talking about my girlfriends…And my next one better be Mexican!"

"What did you just say to me?" Rachel asks, dumbfounded.

"I said I don't care about you!" Emiliano hollers. It's a lie. Of course, it's a lie. One of the biggest lies he's ever forced himself to believe.

"Goodbye, Emiliano."

"What?" he says.

"Just say goodbye. I'm not hanging up on you."

"Well I'm not done ta—"

"Bye." Rachel cuts him off.

"You sound like a child!" he hollers.

After Rachel says one more goodbye, Emiliano mumbles "goodnight" then hangs up the phone. He lets out a sigh and sinks into the couch. He is unsure what all he said. It feels as though he blacked out during the phone call.

Rachel, also unsure of what happened, stands unmoving on the sidewalk in the darkness. She looks down at her feet, unable to think properly. Tears well in her eyes, distorting her vision. A few silent sniffles turn into cries. She stuffs her sleeves over her face. His words about his next girlfriend being Mexican echo through her mind.

Trying to collect herself, she walks toward a street lamp and sits down on a brick wall underneath the poorly lit light. She feels like if love were a potion, theirs is as pure as it comes, yet he is practically begging for the antidote.

A few car lights flash by Rachel on the road. It's past midnight, so she heads down the street toward her house. Unwilling to listen to her anxious brain replay their conversation again, she takes out her phone and puts on "Nobody's Clown" by Los Yesterdays, the perfect song to describe how she feels. She walks into the road and dances, knowing it'll be the perfect cure to get her out of her funk. Not many cars are out, so likely she won't be interrupted. She's hoping to not waste more than a meager moment being sad over a boy. On the double yellow lines, she grooves to the music, twirling, twisting, and feeling her energy.

When the songs final verse commences, Rachel jogs to the sidewalk and turns onto her street. She sees the living room light on through the front window. With her shirt sleeve, she wipes at her eyes to clear any remaining tears or wetness as she opens the front door. Shannon is sitting on the sofa reading.

"Mom, why are you awake?"

"Just checking to make sure you're safe." Shannon looks up from her book and pulls down her reading glasses. "Why are your eyes so puffy?"

"I don't know, Mom…allergies from the pollen," Rachel says with attitude as she sniffles. She feels bad for taking out her frustration on her mother, a completely innocent bystander caught in the crossfire. Rachel wipes her nose with her sleeve as she heads upstairs. "Goodnight."

"What happened, Rachel?" Shannon sets her book down and follows behind her daughter, knowing she has never gotten allergies during pollenating season in the twenty plus years they have lived in Southern California.

"I don't want to talk about it." Rachel rounds the corner toward her room, rolling her eyes. Before Shannon can say anything, Rachel turns around. "Fine. I've been seeing this man. He's the most amazing human I've ever met! I had no idea someone like him could even exist!" She pauses, getting choked up. "And I don't know what just happened."

They walk into Rachel's room and Rachel paces in circles, explaining what transpired during her and Emiliano's call. A few sighs, head shakes, and hand-on-forehead moments tag along for the story. Shannon sits quietly, listening to her distraught daughter who's clearly in love.

"And as someone with a psychology degree, I'm racking my brain, knowing there must be some internal conflict, because I know he cares about me! He's pushing me away because he loves me!" Rachel looks at her mother with helpless eyes.

"That's awesome that you know what could be causing the behavior, Rachel. But…"

"But what?" Rachel looks at her mom, concerned.

"But maybe you just need to look at the facts, honey." Shannon sighs. "He's pushing you away…not pulling you closer."

23 Another World

The heat from the Arizona sun beats on the windowpane. Rachel rolls over, slowly opening her eyes as she pulls the blankets off her body. She looks around at the paintings, the taupe walls, and the brown bedspread. Even after four days of sleeping in this room, she still forgets that she is at her grandmother Tilly's house. Everything has been one continuous blur since the unfavorable exchange with Emiliano.

It's her fifth and final day visiting with her grandmother. The trip has been enjoyable and needed—filled with hiking, arts and crafts, and intellectual discussions about the political state of America and human consciousness. Each morning, Rachel reluctantly recalls how time has been passing in accordance with Emiliano. It's been fourteen days since she has seen him, eight days since they spoke on the phone, and nine hours since he last reached out to her.

Stretching her arms out, she—not so eagerly—sits up and leans against the headboard. Her phone buzzes on the bedside table. After rubbing her eyes, she unplugs it and finds a message from Hannah at the top of the screen.

Where are you and Emiliano? We miss you!

A look of disappointment washes over Rachel; she misses Hannah and soccer. Below Hannah's text is a new one from Emiliano, sent just three hours ago. Rachel clicks on the message, then scrolls through her conversation with him—more so, the one-sided string of messages spanning the last few weeks, in which she is on the receiving end.

I wish we could be cuddled up in bed right now.

I miss you.

Rachel?

So you're ignoring me now?

Please talk to me.

Hey! Read this article. This actress from one of the movies we watched is a therapist (:

Hi…

Rachel, can you please respond?

Her fingers linger over the keyboard for a moment. She desperately wishes to reply, but sets her phone down. The one phrase she didn't see in any of his messages was *I'm sorry*. Additionally, *My next girlfriend better be Mexican* runs through her mind.

Rachel gets out of bed and solemnly walks down the hallway to the kitchen, where a fresh pot of dark roast coffee greets her. After filling a blue ceramic mug to the brim, she slumps down at the kitchen table. Usually, she puts oat milk in her coffee, but she doesn't feel like diluting the energy-giving substance.

"Good morning, Rachel! There should be a fresh pot of coffee ready," Tilly says, coming down the hallway with her cane.

"Good morning, Grandma." Rachel lifts the black coffee to her lips.

"Oh good, you already got some." Tilly smiles and turns into the kitchen. The only noise is the liquid pouring into her mug. "You haven't been your cheery self this entire week." Tilly adds a bit of cream and sugar, then carefully carries her *I love grandma* mug to the kitchen table.

Rachel isn't sure how to respond. She inhales the bitter chestnut smell and takes another sip. "I'm just stressed about my applications."

"You and I both know how brilliant you are. You already know you're going to get into school."

Rachel stares intensely into her mug, the dark liquid resemblant of a black hole. Her mind sinks deeper and deeper into it.

"No." Tilly lets out a slight laugh, shaking her head. "I know that look."

"What look?" Rachel stalls for a beat before lifting her gaze and locking eyes with Tilly.

"You're in love."

"Yeah."

"What's his name?"

"Emiliano."

"What happened?"

Rachel's mouth opens, hesitating. "I'm not…I'm not Mexican."

"Well that makes sense." Tilly sips her steamy coffee. Her slurping fills the silence.

Rachel looks at her grandmother, dumbfounded.

"Do you know everything on our plate comes from the hard work of the bracero?" Tilly says.

"The what?" Rachel asks.

"Bracero…Mexican workers. Whether it's planting, harvesting, picking, animal care, or slaughter, even food packaging."

Rachel takes a long sip of coffee, her brows furrowing. How could food have anything to do with Emiliano not wanting to be with her?

Tilly studies Rachel's face, then continues, "These workers are underpaid, not often given citizenship, treated as underclass or lesser than…And it's not just the food workers. It's many Mexicans and Mexican Americans in general who are treated that way."

"And the American system gives White people the best chance at upward mobility," Rachel adds.

"And they have to be aware of ICE coming into neighborhoods to deport their loved ones." Tilly looks disgusted by the thought of such a program. "These are things you have never had to face."

"So…maybe he has more important things to worry about," Rachel takes a deep breath, "then getting wrapped up with a girl who seems to be from another world…"

Tilly finishes her coffee, then heads into the kitchen to wash her mug. Rachel lifts her leg onto the chair, hugging it tight to her body. She is not pleased with the idea that she and Emiliano cannot be together because of their cultural and racial differences. Tears slowly invade her eyes, nearly mirroring the faucet that is running in the kitchen.

"But I love him!" Rachel hollers. "I would do anything!"

Tilly turns the faucet off and looks down at a kitchen towel. "Are you going to dye your skin and hair and turn into someone of Mexican descent?"

One tear falls down Rachel's cheek and lands on the table. Her chin quivers. "No." She looks down at the ground. "That's impossible," she says, her voice getting smaller with each word. She wipes at her eyes and cheeks. After a few more sniffles and sighs, she is still unsatisfied. "But love can transcend cultural bounds!"

Tilly relaxes her shoulders, allowing the silence to speak. She walks over to her granddaughter and gives her a gentle pat on the back. "Yes…but not if fear is stronger."

Rachel reaches for her mug, now containing only mere dribbles of coffee and a few grainy grounds. She stares into the emptiness, feeling quite empty herself. After twisting the mug in her hand for a few moments, she sets it down and slumps in her chair.

Tilly takes the mug to the kitchen, hoping she didn't come across too harshly. She knows the simple fact of the matter is this: if a man is concerned with her culture, race, or ethnic background, then Rachel should believe him. While cleaning the mug, Tilly notices the unused pans on the stove. "Do you want breakfast before you head out, Rachel?"

"Eh. No thanks, Grandma. I'll get something on the road." Rachel sniffles.

"It's almost eleven. You might beat tonight's rush hour traffic if you leave soon."

"Yeah, I just need to shower and finish packing."

Rachel heads to the guestroom and Tilly continues cleaning the kitchen. As Tilly scrubs the counter top, she can't help but sigh and shake her head while mulling over her granddaughter's predicament. Life is too short to waste time on someone who is unsure about pursuing a relationship. She grabs a few granola bars and dried fruits from the minimal options in her cupboard and packs them in a large Ziploc bag for Rachel, for her drive home.

Twenty minutes later, the luggage wheels bump across the tile down the hallway. Ziploc bag in hand, Tilly rounds the corner, meeting Rachel at the front door. "Please take these in case you get hungry!"

Rachel smiles as she takes the snack bag. The two women make eye contact. Tilly can see the sorrow in Rachel's eyes. "Everything will unfold in due time, sweetie. Thanks for coming to visit." Tilly kisses Rachel on the cheek, then embraces her in a warm, tight hug.

"I'll see you soon, Grandma. I love you."

When they walk outside, they are immediately encircled by the dry Arizonan heat. Tilly sits on the bench in the front yard and blows a few kisses as Rachel backs out of the driveway.

Water fills Rachel's eyes as she pulls off her grandma's street. Yes, the end of a family visit makes her sad, but also their hard talk won't leave her mind. Cultures. Love. Fear. Emiliano. Deciding to leave all her tears in Arizona, Rachel takes a few deep breaths to settle her emotions.

As she calms, she is suddenly made aware of the sweat beads coursing down her back. It feels like there is nothing between her and the scorching sun. She turns on the air, then studies the landscape out the windshield. There's not a cloud in the sky and nothing but orange desert rocks and sand for miles.

She turns onto the I-95, the first of four freeways for the drive home. To occupy her mind, she puts on a true crime podcast. While her trip to Lake Havasu City is coming to an end, her journey home is not simply a return trip, but rather a new beginning. After all, she is bringing new knowledge with her to Old Oak.

24 Derecha, Derecha

The last dribble of cold beer and froth slides down the glass into Emiliano's mouth. He sets the cup firmly on the bar counter, then wipes his lips with the back of his hand. A small burp escapes him, though it goes unheard by the other bar goers. The sports watchers and drunkards around him are much too consumed with cheering, small talk, and clinking glasses.

Ricardo exits the restroom from across the bar and Emiliano watches as his friend sways from side to side, though he can't tell if it's Ricardo stumbling or his own eyesight. As someone who doesn't drink much, four beers in two hours has given Emiliano a strong buzz—meandering somewhere between tipsy and drunk.

"Ay, foo, you wanna get another one?" Ricardo asks as he sits down on a bar stool.

Emiliano lets out a hesitant grumble, his consternation due to the fact that Rachel has been out of town all week. He saw a few pictures she posted with her grandma, and he knows she might finally be home. While it might have been easy for her to ignore him from far away, he is sure that she won't be able to ignore him in the same town. He looks down at his watch that is seemingly blurry and reads that it is almost 7:00 p.m. "Nah, man. I'm real tipsy honestly."

When they get up from their seats, Emiliano kneads his back, attempting to rub out tight knots from work. They maneuver their way around drunk people and sports-filled TV screens and walk out of the rowdy bar. Emiliano drags slowly behind Ricardo: drunk-ish and physically in pain are not a good combination.

As they get into Ricardo's truck, Emiliano pulls out his phone and starts to draft a message to Rachel. Some of his words aren't typed coherently, so he hits the backspace button and retries until his letters and words are in the correct order.

Rachel, Imma call you in fifteen minutes. Please answer.

"Not used to being in your passenger seat." Emiliano looks around the car as he buckles his seatbelt. "So used to Sofía bein' with us."

Ricardo looks over at Emiliano. "You been actin' different, man."

"Nah, fam. I'm aight." Emiliano sighs. "Just buzzin'."

"I'm not used to seeing you drink cuatro cervezas!" Ricardo chuckles as he backs out of the parking spot.

"Just knew it'd help my back pain." Emiliano looks out the passenger window as they drive out of the lot, past oak trees, street lights, and dimly lit lampposts. He scorns as he watches a light flicker. "What is with the lampposts in this town? They all screwed up! How can we see in the dark if there's barely any light?" He feels like he's stuck in the dark with love, with Rachel.

"¿Qué?" Ricardo wonders why Emiliano seems so concerned with such a trivial thing.

Emiliano doesn't reply and just stares out the window.

A few minutes later, they pull into the back alleyway. The old black Firebird is in Emiliano's driveway. A couple of boxed end wrenches are near it on the concrete. Emiliano stares at the unfinished job as he exits the car. "Thanks for pickin' me up, man," he says, giving Ricardo a fist bump.

"No problem! Good luck with your car, hermano. I'm always here for anything."

As Ricardo's pickup truck rumbles down the road, Emiliano glares at the tools, frustrated that he didn't get more done today—he began struggling when Rachel came to mind. The moment was like a portal, resurfacing a memory from a few years prior, when he was fixing cars thinking about his ex-girlfriend.

Working on cars has always come so naturally to him, and he loves getting lost in the meditational aspect of it. However, when going through troubles with women, cars have had the opposite effect. Rather than being a source of calmness while focusing on the minute details, he thinks about all the intangible things he can't seem to fix. And since his mind is occupied, he ignores what he's doing on the car, which leads to him not fixing the tangible things in front of him. The vicious cycle leaves him feeling incompetent and unworthy.

He gets in the driver's seat of his Firebird and puts his hands on the wheel, imagining that his car is running. Images flash in his mind of Rachel and him driving around town together, driving down to the boulevards of Los Angeles. Rachel would be impressed by the low riders. Then *Chicano* couples would pass by in their cars. The females would stare while the tough-as-nails men would use their hydraulic systems to bounce their rides. And Rachel wouldn't fit in.

His fantasy ends. He looks through the windshield as his eyes get watery. With so much frustration building, he leans over and punches the passenger seat cushion. Then, he punches it again. And again. And again.

In the deafening night silence, his phone buzzes. He quickly picks it up, hoping there will be a message from Rachel. It's from his mother saying that she won't be home tonight. His eyes sink. He doesn't understand why Rachel hasn't gotten over their phone call, thinking that if she would just forget about it, then everything would be fine. And then he wouldn't have to say sorry, because acknowledging that he said anything wrong or hurtful, things opposing the man he aims to be, would make him feel like a failure.

With liquid courage, he dials Rachel's phone number. He listens to the monotone sounds, convinced that in thirty seconds he'll reach her voicemail.

"Hello?" Rachel says blandly.

The familiar voice sounds like paradise to him. After a few seconds, he mumbles into the phone, "It's not olden times. This should be OK. I should…we should be able to do this. It's…" Emiliano scoffs. "Things should be different!"

No noise comes from Rachel's end as she merely listens to his plea, knowing he is inebriated and speaking to himself.

"Rachel?" In his tipsiness he forgot she had already answered the phone. "How are you? I miss you…" he whispers.

"Do not ask me how I'm doing! If you're not calling to apologize I will hang up this phone right now!" Rachel pauses, feeling bad for her sternness, but she knows she has to stand up for herself and let him know that she will not be treated poorly. And how dare he try to play down their love. How dare he ever say his next girlfriend better be Mexican. Hearing nothing on the other end, she hesitantly continues, "I will drop you like a fucking penny out of my pocket, Emiliano. And never pick it back up! I will not tolerate that in my life." She hopes her words sound more convincing than they do in her head.

"I'm—I'm sorry, Rachel!" He stammers. "I'm sorry! Baby, I didn't mean any of that stuff I said. I was just hotheaded, frustrated in the moment."

"I don't want excuses."

"Aw, baby." Emiliano sighs. "Listen…I just…I been…tryna convince myself I don't care, that this ain't much...But I know I'm only sayin' that cause I do care." Again nothing comes through the phone from her end, as if they are playing a game of silent tag back and forth. Emiliano continues, "I miss you. I think about you all the time, Rachel...You busy tonight?"

"Not really. Just unpacking my things right now."

"My car's still not runnin', otherwise I'd be at your house." Emiliano gets out of his car and collects the tools. "Can you please come pick me up? I wanna see you."

"Absolutely not," Rachel says with attitude.

"Why not? Baby, please! Please come see me. You know I'd be at your house right now if I had a car!"

"Absolutely not! After what you said on the phone, I have no reason to go out of my way to see you."

"Well...what if I get a ride to you, Rach? Can I come see you if I find a ride?" Was everything he said really that bad? To where she doesn't even care to see him?

"Sure, if you can find a ride."

"OK, Rach...Bye." Emiliano can tell by Rachel's tone that she doesn't think he'll be coming. Little does she know how desperately he wishes to see her. As they get off the phone, his mind races, trying to come up with any possible way to get to her house. Uber? Lyft? Maybe he could ask his mom. Local *raitero* services? Homies? Should he bike? Walk?

He sends text messages out to practically everyone he knows. Keeping his eyes on his phone, he heads into his house to freshen up, anxiously awaiting responses. A few come in back to back. The first one says *I'm sorry I've been drinking I can't drive.* Another says *sorry foo. I'm busy.* Emiliano sits down on the couch and calls Mila over to him. "Hi girl. How's my Mila?"

Mila sits between Emiliano's legs, welcoming his whisker rubs and love. His phone buzzes and he jerks around to look at the screen. One of his neighborhood friends says he's busy getting down in EasLos, otherwise he would drive him. As each "no" comes in, Emiliano sinks further into the couch, feeling smaller and smaller.

Then, another message comes in, this time from Pablo. *Yeah man. I ain't busy. I'll be at your house in five.*

Emiliano gives Mila a pat on the head, then walks to his closet. A little cologne and deodorant, followed by putting on his baseball cap with the red rim, and Emiliano is as ready as he can be. He exits his house and heads down the sidewalk. Shortly after, Pablo rounds the cul-de-sac and pulls up to the front of his house.

"Thank you man. I appreciate you," Emiliano says, jumping into the passenger seat.

The two exchange a handshake before Pablo heads out of Emiliano's neighborhood.

"Where ya goin?" Pablo asks.

"Rachel's."

"I think I remember how to get there, but you maybe gotta help when we get closer."

Emiliano nods, then raps along to Pablo's favorite '90s hip-hop playlist blasting through the stereo. They drive past a slew of dimly lit lampposts. Emiliano looks at them, then looks around the car. He notices a condom in one of the cupholders. "Hey Pablo, can I have that?"

Pablo makes a turn then looks over to see what Emiliano is talking about. He smirks when he sees the condom in Emiliano's hand. "Damn, carnal. It's all yours!"

Nonchalantly, Emiliano slips the condom into his pocket. His heart picks up speed as they get closer to her house. "Derecha, derecha," Emiliano says quickly so Pablo doesn't miss the turn. They skirt onto her street.

Rachel hears tire screeches through her open window. She tosses a dirty shirt in the hamper then skeptically peeks outside, thinking there is no way it's Emiliano. She spots Pablo's brown suburban pulling away and her favorite handsome man standing by his lonesome outside. Without a second thought, she runs out of her bedroom and bolts down the stairs faster than she has ever run, including Christmas morning as a child.

She collects herself before opening the front door. Walking down the porch steps, she remains expressionless, her gaze on Emiliano. He is standing at the foot of her driveway, just fifteen feet away from her.

For a few moments they stare at each other, then Emiliano takes one step up the driveway.

"Can I please hug you?" he asks.

Rachel nods.

They walk until they meet in the middle. Emiliano curls his arms around Rachel's torso, squeezing tightly. She folds into him, then hugs him back. They close their eyes, releasing all the stress from the last two weeks. Each one feeling an overwhelming sense of comfort, as if they have found their way back to their safe havens. The world around them melts away, and all they can feel, smell, and see is one another.

After a few minutes, Emiliano pulls out of the hug shaking his head. A look of concern washes over Rachel. His eyes squeeze shut for a brief moment. "I love you," he whispers. The words somehow make him feel both lighter and heavier. "Rachel, I—I'm in love with you. And it's hard for me to say that."

"I'm in love with you too," she whispers.

Holding each other tightly, they walk hand in hand onto Rachel's porch. Emiliano sucks air through his teeth, grimacing as he puts his hand over his back.

She looks at him as they curl up on the porch swing. "What's wrong?"

"Just messed up my back at work again." Emiliano looks longingly at Rachel. "I'm sorry about what I said and for yelling on the phone." He looks into her eyes, feeling bad that he tried pushing away their love. Of course she was looking for something long-term with him. Of course she feels for him. Of course it was more than just a fantasy to her. He didn't mean any of it, and places a delicate kiss on her forehead so that she knows that too.

"I know." Rachel's gaze lowers. She's glad that he finally apologized, though his phone call statements still make her feel wary.

For a while, they sit silently, grazing their hands against one another's, but not interlocking them. Emiliano feels awkward, out of place. Not wanting to overstay his welcome, he stands, stammering about how he better call an Uber to get home.

"Don't be silly. I'll grab my keys." Rachel walks to her front door, then looks back at him. "By the way, do you want your birthday present? It's not wrapped yet but—"

"You got me a birthday present?!" Emiliano asks.

Rachel huffs and rolls her eyes playfully, wondering why he is so surprised.

He walks to her and places his hands against her cheeks. As he looks into her eyes, he says, "Baby, won't you be with me on my birthday to give it to me then?"

A smile spreads across her face. She nods before walking into the house. Emiliano waits for her at the base of the porch steps thinking about his birthday and how by then he will work up the courage to introduce Rachel as his girlfriend to his family and friends.

After a beat, the door swings open. Without saying anything they get in the car. Emiliano looks over at Rachel as she backs out of the driveway, wondering what is going on in her mind.

"That was nice of Pablo," Rachel says.

"I know." Emiliano reaches into his pocket. "I got this from him too." He holds up the silver condom package.

"So you thought we were going to have sex?"

"Well…no." Emiliano puts it back in his pocket, feeling stupid for having pulled it out. "I just saw it in his car and asked if I could have it in case."

"Oh." Rachel laughs. "So you were trying to impress him?"

"What? No!"

"Well, we haven't used a condom, Emiliano." Rachel glances over at him. "You must have grabbed it to be like 'Hell yeah, bro! Look at me! I might get laid tonight,'" she says, mimicking Emiliano's deep voice.

Ready to defend his actions, his mouth opens, but all that comes out is "Rach, why you so funny?"

She blushes, shrugging. When they pull onto the back alley Emiliano tells her to park against the curb behind his Firebird. They come to a stop, the only sound the low rumbling of the running car. They stare at the world on the other side of the windshield—the peppertrees and oak trees, the condos, the night sky.

"You wanna come in? We can listen to music or watch a movie. Nobody's gonna be home tonight." He opens the passenger door and the car lights go on, illuminating their faces in the darkness.

Rachel bites her lip. Her hands clutch the steering wheel, both body and mind telling her to drive home, to still feel wary about their unfavorable phone call. But her heart tells her to let go of the steering wheel. She loosens her grip and exits the car.

When they enter the living room, all the lights are off and a peaceful silence fills the downstairs. Mila runs over and greets them. They sit down on the couch and, almost immediately, Rachel starts scrolling through the music on her phone.

"So no movie then?" Emiliano asks.

"No," Rachel mumbles, her head lightly shaking.

"All Night Long" by Mary Jane Girls begins to fill the room. Emiliano puckers his lips, looking at her. She smiles coyly, then puckers hers too. Their lips slowly press into each other. Ten pecks follow, where they barely lean out, then press back in—a game of *are you gone?* and *no, I'm still here.* He leans his chest and torso over her body. She slowly leans back, allowing him to get on top of her. Their lips continue to mingle, both of them getting lost in a lustful passion.

"Baby, let's move to the bed." Emiliano gets off the couch and holds out his hand. Instantly, Rachel places her hand in his. They squeeze by the side table, duck under the stairs, and lie down.

One by one, their clothing items are tossed around the room—the edge of the bed, the floor, the couch, the side table. Rachel gets on top of Emiliano's naked body, now in full surrender, openness, and vulnerability. He tucks her hair behind her ear, then gazes at her nakedness straddled atop him. First, her chin, then neck and shoulders, lastly admiring her breasts and lean, feminine hourglass shape.

She watches his jade green eyes, noticing the depth of his masculine presence. Her body gently presses into his. Her wet lips leave lines of love from his cheek to his lips to his ear to his neck. He lets out an aching groan, gently placing his hand around her neck. Their eyes lock—his say, *Baby, let me take you* and hers say, *Baby, please take me.* As Emiliano enters Rachel, they let time slip away, indulging in each other.

"I love you," Emiliano says as they place their foreheads together.

"I love you," Rachel repeats. "I missed you."

"I missed you." Emiliano hugs her tightly.

They continue to echo each other's phrases. Declarations of love are followed with caressing touches, tender kisses, and passionate gazes.

As their bodies rock back and forth, Emiliano holds Rachel's face and looks into her eyes. "Ride me like you missed me, baby," he whispers.

Rachel looks into Emiliano's eyes lovingly. Their bodies move faster and faster, gliding each other into a different dimension, where they join together in a symphony of passionate moans and lustful groans. Between their heavy breathing, their eyes meet again.

"Baby, I love you," Rachel says achingly.

"I want this forever," Emiliano says.

Rachel's body slows as she processes Emiliano's words. She leans forward, cups her hands against his rosy cheeks, and looks into his eyes to uncover whether or not his words were spoken truth. Emiliano stares back, truly looking at Rachel with eyes of forever. He loves her, he truly loves her. His love-radiating gaze is one Rachel has never seen in her entire life—it's a portrait she knows she will never forget.

25 En Caliente Ni Se Siente

"You found her clothes on the living room floor?" Rachel asks, making sure she heard Hannah correctly.

Hannah scuffs her foot against the hiking trail. A cloud of dirt puffs into the air. "Yeah. I got home from work, walked in the living room, and her shorts, underwear, bra, and t-shirt were next to the couch. I sat down and stared at them for at least 20 minutes."

Rachel quickens her pace to catch up to her antsy best friend. Hannah's legs are noticeably thinner—the smallest they've been since the two women were in high school. Rachel wonders if her weight loss is from lovesickness, an eating disorder, or something else entirely.

Hannah continues, "He came out of our bedroom to make dinner…for all three of us. And she came out of her room a little while later. I just couldn't get it out of my head, wondering why the hell her clothes were on the floor."

"Well did she pick them up?"

"Not right away. No. The clothes sat there all during dinner. I didn't talk at all. Only they did. I just stared at the clothes. Stared and stared." Hannah looks down at her dirty running shoes, wetness pooling in her eyes. "Then a couple tears rolled down my cheek. Brax asked why I was crying and I just told them I had a hard day at work."

"So you didn't ask him about it?!"

Hannah abruptly stops, picking a yellow flower off a bush. She faces Rachel, hand on hip with a sassy look on her face. "Of course I did!" She starts plucking the flower's petals. "I asked him to go on a walk with me outside. Then was like, 'Why were her clothes on the floor?' He got *very* annoyed and said, 'I don't know! Why can't you just trust me? I haven't been home all day. How am I supposed to know what she was doing?'"

The flower in Hannah's hand has been plucked to a mere stem. She tosses it over her shoulder and resumes walking. She wants to trust Brax. She kind of does trust Brax. But what is with his relationship with Alexis? It seems like ever since Annoying Alexis came into their lives, Brax has grown distant.

Rachel again hurries to catch up with Hannah's speed walking, their running shoes making crunching sounds against the dirt trail. Not knowing what to say, Rachel takes a deep breath of fresh oak tree air. She looks at the flowering bushes on the side of the trail, glad to see the vibrant colors. The California mountains had been affected by many wildfires over the last few years.

"So what do you think?" Hannah asks nervously, afraid of Rachel's long silence.

"I don't know, Hannah. His story could be true? Who knows if that girl had a guy over during the day. Does she seem like someone who loves attention from guys?"

"Yeah. And she's really pretty. She has perfect skin. Huge double D's. Bleach blonde hair. An obnoxious flirty laugh that goes a little something like this." Hannah giggles with a fake twinkle in her eye. "I've heard it one too many times in this lifetime." She rolls her eyes.

Rachel grimaces, knowing the situation doesn't sound too good for Hannah. When and where would Hannah have heard Alexis's flirty laugh? In their apartment...with Brax?

As they exit the trailhead, walking into the dirt parking lot, Hannah takes off her sweaty shirt, exposing her slender upper arms and stomach. Her ribs are slightly poking out.

"Have you been eating, Hannah?"

"Yeah, I'm fine. I've been eating really healthy so I've lost a few pounds." As the words come out, Hannah internally cringes at herself. She hates being sneaky toward her best friend. And, lately, she's been sneakier than ever—hiding truths or telling half-truths with pretty much everyone who's important to her.

"All right. Well, don't lose anymore...there's nothing left to lose!" Rachel says lightheartedly, knowing her best friend is lying to her. As much as she wants to ask more questions, she won't. She never wants to pry. If Hannah wants to share, she will. And if she doesn't, then she won't. It's as simple as that.

"You know what's funny, Rach?" Hannah says, eager to change topics. "I was thinking...how come we never do group hangouts? Or double dates? I've never even hung out with Emiliano or really seen you two together."

Rachel looks off in the distance as they reach the backside of their cars. "You know...I've never thought about that before, Hannah." She bites her bottom lip. "Now that you say that...I'm realizing Emiliano and I don't *ever* hang out with *anyone*. It's always only us two, which is romantic but...he's never met my family and I've barely met his."

"What? How long have you guys been seeing each other?"

"Around five months." Rachel shoots Hannah a concerned look. She will still hold out hope because she loves him. She loves him enough to wait, enough to keep dreaming of one day. "Now that I think about it, Emiliano and I have never even eaten together inside a restaurant. We always eat in the car. We hang out when and where nobody is around…"

"Damn, Rach." Hannah shakes her head. "What's he hiding you or something?"

"I don't know. I always felt like everything we did was intimate."

"Why are guys the way they are?" Hannah says, rolling her eyes again.

"I don't know. What do you mean?" Rachel asks.

"Like…we are two fucking awesome girls. Why do we have these romantic issues?"

Rachel shrugs, not knowing what to say.

After a few moments of silence, they both rattle off reasons why they better get going—Rachel is heading to Emiliano's because they planned a date to The Peak of the Earth and Hannah has errands.

Rachel follows behind Hannah out of the dirt lot. The clear blue skies, vibrant greenery, and seventy degree weather are beyond beautiful, but she can't focus on any of it. Hannah's comment about "romantic issues" is stuck in her brain. Was Hannah correct in clumping Brax and Emiliano in the same realm? Surely, they can't be. Unless the standard is *men who claim you (1) with integrity (2) to their world*. Perhaps neither Brax nor Emiliano fully fit that definition. Brax doesn't know a thing about integrity and Emiliano hasn't shown his world—his family, friends, and culture—that he loves her.

Suddenly, Rachel's phone buzzes, bringing her into the present moment. When she gets to the stoplight she picks it up. There's a text message from Emiliano.

Hi beautiful. I hope you had a great morning! Are you on your way?

She smiles at the text and quickly responds.

Guapisimooooo! Yes, I'm almost at your house!

When she gets onto his cul-de-sac a few minutes later, he's waiting at the curb.

"Rach, you're too funny," he says as he gets in the car.

"What? Why?"

"How the hell you know the word guapisimo?!" He reaches across the console for their handshake. The movements are now so familiar that it all happens seamlessly, airing more on the stable side of love than on excited lust.

"Well the other day I was thinking I should learn Spanish pet names."

"For real?" Emiliano lets out a chuckle.

Rachel smirks, thinking about the hour she spent at her kitchen table researching the perfect pet names for a Mexican man: *guapísimo, mi vida, mi alma, mi rey, papi*, among others. *Guapísimo* was her favorite because the term is regarded for those with the highest degree of handsomeness. And, in her book, that's Emiliano.

On the way out of the neighborhood, they decide to stop and get snacks. They pass by the *panadería* and Flores de Felicia and pull in front of the grocery store. When they walk through the automatic doors, Rachel looks over at Emiliano thinking about her conversation with Hannah. Emiliano, noticing her intense gaze, playfully pushes up against her as they walk down the candy aisle. She giggles, thinking perhaps she was worried over nothing. Here he is claiming her to the world, right? He's flirting with her in a grocery store in their hometown. Anyone could be here.

While she grabs a family size bag of Takis, he picks up Mike and Ikes and Junior Mints. Then, they head toward the refrigerated drinks, Rachel walking slightly in front of him. He grips the candy in his hands, while keeping his eyes on the real candy: Rachel and her backside, especially how she looks in her tight, high-waisted Levi shorts. She looks over her shoulder to say something and catches him staring.

"Don't mind me...just checkin' you out." Emiliano grins so wide Rachel can practically see all his teeth.

After grabbing a Sprite and a Dr. Pepper, they walk to self-checkout. While Emiliano scans their items, Rachel thinks about how beautiful he looks. Her curiosity about Emiliano being in the same category as Brax has now diminished. Wishful thinking and his magnetism simply melted the thoughts away. A new thought teases her mind: they simply have intimate, one-on-one time. And she doesn't mind their relationship being that way! The card reader beeps, prompting her to help grab their items.

As they walk out of the store, a middle-aged *Mexicano* with a bucket of cleaning supplies approaches them and asks if they need their windows cleaned. Rachel shakes her head as she looks over at Emiliano.

"Rach, I'll pay for it!" Emiliano says.

"Are you sure?" Rachel glances at her car windows; they're covered in bee pollen, dirt, and dust.

"¿Cuánto?" Emiliano asks the man.

"Veinte."

Emiliano gives him a $20 bill before getting in the car. They start jamming out to a playlist of '70s love songs while watching the man spray cleaning fluid on the glass. The dirt and dust wash away as he makes long drags across the windshield. His latex-gloved fingers rub tediously over the stubborn bee pollen. After a few minutes, he manages to scrape off most of it. Emiliano notes how hard it is to remove pollen spots, then Rachel emphasizes how sparkly clean the windshield looks.

The man picks up his supplies and heads to another window. Naturally, Rachel and Emiliano continue watching the oddly satisfying job.

"I really admire this kind of work," Emiliano says.

"Window cleaning?" she questions.

"Window cleaning, shoe shining, food carts, street performers, any sort of street job. Cause none of these people are begging for handouts. They are working hard for everything they got. In Mexico, alotta people are grindin' all day in the hot sun doin' this."

"Sun up to sun down? Yeah, that would be hard…"

"That's why I hate seein' people on buckets begging for money here in the States. They can still find ways to work for money, like this guy who's cleanin' windows!" Emiliano says.

"That's true, I guess. I hadn't thought about that."

As the man takes the cleaning tools to the driver's side, Emiliano opens the door and stands, straddling one foot in the car and one on the asphalt. "¿De dónde eres?" he asks.

"De la ciudad de México, pero vine de Texas." The man rubs the towel in circles soaking up any remaining water, then moves to the backseat window. They converse in Spanish about street vendor work in Mexico, and talk so fast it sounds like they're speaking in tongues to Rachel. The only words she catches are *ciudad* and *trabajo*. When the final window is clean, the man gathers his supplies.

"Hiciste un buen trabajo, hombre. Muchas gracias." Emiliano walks over and hands him a ten dollar bill.

"Ay Dios mío. Gracias. Gracias. This will help me and mi novia. We just stay at a hotel right now while we try to find a place to live."

"I know man. I get it." Emiliano gives him a firm handshake. "You guys are doing great work out here. Buena suerte con todo."

The man waves goodbye, then carries his supplies across the parking lot. As Emiliano gets back in the car, he makes a few kind remarks about the man's effort. Rachel agrees, looking at her sparkly windows.

"Thank you for paying," she says.

"Of course. That was a must." Emiliano buckles, then clasps his hands together on his lap. "Do you remember how to get to The Peak of the Earth?"

"I think so."

Rachel pulls out of the shopping center and heads toward the suburban overlook. She opens the sun roof and cracks the now spotless windows. Her hair flies around in the breeze. Emiliano admires her long tresses. They are bold and carefree, reaching over and touching him the same way Rachel has touched his heart.

He wishes he felt comfortable enough to share that with her, but the depth of it all scares him. So, rather than *tell* her, he takes out his cellphone and scrolls through his music to *show* her how he feels. Most often, he shows her with the way he delicately kisses her and touches her, but occasionally he'll use more subtle means, like song lyrics that mimic his feelings. He raises the volume as "Love…Can Be So Wonderful" by The Temprees comes through the stereo, and tries to convince himself that love really can be wonderful.

Rachel glances over at Emiliano, a soft smile resting below her rosy cheeks. Their eyes lock for a brief moment before she looks back at the road as they head up the windy hill. Emiliano looks out the window skeptically, making sure there are no other cars, no racist White men.

Once parked, Emiliano takes out their snacks. While munching on the junk food they stare out into the wondrous landscape, both recalling the time they shared their first kiss. Here. In this exact spot. Many months ago, on a day when the afternoon sun was so bright it was almost blinding. Now, they gaze into the mass of sunlit trees admiring their natural ebb and flow in the wind.

Rachel reaches for her phone, then pulls back. "Ah, shoot."

"What?" Emiliano asks.

"I was going to google something to show you but there's too much spicy gunk on my hands." Rachel looks around the car but doesn't see any napkins. Her bright red Taki-dusted fingers rest awkwardly in the air. "Can you please look for me, Emiliano?"

"Sure." Emiliano picks up Rachel's phone and navigates his way to the Safari app.

"OK, so just type in—"

"What is this, Rach?" Emiliano asks.

"What's what?"

"Your last Google search." Emiliano eyes the screen suspiciously as Rachel's face slowly grows more red. "Am I…a bad…person?" he reads with a questioning voice.

"Uh…um…er…well…" Rachel stammers. She never intended for him to see her Google search from the night before. "That's hard to explain!" she says nervously.

"You doin' something bad with me? *To* me?" Emiliano asks.

"What?" Rachel says, confused. "No. Of course not."

"Well why'd you look that up?"

"It's just sometimes I get nervous." And she won't go into further detail. What else is she supposed to think when the man she loves is wary about being with her or ditching her last minute? It was only natural for her to go through a checklist of questionable qualities to make sure she didn't in fact have them.

Emiliano continues to look at the odd search. The silence that ensues feels exploratory to him and extremely awkward to her. She gazes out the window, refusing to look at him. Anxiety and embarrassment spread through her entire body like ravaging diseases. Her heart rate accelerates. Her hands get clammy. Her mind starts running—so fast she feels like it has left her body and run down the mountain without her. *He's never going to speak to me ever again* repeats in her mind. For Rachel, the dramatic statement seems to be a very possible reality.

After thirty seconds, that seem like hours in hell to her, Emiliano leans across the console and plops one juicy, sloppy kiss on her lips, even making an audible *mmm* noise. All the tension in her body eases. Emiliano tries to keep a serious face, but his smile spreads like butter on warm toast.

"What?" she asks, feeling shy and awkward.

"It's just…you're *such* a girl." He shakes his head. "Of course you're not a bad person."

It's interesting how his actions are sometimes a cure to Rachel's anxiety while other times they cause it. In this case, Emiliano had the perfect response to her quirkiness. She looks at his shiny white teeth. Now, *I am so in love with you* echoes through her mind. Overwhelmed by the gratitude expanding her heart, she gives Emiliano a peck on his cheek.

"What's that peck for?" he asks.

"Thank you." She leaves another handful of kisses along the sweet treasures that are Emiliano's cheeks and lips, hoping they are hidden treasures for her *only*. Things that no other woman will ever explore.

Enamored by Rachel, Emiliano leans in, placing a hand on her hip. Their eyes close. Their tongues intertwine. He treads lightly though, not allowing himself to get too lost in the beauty of their passion in case someone surprises them again.

After a few minutes, he pulls out of the kisses and scans the area like a security guard. Happy to see no one in sight, he puts his hands against Rachel's cheeks and smooches her waiting mouth. A beat later he looks into her eyes. "So what do you want to work on, Rach?"

"Work on?"

"Like what's one thing you want to work on right now to better your life?"

"Hmm. That's a good question." In deep thought, she looks out into the sky. "Following my intuition…What about you?"

"Get back to doin' my stretch routine before work cause my back's been buggin' me."

"That's a good one!" Rachel says.

"Aight, we gotta do it then! En caliente ni se siente." Emiliano snaps his fingers.

"What does that mean?" Rachel asks.

"Well, it doesn't really make sense in English. Like the words mean 'in hot you can't even feel it.' But it's basically sayin' 'don't stop to think about it or overanalyze it. Just go after what you want. No holding back.'"

He continues staring into Rachel's eyes. Go after what you want. No holding back. Yeah, a stretch routine. Definitely at the top of his list.

"I like it." Rachel smiles. "¡En caliente ni se siente!" She repeats the popular Spanish phrase a few more times as they gaze deeply into each other's eyes. She repeats it until she can properly pronounce it, until it's etched in her memory.

26 The Triangle Structure

Perched at the dining table, Rachel takes one last glance at the birthday card she bought for Emiliano. *Feliz cumpleaños a ti* is written in big bubble letters across the front. She opens the card and gazes at her long message; originally, she was going to write something short and witty, but her love for him is too grand to go unacknowledged. Above her message is a Spanish phrase in cursive. Something about birthdays that she can't understand. After trying to figure it out, she jots down an attempted English translation, then in parenthesis writes *Emiliano, please teach me what this means.*

She puts the card in the envelope, licks the seal, scribbles *Emiliano* and a heart onto it, then tapes it to the gift bag, which is housing two presents: *Portraits* by Gunner Stahl and a packaged black Lakers shirt with a taped note that reads *because this will look soooo sexy tucked in your jeans.* Rachel grimaces looking into the bag, hoping he doesn't already have one or both items, otherwise she will feel embarrassed when he opens it. She lays a few sheets of tissue paper on the top then runs upstairs and puts the present in her closet.

With eagerness and unsettled nerves, she gets ready for soccer. Today she is especially excited because Emiliano invited her to come early while he and Pablo play basketball. While she is looking forward to seeing him play, the bulk of her excitement is over the fact that she'll *finally* get to hang out with someone in Emiliano's life other than his dog.

She hurries out of the house and heads for the park, flooring the gas as she leaves each stop sign and green light. Her overwhelming jitters simply cannot be contained. She skirts into the recreation center and pulls into a parking space just in front of the basketball court. The young men are talking, their backs facing Rachel's car.

Emiliano dribbles the ball down the court, then goes for a lay-up and misses. As he tosses the ball to Pablo, he spots Rachel walking their way. With a smile he says, "Hey! You ready to play some basketball?"

"Hell no." Rachel laughs. "I'm gonna watch!"

"Aw what? C'mon Rach!"

Pablo greets Rachel, then dribbles to the three point line and takes a shot.

After some cordial small talk between the three of them and Emiliano persuading her, Rachel reluctantly takes the ball to the basket for exactly *one* shot—and misses. Figuring it's better to save her energy for soccer, she gladly gives the ball to Emiliano.

"Let's just switch off playing one versus one? Rach, you play too!" Emiliano suggests.

"Let's play pig," Rachel says, smiling, happy with her childhood game suggestion.

"Aight, I'm down for that." Pablo nods, then gets in line behind Rachel.

Emiliano follows along, getting behind his best friend.

Rachel misses her first shot from the top of the key. The ball bounces off the rim and goes straight back to her. She hands the ball to Pablo for his turn and he successfully makes a lay-up. Emiliano chuckles about the easy shot, then makes it as well. When Rachel attempts, she misses. *P* for Rachel.

The following two rounds play out according to that blueprint—Pablo and Emiliano make their shots, Rachel doesn't. *P I G* for Rachel. Already out of the game, as she expected, she sits on the bench and watches the two men, paying extra close attention to Emiliano.

"We should all try to be on the same team today," Emiliano says. He goes up for a jump shot and makes it.

"Hell yeah! I'll make sure Hannah's on our team too," Rachel adds.

"We'll definitely win with all four of us," Pablo says with a chuckle. He does the same jump shot as Emiliano, but misses, accruing a *P*.

"Damn, esé, you gon' let me whoop yo' sorry ass at this game?" Emiliano teases.

"No mames. Este juego es pinche basura and you gonna be oinking by the end of it, güey," Pablo fires back.

While the men continue to banter over their not-so-dramatic game of pig in Spanglish, Rachel drifts off into thought, reflecting over her recent conversation with Hannah (again). On their hike, they were musing that her and Emiliano's love was private, a secret. Now, she is sure she was overthinking, because here she is, with Emiliano and one of his best friends.

Suddenly, the ball flies past her into the grass, bringing her out of her thoughts. She retrieves it for them, then watches the next few rounds as they go back and forth between staying tied or Emiliano having the lead. Eventually both men have the letters *P* and *I*. Now it's just a matter of who will make a mistake first. Pablo makes a three pointer, then so does Emiliano. Taking the ball down the court, Emiliano goes for the reverse lay-up and makes the shot. When Pablo attempts, he misses.

"Nice work, Emiliano!" Rachel calls out.

"Man I haven't played that game since I was prolly ten," Emiliano says.

In the distance, people are gathering at the table and Fabian is setting up equipment.

"We should head over so we can get the same colored pinnies," Rachel says.

They grab their bags from the bench next to the court and head to the field. Once there, Emiliano grabs four blue pinnies from the equipment bag, then hands one to Pablo and two to Rachel before putting his on. The guys head out to the field to warm up while Rachel sits on the grass next to the table to stretch.

"Hi!" Hannah says, coming up behind her best friend.

"Hannah! Hi, how are you?"

"I'm doing all right." Hannah sets her bag down then plops onto the grass. They pull each other in for a bear hug. Some men trailing behind Hannah set their bags down and put on their cleats. Hannah eyes the group until they walk over to the field. "So, I have a story to tell you," Hannah says once everyone is out of ear shot.

Rachel gets perky and alert like a dog sticking its ears up. "Something else happened? What'd he do?" Her tone indicates her pre-annoyance with Brax.

"I got home from work and went in the bathroom to shower. There were three towels in the bathroom. There's always only two. Brax's towel and my towel." Before Rachel can muster a response, Hannah continues. "I was really quiet for a while. When Brax asked what was wrong, I asked why there was an extra towel. He scoffed and said 'I don't know! Why?'"

"He didn't know there was an extra towel in his *own* bathroom?" Rachel questions.

Hannah shrugs, then proceeds to tell Rachel more about the incident. How she told Brax it made her think he was showering with Alexis. How he rolled his eyes. How he pulled the "why can't you trust me" card. How he said he'd move the towel. How she followed behind him as he took the wet mystery item and hung it over Alexis's door.

"So it's her towel?" Rachel asks, confused. She puts on her blue pinny and hands the other one to Hannah.

"I don't know. I was just internally freaking out, staring at it. I hated to see it in our bathroom, but I especially hated to see it on her door." Hannah still can't grasp what that gesture ultimately meant. Was that Brax's way of confessing? That would be cruel, and could anyone be *that* cruel? Suddenly it feels like this is all in her head. She must have been seeing things at her apartment. She must be overthinking right now, reading too deeply into the placement of the towel.

Rachel shoots Hannah a concerned look.

Feeling the need to explain herself, Hannah continues as she puts on her pinny. "I asked him why he hung the towel there! He said, 'So it can dry.' Then I just dropped the subject."

"So do you think they took a shower together?" Rachel stands, unsure how else to continue the conversation about Brax and some woman whom she has never met.

"I don't know. I just can't imagine that he would ever cheat on me…" Hannah gets up and follows Rachel to the field.

"Well, let's just enjoy this game then. I'm sure getting your mind on something else will help."

They were so lost in their conversation that they didn't realize the session started without them. The score is two to two. The white team has six players and the blue team has five. The young women join the game, putting the blue team at seven players. Fabian does a quick head count then offers to be neutral so the teams can be even. He takes off his blue pinny and chucks it behind one of the goals. Meanwhile, the blue team scores again.

It quickly becomes apparent to Rachel that Hannah hasn't gotten much exercise or sleep lately. She misses a lot of her passes and opts to walks more than she usually does. Rachel's focus goes in and out of the game, as she thinks about her best friend's situation and how sports can really be indicators of how people operate in the real world, whether they be tired, angry, aloof, poised, or motivated…or overthinking.

Pablo and Emiliano make a nice play together and Emiliano scores, putting the blue team ahead with four goals. Fabian suggests they play one game to ten instead of two games to five; the faster they finish, the less overbearing heat they'll have to deal with.

Over the next few minutes, both teams score again. Knowing a water break would be right now, with the blue team at five goals, Hannah runs off the field deciding to make her own rules, just as she does with her personal life. She rarely listens to other's thoughts and opinions; the trait proves to be both an asset and a downfall. After a quick sip, she walks back to the field and her game play slowly gets better during the second half of the game.

Some clouds creep in front of the sun, shading most of the field, making it a few degrees cooler. The game continues over the next thirty-five minutes, full of goals, corner kicks, amazing plays, and some mistakes. The blue team dominates with seventy percent ball possession.

The next pivotal play seems to happen in slow motion: Fabian crosses the ball to Rachel and she laces it into the top left corner of the goal. Javier wipes the sweat off his forehead with his white pinny. His frustration grows more visible now that the blue team has nine goals opposed to his team's six.

The white team takes their kickoff. One of the players tries to make a pass out wide, but Hannah steals the ball and sends a perfect cross to Rachel, who one-touches it to Emiliano. He passes it to Hannah as she checks into the center of the field. Hannah, Rachel, and Emiliano move as a unit toward the goal, passing around the white team. Eventually,

Hannah gets the ball again, dribbles past a defender, and scores.

Everyone on the blue team cheers over their win as they take off their pinnies and get off the field. A thought crosses Rachel's mind: perhaps not all sports things correlate to real life. Hannah is a great forward and she works wonders with the triangle structure on the field, but the triangle structure doesn't work so well for her in real life.

Emiliano high-fives Rachel and compliments her skills, then he and Pablo shag balls with Fabian from all the missed shots during the game. While everyone else is busy cleaning up or getting water, Javier walks up behind Rachel. "So are we going out as a group today?"

"Oh...sorry Javier," Rachel says. "I already have plans today. We would need to plan something like that in advance."

"Oh, OK. Good point." He flashes a crooked smile. "Well, hopefully we can really soon. Also, I should have told you this so much earlier, but you are a great forward, Rachel."

"Thanks, Javier." The compliment makes her feel good. She wishes him a great weekend then walks over to Hannah, eager to continue the pertinent hey-you-might-have-a-cheating-boyfriend conversation. "So what do you think you're going to do?"

"About what?" Hannah asks.

"Brax? Alexis?"

"There's nothing to do." Hannah shrugs. "I mean...I'll figure it out. Intuition, right? I better head home. We're all three going to a huge party tonight." She rolls her eyes at the thought of Alexis hanging out with them. "Actually, do you want to come?"

"I already have plans," Rachel says.

"OK. No biggie!" Hannah gives Rachel a quick side hug, then walks up the hill.

Javier slowly gathers his things, wondering if Emiliano has really captured Rachel's attention to the point where she turned down her own best friend. Maybe he will never have his chance with Rachel, after all.

Just then, Pablo, Emiliano, and Fabian walk over and load equipment into the ball bag. "Thanks guys for helping. I appreciate it," Fabian says. They exchange goodbyes and fist bumps, then Emiliano walks over to Rachel, who's been patiently waiting for him at the table.

"So…where should we go for lunch?" he asks.

"I know a great Mediterranean place," Rachel says. Figuring that Emiliano is unfamiliar with the food, she starts listing off items like pita, falafel, kabobs, and tabbouleh, and is confident that Emiliano will find something he likes. The only thing Emiliano has heard of is pita.

Javier eyes them from behind the tree, feeling a tad upset, jealous even. He wishes that he were the one wooing Rachel at a Mediterranean restaurant right now.

27 A Sense of Home

Rachel and Emiliano get in her car, feeling happy that they won't have to wait too long to eat; the Mediterranean restaurant is only a few blocks from the soccer field. At first, Rachel suggests they could eat in the restaurant, but then she remembers that her parents are out of town visiting family in Oregon again. Her eyebrows do a little dance as she emphasizes that they could have uninterrupted *alone time*. Without a second thought, Emiliano agrees that they should definitely take the food to go and eat at her place.

"Maybe we can pick up some Cacti too," Emiliano says.

"Why do you want to get a cactus?" Rachel asks as they pull into the parking lot.

"Rach!" Emiliano laughs. "Cacti is the new Travis Scott drink. It's a hard seltzer."

"Hmm. I never can keep up with these things."

After a quick trip into Baba's Kitchen and the liquor store beside it, they head back to her car with a case of Cacti and to-go orders of beef and salmon shawarma. Emiliano eagerly opens the take-out box to examine the food: yellow rice topped with grilled onions and meat, a pile of garlic hummus, and a Mediterranean salad consisting of various greens, cucumbers, and tomatoes. He's a picky eater, which means only some of the meal will suffice.

"Ick. I'm not eating salad," he says.

"It's good for you, Emiliano! I thought you liked the idea of suh-lads?"

He chuckles as he closes the lid. "Laughing about 'em. Not eating 'em…Speakin' of food, I never seen you eat something that isn't vegan. And here you are ordering fish."

"Well it is a rare occurrence," Rachel replies as they head out of the parking lot.

"Rare occurrence? Rach, you're too funny."

"You always say that. Why am I so funny?"

"Just the way you say things."

When they get to Rachel's house, Cece barks with excitement, greeting them at the front door. She sniffs Emiliano, then runs over to her bucket of toys, pulling out a stuffed animal sting ray. They head into the living room—promising the dog that they'll play with her later—and start eating.

Rachel looks over at Emiliano, her mouth full of rice, eager to see his reaction to the food. He always introduces her to new things and it feels good to introduce him to something.

"This is delicious, Rach. I've never tried anything like it before."

"Phewph! I would have felt bad if you didn't like it."

"Do you like the drink?" he asks.

"Yeah these are good. They don't even taste like alcohol." Rachel finishes her first seltzer, then pops the top of her second can. She already feels a slight buzz; she doesn't drink often and is considered a light weight. A bubbly giggling overcomes her. "I'm full…and I think I'm tipsy," she says.

She leans back, sinking deeply into the couch. Emiliano lies down with her, nestling into her, putting his head on her chest. She wraps her arm around him and combs through his hair. For a few minutes, they lie peacefully, enjoying the silence, the resting, each other.

"We should play Dance Dance Revolution!" she exclaims.

"You have that game?"

"I've played it my whole life."

Hastily, she sets up the electronics, eager to show Emiliano her moves. Rarely would she consider showing someone her dancing skills (more so, foot stomping skills with this game), whether or not she has had anything to drink.

As the main screen comes on, the background music blares through the surround sound system. Rachel puts the game on the hardest level, then chooses one of those funky Dance Dance Revolution songs that nobody would ever hear of except for on this game. Emiliano intently watches as her feet stomp furiously around the dancing mat. They move at a speed Emiliano didn't know was possible, hitting the front, back, and side arrows almost always on cue.

"What the heck, Rach! How did you learn this?" Emiliano laughs, stunned at what he is seeing.

"I just practiced all the time when I was little."

The song ends and Rachel continues staring at the screen as her score is tallied. The result comes in and she receives a B+, which she hates as a straight-A student. Emiliano claps and congratulates her.

"No, I should have gotten an A." Rachel shakes her head, then takes a sip of her seltzer. "Your turn!"

"Oh…I'm not playing." Emiliano laughs awkwardly.

"Come on, Emiliano! For me?" Rachel smiles.

"Fine. I'll try once but you gotta put it on the beginner level."

Rachel adjusts the game settings on the dance pad.

Emiliano opens a second seltzer, then walks over to the mat and awkwardly stomps his feet against the pads looking through the songs. "I know this one!"

Rachel chuckles, amazed that Emiliano would know a Dance Dance Revolution song. She looks at the screen and sees "Burn for You" by Kreo on display.

Emiliano looks around, wondering how to start the game.

"Press the green button on the mat," Rachel says.

The song begins and Emiliano bobs his head to the beginning instrumental. The arrows come up on the screen and Emiliano hurriedly stomps his feet. Sometimes he misses the correct arrow. Other times he hits the correct one too late. Rachel giggles, then starts clapping for him.

After one minute *failed* comes across the screen and everything fades to gray. Emiliano scores an E, the lowest possible score.

"Aight, well this ain't dancin' anyway." Emiliano scoffs as he gets off the mat. "I'm a great dancer." He picks up his drink and looks at Rachel. "I know a whole bunch of quinceañera dances."

"Really? Show me one of them!" Rachel bites her bottom lip, smiling.

Emiliano steps into the foyer, in front of Cece's bed, and hums a tune. He spins in circles, claps his hands, crosses his feet one over the other, turns, and repeats a sequence. "I been to so many quinces," he says without stopping the flow. He takes a sip and continues for another few rounds, making his way around the foyer and living room.

Rachel intently watches, thinking about how incredible he looks performing line dances *just* for her.

"Thank you, thank you," he says with a bow.

Rachel shakes her head, smirking. How is it possible for someone to be *this* mesmerizing? "I wonder if this game has any songs that I know," she says. She stamps her foot against the dance pad, scrolling fast through the music library.

She pauses on "I Was Made For Lovin' You" by KISS. A sample of the track fills the living room. She knows this one, and she believes she was made for loving Emiliano.

Emiliano bobs his head to the beat. "Rach, this is one of my favorite songs." Spotting a lint roller nearby on the TV stand, he picks it up and pretends it's a microphone. As he starts singing the chorus, he looks over at her.

She laughs. Two performances in a row? It must be her lucky day. He bobs slightly harder and his hair cascades down the front of his face. She pays such close attention that it seems like his hair flip happens in slow motion. Just like something from a movie. Immediately, she recognizes this is one of those Emiliano moments that she will cherish forever. All she can think is that he is the most gorgeous creature alive.

After flicking his hair back, he walks over to Rachel, still singing into the lint roller. He dances next to her for a verse then extends his hand to her. Her cheeks flush a deep pink hue. She doesn't take his hand.

"Come on, Rach!" Emiliano says.

"I can't...I'd feel too embarrassed!" In truth, she is apprehensive toward dancing with him because they've never danced together before, and it will only make her fall even more in love with him.

He sets the lint roller down, then sits next to her, offering another drink. She shakes her head vehemently because she already feels tipsy enough. "We could rent a movie from our list?" he suggests. "I'm thinkin' you'd like *American Graffiti*."

Nothing gets Rachel more excited than checking off a movie from her and Emiliano's list. He didn't need to say anything more to get her moving; she puts the dancing game away, turns off the lights, grabs a blanket, and gets the TV ready for movie night. Cece jumps on the couch and curls up next to Emiliano.

They settle in for The George Lucas comedy. It revolves around high school seniors in the '60s. Emiliano emphasizes the style of the cars, clothes, and music of the decade—how it had so much more personality than today.

Midway through the movie, one of the main characters gets into an issue with a group of greasers.

"Masculine brawls seem so exaggerated compared to real life, whether in the '60s or today," Rachel says.

Emiliano pauses the movie. "Nah things can get pretty serious for any male group from greasers to gangs. If your masculinity is challenged by other men it's the kind of thing you can't just back down from." Reluctantly, he shares the story about what happened to him a few months ago when the young man from a local gang entered his neighborhood and approached him.

Rachel gasps. "Emiliano! Why didn't you tell me?"

"Guess it never came up." Emiliano shrugs. Not wanting to discuss it any further, he presses play.

As they continue watching, Rachel thinks about the gang member who came into Emiliano's neighborhood. About how Emiliano must have felt during the exchange. About how that is something she would never experience in her neighborhood. About how masculine Emiliano is at such a young age.

After the movie full of love and laughter ends, Rachel suggests they go upstairs to relax—and to maximize on their opportunity for alone time. Without hesitation, Emiliano follows her up the stairs, with Cece close behind.

"I'm sorry Moo, you can't come in," Rachel says when they reach the bedroom.

Cece whimpers, then lies down as Rachel closes the door.

Emiliano sits down on Rachel's bed, staring at her longingly as she starts removing her clothing. She takes off her shirt, then slips out of her shorts. Almost immediately, he follows along, removing his garments.

When they are entirely naked, Rachel straddles Emiliano on the edge of the bed. He looks into her eyes as his hands explore her skin. They kiss each other delicately, then Emiliano sucks on Rachel's neck. His mouth moves down to her collar bone, then down to her breasts. Slowly, he looks up at her, in awe of her femininity. Then his eyes continue wandering across her body, down her torso and belly button over to her outer hips. Delicately, he moves his fingers across her thin white stretch marks. "Baby, I love your tiger stripes," he whispers.

Rachel blushes. Her arms wrap tightly around him as she passionately kisses his cheek and forehead. Then she pulls him in for an even tighter hug. Their naked bodies press together; in each other's arms they again feel a sense of home. The energy between their bodies undulates as they entwine. Their hearts beat at the same cadence. Their breathing patterns synchronize. Seamlessly, they become one.

28 All Eyes on Him

With two bags of groceries in hand, Adriana walks through the front door, immediately noticing Emiliano still asleep underneath the staircase. His body is sprawled out, limbs hanging off the sides of the bed. "You gonna sleep through your whole birthday, vato?" she hollers, clunking the grocery bags against the kitchen counter. In a loud obnoxious tone, she begins to sing "Las Mañanitas."

Emiliano grumbles, rustling around in the blankets and sheets for a few moments. As he opens his eyes, squinting from the light, he stretches out his arms. "¿Qué hora es?"

"Why don't you get up outta that bed and find out!"

"Sassy even on my birthday, Mamá?"

Adriana walks over and squeezes him in a tight hug. With a kiss on the cheek, she wishes him *Feliz cumpleaños*, then walks to the front door. "Now come help me with the rest of these groceries."

They grab the remainder of the bags from Adriana's trunk and bring them into the kitchen, sprawling the food across every counter. While they unpack everything, Adriana reminds Emiliano about his birthday celebration at his grandmother's house, though he of course didn't forget about it. She suggests he wear a collared shirt since they will be taking family photos.

"All right, Ma." He complies, though he hates collared shirts and family photographs.

After they finish putting the groceries away, Adriana heads upstairs to get ready, while Emiliano grabs his phone off the charger in the living room. There are four missed calls and twelve text messages, most of which pertain to his birthday. The first text he opens is the one from Rachel.

Happy Happy Birthday! Hope you get some birthday sex today ;) lol.

Almost instantly, a smile crosses his face. He quickly types a thank you response, making sure to add that he hopes he gets birthday sex as well. For nearly thirty minutes he sits on the couch, replying to birthday wishes and making quick phone calls to the friends and family members who reached out while he was sleeping. Right as he is about to put his phone down, another message comes in from Rachel.

I'm pretty busy today but I'd love to see you for at least a little bit! Can I take you out for some ice cream and give you your present?

Truly, Rachel isn't all that busy; she texted this because she doesn't want to put any added pressure on him. If it were up to Rachel she would spend the whole day with him, shower him with kisses and hugs, and celebrate with his family.

Before replying, Emiliano takes a moment to think. Of course, he would love to see her. And he did promise that he would see her on his birthday. *But* he has things to do with his family and friends. He can't mix Rachel in with his family and friends. Maybe he won't have time. Then again, couldn't he make some time?

Thanks. You're too sweet, Rach! I'd love to see you. How bout in the evening?

Adriana comes walking down the stairs, putting on a pair of dangly earrings. She is appalled to see Emiliano still wearing his pajamas. "Mijo, you're still not ready?"

"I'm going right now, Ma. I'll get ready quick." Emiliano heads to his closet in the kitchen still immersed in his phone and virtual world. He slings a blue button-up shirt and black jeans over his shoulder, then grabs hair gel and deodorant. As he looks up, his mother's flattering black blouse catches his eye. He quickly snaps a photo with his phone.

"And what do you think you're doing?" she asks.

"Mamá, you look so beautiful!"

Adriana blushes. She looks at her son, wondering how she got so lucky, wondering if luck is really even involved at all. He turns the phone around so she can see the picture.

"Ah yes, this blouse does look good on me, no?" she says.

Emiliano smiles, then puts his phone down and heads upstairs. Twenty minutes later, he emerges from the steamy bathroom, dressed and cleaned. He pats at his gelled hair as he hurries to gather his things. Realizing his mom must be in the car, he picks up his leather Converse and rushes past Mila out the door.

"I'm glad I don't have to knock you silly on your birthday!" Adriana says jokingly out the window.

"Me too," Emiliano hollers.

"We can't be late to your own celebration, mijo."

As soon as he buckles, Adriana backs out of the driveway. Emiliano looks out at the passing trees thinking about his love-hate relationship with birthdays. It's great to see his family, but he doesn't like having all eyes on him. It makes him feel uncomfortable, like he has to perform or entertain. He finds it nerve racking to be the center of attention since he's used to being so private.

When they pull onto Martina's street, they pass a few handfuls of recognizable cars and spot some of their family members. Samanta and Marcos are walking up the driveway and Emiliano's younger cousins are running around on the front lawn. As Adriana parks, Emiliano looks out at the familiar faces. Truly, all eyes will be on him. Yet, he also feels lucky to have such a large, loving family.

While Adriana unloads a few birthday supplies from the backseat, Emiliano greets his family members with hugs and kisses. His younger cousin, Alicia, runs over and immediately begs to show her skateboarding skills to him. He gives her a high five and tells her they will definitely skateboard at some point today. She smiles wide and Emiliano notices a prominent gap in her top row of teeth.

"Did you lose a bebé tooth, Alicia?"

She nods.

"Did you leave it under your pillow for Ráton Pérez?"

"Sí."

"Did he bring you a gift?"

"I wrote Ráton Perez a letter. I told him I'm from the United States and that I wanted pesos for my gift."

"That's una gran idea, Alicia. Did you wake up to some pesos?"

She nods again. Somehow, her smile is even wider than before. Alicia reaches into her pocket and flashes a $2 *peso*. A stainless steel outer rim wraps around the aluminum bronze core. Emiliano holds out his hand and she carefully gives it to him, making sure not to drop it in the grass where it could get lost. He looks closely at the detailing on the front. *Estados Unidos Mexicanos* is engraved on the outer rim.

"Very cool." He gently hands Alicia her precious coin.

The front door opens and Martina comes outside, followed by Emiliano's *tíos*, *primos*, and *padrinos*. The group walks over to an oak tree on the far side of the lawn while Martina hollers for everyone else to head over for photographs. She doesn't want to wait until after they eat in case anyone spills on their outfits. Emiliano, Samanta, Marcos, and the younger cousins all walk over. The children groan along the way, rejecting the idea because they'd rather continue playing.

Everyone lines up in two rows and Emiliano gets to stand in the center. He swivels around and makes quick greetings to the family members he hasn't had a chance to see yet. Cheerful smiles spread contagiously across the family.

After taking ten or so photos, Martina releases everyone to go back to what they were doing. Emiliano heads for the front door when he feels a tap on his shoulder. He turns to see his *abuela* standing behind him. In Spanish, he thanks her for throwing him a birthday celebration.

"Claro que si, nieto." Martina holds out the camera and shows Emiliano one of the family photos. "¿Quién falta en la foto?"

Emiliano looks quizzically at the picture, scanning the faces. What does his *abuela* mean that someone is missing? He tries to figure out which family member isn't present. Everyone who lives in close driving proximity is already at the party and is in the photo.

"Una mujer hermosa…para ti," Martina says, breaking the silence.

Emiliano anxiously laughs. She wants to see a beautiful lady, a girlfriend, in the photo?

"Las chicas probablemente son tímidas porque eres guapo."

Emiliano nods, though he doesn't believe what he hears. He thinks there's no way women could be intimidated by him, and also what about Rachel?

As they enter the house together, mariachi music fills the air. A delectable aroma of *al pastor* and *carnitas* tacos wafts through their noses. Sweet dishes, including *arroz con leche* and *flan*, are spread across the kitchen counter. A few family members walk in the house after them. Tía Camila starts singing "Feliz Cumpleaños." She doesn't stop until Emiliano turns around and gives her a big smile. They walk toward each other with open arms. As the two embrace, Camila whispers that he looks extra handsome in the button-up shirt.

"¡Dios mio! Emiliano, you are so grown up." She shakes her head as she looks him up and down. "I remember the day you were born you know!"

"I know," Emiliano says. "Alicia showed me the *peso* she got from Ráton Pérez."

"Ah, sí. Me and Antonio were thrilled when we read her letter. We gave her a peso from a jar in our bedroom."

"I miss Mexico, Tía Camila. I want to visit real soon!"

"Yo tambien, child. Yo tambien."

They both look at Martina as she walks past them with a stack of paper plates. "¡Ven a comer!" she hollers, lifting the plastic lids and aluminum foil off the containers of food.

Everyone who hears her makes their way through the kitchen, scooping small bits of each fiesta item onto their plate. Still dressed in her apron, Martina marches outside and yells to the adults mingling and children playing. She tells them the food will be cold and gross if they wait any longer. They funnel into the house and squeeze past one another in the hallway.

After piling their plates with savories and sweets, each person grabs a soda can or *cerveza* from the cooler. When all the seats in the living room, dining room, and outdoor patio are taken, Tío Antonio stands, clearing his throat to make a toast to Emiliano. Everyone holds their glasses in the air.

"¡Salud!" Antonio hollers.

Glasses clink as they drink to their health. Forks are grabbed and chatter echoes through the rooms. A few party goers yell *Feliz cumpleaños* to Emiliano across the table as they eat. Antonio brings out a bottle of Corralejo Resposado, fills two shot glasses, and motions for Emiliano to come to the head of the table. After taking a bite of a taco, the birthday boy walks over.

"Twenty-three already? ¡Feliz cumpleaños, mi hombre!" With the back of his fingers, Antonio slides one of the shots across the table.

Without asking questions, Emiliano lifts the glass. Both men look at each other as they clink the glassware, then tilt their heads back, welcoming the fiery liquid down their throats. When they slam the empty glasses against the table, Emiliano does not shutter and cough like how he did on Epiphany.

"Someone's been drinking!" Antonio exclaims as he pats Emiliano's shoulder.

"Un poco, Tío."

"Good! Now I know you really are mi sobrino!" Antonio takes a large bite of *arroz con leche*. As he chews he tells Emiliano he'd better go finish his food before they bring out the cake.

Suddenly, music blasts from the backyard. Emiliano whips around to see his older cousins dancing on the patio, *cervezas* in hand. Some people in the living room take a break from eating and go outside to let loose on the dance floor. One cousin hollers for Emiliano to join them.

Emiliano grabs a soda from the cooler, then goes outside. His cousin DJs, putting on all the hottest, modern Spanish hits. Everyone claps and jumps around as Emiliano goes to the center of the dance floor. After a few minutes of tapping, twisting, and grooving, he pulls at some family members arms. They take turns rotating into the center, everyone on the outer rim hyping up whoever happens to be in the middle.

Sweaty and tired, Emiliano walks into the house and goes back to his seat. He finishes a taco and takes a few bites of the sweet dishes. Shortly after, Martina emerges from the kitchen carrying the platter of *tres leches*. Adriana hovers over the candles to make sure they don't get blown out.

Everyone dancing comes inside and the entire family circles around Emiliano as the cake is set in front of him. Together, they sing "Las Mañanitas." Emiliano stares at the dancing flames atop the cake, a soft smile crossing his cheeks. He lifts his gaze and admires the sea of brown faces. He appreciates that in his culture birthdays are known for being family affairs above anything else. There is nobody he would rather spend his birthday with than the people who are there for him through life's highs and lows. He blows out the candles as the song ends and Martina almost immediately begins removing them.

Everyone claps, then begins chanting "¡Qué le muerda, qué le muerda, qué le muerda!"

Emiliano leans forward to take a bite of the cake (to take the first bite without utensils brings good luck). He already anticipates what is coming as he leans forward. Tío Antonio gently pushes the back of his head. Laughter erupts across the room as small bits of *tres leches* cover Emiliano's nose and mouth. One family member hands him a wet wipe to clean the frosting off his face.

After Martina cuts the cake, she gives Emiliano the remainder of the slice that he already bit. Each person picks up a piece and begins devouring the moist delicacy. Alicia makes sure to sit next to Emiliano to confirm that they will go skateboarding before the party is over. He tells her as soon as they finish their last bite, they are heading outside. Hearing the incredible news, Alicia wolfs down the cake, not taking time to enjoy the flavor between bites.

"OK, I'm done! Are you ready?" she says, grinning wide.

"Yes, Alicia. Let me finish this."

Alicia runs into the other room to grab her helmet while Emiliano takes the last few bites. The two meet at the front door and head outside together. She runs ahead of him and jumps on her skateboard.

"Wait for me, Alicia!" Emiliano runs down the grass to catch up to her.

"Watch this…I can pull a manny!" Alicia leans back and the front wheels lift off the ground. She glides down the sidewalk balancing on the back wheels. After a few seconds, the front of the board clunks down. Instinctively, her arms shoot out and she manages to keep her balance.

Some partiers begin leaving, interrupting Alicia's skateboarding session. Emiliano exchanges goodbyes with his family members and close family friends, thanking them for attending his birthday party. Before he can turn around to tell Alicia good job on the manny, she already sets her mind on performing her next trick.

"I also learned to Ollie!" she hollers as she gets on the board.

After pushing fast off the ground, she crouches, putting extra weight on the back end of the board as she jumps. The board stays with her as she flies angelically through the air. She looks up to Emiliano, hoping he is impressed by her new skills. When the board hits the sidewalk, she leans too much weight on the heels of her feet and loses balance. She falls backward and her backside smacks against the concrete.

Emiliano's eyes widen. He rushes over to help her off the ground. "Alicia! You all right?"

She gets up before he can lend a helping hand. Her clothes have slight tears from skidding. Wiping the gravel off her hands, she lets out a laugh. Emiliano is relieved that she isn't hurt, and admires her for being such a daredevil.

Alicia pats at the backside of her shorts and doesn't feel the *peso*. Hastily, she looks around the grass and sidewalk, checking every square inch of the area where she fell. She comes up empty handed. Tears pool in her eyes.

Not knowing whether she is hurt, Emiliano crouches next to her to help. Her crying grows louder and louder.

A few moments later, Tía Camila comes running out the front door, having heard Alicia's cries. "¿Qué pasó? ¿Qué pasó?"

"No lo se, Tía." Emiliano shrugs.

"¡Mi peso!" Alicia cries.

"Mija, we will find it." Camila gives her daughter a warm hug.

All three of them scour the front lawn and sidewalk. With each passing minute, Alicia's anguish grows. The coin doesn't turn up anywhere.

As they head inside the house, a few people walk past them to leave, including Samanta and Marcos. Samanta notices Alicia's puffy red eyes and stops walking. "What happened? Is she OK?" she asks Emiliano, watching Camila clean off Alicia's scrapes.

"Yeah…she's not hurt too bad. Her peso from Ráton Pérez is gone. We couldn't find it."

"What kind?" Samanta mouths silently, so Alicia won't hear.

Emiliano holds up two fingers to indicate it was the $2 *peso*.

"I'll be right back," Samanta says. "Gimme a few minutes, Marcos."

Her boyfriend nods. He and Emiliano head into the dining room to mingle with the family members who are still at the party.

Samanta opens the front door and heads for her car. A heaviness overcomes her. It feels like her heart is being anchored into her stomach. She thinks about the anguish Alicia must feel. A memory from grade school comes to mind: Samanta had eagerly brought a *peso* to school. At recess it was stolen by a group of young White girls. She had begged for them to hand it back to her. They all giggled and one said, "You can't use this in our country." The cocky tone is still etched in Samanta's brain. After that, the girl threw the coin over the fence and into a ravine.

Samanta shakes her head as she reaches her car, releasing the bad memory. She leans in and thumbs through the center console. It is mainly filled with quarters and nickels. Every so often she stumbles upon a gum wrapper or other oddity. A few *pesos* are in the pile. Luckily one of them is similar to the one that went missing. She puts it in her pocket then heads back to the house, noticing Ricardo's truck parallel parked on the street.

When Samanta walks inside, most of the party attendees have left. The only people still at the house are Tía Camila's family and Adriana's. Samanta looks around for Emiliano to let him know Ricardo is outside, but can't find him. She checks the backyard and spots Alicia. "What are you doing out here all by yourself?"

Alicia doesn't answer. She keeps her gaze fixed on the cloudy glass table below her elbows.

"I found something," Samanta whispers. She reaches into her back pocket and pulls out the *peso*.

"Where did you find it?!" Alicia excitedly cradles the coin in her hands.

"Rátón Pérez found it! He told me to tell you that home is a place inside every human heart. That means it's not something you can lose. It's not something others can take away." Samanta gently taps her index finger to Alicia's nose.

Alicia giggles. "Gracias." She stands and wraps her arms around Samanta's torso before hurrying inside to show her mother that her *peso* was found. Samanta follows behind, finally spotting Emiliano in the living room. "Hey, I've been looking for you."

Emiliano turns around. "What's up?"

"Your friend's truck is outside. Think they've been waiting for you." Samanta glances at Marcos, who is watching TV. "Lo siento. I'm ready now."

Adriana and Martina start cleaning up. Emiliano kisses both of them on the cheek, thanking them for the beautiful party. He also gives Alicia and his other family members hugs and goodbyes, then walks outside to meet up with his best friends.

29 The Long Trail of Ys

"Happy birthday, hermano!" Pablo hollers out the window.

"Thanks man." Emiliano gets in the backseat of Ricardo's truck. He gives fist bumps to Pablo and Ricardo, then offers Sofía a nod. As he buckles in, Ricardo makes a U-turn and exits the neighborhood.

"Soooo what about me?" Sofía says from the passenger seat.

"What? You want a fist bump?" Emiliano asks.

"Am I not allowed to because I got a vagina or somethin'?"

"No, Sof. That ain't got nothin' to do with it." Emiliano playfully rolls his eyes and holds out his fist.

Sofía doesn't turn around, leaving his hand alone in the air.

"Sof?" Emiliano says.

She looks out of the corner of her eyes as she chomps her gum. "No thanks, I changed my mind."

Emiliano smacks his lips as he leans back in his seat. Looking out the window, he begins guessing where they are taking him. His first two thoughts are the lake in Echo Parque or the Hollywood sign. Pablo shakes his head while Ricardo teases him about his guess. When he finally says El Pino, everyone chimes in with some version of *yes, of course, where else would we take you.*

"So where's your make believe girlfriend?" Sofía asks, smiling sassily at Emiliano.

"Make believe?" Emiliano says.

"Yeah, I mean…I don't see her here." Sofía lifts a water bottle from the cup holder and pretends to look for a woman underneath it.

"Ha. Funny, Sof." Emiliano looks at the clock on the dashboard; it's almost 7:00 p.m. He feels guilty for not messaging Rachel yet. "She does exist," he tells Sofía. "Pablo's met her."

"Right…I'm sure." Sofía squints, unconvinced. "You know, if you wanna stop pretending I can hook you up with mi amiga, Jemma." She turns on the radio and skips through all the unwanted stations until "Today's top hits" fills the car.

They drive past long lines of tall palm trees and a "Welcome to Los Angeles" sign. A few minutes later, they pull onto Indiana Street and drive up to El Pino. The sun starts sinking over the East Los Angeles mountains. Ricardo opens a small cooler full of Modelo beers. He pops the top of his, then passes the bottle opener to Sofía. When everyone's beer is open they do a cheers for Emiliano's birthday.

After taking long, good looks at El Pino, everyone sits on the ledge in front of the tree. Sipping on their *cervezas*, they stare out into East Los Angeles. There is a peaceful breeze blowing. All four of them can feel it.

"Wish we could take that golf cart for a spin on these streets," Pablo says to Emiliano.

"Too bad you ruined it, esé!"

Both men laugh.

"¿Qué? What golf cart?" Ricardo asks.

Emiliano shakes his head. "Just gotta show you and Sofia." He swigs his beer as he searches through his phone. When he finds the video of Pablo and Jimmy, he plays it for everyone. At first, the video appears wobbly since Emiliano was jogging when he recorded it. Though, when he gets closer to Pablo and the cart, everyone can clearly see the shoe fly off his foot. As Pablo falls in the video, the three men laugh. Ricardo tells Emiliano to rewind and play it in slow motion. Right as Pablo hits the ground, Ricardo spits out his beer from laughing so hard.

Sofia watches as the men play and replay the video. She hasn't laughed once. Each time the cart hits the trash bin, she rolls her eyes. "I just don't understand men," she says. "So you ruined this cart for no reason?"

"No, it wasn't like that Sof!" Emiliano pauses, thinking about how to explain it.

Pablo looks over at him, then over at Sofia, deciding to take the lead. "Yeah when we got to work that day, we saw the old abandoned cart. It was almost ready for the dump anyway. Nobody on the property owned it. We double checked with my dad. We wouldn'ta done anything if the cart belonged to anybody."

Sofia's head tilts as she reasons with their explanation. Her stomach growls, loud enough for the men to hear.

"We gotta get food," Ricardo says. "My girl never gonna be hungry like that."

Emiliano tilts his beer back, pooling the last sip of birthday juice on his tongue. Then, he collects everyone's empty bottles and puts them in a box in Ricardo's truck. "You good to drive?" he asks Ricardo.

"Sí, definitely."

Everyone hops in and they take one last look at El Pino before exiting the street. Emiliano stares longingly at the cream-colored house when they pass it. One day he will live there. No matter what.

"Should we get El Huero?" Pablo suggests. "Since it's somewhat on the way home?"

"Sí, por favor, mi favorita," Sofía says.

For the next fifteen minutes they sing along to their favorite Spanish tunes. When Ricardo pulls into the drive-thru, Sofía lowers the stereo's volume and everyone peers at the large menu.

"Vegetarian? Did they have that here last time? Ha, I would never!" Sofía says, looking at the few meat-free options.

"Yeah, who eats that shit?" Ricardo laughs.

Emiliano let's out an awkward laugh. Rachel does. She eats that shit. "I'll get a carne asada burrito."

"Same," Pablo chimes in.

"Yeah, I think I'm feeling a burrito tonight too," Ricardo says before looking over at Sofía. "What do you want mi amor?"

"I'll get the taco salad." Sofía smirks.

"Salad?" Ricardo questions. "Get the fuck outta here!" He snickers between each word. "What do you really want?"

"Onion rings, tres tostadas, y…nacho fries."

Ricardo scowls, questioning if Sofía could really eat all that.

"Don't give me that look! I'm hungry!" she says.

"All right, baby. I'll get it all." Ricardo rolls down the window and orders the long list of items. As he pulls his car around the building, he tells everyone that dinner is on him for Emiliano's birthday.

After getting their meals, everyone grows silent as they eagerly open lids and unwrap foil, taking their first few bites of food.

"Mmm," Ricardo mumbles. "Emiliano you know what this burrito reminds me of?"

Emiliano looks up from his food. "¿Qué?"

"That food truck we tried at that car show last year, remember?" Ricardo briefly looks at Emiliano through the rearview mirror, then looks back at the road.

"So that was right before your life became amazing," Sofía says.

"Why is that?" Ricardo asks.

"Cause that was right before you met me!"

"Ohhhh. Well, yeah…I love having you in my life." Ricardo chomps down on his burrito.

"Don't suck up to me, Ricardo." Sofía blushes. She twirls an onion ring around her finger before munching on it.

Emiliano takes another bite of his food, thinking about what Ricardo said. "Yeah, man. I think it's the way the meat was marinated. It does taste like that food fosho."

"All four of us should go to a car show soon," Ricardo says.

Everyone in the car agrees, each bringing up memories of their favorite car shows, talking about the most tricked out rides and the ones with the best hydraulics. Sofía mentions it would be especially fun to go with Emiliano and Pablo since they know so much about cars.

As they exit the freeway, Emiliano stares out into the pitch black night. He feels that his birthday was somehow the longest day ever but also just a moment in time. The only person he hasn't seen yet is Rachel. At least there are still a few hours left on his birthday. Maybe she will still be willing to see him. Maybe she hasn't gone to bed yet. Maybe she will forgive him for being a few hours late to their plan.

It's almost 9:30 p.m. Rachel thinks to herself as she looks down at her watch. She taps her fingers against the kitchen table, wondering why Emiliano hasn't called her yet. He said "evening" and now his birthday is almost over. She looks up at his birthday present, feeling like it's mocking her. Two thoughts keep circulating through her mind. *I must not mean anything to him if he doesn't care to see me on his birthday* and *I must not mean anything to him if he doesn't care to keep plans with me.*

Deciding that she won't let the situation get her down, she picks up a pen and continues journaling, her favorite form of self-therapy. She journals about her mood, then writes down her favorite memory of the day. Today, her favorite event was getting a vegan ice cream sandwich. Since she didn't hear from Emiliano, she went to get ice cream without him—her way of refusing to stop her life for a man.

Abruptly, her phone buzzes. The pit of her stomach feels knotted up. It's a message from Emiliano.

Heeeyyyyyyy. What's up?

She stares at the long trail of *y*s sensing his guilt through the phone. There is no way she is going to be someone's afterthought, someone's vague or cancelled plan, someone's late night girl. Without responding, she tucks her phone in her back pocket. Taking another look at the present, she scoffs under her breath. Just as she begins journaling again her phone buzzes. Frustrated, she whips it out. It's another message from Emiliano.

Please don't be mad I didn't see you today. It's just my birthday.

Rachel's eyes slowly fill with tears until she can no longer read the message. She stands, yanking at the gift bag handles. In this moment, she feels sure Emiliano doesn't really see himself being with her long-term. She trudges up the stairs and puts the present on the floor next to her bookshelf. "Cece, come on!" she hollers. Her dog immediately runs to her.

Knowing that journaling won't suffice, Rachel decides to go for a late night walk. She hurries down the stairs, swiftly grabbing the harness and leash, then they head out the front door. Since the lampposts are poorly lit, Rachel lets Cece wander far in front, taking the lead. The dog sniffs along the grass as they walk around the neighborhood. The only thing on Rachel's mind is the fact that Emiliano made multiple plans to see her on his birthday and deferred. When he declined the offer of her present and the ice cream date, she felt that he was rejecting her love.

She wonders if the three strike rule should move into effect. Strike one: His abrupt change in behavior when his sister interrupted their sleepover. Strike two: He was rude on the phone and told her his next girlfriend better be Mexican. Strike three: His entire birthday is strike three. Then she considers the millions of beautiful things and attributes that make up Emiliano. Surely everyone makes mistakes. Perhaps, there should be no strike system, she muses.

Rachel walks past Cece and the leash pulls at her arm; Cece firmly holds her ground, sniffing something in the dirt. Rachel continues staring out into the dark world. Her biggest fear is giving her all to a man who doesn't feel the same way about her. She already knows she would give everything for Emiliano. Would he do the same? Is he doing the same?

Fear blankets her chest. Either way, she feels like she is screwed. Real love terrifies her. The idea of someone seeing her fully and still being there makes her want to peel off her outer layer of skin and hide inside of it. Fake love terrifies her too. The idea of two people using each other for the time being makes her want to gauge out her own eyeballs and steep them in tea. But what terrifies her the most is real love being paired with fake love. If he doesn't love her the way she loves him, she'll have to force herself to stop loving him—but how could she do that? How could she move on from the person she could see herself with forever?

Realizing her and Cece have been standing in the same spot for a few minutes, Rachel gently tugs at the leash. Cece again firmly fixes her stance in the dirt. Finally, Rachel looks down to see why her dog has been sniffing the same spot for so long. There is a freshly dead crow lying on its belly.

30 Five Deep Breaths

Pulling into the parking structure at Hannah's apartment complex, Rachel ponders how her best friend was able to talk her—of all people—into coming to a party. Though, she is glad Hannah did. She's been ignoring Emiliano for a week, and it's hard to keep herself from contacting him. She misses him. She aches for him. And too much of her time has been spent in a bubble of sadness that so desperately needs to be popped.

After putting her car in park, she takes an extra moment to admire the swaying palm trees through the concrete slats. The elevator door opens and Hannah steps out dressed in a light yellow crop top, a tight black jean skirt, and black high heels. Her makeup looks as extravagant as her ensemble. Rachel waves to Hannah, then looks down at her own outfit—a flannel and boyfriend jeans. She hopes she isn't too underdressed for the bar they'll be going to in a few hours.

"Hannah, you're looking a little too good!" Rachel hollers as she opens the trunk to collect her sleepover items.

Hannah giggles, embracing Rachel in a warm hug. While they gather Rachel's pillow, blanket, clothing bag, and makeup, Rachel tells Hannah that she went to see another tarot reader because of all the confusion going on with Emiliano.

"OK. Tonight is going to be about Rachel Storytime then," Hannah says. "Who did your reading? Was it a woman or man? Old or young?"

"It was a young woman this time! I can definitely give you the full details, but basically some of it was to a T what the first reading said. The woman told me two men will be contacting me, some sort of triangle between us. And I am still just as confused as ever because obviously if I had to choose between two men I would always pick Emiliano. Hell, if I had to choose out of every man on the planet I would pick Emiliano!"

"Yeah, you would," Hannah says with a chuckle as they get in the elevator. "Well, this is juicy and I'm anxiously awaiting with you. Definitely keep me updated on the triangle stuff."

As they ride to Hannah's floor, Hannah tells Rachel about the party: people will start arriving in thirty minutes, there will be lots of booze if Rachel decides to drink, and Brax is currently lighting up hookah coals. "It'll basically be a typical college party," Hannah says, as they reach the front door. "Full of whatever substances it takes for everyone to let loose or hide from their pain."

As they step inside the apartment, Hannah holds her breath, immediately sensing something off in the atmosphere. Rachel doesn't notice it. The only thing she notices are the hookah coals burning on the stove.

Hannah stealthily moves toward her bedroom door that's cracked open. Abruptly, Alexis's baseball-capped head pops out with an insincere smile. Hannah fake smiles back, thinking that Alexis looks like a squirrel. Brax walks out of the bedroom, past Alexis and Hannah, without saying anything, into the kitchen and gets the hookah ready.

"Brax was just showing me something funny on TV in your room," Alexis shares with Hannah.

Even though Rachel has heard questionable things about Alexis, she figures it is best to be cordial for Hannah's sake. She walks over with a friendly smile. Hannah quickly introduces the two, not so eager to have her best friend meet her frenemy. After Alexis gives a typical *oh-my-god-you-are-literally-so-pretty* compliment to Rachel, she walks down the hallway to her bedroom to get ready for the party.

Dispersing throughout the apartment, everyone awkwardly does their own thing. Rachel touches up her mascara in Hannah and Brax's master bathroom. Brax blows *O*s with the hookah pipe. Hannah happily cracks open a spiked seltzer and chugs it. After a few minutes, Alexis walks out of her bedroom in a tight tube top and mini skirt—an outfit that looks oddly similar to Hannah's. She walks through the living room holding a gold necklace between her fingers.

"Brax, could you put this on for me?" she asks in a giggly high-pitched voice.

Letting out one more round of smokey *O*s, Brax walks into the living room and takes the necklace. He slowly scoops her bleached blonde hair over her shoulder, his fingers grazing against her neck as he clasps the necklace. Rachel walks into the living room, only catching a small glimpse of the slightly sexual exchange. From the kitchen, Hannah watches, swishing hard seltzer around her gums.

A knock at the door briefly disassembles the tension. Hannah hurries over and greets Brax's friends, men he met during his studies at USC. Some of them have 30-packs of beer, others have liquor bottles. "Can I have a shot of that?" Hannah asks one of the men.

He nods, handing her the bottle of apple flavored Crown Royale. Hannah takes out three shot glasses—one for her, one for Rachel, one for the owner of the liquor. The man takes the shot, then grabs his bottle and heads into the living room with his friends. They turn on a speaker and blast modern rap and hip-hop.

"Wanna take it with me, Rach?" Hannah hollers over the loud music, pointing to the two full shot glasses.

Rachel looks at the dark liquid, knowing it will only lead to poor decisions and reduced memory. "I'd rather stay sober and be the designated driver."

Hannah shoots the first shot down her throat. Her tongue protrudes from her mouth and her eyes squinch while she tries to process the stinging alcohol. After a quick shudder, she takes the second shot. Rachel watches, feeling the burn of toxic love in her own throat as Hannah coughs. While Hannah's body processes the second shot, Rachel wonders if this is the new norm for her best friend.

The doorbell rings and Hannah quickly turns around. Before even making it down the hallway, the door swings open. A large group of young men and women come inside, offering head nods to Hannah and Rachel as they walk past them.

"Who are all these people?" Rachel whispers to Hannah.

"Some are Brax's friends. Some I don't recognize." Hannah shuts the front door. "I'm gonna smoke some hookah if you want to join."

The two women sit next to Brax at the kitchen table. He double fists the two hoses for a long toke, inhaling the vaporized blueberry flavored shisha. With the smoke marinating in his lungs, he passes a hose to Hannah, then exhales.

The water in the hookah bubbles loudly as Hannah takes a long drag. She slowly exhales, letting out a slight cough. As she is about to hand the hose back, she decides to keep it for another hit.

Just then, Alexis walks into the kitchen holding a tray of leftover dinner food.

"Do you want a bite of my biscuit?" Alexis giggles, batting her long eyelashes at Brax. "I know how much you love them!"

Brax reaches his hand across the table and picks up the remainder of the buttery, flaky biscuit.

Hannah watches him take a bite, then loudly chokes on the hookah smoke, thinking to herself, "What the fuck is he doing?" With a quick glance at the hookah, she notices the coals are covered in a layer of ash. She picks up the tongs and knocks a coal against the metal until the outer black layer fades and the glowing red is exposed. She rotates it on the foil, then goes for the second coal. It accidently falls on the table, tumbling a good few inches away from Brax. Within seconds, black singe marks form on the wood.

Brax scoffs, shooting a look Hannah's way that makes it seem like he wishes he could put black singe marks on her. "Are you fucking kidding me, Hannah?" He rips the tongs from her and puts the fiery coal back on the hookah.

Hannah stares into the crowd of people in the living room. "Hey Cheech!" she yells. Brax's friend looks over his shoulder. She gestures for him to come over to the kitchen table. "Do you have anything I can buy off you?"

He opens his backpack, showing her various pill bottles, Ziplocs full of marijuana, and tiny resealable jewelry bags full of cocaine. Rachel looks over curiously. For one, she has never seen cocaine before. Secondly, she is officially worried for Hannah, wondering if this downhill trend has been consistent in her life the last few months and if drugs have been a factor in Hannah's becoming so skinny.

After holding up a few of the prescription bottles, Hannah asks Cheech about the Vyvanse pill. He explains that it's essentially like Adderall but stronger and tells her she'll be full of energy. Hannah quickly exchanges money for it. Most of the time, Hannah chases alcohol with soda. Tonight, she finds herself chasing alcohol with Vyvanse.

Abruptly, Brax leaves the table. In the living room he mingles with men and women, telling everyone a story about Hannah being drunk when they were first getting to know each other. He intentionally dramatizes some of the elements, sharing that he had to help her home and that she got blacklisted from a bar. A few people laugh. Rachel looks over to her best friend, knowing the story doesn't sound factual.

Hannah's face grows hot and uncomfortable. "Stop making shit up! That's not even what happened!" she blurts out.

For the first time, she finds herself standing up to Brax after months of mistreatment. Initially, it feels good, but when she looks into Brax's eyes, she instantly regrets uttering a single word. His gaze is piercing. She's all too familiar with the story behind his eyes. They are sending her a look of all consuming disappointment and repulsion. In a calm—yet grim—tone, Brax tells Hannah he needs to talk to her alone in their bedroom. Nervous, she hesitantly walks over, staring into the dirty brown carpet, biting the inside of her cheek.

Rachel looks over as Brax shuts the bedroom door. Questions fire in her mind about Hannah's living situation. Eager to get to the bottom of the love triangle, she looks over at Alexis, who is squeezing between two men on the couch. Luckily, she is within ear shot, and listens as Alexis suggests to the men they all play a drinking game together.

The classic game they decide on is truth or dare with a twist. If someone doesn't complete the truth or the dare, they have to take a sip of their drink.

"I want to go first and I already know I'm choosing truth," Alexis says.

"How many people have you fucked?" one of the boys asks.

Alexis giggles and they prod her to answer the question.

"Well, it's so funny you ask that because me and Brax were literally talking about this last week. So ironic but we've both had sex with 26 people."

"Woah. Only 26? Bruh, I'm at 38," one of the boys brags.

Rachel stops listening to the sex conversation as Brax's voice grows louder from behind the bedroom door. Somehow, Rachel is the only one who seems to notice. The drunkards continue singing along to the music, playing beer pong, and chugging drinks.

"You will not speak to me like that under my roof!" Brax hollers. "And stop being so sensitive! Learn how to take a joke!"

The door opens. Brax walks out calmly, drink in hand. He shoots a smile to Alexis across the room. Shortly after, Hannah walks out, teary eyed. She heads to the refrigerator and grabs another seltzer and starts chugging it.

Rachel watches her best friend, feeling uneasy. "Hannah, will you come outside with me? It's really hot in here. I need some fresh air."

After one more swig, Hannah agrees. They step outside into the breezeway. Rachel paces, then puts her hands on the rail and leans out into the cold wind. Hannah nonchalantly sips her drink, drunk and unaware of her best friend's frantic concern.

"I'm going to knock his head off!" Rachel yells.

"No, please…It'll only make things worse!" Hannah says nervously, leaning up against a wall. A sullen look is plastered on her face. Water pools in her eyes. The weeping starts before the tears fall. "I don't know what's wrong with me," Hannah says between sobs. "He used to treat me like a queen. What did I do wrong? Why am I so unlovable?"

Rachel walks over and wraps Hannah in her arms, cradling her while she cries. The shoulder of Rachel's flannel gets soaked with tears and snot.

"What should I do, Rach?" Hannah mumbles into the flannel.

"You're my best friend, Hannah. I love you and want the best for you…This isn't it."

Hannah looks up, sniffling. "What do you mean?"

"Well…why are you dating someone who might be cheating on you? Who gaslights you? Who embarrasses you? Who tries to ruin your reputation?" Disgusted, Rachel shakes her head. "You deserve so much better."

Hannah rolls her eyes as she leans back against the wall. She doesn't want to listen to Rachel's tough love. Not one ounce of her wants to believe that Brax is cheating on her. "Why don't you take your own dating advice," Hannah retaliates, her words a bit slurry. "Why are you dating a man who didn't even care to see you on his birthday? Who clearly has an issue with your cultural differences? Who's not even educated? Who has kept you on a string for months?"

Letting out an awkward laugh, Rachel cannot believe what she is hearing, all because her best friend can't stand to hear the truth. Rachel defends Emiliano and his intelligence. Pointing her finger sharply at Hannah, she says, "People don't need to go to school or have degrees to be intelligent. Emiliano is the greatest man I've ever met. It's a privilege to love him." Rachel pauses as tears fill her eyes. She looks out at the palm trees illuminated by the lights of Los Angeles. "I don't need to explain myself. You don't even know him."

"Well of course I don't know him! Your love's been a secret to the entire world!" Hannah lifts her arms with attitude.

While the other comments didn't affect Rachel, this one feels like a bee sting straight to the heart. The women stand in the breezeway, staring at each other. Both are somewhere between anger and sadness. A long uncomfortable silence fills the atmosphere.

Rachel checks her jean pockets to make sure she has her phone, wallet, and car keys. "I'm going home." Without saying goodbye, she walks toward the elevator.

"What about your sleepover bag?" Hannah hollers.

Rachel doesn't turn around. She presses the elevator button and stares at the metal doors. Drunkenly, Hannah yells something that Rachel can't quite understand, then she goes back into her apartment, slamming the door behind her. The elevator dings. Before entering, Rachel looks back to make sure Hannah got inside safely.

Once in the parking structure, Rachel storms to her car and peels out of the apartment complex. Typically, she hates leaving Los Angeles and Hannah's place, but right now she couldn't be more thrilled to get home. She blasts music, skipping over any songs that remind her of Emiliano or romantic love.

The entire drive is consumed by thoughts of her love life. The majority of the men with whom she had been intimate were full of broken promises, only seeking situationships or flings. And then, there's Emiliano, who she thinks is different, and worth waiting for. Emiliano—sweet, trustworthy, beautiful, authentic, goofy, intelligent Emiliano—is everything to her.

Rachel pulls into her driveway, wondering how the drive went by so fast. She hurries inside the house and calls for her dog. The last thing she wants to do is sit at home and continue to let her thoughts ruminate. She grabs the harness and leash as Cece comes running down the stairs barking with excitement.

They walk outside, ready for their nighttime loop, and head for the main road. Behind them, leaves crunch and footsteps pitter patter. Rachel turns, but doesn't see anyone. She feels a bit scared, but not too scared; the most terrifying things about this walk are all the thoughts in her head. As Cece sniffs along the dirt, Rachel continues reflecting on romance, wondering if there will be a day when a man will fight for her and love her—even after there is a ring on her finger. She wonders if that man could be Emiliano.

Annoyed by her racing thoughts, Rachel decides to implement a therapy tactic on her walk: the five senses grounding technique. She takes five deep breaths to center herself, then examines the scenery around her. Name four things you can see. The moon. Houses. Lampposts. An oak tree. List three things you can hear. An owl. The wind. Leaves. Two things you can touch. Cece's fur. The leash. One thing you can smell. Rachel wishes she could smell Emiliano, then inhales, catching a whiff of rotting flesh. She looks down. Cece is, again, hovering over the same dead crow.

Rachel pulls at Cece's harness to move her away from the possibly contaminated bird, then bends down to examine the animal. She turns her phone flashlight on, finding it odd that both times she's walked by the crow, Emiliano has been on her mind. Its feathers are looser this time and a few rib bones are poking out.

"By the time this crow is gone, he's going to realize our cultural differences don't matter," Rachel says into the night air. "He won't just *tell* me he wants this…he'll *show* me!" She stands, still staring at the bird, wondering how long it takes for a crow to decompose, as her future is now symbolically tied to it.

Then she considers if the crow will ever truly be *gone*. Won't all of its parts simply be recycled back into the Earth for other purposes? "And—and as long as any part of this bird exists, then our love exists!" she adds, relieved to now have covered all her bases.

One final look at the bird, then the two continue down the dark sidewalk. A premonition comes to Rachel's mind. There will be no more shackles on her and Emiliano's love. A vision follows. Her arms are stretched wide. Wind blowing through her hair. She's on a mountain. And they are free to love.

Staring out at the Santa Monica mountain range from the freeway overlook, Emiliano says a prayer to *La Virgen de Guadalupe.* He asks for guidance and patience, and for Rachel to come back to him. Then, leaning further back on the hood of his mother's car, he thinks about how Rachel still hasn't responded to his text messages. After all, it was just a day, right? Does he really deserve the silent treatment?

His phone buzzes. He pulls it out of his pocket, hoping it's Rachel. The text is from his mother asking when he'll be home with her car. Quickly, he responds, letting her know he'll be there in twenty minutes.

With a sad sigh, he puts on one of his favorite songs: "Everybody Wants To Rule The World" by Tears for Fears. As the first verse starts, he decides to text Rachel again. He is embarrassed to reach out, since she hasn't responded to his texts all week. After typing a few sentences, he presses the backspace button. A few more attempts play out the same way. He stares at the empty text for a few moments, then types again.

Rach, I'd love to see you soon. Been tryna give us time…I don't know if that's right…I'm always tryna do right.

A few moments later, Emiliano's phone buzzes. He is surprised to see Rachel's name pop up on his phone.

No. Telling me something isn't enough. You showed me where I stand in your life.

Emiliano furiously taps the screen.

No I didn't, Rach! I didn't show you anything!

A moment later, a new text from Rachel pops up.

Exactly.

Emiliano stares at the screen, at the one word response. He feels like he doesn't understand Rachel at all. Like Rachel doesn't understand him either.

31 A Bittersweet Feeling

With beer pints in each hand, Adriana and Emiliano squeeze through the aisle of nose bleed seats and hand Samanta and Marcos their beverages. "Thanks for the refills!" Samanta says. "You guys missed the entire eighth inning. It went by fast, though. Nobody scored. We're still tied two to two."

During the top of the ninth, they eagerly watch each of the Cubs' hitters at bat while finishing their meager snacks. Samanta and Marcos munch on a small box of cracker jacks and Emiliano picks at a bag of blue cotton candy. Thankfully, the Dodgers hold the Cubs and the score remains tied.

The announcer's animated voice sounds through the stadium encouraging the Dodgers' fans to chant for the bottom of the ninth. The home team's roar is accompanied by boos from the Cubs' fans. Pollock goes up to the plate and grounds out on the first pitch. Beaty is up next. He smacks the ball to the outfield, but the center fielder catches it. Sighs from the Dodgers' fans ring across the stands.

Adriana cups her hands at her mouth and screams for the Dodgers. Some of her beer spills, dripping onto the ground. Lost in the excitement, she doesn't notice.

The next player, Bellinger, walks up to the plate. Silence sweeps through the stadium. Two balls, a strike, then another ball—almost a full count. On the next pitch, Bellinger smacks the ball to center field. It flies well over the Cubs' outfielders and lands over the fence in the stands: a walk-off homerun. Immediately, music starts playing and the announcer raves about the hit. All the Dodgers' fans go wild. Emiliano, Adriana, Samanta, and Marcos exchange smiles and high fives. Bellinger rounds third and heads home.

Elated, no home team fan leaves their seat for the next few minutes. People holler through the aisles to other fans, sharing in the winning atmosphere. Adriana and Samanta chat about how nerve racking the ending was, how they were *literally* on the edge of their stadium seats.

When Emiliano's family heads out of the aisles, they walk slowly among the Dodgers' ecstatic fans and the Cubs' disappointed fans, stopping a few times to take pictures in front of murals and signs. Samanta and Adriana examine each photo to see if they like any of them.

Once at Adriana's car, they put their souvenir beer cups in the trunk before piling in.

"Where should we go for dinner?" Adriana asks.

Each of them had wanted to get the nearly foot-long Dodger dogs, but the food lines had been too long, which is why they settled for the in-seat snack service. Plus, they had been so invested in the thrill of the game that they stayed glued to their seats unless necessary.

"That one Mexican taqueria in the valley?" Samanta muses.

"Or maybe that food truck, Hecho Con Amor? They have the best quesabirria tacos," Marcos suggests. "'Cept, it takes forty-five minutes to get food there cause their line always so long."

"We can go to Cinco Puntos." Emiliano looks at his mother, than Marcos and Samanta in the back seat. Everyone agrees since it's only a few miles from the stadium and it's one of their family's favorite spots.

After thirty minutes of honks, blinkers, eye rolls, and minimal tire movements, they break away from the Dodgers' stadium traffic. Emiliano stays quiet, looking out the window at the Los Angeles signs, palm trees, and graffiti tags on the walls. He admires each work of art, and the ingenuity the artists put into them. It makes him upset to see that some pieces have been covered up by the city.

Adriana glances at her son, wondering why he has seemed different, more melancholy, over the last few weeks. She wonders if it has anything to do with the girl he has been seeing, who hasn't been around their house lately.

As they pull into Cinco Puntos, Adriana looks at Samanta and Marcos in the backseat, her eyebrows raised. "Let's eat here, huh? I don't want food spilling in my car."

"Madre, Cinco Puntos es un mercado....there's no indoor seating aquí," Samanta says.

"So we'll perch against the ledge out front. Just order something fácil." Adriana opens the door and walks across the parking lot. The three others quickly follow.

Inside, they are greeted by friendly faces behind the counter. Some of the workers give them head nods, recognizing Emiliano's family.

"¿Vinieron del juego?" a young male cashier asks, noticing their Dodgers attire.

"Sí, fue un gran juego." Adriana smiles, reminiscing over the final play.

The young man asks Adriana questions about the game as he takes their large order of tacos, burritos, and quesadillas. While the couple steps outside, Emiliano waits with Adriana for the food. He tucks his hands in his pockets and looks at the tile floor. It feels weird to him that no matter what he does, where he goes, or who he is with, Rachel is on his mind. He looks outside, spotting Samanta and Marcos kissing. Immediately, he looks down at the tiles again.

A few minutes later their food is ready. Adriana thanks the workers, then Emiliano thanks his mother as they carry the food bags outside. They all unwrap their cheesy and greasy items against the ledge.

"The weather is amazing tonight," Adriana says.

"And we got to see such an awesome game," Emiliano adds.

"That will probably be one of the most exciting games of the summer." Samanta takes a bite of her quesadilla, then looks over at Marcos. They do the silent talking thing that couples do—eyes locked, mouths closed, yet somehow communicating.

Emiliano looks over for a brief moment, then takes a bite out of his taco. "Will never get over how damn big that trees is," he says.

They all glance up. From where they stand, they have a perfect view of El Pino. Emiliano takes another bite of his taco while he admires the tree: the ultimate symbol that represents East Los Angeles's *Chicano* culture. His eyes shift across the landscape until he's looking at El Super, where he and Rachel had parked. Then La Princesita, where he and Rachel went for drinks before going to El Pino. A bittersweet feeling comes over him. The day he had brought her here was the day he knew he loved her, *really* loved her. While finishing his taco, he wonders where Rachel is on such a perfect Saturday night.

With a paper plate in hand, Rachel stares out at the setting sun over the mountains. A few of her neighbors are in front of her in line, piling their plates with the odd assortment of entrees: hot dogs, orange chicken, pasta salad, chicken nuggets, Caesar salad, veggie burgers, and more. When she gets to the front of the line, Shannon walks over and joins her. They walk down the tables, filling their own plates and one for

Charles. In their hunger, they add so much food their plates become flimsy and overloaded.

Next to the fold-out food tables are a few ice chests filled with sodas, waters, beers, and seltzers. Even though the neighborhood block party started only thirty minutes ago, the recycle bins are nearly filled with empty bottles. Everyone was keen on rehydrating after the annual neighborhood hike to the top of Bluffs Peak. And they continued, drinking in their lawn chairs sprawled along the street, sidewalk, and freshly manicured lawns.

As Shannon and Rachel head to their chairs, a young woman from their neighborhood, a few years older than Rachel, eagerly runs over waving. Rachel tells her mom to go on without her—not only is Casey a chatterbox, but one of the most annoying people Rachel has ever met.

"Hey, Casey," Rachel says. "What's up?"

"Hey, girl! Haven't seen you in sooooo long." Casey wraps her arm awkwardly around Rachel for a quick side hug. "Well, actually...I saw you kinda recently by Baba's Kitchen. You were with, um, with a Mexican guy?"

"Oh, you did? Yeah, that was...a great day." Rachel smiles, for a moment reminiscing over her date with Emiliano. "Surprisingly, he had *never* had food from there before!"

"Yeah, I've never had food from Baba's Kitchen either. Grooooosssss." Casey fake smiles, then mutters under her breath, "Funny...wouldn't think me and that guy have anything in common." Before Rachel can respond, Casey continues, "Well, just be careful, OK?"

"Careful?" Rachel questions.

"Yeah. I heard that Mexican men are *not* faithful. It's just part of their culture. They have a wife and multiple girlfriends on the side."

"Where did you hear that, Casey?"

"My mother. And, anyway, it's just something everyone knows, Rachel."

"So you believe something simply because it was told to you?" Rachel scoffs. "How many Mexicans or Mexican Americans do you even know, anyway?" Rachel's rapid-fire questions come at Casey so fast, she doesn't know how to respond and just stares at Rachel blankly. Rachel gives her a half-hearted goodbye and heads over to her family, rolling her eyes. Talk about ignorance, stereotypes, and racism. People like Casey are the reason why Emiliano doesn't trust White people.

As she sits down in her lawn chair, everyone cheers for the off-pitch middle schooler singing on the karaoke machine. Shannon and a few others chat about the neighborhood gossip—who's off to college, who's getting married, who's having children. They find that so much has changed since their last neighborhood get together.

Charles sips on his beer and watches the Dodgers' highlights on his phone. "Oh yeah! And that's the ball game!" he shouts excitedly as he watches the homerun hit at the bottom of the ninth.

Rachel picks at her food in silence. Not only did the interaction with Casey make her queasy, but she hasn't felt too hungry the last few weeks—it's just something that comes along with lovesickness. A glob of ketchup spills on her sweaty Yosemite t-shirt. She considers going home to change, but is too tired from the day's hike, so she wipes it with a napkin and leaves the crimson stain there. She sets her veggie burger on the plate and looks around the cul-de-sac.

There is so much going on around her. An older man is now up at the karaoke, singing a '60s song that only a few people know—she is one of them. It's a song Emiliano once showed her. A group of kids are playing kick the can. Memories flash in Rachel's mind of her childhood, playing that game along with capture the flag, bloody murder, and red rover. A small white Toyota truck filled with landscaping tools drives by. The smell of grease and salt waft through the air. There's a group of moms huddled on one lawn laughing and playing Bunko. Their ages, skin colors, sizes, shapes, and sexual orientations range in every way. Rachel watches them for a few moments, recognizing that not everyone is like Casey from her middle-class American culture. Finally, she's really, truly, noticing the world around her. All at once, it clicks in her mind: every color, gender, race, culture, nationality has racist people; and, likewise, all have non-racist people.

"Will you play kick the can with us?" a young girl asks Rachel, interrupting her people watching.

Rachel looks down at her almost full plate. "After I finish all this I'll definitely come play!" She smiles at her young neighbor and gives her a high five before watching her run off toward the other kids.

For a few moments, Rachel stares at her plate. As much as she feels like she can't eat from missing Emiliano, she tells herself she must eat. Her health doesn't deserve to diminish because of her love life. She takes a small bite of her veggie burger, then considers, perhaps her dad will help. He loves seconds and hates wasting food.

"How's the burger, Rachel?" Shannon asks.

"It's good, Mom." Rachel makes a somewhat melancholy smile, then takes another small bite before offering some to Charles.

Shannon watches, feeling both proud of her daughter and concerned. Proud that she is an independent woman who tries her best no matter what life throws at her. Concerned that she has been awfully quiet around the house recently. "I'm glad we were all able to make it this year to the hike," Shannon says, shifting her gaze from Charles to Rachel.

"Me too, sweety." Charles continues watching the ESPN highlights.

Rachel smiles, tightening her ponytail. As she reaches for her soda can, a loud engine rumbles somewhere in the distance. It sounds just like Emiliano's car. Rachel swivels around; her eyes widen. An old black Firebird comes up the street. Her mind starts running at the pace of 300 thoughts per minute. *Is that Emiliano? Am I dreaming? Why is he here? What am I going to say? Is he ready to really pursue this? Should I tell him I love him? How did he get his car fixed?*

The car pulls against the curb at the bottom of the street. A man with long red hair in his late twenties hops out. Rachel sighs, watching him walk up a driveway. She wishes he were Emiliano. When the man goes inside the house, she looks at the car again, wondering what the chances are that someone in her neighborhood has almost the exact same car as him. Internally, she asks the universe why it would play such a cruel trick on her. Then, she thinks, perhaps it's not cruel, as all her times with Emiliano formed some of her most cherished memories. The slightest smile rounds the corners of her mouth as she thinks about the time he spilled fries everywhere, when she got a nice view of his well-shaped backside in his Levi jeans.

Abruptly, Rachel's phone buzzes in her backpack. She unzips her bag, hoping it's Emiliano. On the screen is a number she doesn't recognize and the first few lines of a text message. Curious, Rachel clicks on it.

Hey, Rachel. I hope you are doing well. Next time we play can we be on the same team? I'm tired of losing and know I'll win if I'm on your team ;)

Since she doesn't have the number saved, she assumes the person got her number from the SSS group chat. It wouldn't be Fabian, or Emiliano, or Pablo, at least she doesn't think it would be any of them. She thinks about the other regulars and then Javier's name pops into her mind.

Is this Javier?

Not even a minute later, a response comes through.

Lol, yes. Sorry, I forgot to mention that! Also, do you have plans this weekend? I was wondering if you would want to go get some ice cream, my treat?

Rachel puts her phone in her backpack. She is not in the mood for any man who isn't Emiliano. And Emiliano's nowhere to be found. A beat later, her phone starts ringing.

She wonders if Javier is calling her. Except it's not Javier—this time, it is Emiliano.

She heads down the street, away from the block party, staring at his name for a few seconds before answering the phone call.

"Rachel?"

"Emiliano?"

A long pause rests between them.

"It's great to hear your voice," he says achingly.

"Emiliano." Rachel sighs. "Why are you calling me? If you're not going to pursue this long-term then don't reach out to me anymore."

"Well, I'm tryin' my best! Can't we be friends?" And that's true—he is trying his best.

The word "friend" echoes in Rachel's brain. There he goes again, keeping her on a string, she thinks. "We made love Emiliano. I am not your friend! How am I supposed to just be your friend when I'm in love with you? This isn't something little to me."

"What do you mean, Rach?"

"It's not a rock, it's a boulder. It's not a hill, it's a mountain. It's not an appetizer, it's a full-course meal...I mean, you're...you're nothing like a love poem."

"What?!" he says, confused.

"You're not a love poem! You're an entire fucking romance novel."

"How am I supposed to know what you mean by that?" he questions.

"You once spoke to me using a metaphor, Emiliano. Think about it."

And, with that, Rachel hangs up. His texts, his calls, his pleas are just words. Not proof to her, not action, therefore not convincing. She doesn't know what it would take, but after so much rejection toward their differences, a phone call is not enough. She's putting her foot down and demanding better.

As she walks back to the block party, she wonders if this is the moment the tarot readings were referring to—two different men reaching out to her. Maybe this is the start of the oddly shaped triangle. Her first instinct is to text Hannah since she wanted an update. Though, she hesitates, marinating on their fight. The only big fight they've ever had in their friendship. Every other one was something easy they could mull over like borrowing a shirt for too long or neglecting to listen to a story with close enough attention. This fight isn't something they can just bounce back from, right? Since Hannah is her best friend she decides to text her anyway, and she doesn't mention anything about their fight.

It looks like the triangle is starting. Javier texted me saying he wants to go to ice cream?! Right after, Emiliano called me saying we were friends, and that he is trying his best. I have no idea what to do. Help!

Thirty miles away, in Los Angeles, Hannah is packing up the remaining items of her soon-to-be old life. She has been sleeping at her parents' house this week, and is moving back in with them. After Rachel had left Hannah's apartment the previous weekend, Brax ignored Hannah all night at the bar, went home without her, and locked her out of their apartment. She cried on the concrete breezeway until 4:00 a.m., until a kind soul in a nearby apartment let her sleep on the couch after she distraughtly explained that her boyfriend locked her out on purpose. That was the final straw, that was what finally made Hannah wake up.

Now she is at her apartment for the last time. Brax and Alexis silently watch as she packs up her TV, Roku, and last duffle bag of clothes. As Hannah makes it into the breezeway, with puffy and teary eyes, she notices Rachel's text. She wants to respond, but simply can't right now. She is a bit too lost, disoriented, and preoccupied with her own life.

32 The Path in Front of Them

Just as Javier had wanted, he and Rachel are on the same team today. However, she didn't plan it or try to make it happen; Fabian had just happened to hand them the same colored pinnies.

Rachel spots Javier open on the far side of the field and attempts to cross him the ball but shanks it to Pablo on the other team. Quickly, Pablo starts a counter attack and pings the ball to Fabian who dribbles around a defender and scores.

Immediately, Rachel walks toward the table, staring at the unkempt dirt patches on the field. Everything about the game felt off from her poor passing to her incessant agitation. One of the guys from her team pats her on the back, telling her everyone has off days. His kind gesture falls on deaf ears. Her team lost and she was at fault for the final play. She sits down on the grass and takes off her cleats.

From underneath the tree, Javier scans the crowd. A few things immediately work their way through his mind.

One: Rachel didn't play well today. Two: Hannah is not here. Three: Emiliano is not here. Maybe these things are related, maybe they aren't. Either way, he might finally be able to talk to Rachel. He slings his bag over his shoulder and joins the others at the table, his back facing her.

"We should all go out to the bar for lunch," one of the young men suggests.

"Oh yeah. There is nothing like boozing after sweating so hard during a match," Fabian says. "Who's in?" Everyone except Javier and Rachel raises a hand. "First round's on me!" Fabian hollers.

The group heads to the parking lot, taking all the chatter with them. As Rachel stands to follow the crowd, she overhears Javier mumbling to himself and stops to listen. "Life is too hard," he whines. "I think I just want to end it all." With her copious amount of psychology and therapy knowledge, she walks over, hoping to offer help.

Hearing approaching footsteps, Javier looks over his shoulder. "Oh god. Rachel. I didn't know anyone was still here."

"Sorry, I didn't mean to eavesdrop." Rachel sits across from him at the table. "I heard what you said and just wanted to let you know I'm here if you need anything. I know what it's like to struggle with mental health." After a few moments of awkward silence, Rachel smiles softly.

"Thanks," he says. "Hey where's your boyfriend today? Sucks he couldn't make it."

"Boyfriend?" Rachel questions. "I don't have a boyfriend."

"Oh I thought you and Emiliano were——"

"No." Rachel cuts him off. She says it in a sad tone, which tells Javier that if it were up to her, Emiliano *would* be her boyfriend.

"Sorry to hear that. If it makes you feel better, he's an idiot for not being with you. You're a total catch."

Rachel smiles softly; though, behind her smile is a sad musing. She wonders why other men can see her worth, but Emiliano can't. Before she can respond, Javier says, "Well, I know something that could help cheer you up. Are you free today, Rachel?"

"Uh…" Rachel looks down at the grass, thinking about Hannah and Emiliano—the two people who she would typically have plans with. She isn't talking with Emiliano, and Hannah isn't talking with her. "Yeah, actually I am free, Javier."

"Cool. I got a group together for a hike. I'd love for you to come." Javier smiles softly.

"I love hiking!" Rachel says. She would rather go with Hannah or Emiliano, but both of those options aren't possible right now. "Which trailhead should I drive to? I'm familiar with all the ones in the area."

"Well, it's forty miles away. My friends and I can pick you up." Javier says. "I just have to go home to get my backpack, then we'll be at your house."

"OK, that works." Rachel starts to walk toward her car, then turns around. "Wait, don't you need my address?"

"Oh yeah…I totally forgot! An address would be good," Javier says with a chuckle, even though he would probably know the way to her house blindfolded.

Rachel laughs. "OK, I'll text it to you."

She hurries home and changes into an athletic top, shorts, and running shoes, then rummages through her closet for her hiking backpack. When she finds it, she checks if her hiking materials are still inside from the annual neighborhood hike. It's still full, with everything from granola bars and headlamps to a rape whistle and pepper spray. Hearing a honk, she zips her bag in a rush and heads outside.

Javier gets out of his car wearing jet black sunglasses. "So unfortunately, all my friends bailed. It'll just be me and you," he says, looking disappointed.

"Aw darn! Well, that's all right. Should we head out?"

"Well, another thing Rachel…I'm low on gas. You should drive," he says.

Rachel playfully rolls her eyes. "No friends, no gas? Looks like we could have just met at the trailhead."

They get in her car, and—more than anything—Rachel hopes it won't be awkward, hopes that Javier will be able to keep a conversation going. He shows her the coordinates for the hiking trail and the GPS says it'll be a thirty-five minute drive with minimal traffic.

"I'm starving. I haven't eaten anything all day," Javier says.

Before pulling out of the driveway, Rachel digs for a granola bar in her bag and hands it to him with a friendly smile roaming across her lips.

As Javier unwraps it, his nerves begin jittering with excitement. It feels like his fists could explode. Like he could grip something so tight until it turns blue. "You know, I love learning about the psychology of the mind," Javier says. "And I love the outdoors. That's where my spiritual life is so…vibrant." Before Rachel can say anything, he continues listing off traits he possesses. "Also, I love vegan food. It's my favorite."

Rachel nods, awkwardly smiling. For one, Javier is way more talkative than she imagined. Secondly, it seems like they oddly have a lot in common. She's never heard him talk about any of those things at their games over the last eight or so months that they've been playing soccer together.

"Can I play music?" Javier asks while they are in a light pocket of traffic.

"Of course."

He raises the volume on the stereo and puts on electronic dance music (EDM), the genre played at rave festivals—think bright lights, lots of skin, dancing, drinking, drugs. A different world than Rachel's. She doesn't know a single song that he plays.

"What kind of music are you into?" he asks, noticing that she hasn't been singing along.

"I like '50s, '60s, '70s and '80s," Rachel says, Emiliano crossing her mind. "Um, also, indie and alternative."

Immediately, Javier puts on modern alternative tunes. "Oh yeah, I love alternative. It's crazy how we even have our music taste in common too."

When they arrive, the dirt parking lot is full, except for one potentially illegal spot directly in front of the trailhead sign. Javier encourages Rachel to park in it. She nervously obliges hoping they won't get a ticket. Both of them lather their faces in sunscreen before heading into the wilderness.

She looks at the trickling creek, the heavily wooded area, and the bits of light peeking through the oak tree canopy. All the while, she thinks about Emiliano and wishes he were here with her instead of Javier.

A broad ancient-looking oak tree suddenly catches her attention. She squints. The scenery looks oddly familiar. Except she has never been here. "Is this the mountain where that girl's body was found?" Rachel asks.

"Which one?"

"I don't know, um…I only heard of that one case from last December?" she says.

Javier shrugs. "I have no idea."

Her attention veers from the odd mystery to the breathtaking scenery around her. The creek is subtle. The water sounds therapeutic with how it flows and glides down the rocks. Birds sing as they perch on trees. A few squirrels run across the trail. She inhales, breathing in the freshness. She holds out her arms and remarks that the Earth is stunning.

"Don't get too excited. This won't be easy and you're going to be out of breath. You know it's a ten-mile round-trip journey into a canyon?"

Silently, she continues her nature worship as they walk, wondering why he suddenly has an attitude. "So have you been here before?" Rachel asks.

"Yeah, I've hiked to this swimming hole six or seven times." Javier points at the creek. "This comes from the waterfall. We'll be next to it the whole hike."

For a few miles they continue walking in and out of the shaded tree canopies. They traverse a wide variety of terrain from the dirt to the creek bed, even scaling up large boulders. Then, they break for water at a not-so-obvious fork in the trail. To the left, there are large rocks next to the river. To the right, the dirt trail continues.

Rachel takes out her phone to see if she has any text messages or missed calls. No notifications pop up on her screen. The service bars aren't lit up, and she realizes they have lost service. There must be no cell towers this deep in the mountains. She puts her canteen back in her bag, then walks down the dirt path.

"That's not the way to the water hole. From here we climb up these rocks and we'll reach another trail," Javier informs her.

Since he has been here many times, Rachel follows him. When they get to the top of the rocks, they start trudging through bushes. Rachel looks down and notices the dirt beneath them has no traces of any other shoe prints. A thought passes through her mind that just because she plays soccer with Javier that doesn't mean she really *knows him*. "I don't hear the water anymore, Javier. Maybe we should turn around."

"No, this is the right way. Trust me."

Silently, they continue walking. Rachel listens to the chirping birds and the wind blowing through the leaves.

"I have tie wire and a pocket knife," Javier says, out of the blue.

Rachel walks slower, staring at the back of Javier's body, wondering why he would say that so randomly. Her gut instinct tells her that something is off, and to remain calm. "Wire? Why would you need wire?"

"Cause you never know when you need to tie someone up." Javier continues trail blazing, leading Rachel farther and farther into the wilderness.

Her intuition kicks her from the inside of her stomach. While Rachel isn't street smart in the typical sense, she is intelligent. She tells herself to think one step ahead of him. "Well that's great you brought those Javier. I have a rape whistle, pepper spray, and a pocket knife too. If we run into any mountain lions or armed humans, we'll have a chance at fighting them off together."

Javier stops walking. He looks to the right, to the left, and then to Rachel. "You know, I'm thinking maybe we did take a wrong turn. I'm gonna keep going for a bit to see if there's another trail. Just wait for me here."

When he goes out of sight, she hops onto a nearby boulder to keep an eye on him in case he goes into his bag for the wire or the knife. She squats down and slowly unzips her backpack. While keeping her eyes on him, she fusses through her things until she finds the pepper spray. She tucks it under her sports bra as she watches Javier peer around the bend in the mountain. Soon after, he turns to head back toward her.

Quickly, Rachel jumps off the rock, letting out a sigh of relief. From what she had seen up there, he hadn't gone into his bag for any of his crazy materials. At least not yet, anyway.

"Yeah, it looks like we went the wrong way," Javier says, coming around the large boulder. "Ladies first." He motions for Rachel to walk in front.

A vision flashes in Rachel's mind of Javier wrapping wire around her neck from behind. She takes a step back, crunching the leaves below her feet. "No, that's OK, Javier. I don't know these canyons the way you do." She gestures for him to walk in front.

Reluctantly, he takes the lead. They walk back through the area where they trail-blazed and climb down the same grouping of large rocks. Rachel keeps fifteen feet between them, that way if he were to make a swift move, she would have time to whip out her pepper spray. Javier gets off the last rock, returning to the main trail, then watches Rachel slowly climb down.

"Why are you so far behind me?" he asks.

"You know…I'm actually kinda out of hiking shape. I'm not used to so much rock climbing." Rachel jumps down from the last rock, hoping he'll believe her bluff.

She is happy to be near the creek again, to be back on the main trail. As they round the next corner, they meet another, more obvious, fork in the trail. The path in front of them continues with no elevation. A second one, to the right, has switchbacks going up a mountain. Javier leads Rachel to the right.

As they hike up the switchbacks, Rachel looks out at the creek that is, once again, getting farther away as they go higher in elevation. It doesn't make sense to her that a water hole could be at the top of a mountain. Then she wonders if, perhaps, there is no water hole at all.

Four teenagers come into view at the top of the hill. Rachel is glad to see other humans for the first time since they've been hiking. As they get closer, she makes note that none of them have towels or look wet from swimming. Javier waves and nods as he passes the teenagers.

"Hey, is the water hole up this way?" Rachel asks them, pointing up the trail.

"No, there's no water hole up there," one of the girls says in passing.

Rachel thanks her for the information, then looks at Javier, disappointed. "Looks like we went the wrong way again. Let's follow them down." She begins following the teenagers, feeling safe to be in close proximity to a group of people.

When they get to the bottom of the hill, the four teenagers turn to the left, in the direction of the parking lot.

"Well…we won't make any more mistakes on the way to the water hole. It must be this way," he says pointing down a trail.

Rachel looks at the teenagers as they fade in the distance. While she would want to protest and follow them out of the canyon, she decides not to say anything since she doesn't know the way. After the multiple wrong turns, the crossing of the river, and the climbing up various rock formations, she lost track of the directions. She follows behind Javier, thinking about how unfortunate it is that her only way out of the canyon is to rely on the very person who is making her feel uneasy.

For another mile they follow the main trail alongside the creek. Eventually, they pass bigger pockets of water. The stream gets faster and louder. They climb up and around a few more boulders and make it to a water hole.

Immediately, Rachel feels safe. The water hole does exist. And some men are hanging out in the water. She sets her bag down and admires the large rocks that jut out from the surrounding mountains. One of the slabs of rock makes a natural water slide, the waterfall stream passing right over it.

"I'm surprised you said you don't feel fit. You look more fit than you used to," Javier says as he takes off his shirt. "Your legs have leaned out."

Rachel laughs, feeling uncomfortable, yet happy to hear a compliment. Although, her weight has only fluctuated a few pounds, if any. Why has he been paying that close attention to it? How could he notice such a minute difference?

"Wanna hear something funny, Rachel?"

"Uh, sure…What is it?"

"I used to have a crush on you. Not anymore though, I have a girlfriend."

Rachel doesn't know what to say, as she is not, nor ever would be, interested in him romantically. She takes her shirt off, making sure to wrap the pepper spray inside of it, then walks into the water in her sports bra. Javier takes off his sunglasses, then follows. He splashes her with water and flirtatiously jokes with her.

"So, who is your girlfriend, Javier? How long have you been dating?"

"A few months. You don't know her."

The group of men all head over to the natural water slide, each taking a turn gliding down the rock and into the water. Rachel swims over, climbs up the slippery slab, and waits in line behind them. Javier wades in the water, watching as they go down one by one. As Rachel flies in and makes a big splash, another, even larger, group of people come hiking into the sanctuary.

"There's too many people here. We should head out," Javier says.

"I guess. I mean…yeah we still have another five miles ahead of us," Rachel replies.

While they dry off, the strangers pass by and say hello. Everyone in the large group sets down their bags and cannonballs into the water. Rachel quickly grabs her bag and moves so she won't get splashed. She walks behind a boulder, puts her t-shirt back on, and tucks the pepper spray in her damp sports bra. A few seconds later, Javier comes around the bend. His backpack is fastened tightly around both shoulders and his dark shades are back on his face.

They leave the water hole and start their trek out of the canyon. For the first few miles, they make small talk about soccer and music. While Rachel admires the canyon's beauty, Javier admires Rachel's body. She continuously looks over at the creek, making sure it is still there, and feels relieved every time she glances at it.

"What if something crazy were to happen, like you go missing here or something?" Javier asks, nonchalantly.

Rachel laughs, hoping he's just speculating. "That could never happen. I know my way out of the mountain."

Again, she hopes he believes her bluff. "Also, if you mean today…my car is here. Police or rangers would find it. And it wouldn't be long before my parents would search for me."

"So, what about your love life? I'd love to hear more about it," Javier asks.

"Well…I *was* seeing Emiliano." Rachel looks down at the dirt, sad to be talking about their love in the past tense.

"I already know that about your love life." Javier spits into a bush. "What did you see in him though? He's fucking ugly."

Rachel scowls. He must be jealous of Emiliano because Emiliano is a knock out and he isn't. "Emiliano was everything and more. One of my favorite things about our romantic relationship was that it wasn't built around lust and sex. We truly enjoyed each other's company as friends, first and foremost, above everything else."

Javier scoffs. "You're naïve."

She looks at him, confused.

"No man can go more than a few days without having sex. Emiliano was definitely sleeping with other women. He didn't love you…He was just using you."

Rachel shakes her head and continues walking. None of his statements are true, right? Suddenly, tears flood her eyes. She feels worse than she's ever felt. The mere thought of Emiliano sleeping with another woman feels like someone's squeezing the blood out of her heart. Or someone forcing her to throw up. Or a knife carving through her brain.

"Oh my gosh, are you crying? Come here." Javier holds out his arms.

Rachel hugs Javier, thinking it's kind of him to comfort her, not realizing in her distraught state that his words are what made her cry. She wipes her tears with her shirt.

"I am absolutely ravished." Javier says. "Nothing seems to shake my hunger."

"I know a great food spot that's right on the way home," she says. The place she has in mind is the food court with Thai, American, Mexican, and Korean, where she once took Emiliano.

Once they are in the car, pulling out of the dirt parking lot, a sense of relief shudders through her body. Then an overwhelming sense of guilt takes over. She thinks perhaps she's been cruel and misjudged Javier. After all, she came out of the hike alive. Plus, he apparently has a girlfriend and surely that means he doesn't have evil intent. She must have been overly alert because she listens to true crime podcasts. They roll down their windows as they get on the main road and she lets Javier blast his EDM music for the entirety of the drive.

When they pull into the food court lot, Rachel looks at Elations Outreach Church, remembering Emiliano's story. She hasn't been here since the time she brought him. Javier quickly gets out and heads toward the food hall, Rachel following close behind looking at the sky. She remembers when she and Emiliano had tripped over the planter together. Today there are no clouds, no special colors, and there's no immaculate sunset.

Inside, she doesn't mention anything about the American vegan place. "This place has a big menu," she says, pointing to the Mexican spot.

They order separately—both in English—then sit across from each other at a table. A few minutes later their steamy food comes out. Rachel notes that Javier's tacos have the same ingredients that were on Emiliano's nachos. Before she takes a bite of her shrimp taco, she watches Javier pick up and examine his food. He crunches down on the shredded chicken, rice, beans, jalapeños, and green salsa.

"Wow…This is really good Mexican food!" he says between chews.

"Huh…really? You think so?" Rachel watches him take another bite, then tries her taco, thinking about how Emiliano had such a different opinion.

33 Just a Few Feet Away

While taking a long sip of soda, Emiliano scans the banquet hall from his seat. The decorations on the walls and tables are light pink and gold. On the stage is an enormous pile of presents. Behind them is a large three tiered pink cake. In front of them are large glitter block letters that spell *Bianca*. A mariachi band stands to the side of the stage, serenading the crowd with *boleros* and *baladas*. At Emiliano's table sits Samanta, Marcos, Adriana, and another family from their neighborhood.

"Everything looks stunning," Adriana remarks, touching the centerpiece of the table—a chandelier modeled vase that holds a bouquet of pink roses.

Suddenly, everyone's attention veers to the center of the dance floor as the DJ begins announcing the court of honor. There are six pairs of *damas* and *chambelanes*. The *damas* are wearing light pink dresses with sparkles. The *chambelanes* are wearing fitted black tuxedos. They each have light pink bow ties, except for the main *chambelan* who has a gold bow tie.

All the girls stand on one side, and the boys stand on the other. Friends, family, and other partygoers clap for the court.

Emiliano smiles, recalling his teenage years, attending these birthday events and being part of them. He got asked by many girls from his neighborhood or from school to be part of their *quinces* growing up. In some way, he knew the girls wanted to be closer to him, or had crushes on him. He would politely decline, unless it was a good friend. And, once, he accepted to be the main *chambelan* for one girl he considered to be a best friend.

"¡Y la quinceañera, Biancaaaaa!" the DJ hollers.

As the fifteen-year-old walks into the banquet hall, the music begins. Her pink ball gown looks exactly like something a Disney princess would wear, and she looks like a Disney princess in it. The dress hugs at her torso, then flairs out at her hips, commanding every square inch of the floor in a two-foot radius. Additionally, she is fashioning dangly gold earrings, a short gold necklace, and a gold bracelet.

When she sits down on a chair in the center of the dance floor, people begin to cheer. Her mother and father get up from the head table, each holding pillows with different ceremonial items. Her mother walks over, sets the pillow down, and picks up a gold tiara. She places it on Bianca's head, kissing her daughter on the cheek. Her father sets the second pillow down and picks up gold and glittery heels. Lifting the bottom of Bianca's fluffy dress, he pulls off her pink Vans sneakers and replaces them. The crowd claps for Bianca's emergence into womanhood.

"It brings tears to my eyes! It's just so amazing," Adriana whispers to Emiliano. He pats his mother's shoulder, offering comfort. She loves the atmosphere, the decorations, the dresses, the important tradition for women. She never got a *quinceañera* of her own—since her family came across the border when she was nine, they didn't have enough of a foundation in the States or money to throw her a celebration when she turned fifteen. She feels proud and overjoyed every time she gets to celebrate any *Mexicana* or *Chicana* whose family can afford a *quince*. It gives her hope for future generations.

"Tu Sangre en Mi Cuerpo" by Ángela Aguilar begins playing through the hall. The main *chambelan* removes Bianca's chair from the dance floor as she takes her father's hand. Together they perform a father-daughter waltz. Their dancing captures the whole room's attention. "I am so proud of you. I love you so much. You are an incredible young woman," he whispers in her ear. They both pat at their eyes, trying to keep from crying.

When the song concludes, her mother comes out for a mother-daughter waltz. It lasts for half a song and is filled with laughter and tears. Bianca's two younger sisters walk out next. She holds onto both of them as they lightly spin in circles, grooving to the beat.

Over the next twenty minutes, Bianca dances with the rest of her family members, including her *hermano*, *tíos*, *tías*, and *abuelo*.

"This is way too emotional for me. Imma need another beer," one of Emiliano's neighbors says to the whole table.

"No mames, guey," Adriana says jokingly.

Emiliano, Samanta, and Marcos all chuckle, Marcos tilting his beer toward the neighbor in agreement.

"Déjate sentir," Adriana adds. "Didn't your daughter just have her quince a few years ago?"

"Sí, and I was hammered for that too," the man jokes.

"¡No manches!" Adriana shakes her head. "¿Dónde esta tu corazón?"

Emiliano's eyes shift back and forth between his neighbor and mother. He loves the banter, the playfulness, the realness.

As Bianca's family sits down, her *damas* and *chambelanes* stand and make their way to the dance floor. While they slowly sway and bob their heads, Bianca and her mother head to a separate room at the venue to change outfits for the *baile sorpresa.*

A few minutes later, the crowd watches the double doors as Bianca's main *chambelan* escorts her back into the banquet hall. She is wearing a gold dress, about mid-length, like her *damas'* pink dresses.

A music mash-up of modern Spanish and English pop music plays. The entire court lines up in their positions around the dance floor. Together, they perform a choreographed dance. Sometimes, the *damas* and *chambelanes* have their own moves; other times they pair up with one another. The attendees can tell that the young group must have worked hard during their dance lessons over the last several months.

At the end of their dance, the court stands in a line behind Bianca. Each of them is given a glass with non-alcoholic champagne. Bianca's father comes to the dance floor once more to make a toast to his daughter. "Mi niña ahora es una mujer. Bianca...eres inteligente, hermosa, divertida, y talentosa. Esto es para ti. ¡Saludos!"

The DJ follows with another Spanish speech about *quinceañeras* being a special once in a lifetime birthday celebration, so everyone better shower Bianca with love tonight. "¡Arriba, abajo, al centro, y para adentro!" he hollers. The court, and every fiesta attendee with a drink, motions their cups up, then down, to the center, then drinks.

"Bianca looks so stunning," Adriana says to Samanta. "¿Verdad, mija?"

"Sí. Her dress looks kind of like my quince dress, no?" Samanta smiles, recalling her own *quinceañera* that took place around ten years ago. "Maybe Bianca will end up with one of her chambelanes too." She nudges Marcos's shoulder.

He softly smiles, combing his hands through his hair.

The pop music continues playing through the speakers while the *quinceañera* and her court begin making their way to their seats for the feast. At one of the tables, a family stands and exits the banquet hall, heading toward the kitchen at the venue. They return a few minutes later with fresh food, utensils, and gloved hands. Trays and trays of hot meal items are lined across a few tables. Pitchers of spritzer and juice are placed at the end of the food line.

Emiliano takes a sip of soda, looking at the backs of the family's heads, wondering why party attendees would also be catering the food. "Fancy dresses and white button-ups. These guests caterin' the food or qué?" Emiliano questions.

"No sé, vato." Adriana shrugs.

"I would hate to attend an event and also work it," Samanta says, her brows furrowing.

Tables are called one at a time by the DJ to get their meals. The *quinceañera* and her court are the first to pile their plates. A few more tables get food before Emiliano's table is announced. His family follows behind one another across the room, swaying and bopping to the music.

A screen is lowered in front of the stage and a slide show starts with pictures of Bianca and her family, friends, neighbors, and other loved ones. Everyone *oohs* and *awes* at the walk through her life. Emiliano glances at the screen then looks at the food containers. He piles his plate with a little bit of everything—*enchiladas, arroz, frijoles, tamales, cabrito,* and *pan de polvo.*

"Mira, mijo. ¡Mira!" Adriana points to the screen.

Emiliano looks up to see a photo of him and Bianca. Eight-year-old Emiliano is holding baby Bianca after her baptism. His bottom tooth is missing, his shirt is dirty from playing outside, and Bianca barely has any hair. A soft smile and warm feeling overcome him, though he has no memory of taking the picture.

He carefully carries his full plate back to his seat, Adriana following close behind with hers. "¿Quién es ella? Tan bonita," she says, looking at a picture on the screen. It's a recent photo of Jemma and Bianca hugging.

Emiliano sits down and scans his delicious plate of food. "¿Quién?" He looks up. The picture has already faded and been replaced by a photo of Bianca and her father.

"A young woman about your age. You missed it." Adriana sits down next to her son. Shortly after, Marcos and Samanta come over with full plates. Everyone chats, jokes, and laughs with one another as they enjoy the catered food and watch the remainder of the slide show.

Once people start setting down their forks, the DJ raises the volume and puts on "No Rompas Mi Corazón" by Caballo Dorado. "Necesito a todos los niños y niñas, a todos los hombres y mujeres aquí bailando," he hollers.

Chairs screech against the floor as people excitedly leave their tables. Emiliano, Adriana, Samanta, and Marcos line up next to each other for the Caballo Dorado line dance. Everyone begins pumping their fists in the air. At the top of the eight count, they begin moving: two steps right, two steps left, two back, two forward, turn counterclockwise, then repeat. Some people add in a spin during the turn, including Emiliano. A memory flashes in his mind, when he was performing this for Rachel in her living room.

When the song is finished, the DJ puts on "Payaso de Rodeo" by Caballo Dorado. Samanta and Marcos return to their seats, while Emiliano and Adriana stay on the floor for the faster version of the line dance. They laugh together as their side steps turn to gallops and their step dancing turns into a workout. When they get close to Bianca, they each congratulate her.

"Orgullosa de ti," Adriana whispers to Bianca, as she squeezes her tightly in a hug.

"¡Ahora, todos ustedes traigan un compañero a la pista de baile!" the DJ yells.

Husbands and wives, boyfriends and girlfriends, and other pairs of two walk to the dance floor. As Samanta and Marcos get up to dance, Emiliano sits down at the table and takes a sip of soda. Pairs of two. All he can think about is

Rachel. They were a real pair of two. Taking it slowly. Really getting to know each other. And now she won't even speak to him or see him. What is he supposed to do? There's nothing more he can do, right? His heart aches as a slow song starts. He watches the couples on the dance floor sway to the music.

A few minutes later, Adriana finishes her conversation with Bianca and walks over to Emiliano. "You don't want to dance, papi?"

Emiliano shakes his head. He takes another sip of soda, then scans the crowd. He watches the catering family clean up the meal and replace the empty food containers with desserts. Again, he wonders who they are and why they are catering if they are also guests.

Jemma turns around and throws her gloves in the trash. Then she walks over to a woman on the far side of the dance floor. Emiliano catches a glimpse of her face. She looks familiar. Very familiar. The woman whispers something to Jemma, then Jemma looks over at Emiliano. Immediately, he breaks eye contact. Soccer. That's where he had seen her. Javier used to invite her to watch them play.

Emiliano takes another sip of his drink then watches the people slow dance. Maybe in a few months, that could have been him and Rachel out there. Once she got to know him more. To trust him more. To understand his culture. Eventually he would have let her in fully, right? Why couldn't she just be more patient? All he can feel is sadness. And anger. Frustration. Nervousness. Truly, a mixture of many unfavorable emotions.

Finding Jemma to be intriguing, he steals another glance. A few moments later, she looks over to him. Their eyes lock. They exchange smiles from across the room. Now that's a girl who would probably understand him. She knows the culture. She is *la cultura*.

He excuses himself from the table, and makes his way across the banquet hall. Makes his way toward *her*. He needs to get Rachel off his mind anyway. Rachel hasn't spoken to him. Clearly, he needs to move on. Needs to put himself out there. Needs to take risks and do new things.

Again, the woman next to Jemma whispers something in her ear before vanishing. Jemma turns around and Emiliano is standing there, just a few feet away. For a brief moment, they just look at one another without saying anything.

"I—I remember you from soccer," Emiliano says.

"I remember you too." Jemma tucks her hair behind her ear. "I watched you play. Eres muy bueno."

"Gracias." Emiliano smiles. "How do you know Bianca?"

"Ella es mi prima. How about you?"

"Bianca's my neighbor." Emiliano studies Jemma's facial features—kind dark eyes, soft pink lips—then glances at her long and thick dark brown hair. "Quieres bailar?" he asks, offering his hand.

Jemma blushes, slipping her palm into his.

Emiliano leads her onto the dance floor as "Mujer Mia" by Joe Baton begins. Together, they sway to the left and right, then back and forth. The rhythm of their slow dance is so in sync, it looks like they have danced together before.

34 In Such Close Proximity

Emiliano straightens the pillows on the living room couches, then walks into the kitchen. The sink is full of dishes. He considers cleaning them, but a knock on the door interrupts his thought. Jemma waves through the square window. He walks over and opens the door.

"Hola," Emiliano says.

"Hola," Jemma replies with flush cheeks.

"Please come in," he says, giving her a quick, friendly hug. "This is Mila." He gestures to the dog who is cowering behind him. Jemma pets her, complimenting her gray coat.

"So, how's everything been since the quince last weekend?" he asks.

"Muy bien. ¿Y tu?"

"Bien." He looks into her eyes, smiling. A fresh and content smile, one that comes from a place of comfort. "You seen Bianca at all this week?"

"Sí. I took her out to lunch for her birthday."

He nods. For a moment, silence blankets the room. The two didn't talk much at the *quince*. Most of their time together was spent slow dancing, line dancing, laughing, and exchanging glances. He's not sure what to say, or where to begin. She's radiant and beautiful, like Rachel. And she speaks Spanish.

"Oh, and here's this." She reaches into her bag and pulls out a DVD.

Emiliano scans the front cover of *Y tu mamá, también*, looking at the female actress sandwiched between the two male actors. Then he turns the case over and reads about the provocative, coming-of-age film. "This was nominated for a Golden Globe?" he asks.

"Sí. That's why I wanted to show you. It set the record for highest box office sales in Mexican cinema...It was actually nominated for a few awards." Jemma looks over Emiliano's shoulder at the back cover.

"Is it a romantic comedy?"

She shakes her head. "It's a road film. I can't tell you more because then the movie won't be a surprise."

"Road film? That's coo. I love cars...There's this movie...*American Graffiti*. That's an American road and coming-of-age film. Who knows, maybe we have the same movie taste." Emiliano eagerly sets up the DVD and shuts off the lights. "We can sit anywhere you like." He motions to the couches and his bed.

"Gracias. I'm kind of cold. Could I use a blanket?"

"Sí. Of course."

Jemma takes her sandals off, then squeezes by the side table and sits on the bed under the stairs. Emiliano joins her, remote in hand.

As he is about to press play, Samanta comes through the front door. She looks at Emiliano, then Jemma, then the spotless floor around them. "Come on, Mila. Let's go to the park," Samanta says.

After picking up the leash and a toy ball, Samanta looks back at Emiliano and Jemma again. Without saying a word, she and Mila head out to the car where Marcos is waiting for them.

"Sorry…Sometimes she's not the friendliest. Trust me though…I've seen worse." Emiliano awkwardly laughs, then presses play.

The first scene: sex. Two lovers promise they won't sleep with anyone during their summer away from one another.

Emiliano raises the volume so he can hear more clearly. It's been a while since he has watched a movie fully in Spanish. Jemma pulls a blanket over her legs, then glances at Emiliano briefly before focusing on the film. Over the next hour, they watch raunchy young boys partake in sex, drugs, and an unexpected road trip with a beautiful older woman.

Outside, someone jangles the door knob. Emiliano pauses the movie so they won't miss anything. A few moments later, the young boy who lives at Emiliano's walks into the house. He smiles at Emiliano, looks at Jemma, then walks upstairs to his bedroom.

"Is he your little brother?" Jemma asks.

Emiliano shakes his head. "No, we aren't related. He and his mother rent a room from us."

"Ah, sí." Jemma nods.

They exchange smiles, then Emiliano presses play, hoping their movie date won't be interrupted by anyone else. *Date.* Well, they're friends. A friendly date. It's not like he can move on that fast from Rachel. But also Rachel didn't understand his culture, didn't understand him, right?

He tries his best to stay focused on the film, even though Rachel keeps coming to mind. Jemma studies his facial expressions at each of the movie's unexpected plot twists, including when two male best friends get drunkenly intimate with one another and when one character gets a cancer diagnosis.

When the credits role, Emiliano says, "Honestly, I've never seen anything like it before. Thanks for showin' me."

"Did you notice all the events going on in the background with the police and the government? It takes place after seven decades of el Partido Revolucionario Institucional dominating the political scene."

"I don't know much about Mexicano politics." Emiliano is taken aback, intrigued by Jemma's intellect. "I'd love to learn more."

"Sí. There's so much I can show you," Jemma says, crouching out from under the stairs. "Tengo hambre."

"We can go get lunch." Emiliano follows behind her.

"I know a good Japanese place at the mall," she says.

After putting on their shoes, they leave the house and walk down the street to Jemma's silver Corolla. A neighbor walking a dog smiles at them, saying *Buenos tardes*. Jemma and Emiliano both recite the afternoon greeting back to the neighbor before getting in the car.

"Jemma, I forgot to ask at the quince, pero why was your family catering the food?" Emiliano asks as they pull off his street, heading toward the town's mall.

"Mi familia owns a restaurant. It was inherited by my parents from mi abuelo when I was just a baby. Time flies though…I've worked as the main book keeper and manager for four years, ever since I turned eighteen."

"That's awesome." Emiliano looks out the window at the palm trees passing by. Jemma knows hard work. She knows because she is *la raza*, just like him. "Y'know, I kept forgettin' to ask about that cause I was jus' so in the moment with you. You're a great dancer."

Jemma giggles. "Gracias."

"So whatever happened with you and Javier? Were you two together? You stopped coming to soccer."

"No, we were just friends. I met him when my family was catering a quinceañera. He told me that he played soccer and I'm a huge fan, so we bonded over that. We never kissed or anything. He came on really strong a few times and I didn't like that. I got a bad gut feeling about him and just stopped talking to him."

Emiliano nods, wondering about the gut feeling as they turn into the packed structure and head to the second floor, the closest parking to the food court. After driving past a string of cars, Jemma squeezes into a compact spot. It's so tight that Emiliano almost hits the car next to him as he gets out.

When they head for the entrance, Jemma accidentally bumps into Emiliano, tripping him. A thought of Rachel flashes in his mind. The planter. Mexican Food. Vegan Sushi. Orange, pink sky. Sunset. Fixie Bikes. Then, just as quickly, the images leave his mind. With Jemma's help, he catches his balance and doesn't fall.

"Sorry. Excuse me, Emmy," she says, firmly gripping his shoulder. "Oh sorry. That just slipped out…Emmy."

"And I'll call you…Jemmy." Emiliano grins, showing off all his teeth. At the same time, they both laugh. "I'm just kidding. Emmy is great. I love nicknames."

They walk through the automatic doors and head to the Japanese restaurant. He orders beef teriyaki; she orders chicken teriyaki. Then Emiliano adds two fountain drinks to the order. While he pays, Jemma finds an empty table for them to eat.

"¿Qué bebida?" Emiliano hollers.

"¡Sorpréndeme!" Jemma winks from across the room.

Emiliano fills both drinks with Dr. Pepper, then joins her at the table.

"Gracias por la comida. Someday I'll cook you a delicious meal from our restaurant," she says, her glossy brown eyes looking into his. She takes a few sips of her drink, then excuses herself to the restroom. He watches her cute, petite figure, enjoying the way her skinny jeans hug her waist. When she walks out of view, he watches a TV in the food court and sips his drink.

Inside the restroom, Rachel finishes drying her hands, then picks up her Adidas bag. As she turns around, Jemma is walking in. Recognizing each other, the women exchange smiles as they cross paths.

Rachel exits the bathroom thinking *maybe if I were more like her, I could be with Emiliano.* Then, suddenly, she drops her shopping bag. Her mind and heart halt as she glances out into the food court. Emiliano is at a table with *two* drinks. Quickly, she scrambles to grab her things, then rushes through the automatic doors, not wanting him to see her.

A few minutes later, Jemma walks out of the bathroom and rejoins Emiliano. "I think I saw a girl from your Saturday soccer group in the restroom!"

Emiliano looks around the food court, then their order number is called over the loud speaker. He stands to get their food, wondering if Jemma is referring to Rachel, wondering if Rachel is really in such close proximity to him right now. He feels guilty. He misses her, of course. But she kept ignoring him and gave him the cold shoulder.

Just outside of the automatic doors, Rachel is inside her car, crying and unable to drive. Her mind won't stop bombarding her with thoughts about what she saw inside the mall. Maybe Emiliano was just really thirsty. Knowing that couldn't be it, she wonders if he was with a guy friend. Tears stream down her face. She doesn't believe that scenario either. Maybe Emiliano was there with *Jemma.*

Rachel places her hand over the lever to back out, but can't get herself to drive. Again, she folds over in tears. Her cries get louder and louder, then she smacks the wheel.

The internal noise in her mind is on full blast when her phone starts ringing, which annoys her. She doesn't need any external noise right now. She takes a deep breath and wipes her tears. Rustling through her purse, she finds her cell. It's Javier. Rachel clears her throat as she answers.

"Hey, Rachel. What are you doing tomorrow?"

"Uh, I don't know. Why?" Rachel looks in the rearview mirror, patting at her red puffy eyes as she continues thinking about Emiliano.

"I was calling to invite you on a night hike. We can stargaze too," Javier says.

"Yeah. Sure. Why not? I'm free." Rachel reaches into her glove compartment and pulls out a wadded up, already used tissue. "I gotta go, Javier. I'll see you later." She hangs up the phone and blows her nose, her mind still all-consumed by the two-cup mystery.

After a few more ugly cries, she tells herself she must get it together. She leaves the parking garage, glancing over at her Adidas bag on the front seat. Buying new cleats was the highlight of her day. Seeing Emiliano with two cups was the downfall of her day.

She has a hard time paying attention to the road on her drive home as memories of Emiliano surface like bubbles in boiling water. His big smile. His perfect teeth. His laugh. His sweet eyes. The way he puckered his lips. The time he sang to the moon. The time he ran with the dogs. The time he did karaoke with the lint roller. The time he said *forever*. Did all of it mean nothing?

35 The Setting Sun

As Rachel looks at her wet, freshly showered hair in the mirror, she thinks about how things aren't always as they appear. While she may look put together, *normal*, she feels empty and disgusting on the inside. With no desire to dress up for Javier, she throws on a pair of Adidas sweats and an oversized gray t-shirt with a light coffee stain on it. Then, she sprawls across her bed, cuddling with Cece. She counts her blessings—her dog, her parents, soccer, and education. Regardless of who comes and goes, those pillars are always constant.

A car honking interrupts her thoughts. Javier's modern black Nissan is parked along the curb. She stares at it, wishing it were Emiliano's car. Same size. Same color. None of the personality. None of the class.

Rachel gives Cece a kiss on the forehead, then glances over to her bookshelf. Emiliano's birthday present is still sitting there on the hardwood floor. She saunters downstairs, not even sure if she is ready to stargaze. If it were Emiliano here, she would already be outside. Javier can wait. He is *not* Emiliano. Nothing like him. His company is just a time-filler, postponing her feelings of loneliness and sadness. It's not the best strategy, and she knows that. It's like using rubber bands to strap a broken heart together, and then calling the heart whole.

As she gets to the front door, she notices her hiking backpack sitting on the piano bench. Pepper spray comes to mind. Should she bring it? He was so weird on their first hike. No. She'll be fine. Suddenly, her intuition sounds her entire system like an alarm at a jewelry store. Just in case, she shoves the pink pepper spray in her purse, then walks out to Javier's car.

First she notices his shades, then his full tank of gas, which means she won't have to drive. As she buckles, she spots two empty drinks in the cupholders. Again, she thinks of Emiliano and what transpired at the mall.

"Yeah, me and this girl I know went to lunch today," Javier says, noticing Rachel staring at the cups. He zips off her street and onto the main road. "Could have just as easily been another girl though. I got lots of girls after me."

Rachel nods, then looks out the window at the setting sun. God. Of all the people she could waste time with. Javier seemed so normal for months at soccer, and even when he said he was experiencing depression. Now, he is just getting weirder and weirder the more time she spends alone with him.

"So…Rachel…What would you rate me on a scale from one to ten?"

"No thanks, Javier. I don't want to play that game." Rachel sighs. There are multiple reasons she doesn't want to play. For one, she doesn't want him getting any ideas about their friendship being something more. Also, she is not attracted to him and thinks her rating would hurt his feelings. (She would rate him a three.)

"Hmm. Well…what would you rate yourself from one to ten?" Javier asks. He switches lanes and turns onto the freeway.

Initially, the number nine pops in Rachel's head. She knows she is an attractive girl. But…she also knows a thing or two about modesty. "I'm probably about a seven, Javier."

"Ehhh. Nah you're more like a six," he says, looking her up and down. "Now rate me!"

Without looking over at him, Rachel mutters six. She figures it's the safest number. It's high enough to where it hopefully won't hurt his feelings. Low enough to let him know she's definitely not interested.

Javier scoffs, hearing her middle-of-the-scale rating. "Nah, I'm a nine. It doesn't bother me that you said six." Except, it does bother him.

Rachel peers out the window pondering about how Javier rated her exactly half what Emiliano once had. When she tunes back in, Javier is still talking about how attractive he is. He complains that so many women find him attractive that it's hard to stay faithful to his girlfriend. Everywhere he turns, there's hot women—Caucasian ones, Asian ones, Mexican ones, and European.

"You should break up with your girlfriend if you aren't planning on staying loyal," Rachel says. Truly, though, she doesn't think he has a girlfriend. If he did, wouldn't he be with her instead of Rachel right now?

Javier smirks. Rachel must be flirting with him. She must be saying to break up with his girlfriend because she wants to sleep with him. "Well, me and my girlfriend are actually on a break," he says flirtatiously.

"Good," Rachel says firmly.

They exit the freeway, make a few turns, and drive up Topanga Canyon. The sun finishes setting during the first few twists and turns up the mountain.

"Did you tell anyone that we're hanging out tonight?" Javier asks.

"No," Rachel says, hoping Javier isn't thinking that they are starting to become an item. "Also, why forty minutes away to stargaze, when we could have just done that in the suburbs?"

"This is the best mountain for stargazing. I *love* watching the lights go out." He looks down at his phone, messing with the music and Bluetooth, then puts on "Closer" by Nine Inch Nails.

What the hell is he talking about…houses, stars, city lights? She tunes out the music, sure that it's not intriguing in any way. She looks out into Los Angeles as she thinks about Emiliano's soft lips. Then she lowers the window and leans out, taking a deep breath of fresh air.

As she looks up, she notices it's foggy. So much for star gazing. There is only one visible star. A nursery rhyme from her childhood pops into her head. *Star light, star bright, first star I see tonight. I wish I may, I wish I might, have this wish I wish tonight.* She closes her eyes and wishes for Emiliano to be close to her, to love her, to choose her, to let her in fully.

Right as the wish ends, her phone rings. She picks her purse up, wondering if wishes really work that fast. Could it be Emiliano? Surprisingly, it's Hannah. Her best friend's name makes her smile. It's the first time Hannah's reached out since their fight and she's eager to hear her voice.

As she answers the phone, Javier whips around a curve and the call fails. They're so high up that there's no service. An uneasy feeling churns in Rachel's stomach. Both times she has been with Javier, there's been no cell reception. And they've been to locations Javier is familiar with—places she has never been.

Javier rounds the last bend and parks at the top of the mountain. A couple is parked there with their windows down. The man and woman are sharing a tray of In-N-Out fries. Rachel hugs her purse tight to her as they exit the car, sit down on a bench, and stare upward at the fog that blocks the stars.

After a few minutes of sitting silently, Javier playfully pushes Rachel and tells her to loosen up. She giggles half-heartedly, still clutching to her purse. The other car's headlights turn on, blinding them for a moment. Rocks and dirt crackle below the tires as the car turns onto the asphalt and disappears down the mountain.

"I've really wanted to kiss you for a while now," Javier says, straddling his legs on each side of the bench.

Rachel tucks her hair behind her ear, immediately feeling a slew of emotions. For one, she feels bad—she only sees them as soccer friends, or acquaintances, nothing more. Secondly, she feels uneasy—she remembers that there is no cell service and Javier has said really odd things in the time they've spent together. Then, part of her feels pleased—it's nice to feel beautiful and wanted. Truly, the biggest emotion she feels, however, is anger—toward Emiliano. How could he deny their love? How did he make plans and promises he knew he wouldn't keep? How did he let Rachel fall, and not catch her? How could he, with Mexican blood, be skeptical of being with her, yet Javier, with Mexican blood, isn't skeptical?

In the long awkward silence, they both lift their gazes. Rachel looks into Javier's eyes, searching for Emiliano. She doesn't see anything inside of them. She doesn't feel anything. His eyes are like black holes, sucking her into nothingness. She awkwardly smiles, then looks at his facial features. His unsymmetrical face. His slightly crooked front tooth. His eye that is a little higher than the other one. Nothing about him—personality or looks—is attractive.

Maybe it's because she feels bad, maybe it's because she's scared of rejecting a scary man, maybe it's because she's angry, maybe it's because she's full of unanswerable questions, maybe it's because she's vulnerable, maybe it's because she's heartbroken, maybe it's a combination of all the above—she looks at Javier, and with no desire to actually kiss him, she says, "I guess we can try it and see if there's a spark." Plus, what's the harm in one kiss? She obviously won't do anything else with him.

Javier leans in and kisses her. Rachel immediately hates the taste of his lips and their lack of chemistry. Before she has the chance to say anything, Javier swiftly lifts her shirt and starts sucking on one of her nipples.

Speechless, Rachel pulls her shirt down and scoots farther away from him. "I do not move like that, Javier. Do not go underneath my shirt."

Javier hates rejection. "You like being choked?"

"Um…What?"

"Here's how to choke someone." Javier wraps his hands around Rachel's neck, then slowly squeezes. "Like this, they barely lose consciousness," he whispers. For another second, he squeezes tighter. "And then, you let them regain it." Slowly, he let's go.

Rachel takes a deep breath, trying to stay calm. Now, all she feels is scared. She can't run down the mountain for 20 miles. She can't call anyone—she has no service. She can't run away from him, he's faster. She can't fight him, he's stronger. She can't pepper spray him. Can she? Should she? Maybe the only way to get home safely is to oblige by what he says. To not anger him. To not fear him. To let him down gently.

Hoping to change the subject, she mentions whatever constellations and planets she can think of—Mars, Venus, the little dipper, the big dipper, Orion's belt, Saturn—though it's hard to see any of them through the foggy haze.

Javier leans over and sticks his hand in Rachel's pants. Instantly, Rachel pulls his hand out, reminding him, nicely, that she doesn't move like that. He chuckles, believing she is just playing hard to get. Once more, he reaches inside her shirt. This time, maneuvering around her breasts.

"Javier! I said no. Please stop touching me." Rachel pulls his hand out.

"But I wasn't even touching your tits, I went around them," he argues.

"It's still a no. I don't do any of that unless I'm in a serious relationship with someone." Rachel pushes against the bench, starting to stand.

Javier *really* hates rejection. He bends down and grabs Rachel's ankles, then pulls her toward him. Her butt slides against the bench, until she rams into his crotch. Promptly, he begins thrusting into her with his clothes on.

In shock, Rachel doesn't do anything, unsure what to do.

Javier wraps one arm around her throat. "You like that, don't you? You like that?" With his other arm, he rips at the neck line of her t-shirt.

In an attempt to get him to stop, Rachel jerks sideways, landing on the dirt next to her purse. Javier falls on top of her, compressing her lungs, causing the wind to get knocked out of her. When she comes to, she coughs, then squirms and reaches for her bag. He pins her arms down, his sweaty, clothed crotch dangling in her face. Rachel turns her head.

Swiftly, Javier reaches for her purse and throws it over the side of the mountain. The clasp unhooks and its contents fly everywhere. Tampons in bushes. Napkins on dirt. Cellphone down the hillside. Pepper spray caught on a small branch.

Rachel lets out a yelp.

"Shut up!"

She starts crying as he briefly gets off her, only to rip her pants down, making sure her underwear comes with them. He jerks himself between her legs, then starts choking her as he forces himself into her. With each pound, he grips her neck squeezing tighter and tighter.

Hoping to finally see fear from Rachel, he looks into her eyes. Her gaze is on the sea of lights in Los Angeles. A tear trickles down her cheek and lands on the dirt. She feels her own light beginning to fade. Rachel's body scratches against the pebbles and rocks as it is jolted forward and backward.

Her mind is saying Emiliano was wrong—*El Cucuy* does exist. It's not just children that the boogeyman haunts, it's women. Javier's hands grip tighter and tighter around her neck, blocking the blood flow from her brain. Drifting off, Rachel feels herself becoming lighter, lighter, lighter. A last exhaled breath. Her arms are stretched wide. Wind blowing through her hair. She is on a mountain. She is free.

Why is he inside of me? What is he doing to me? The pain is too great. Javier…you've made it so I can't come back. I can't. I can't. And I didn't get to say goodbye…I tried to answer the phone, Hannah. How will I play soccer? Cece…where's my Cece? I hope my mom and dad know how much I love them. Where's Emiliano?

"Yes, Mamá. I'm getting the vase for your flow—" The vase tumbles out of Emiliano's hands and crashes onto the floor, shattering. Crystalline pieces scatter across the kitchen. Emiliano stares at the mess, stunned. "What just happened?" he whispers, feeling an excruciating ache ripple through his heart.

EPILOGUE

SIX MONTHS LATER

Hearing the chorus of "Steppin' Out" by Joe Jackson, Hannah rolls over and slaps her alarm clock. Abruptly, the music stops and her room returns to silence. In her sleep fog, she wonders if she had a nightmare. After rubbing her eyes awake, she remembers that her life is the nightmare, that this is reality.

"Today is the day." Hannah sighs, thinking about the memorial soccer match being held in Rachel's honor. She hasn't seen Fabian, Emiliano, or any of the other players since everything happened. Slowly and groggily, she stands and makes her bed. A pile of bills are on her night stand—water, electricity, rent. Due dates seem to come faster now that she's paying for her own things. Walking over to the window, she's instantly glad to not see the view from her childhood bedroom or the smog of Los Angeles. Her new apartment is in the suburbs.

Just as she does every morning, she walks over to the framed newspaper article above her dresser. The bold heading reads, "Best Friend Seeks Justice—Helps Find Murderer." It discusses Hannah's tenacity with solving the case, even when authorities doubted her evidence: clues from a tarot reading and a text Rachel had sent her about a week prior to the rape and murder. Hannah stares at the photo of her and Rachel, still wishing she could say goodbye, knowing the ache is a hole she can never fill, never patch, never drink away.

When the anger rises, as it does every morning, she opens the top drawer of her dresser and pulls out the only thing inside of it: another newspaper article. It's titled "The Mountain Murderer." Hannah takes out a lighter and sparks the edge of the paper, letting it burn for a few seconds as she stares at what's left of Javier's mugshot.

Though it's no longer legible, the *Los Angeles Times* article discusses that once Javier was linked to Rachel's death, his house was searched and inside his nightstand were the thongs from each of his victims. Also lying with the undergarments was one cut piece of a gingham red and white dress. The police found four other bodies—three in Topanga Canyon, one by the water hole. Javier is also considered the prime suspect for the unsolved December murder from the previous year. As the news about Rachel spread, nine other women from the community came forward with rape accounts against him.

Wanting Javier to burn slowly, Hannah blows out the fire when it singes just past one of his eyes. She throws the lighter and article into the drawer and slams it shut before opening another drawer full of athletic clothes. She stares at them, wondering how this day came so fast. It seems like it was yesterday when she got the call about what happened to her best friend. And now, somehow, months have seemed to fly by. Hastily she gets ready and grabs her bag. As she is about to leave, her ball falls out of her closet and rolls toward her. She stares at it for a few seconds before picking it up. When she opens the bedroom door, her new roommate is sitting on the couch.

"I hope the memorial game goes well, Hannah. Call me if you need anything."

Hannah thanks her roommate and heads out of the apartment. She jogs down a flight of stairs, eager to get to the florist shop. Each person coming to the game is bringing a bouquet of flowers that remind them of Rachel. Hannah ordered a bouquet of pink Dahlias: the national flower of Mexico. She chose them because to her they represented Rachel's unwavering love. As she gets in her car, she thinks about Rachel's family. She's eager to see them at the event.

Shannon, Charles, and Tilly admire nature's subtleties as they walk the dog around the neighborhood. Fresh air. Sunshine. A light breeze. No one utters a word.

Occasionally, they exchange glances. Each of them has teary, puffy eyes. Cece pulls Shannon as she sniffs everything in sight. Suddenly, her collar tag stops jangling as she plants her paws firmly in the dirt. Charles and Tilly walk ahead as Shannon's arm is pulled back from the leash.

"Ahh, Cece? What are you sniffing?" Shannon says.

Cece caught a scent right where the black crow used to lie. After a few moments of hard sniffing, she begins digging and digging, then rolls over and rubs herself in the odor. Proof that the essence of the bird lives on. Proof that Emiliano and Rachel's love lives on. Somewhere in realms unseen, where there are no egos, no human shackles. Somewhere where their souls are free.

"Cece stop that." Shannon tugs at the leash.

When they get far enough away from the mystery scent, Shannon takes Cece's harness off. The dog runs around the corner toward their house, tail wagging. They each stare at her dirt-filled fur coat as she passes them.

When they get inside, Charles gives Cece a treat. Immediately, the dog runs upstairs and eats in front of Rachel's locked bedroom. Taped to the door is an acceptance letter to Boston College. Cece paws at the door and whines. Behind the door, next to the bookshelf, is Emiliano's birthday present, full of dust, and their list of movies, with only half of them crossed out.

"We'll be home later, Cece," Shannon hollers up the stairs.

The dog comes running down as they leave. Each of them holds their bouquet of flowers: purple lily's from Shannon, a symbol of sweetness and innocence; white carnations from Charles, a symbol of pure love; and sunflowers from Tilly, a symbol of loyalty and adoration. They get into Charles's car, heading for the memorial game.

"Does anyone have paper?" Tilly asks.

Shannon thumbs through her purse, then passes her a small notepad. Tilly scribbles a message to Rachel. *A mother should never have to bury her child, nor should a grandmother.* Tears well in her eyes. She hesitates for a moment before continuing. *Grief wears many faces, my child. Just know we all miss you.* With shaky hands, Tilly folds the note a few times over, then tucks it into the bright yellow bouquet. She blows her nose, then wonders if she will be able to recognize Emiliano, the love of Rachel's life, at the game.

Emiliano opens his eyes and looks around the small bed underneath the staircase, thinking about how he and Rachel once made love here. Just as many other times, he begins to feel her presence, swearing he can hear the sweet hum of her laughter.

Despite the fears that rattled their bond like a wrecking ball, he deeply loved her. He loved her so much, in fact, that he fought through that fear, knowing he was swimming against a current going in the opposite direction. What they shared was true, albeit juvenile—but young love is still real love.

Her laughter begins to echo in his mind again. Memories flash of her quirkiness. Her intellect. Her kisses. Her loving caress. Her sensual dance to a Prince song. Her soul making love with his. The pain is too great. He gets up and walks into the kitchen to find his car keys.

Adriana, Samanta, and Marcos are chatting at the dining table as they eat breakfast. Samanta feeds Mila a strip of bacon. Adriana takes a bite of a pink *concha*, then urges Emiliano to eat. He shakes his head, promising he will later.

After saying goodbye to everyone and giving Mila a noogie, he walks outside to his car fully dressed in his typical get-up—Lakers hat, Lakers hoodie, black belt, dark blue Levi's, and black leather Converse. The sun shines on his car's new black paint. Emiliano half-smiles. "You've come a long way," he mumbles, patting the roof of the Firebird. He takes a deep breath as he gets inside. Slowly, he pulls off the curb and drives down the road, waving to his neighbors and the children running around on the grass.

When he exits his neighborhood, he pulls into the shopping center parking lot and parks right in front of Flores de Felicia.

"Hola, Emiliano. ¿Cómo estás?" Felicia says as he walks in.

"Estoy cansado." Emiliano doesn't feel like talking, but also doesn't want to be rude. "¿Y tu? ¿Qué pasa, Felicia?"

"Estoy bien, Emiliano."

They both smile and nod. Emiliano pulls out a wad of cash. Felicia takes the money and exchanges it for two bouquets of white roses, which symbolize young love and eternal loyalty. He holds them both in one arm, leaning them against his chest as he collects the change.

"Ahora, ¿es uno para tu mamá, uno para tu novia?" Felicia chuckles.

"Somethin' like that." Emiliano knocks his fingers against the counter, then exits the flower shop. One bouquet is placed in the backseat, next to his dusty soccer bag, for Rachel. He doesn't play soccer anymore. The other bouquet is placed on the passenger seat, next to his basketball, for Jemma.

Also on the seat is a wrapped present for Jemma's birthday and an engagement ring. He picks up the small square box, testing how it feels between his fingers, then glances at the polaroid picture of Jemma and himself on the dashboard. He smiles, reading her note in black marker that says *Love you, Emmy!* across the bottom of the picture.

After putting the engagement ring down, he backs out of the parking lot. His phone starts ringing and he answers the call.

"Ay, esé."

"Pablo?" Emiliano questions. "My man, you be soundin' different."

"It's the new job I just got, hombre. Don't feel like a little kid anymore workin' at my Dad's shop."

"That's great, bro. You like the job?" Emiliano asks.

"Sí…Wish I wasn't workin' today, Emiliano. You know I'd be at the game."

A long silence comes through the phone.

"I know, Pablo. Thanks. I appreciate it."

As the men exchange goodbyes, Emiliano looks over at the passenger door panel, now completely repaired. Sometimes he forgets how much work he has put into his Firebird over the last several months. He looks at the engagement box again as he pulls up to the stoplight just before the park.

Not wanting to sit in silence, Emiliano turns on the radio. He holds his breath, hearing the starting chords of "Major Tom" by Peter Schilling. Lost in a trance, Emiliano lightly bobs his head to the beat. Then, slowly, he gazes diagonally to the left of the intersection.

There is no white car.

Acknowledgements

Over the course of nearly two and a half years, I obsessively worked on this book. Sometimes I forgot to eat. Sometimes I worked from dawn to dusk without seeing the sun. Sometimes I got stuck on Spanish dialogue and did hours and hours of research. Sometimes this tale was the only thing I could talk about with those around me. Thus, there are many people I want to thank for helping bring this book to life. Thank you to my grandmother, Maureen Hammond, for encouraging me to start writing fiction. Her belief in my storytelling is what helped me write the first scene. During the process of writing the initial draft, I would bring piles and piles of papers to her house that she would almost immediately read and give feedback on. This book would never be what it is without her. Thank you to my father, Chris Hammond, for being my second reader. He sat down and read my first full draft in just three days. I knew my book had true power when he—a man who doesn't cry—cried at the end. Thank you to my mother, Sandra Hammond. Not only did she hear me yap about the book 24/7, but she would listen to chapters out of order or take time out of her day to edit sections of the book. Thank you to Maria Nava for not only being a beta reader but also for editing the Spanish in this book. Thank you to Edward Lugo for listening to early drafts, offering Spanish help, and helping with the back cover blurb. Thank you to the following people who read the novel, or portions of it, and gave early feedback: Alex Tessier, Robert Hammond, Robyn Hammond, Kyran Hammond, Jayd Hammond, Isaias Magallon, and Jenna Harry. Thank you to my advanced readers for reading the book a month prior to the release date, providing honest reviews, and helping me build intrigue for the novel. Thank you to everyone who has encouraged or inspired me in some way during this incredible journey. I have a deep appreciation for each of you.

About The Author

Ryanna Hammond is a human being, who is probably "being" just like you—with unique quirks, flaws, passions, and unanswered questions. Truly, she believes we are all brothers and sisters and siblings of the Universe, all experiencing this peculiar human existence during a peculiar time in history. Thus, she writes with the aim to shed light on the modern human condition, and to connect with others and help them feel less alone. She has a BA in Psychology from UNC Asheville (May 2019) and an MFA in Creative Writing from Emerson College (May 2024). This is her first fiction novel, and she has five collections of poetry. Many more books are sure to come.

Connect with Ryanna on Instagram: @itsryannahammond
or TikTok: @poemsinprettyplaces